WHA-CKED
(White House Attorney-Counsel Killed)

JED O'Dea

ALSO BY

Tucker's Discovery

Deadly Cold

Unsustainable

WHA-CKED

JED O'DEA

WHA-CKED
(White House Attorney-Counsel Killed)

JED O'Dea

Published by

ISBN-10:0-9974555-0-0
ISBN-13:978-0-9974555-0-2

This novel is a work of fiction inspired by a true story. Names, characters, places, and incidents either are the product of the author's imagination or are used fictitiously.

iii

WHA-CKED

JED O'Dea

(White House Attorney-Counsel Killed)

*This Book Is Dedicated to
Kenda Rose Hurt
who is the inspiration for the
character, Star.*

White House Counsel:

"I was not meant for the spotlight of public life in Washington. Here, ruining people is considered a sport."

Albert Einstein:

"I never made one of my discoveries through the process of rational thinking."

WHA-CKED

(White House Attorney-Counsel Killed)

JED O'Dea

Main Characters

Tank Alvarez – Founder of *White Knight Personal Security Services, LLC*

Jolene Landrieu – *White Knight* Security Officer, Significant Other of Tank Alvarez

Tucker Cherokee – CEO of *Entropy Entrepreneurs*

Powers – Former Special Forces, Former U.S. Senator, and Co-Owner of *White Knight Personal Security Services, LLC*

Maya Li Cherokee – Physicist, Former National Science Advisor, Wife to Tucker Cherokee and Mother to Star

Star Cherokee – Daughter of Tucker and Maya Cherokee

Lucas Justice – *White Knight* Security Officer

Viktor Soroson – Megalomaniacal billionnaire

Other Characters

AG – Attorney General for the State of Maryland

Ahmed Mohammad – The man who uses Soroson's billions to rally ISIS against Germany

Brian Richmond – Agent-in-charge of the investigation into the death of the White House Counsel

Byron Chism – Architect of the Capitol and Co-owner of the *Brown Leaf Cigar Bar*

Casey Robinson – Scientist at *Entropy Entrepreneurs*

Chef Rhino – Chef at the Cherokee Estate

WHA-CKED

(White House Attorney-Counsel Killed)

Clinton Auclair – Director of the Library of Congress (Librarian of Congress) and Co-owner of the *Brown Leaf Cigar Bar*

Damian LaTorre – Former Director of the FBI

Elliott Brave – CEO of *Brave Chicken Corporation*

Fischer Men – Viktor Soroson's group of hired 'hit men' to include Rook, The Bishop, Queenie, Kingster, Pawn, and Horse

Forrester True – Investigative Reporter for the *Washington Press* into the death of the White House Counsel

Gina Goodman – Chairman of the Board for the Smithsonian Institution and founder of the Washington Mystery Club

Gunter Korf - Henchman for the Deutsch Chamber and kidnapper of Jolene

Harold Andrews – Attorney with *Andrews, Crosby, and Underwood* and the person who hired Richard Kingsley

Jimmy Ma – Employee of *Entropy Entrepreneurs* and expert at following financial transactions JJ (Jimmy Jordan) – Handicapped Executive Assistant for the *White Knights*

Kristen Brown – U.S. Park Police Officer in charge of the investigation into the death of the White House Counsel

Mark Vintage – FBI Special Agent in charge of investigating the kidnapping of Jolene

Marsha Katz – Holocaust victim, Viktor Soroson's mother

Melody – Richard Kingsley's friend

Meng Wong – President of *China Methyl Ester, Ltd.*

Niu Boa – Meng Wong's enforcer

Ram – K-9, German shepherd, trained by Powers, given to Tank and assigned to protect Star

Randoph Randolph IV – Member of the House of Lords

WHA-CKED
(White House Attorney-Counsel Killed)

JED O'Dea

Ray LaSalle – Former Pentagon strategist, creator of algorithms that predict consequences of actions, and friend of Tucker Cherokee, Powers and Tank Alvarez

Richard Kingsley – Robert Kingsley's son, the blond man

Robert Kingsley – First person on the scene of the death of the White House Counsel

Rook – Soroson's hit man, Duke Dillinger, leader of the Fischermen

Sam Pearson – Attorney for *White Knight Personal Security Services*

Shelby Viking – Former First Lady's campaign manager

Sonja McLeod – Powers' daughter and Israeli sniper

Stone Garry – MI-5 agent

Theodore Rich – Chief Medical Examiner during the investigation into the alleged suicide of the White House Counsel

Tony Vinci – Chief Scientist, *Entropy Entrepreneurs*

Wilhelm Soroson – Research Medical Scientist at Auschwitz

Yuri Prociv – Russian Priest, Master Chess Player, and Keeper of Russian Archives

WHA-CKED   JED O'Dea
(White House Attorney-Counsel Killed)

PROLOGUE -- THE WHITE HOUSE COUNSEL'S EPIPHANY

McLean, Virginia, 1993: He sat on a rusted and sagging lawn chair, subconsciously fingering the recent tear in the sleeve of his Brooks Brothers' suit jacket and stared down at his bare chalk-white feet immersed in the cool water of the Potomac River. He had never done this before -- he'd never escaped from the political circus in which he found himself, just to be alone to meditate, collect his thoughts, assess his situation, and figure out his path forward.

An odd sensation swept across his face as he contemplated his enlightenment -- he was exercising atrophied smile muscles. He had an epiphany, a sudden insight, a eureka moment with clarity of vision. He no longer gave a flying fuck or a rat's ass about his career, or about his influence on the world stage. He couldn't remember why his White House job was so damned important to him, and concluded that his prior depression and job-related misery was self-inflicted. Even earlier today   just this morning -- he still drove himself hard to be important to people who used him.

The newly-unburdened Deputy White House Counsel now contemplated leaving his highly visible and prestigious job with the current administration. Yesterday, he had believed that he was between a rock and a hard place, and had expected to be subpoenaed to testify before Congress.

What fun that would be!

His choices had been either to lie under oath **or** incur the wrath of the two most powerful people in the world, and receive in the process an enlarged anal orifice from the administration-friendly, Kool-Aid-drinking news media.

But now, after his epiphany, he actually looked forward to leaving his current contentious job and, after all the dust settled, making the big bucks as a lobbyist on K-Street. He wasn't sure where he'd heard it, but he thought, "All I ask for is the chance to prove that money won't make me happy."

The rumbling of sounds overhead from another world, the hectic sounds of traffic crossing on the Chain Bridge on their commute between Virginia and Washington, D.C., disrupted his pensiveness. He tried to imagine what the sounds were like in 1810 when the bridge was actually supported entirely by chains.

It had truly been an unusual adventure for him just to get to this spot after negotiating the steep rocky incline from Chain Bridge Road down to the water's edge. He fell twice on his way down, as his slick Italian leather wingtip dress shoes slid on the dirt.

As he happily contemplated his numerous upbeat options for the future, he noticed that the sky was darkening and an afternoon thunderstorm was brewing. He put his socks and wingtips back on, tucked his blue silk tie into his long-sleeved-button down white shirt, and started up the rocky bank. He struggled to drag his out-of-shape six-foot, four-inch frame up the incline, and wandered onto a narrow pathway overgrown with kudzu and briar, walking in the direction of the old Civil War era fort. He wiped spider webs from his face as he grabbed onto a dogwood tree for support and slowly progressed in his half-mile trek up the steep rock face back to the road and to his rendezvous point.

As he reached level ground, he thought about spending some quality time alone with his beautiful, sexy wife. The two of them damned well deserved it. That thought brought back another broad smile.

It was his last thought.

PART I

CHAPTER I – DISCLOSE THE TRUTH, OR ELSE

Wiscasset, Maine: My sides are killing me and I'm having trouble breathing, but I can't let him know; the devious bastard will go for the kill.

"Tank, you know you can't win," boasts my nemesis in his hoarse-like guttural voice. "Just surrender to me before I make you suffer even more. Maybe, the next time I drive you into the wall it might knock some sense into you. Your freakish size won't help you this time."

Possibly, he's right. I have trouble keeping my weight down to 310 pounds. At six feet, seven inches tall with a wing span of almost seven feet, I shouldn't have to move much in this claustrophobic-size racquetball court -- especially playing against a slower man who is fifteen years my senior. I have to stop on a dime, reverse directions, run as fast as I can, then stop and reverse directions again and again. That's tough when you're carrying around my weight.

"Experience and treachery will beat youth and vigor every time," Powers says with confidence. In his former life, Powers was a commander of Special Operations and a trainer of Army Rangers in hand-to-hand combat. He is short by my standards at five feet, eleven inches tall and small at 190 pounds -- but he is as soft as a wire brush and as gentle as a junk yard dog. The Bob Seger song, "*Like a Rock,*" comes to mind when thinking about Powers. I'm glad we're partners, because I wouldn't want him as my enemy.

Years ago, I, Jorge (Tank) Alvarez, was once a bodyguard for and saved a sexy young country singer from an inebriated and aggressive redneck. The incident was viewed live on national TV. I leveraged my "fifteen minutes of fame" into a

3

personal security business and hired Powers to train me and, eventually, all of our guards, investigators, officers, and operatives. The rest is history -- and our firm, *White Knight Personal Security Services, LLC,* is now the most-respected security firm in the nation.

I suppose I have too much pride, but I tend to fight to the finish. It's time for me to put my racquetball skills where my mouth is, or better yet, where Powers' mouth is. The sport requires the execution of a strategy using skill-based tactics, some of which are within legal racquetball rules. It's a sport where patterns have to be disrupted, predictability removed, and players must have eyes in the backs of their heads.

Powers serves hard and low to my backhand expecting the serve to be impossible to return. But I anticipate his serve, step an arm's length away from the corner, and return the serve with all the arm and wrist strength I can muster angled across court low intended for the right front corner.

"Ahhhhh," screams Powers, holding his right side kidney area. "I've been fucking shot. Tank, damn it, you're not allowed to have weapons in here."

Apparently my shot didn't make it to the right front corner; someone got in the way. "But Powers, isn't it you who says, 'this is the only time blue balls are fun?'"

"Honestly, Tank, I've been gun-shot multiple times and being shot didn't hurt as much as your power shot when it hit the fatty part of my side. Maybe, we should consider using racquetball as an interrogation technique. Hell, it hurts more than being water-boarded.

"You've pissed me off now; this is war!"

But someone is pounding on the back wall of the racquetball court. I look back to see that outside the Plexiglas back wall is our *White Knight* Operations Coordinator, Jimmy Jordan, whom we call JJ. Though he is in a motorized wheelchair, equipped with the most advanced technology, he still uses the old non-technical method of pounding on the window to get our attention.

His eyes tell a story I know I don't want to hear. The expression on his old country boy's face is dour. Something is wrong, big-time. I reach the back wall, flip the door handle up, turn it, open and duck through the door to see his sad eyes.

"What is it, JJ?"

He sighs, reaches into an old leather satchel which is attached to his wheelchair, pulls out a piece of paper and hands it to me. I towel the sweat off my hands and accept it with trepidation. As I open the folded sheet of paper, JJ says, "This here is a printout of a message left on y'all's company website."

I turn and read it out loud, to share the message with Powers.

"We have Jolene. Nothing will happen to her as long as you follow our instructions. Check the bed of your truck."

Jolene is the love of my life.

"Dammit," I yell; "this can't be happening to her again. I'll tear the head off of whoever has kidnapped her." She was abducted once before and used as bait, intended to draw me out into the open.

I sprint as fast as I can out of the athletic center into the cool Maine air until I reach my truck. Powers is behind me, struggling to keep up. In the bed of my truck is an unfamiliar beat-up red metal tackle box. I step onto the bumper, over the tailgate, and then into the truck bed. Powers yells, "Slow down big guy -- check that box to make sure it's not booby-trapped."

There are no visible wires or evidence of an improvised explosive device, so I grab the box handle, lift its hinged top open and find that it's ... empty except for a small portable electronic data storage device -- a thumb drive -- in its top tool tray.

5

She wiggles her toes, flexes her fingers, and moves her throbbing head from side to side. The former Marine lies still on her back with her eyes closed and assesses her physical condition. Despite her excruciating headache and upset stomach, she concludes that she's at least in one piece. As Jolene is crossing the boundary between being knocked unconscious and wakefulness, she wonders who glued her eyelids shut.

She has no memory about what has happened to her. She lifts her right arm -- which feels like it weighs a ton -- and drags it to her face. She uses her fingers to force her eyelids open. She discovers with her blurred vision that the room is either moving, or she is dizzy.

Her last memory before her surreal awakening is that of confronting the leader of a mob of animal-rights activists. The CEO of a poultry products company needed protection and it was Jolene's job to provide it. Jolene Landrieu is a *White Knight* operative and Tank's long-time girlfriend. She is a six-foot one-inch former Olympic beach volleyball silver medalist, blond, green eyed, muscular, and intimidating -- unless you're a six-foot seven-inch-tall, even more intimidating Tank Alvarez.

Instead of worrying about herself, she lies there and worries about the person who hired *White Knight* for personal protection. "Is Elliot OK; what the hell happened?" She's never before failed a mission. She hopes that he's safe.

"Why can't I remember how I got into this bed?" Jolene struggles to sit up, looks around, her vision clearing slightly, but her head is still pounding like she drank too much alcohol.

It's not her bed; it's not her home. "Where the hell am I?"

(White House Attorney-Counsel Killed)

She is hesitant to stand up.

"Tank, are you here?" There is no answer.

"Anybody here?" Still, there is no answer.

Her stomach begins to roll, as if she is trying to digest a live eel. Jolene cautiously tries to stand up, only to fall back awkwardly onto the hard bed. She needs to get to a bathroom, urgently. Her vision clears marginally as she looks around. She is in a large room, 20 feet by 20 feet, with a high ceiling and three doors. One door is open; the other two are closed. She hopes the open door goes to a bathroom. She rolls clumsily off the bed, lands hard on her side, crawls to the open door, finds the porcelain, and vomits.

She flushes the toilet and while holding onto the bathroom sink; she struggles to stand up in front of the mirror. Her face doesn't have cuts or bruises, so she concludes that she hasn't been in a scuffle, she is unhurt, and there is no evidence of a line-of-duty type confrontation. Though her shoulder-length blond hair looks like she slept on it, there are no signs of blood in her hair from head injuries. Her eyes are red and the crow's feet remind her that she is no longer a spring chicken.

She concludes that she has been drugged -- with something which wipes out short-term memory.

The taste in her mouth is disgusting, so she turns her attention to the sterile, immaculately clean, spacious, and well stocked bathroom in search of mouthwash. On the counter next to the sink she finds an unopened packaged toothbrush, toothpaste, Listerine, Bayer aspirin, dental floss, and a hairbrush -- all new. There are washrags and towels in the bathroom closet along with lots of soap, toilet paper, and tissue. The bathtub is large and deep with bubble bath, shampoo and conditioner next to the faucets.

Though still unstable, she wanders back into the main room, only to observe that everything in the room is new and has been cleaned by someone obsessed. She stumbles over to a chest of drawers and opens the top drawer to find underwear and bras in her size.

She wobbles over to the closed closet door, opens it and finds a walk-in closet with clothing of all types. Everything is in her size -- including sweaters, blouses, jeans, shoes, tee-shirts, shorts, and even house slippers.

She looks at the closed door. "What's behind that door? Is it locked? Is it a way out?"

She musters up the strength to check out the door. It cracks open; it's not locked. Jolene takes a deep breath, opens the door fully and peers inside.

She walks into the perfect woman-cave. It contains a spectacular kitchen with all the latest appliances, a fully stocked refrigerator/freezer and pantry, and a wet bar. On the other side of the room is a 75-inch flat screen TV with a DVD-player with Blue-ray, and hundreds of DVDs.

One very important thing is missing, something that screams volumes about her current situation. There are no windows.

Jolene becomes sick to her stomach again. This time, she doesn't think it has to do with the drug she's been given.

"What the fuck? Something really bad must be going down."

Wiscasset, Maine: My laptop is in the truck but my keys are back in the safe-slot in the racquetball court. I start back, until I hear the truck unlock. JJ has a set of keys with him and has pushed the fob to open the door to the truck from 50 feet behind me.

I swing the back door to the truck open and grab my computer bag, open my Toshiba laptop, and wait for the computer to start up -- it seems to take forever, but it takes only 30 seconds. JJ catches up with me and wheels within fifteen feet of the truck by the time Windows desktop screen appears. I insert the thumb drive into one of the laptop's USB ports.

JJ is parked beside me now and says, "I have an active AT&T hot spot with me. You have live internet access." It's a good thing because the first file on the drive contains a web address.

I click on the link to open the website to find myself watching Jolene, live, in real time it seems. She is sitting on a bed, looking a little disoriented.

Then the website goes dark. A message flashes across the screen: *You get 10 seconds each day. It's proof of life. Open the next file entitled, 'White Knight Assignment'.*

I open it.

Powers, who followed close behind me on the run to the truck, tries to look over my shoulder to read the text. I move the laptop screen at an angle so that both of us can read it together.

We will hold Jolene Landrieu hostage until you complete your next assignment. We selected you for the assignment because White Knight is reputed to be the best personal security and investigative organization in the United States. Included on this drive are multiple files including forensic analysis, an FBI investigative report, and an autopsy report of the deceased. Though the case has been closed for over twenty years and the death was declared a suicide, we know better. Your job is to uncover and disclose the truth.

Powers and I have provided security advice to numerous customers in similar kidnapping situations. There's something unique about every kidnapping/ransoming crisis. Sometimes the best thing to do is pay the ransom, and sometimes the best thing to do is notify the FBI. And, then again, sometimes, the best thing to do is handle it yourself.

"JJ," I say, "see if the athletic facility's surveillance cameras picked up who put the tackle box in the truck bed.

"And Powers, do you think your FBI or NSA buddies can figure out who owns the web site and track down where that video cam is located?"

"I'll make a few calls," answers Powers.

"I'm going to rally the troops and read the files on the thumb drive. I'm damned well going to get Jolene back and the kidnappers are going to pay dearly.

"They just shit in their mess kit."

CHAPTER 2 -- A CROSS TO BEAR

Wiscasset, Maine: She is both blessed and cursed. The blessings are obvious, as twelve-year-old Star has loving, protective, and attentive parents; the curse is opaque, almost invisible.

She is blessed with good health, intelligence, and beauty -- her long red curly hair, snow-white teeth, flawless complexion, lithe little body, penetrating blue eyes, and contagiously happy disposition make her easy to love. But she has a cross to bear.

She is blessed with friends, purpose, and all the advantages of excessive wealth. But ... as fate would have it, she is also damned with an unfair burden.

It is impossible for Star Cherokee to lead a normal life with her paranormal, extrasensory-perception powers, which include the ability to read the thoughts of others, the ability to sense the feelings of animals, and more. She's been very careful, ever since she was just five years old, not to share with others the knowledge of **all** of her unnatural paranormal skills.

Her parents, of course, know about her mind-reading skills. But, because she also reads *their* thoughts, she understands their fears. As scientists, Tucker and Maya -- Star's parents -- know the potential consequences to her from cold, ambitious and calculating scientists under peer pressure in search of rewards from the scientific community. Star's potential for being experimentally abused is too high to allow disclosure of her talents. They have every reason to be afraid that she will become a lab rat of sorts -- an anomaly who **must** be scientifically investigated.

Star shares that anxiety. But her competing fear is that Jolene's life might be at risk if she keeps quiet about what she has learned through an undefined sixth or seventh sense.

11

Her one-hundred-pound well-trained guard dog and friend, Ram, senses her discomfort and lies protectively beside her.

At least she isn't at risk of being stoned to death like her misunderstood great-great-grandmother, who was accused of being a witch, and from whom her parents believe Star inherited her unnatural talents. Star knows that she has to "bite the bullet" and tell her parents about Jolene. She owes it to Tank whom she loves like an uncle. Shaking with anxiety, Star leaves her shielded bedroom with Ram by her side, and walks in the direction of her dad's office.

Her dad is working "as usual" in his home office and "as usual" is on a Go-To-Meeting video conference with a business associate. Though Tucker doesn't prohibit Star and Ram from entering his office, it is an unspoken rule that she is not to interrupt him unless it is an emergency. Star tentatively turns the door handle, nudges the door open, and sticks her head into her dad's office. Tucker sees her immediately, recognizes anxiety on his daughter's lovely face, and speaks into the mic attached to the monitor, "Tony, I have to go. I'll call you back," and he immediately disconnects the call.

Tucker sees the trembling chin and expression on Star's face -- something serious is troubling her. "Come on in, sweetheart. It's always a special event when you and Ram visit me here. Have you gotten too big to sit on my lap?"

Though Star isn't a crier, tears water Star's royal blue eyes. Tucker stands up, picks her up, and gives her a big hug. "What's the matter, baby?"

"I need to tell you and Mom something about Jolene. I think Mom is in the gym. Will you come with me so I can tell you both at the same time?"

Their gym is in the basement where Star's mother is working out. Tucker holds Star's hand as they both walk into the gym and observe Dr. Maya Li Cherokee double-timing it on the stair-step machine, while reading a non-fiction book about "dark matter" on her Kindle. She stops climbing immediately when she sees the two people she loves most in the world looking anxious. The contrast of seeing her tall handsome, fit, and well-dressed husband wearing a fake smile while her beautiful twelve-year-old is wearing only tights, a T-shirt, and a serious expression ... is disconcerting.

Star always looks people straight in the eye. Something about the intensity of her gaze usually makes the recipient feel a little uncomfortable. This is one of those times. But Maya doesn't look away; rather, she concentrates on Star's expressive sparkling blue eyes.

While Star and her mother size each other up, Tucker is observing the entire spectacular person who is his wife. She is stunningly and naturally beautiful all the time, under all circumstances, and in any environment. Today is no different. The sweat from her workout makes her skin glisten and appear moist and soft. Her five-foot, nine-inch-tall frame is covered by black tights and a black tank-top, which highlights the texture of her waist-long jet-black hair, tied with a band into a pony-tail. Her features reflect the exotic mixture of her Chinese and Norwegian heritage. Tucker's heart still races every time he sees her. He also knows that her heart is as beautiful as her outwards appearance, and has always felt blessed to have her as his wife.

Star suddenly blurts it out in hyper-speed: "Jolene is in trouble. She is scared and alone and feeling sick. You need to call Tank. Please, I'm afraid for her. I think she has been kidnapped or something."

"Whoa, sweetheart. You need to slow down a little. Let's start with why you think she's been kidnapped."

"Daddy, please can we call Tank, now?"

13

Maya steps off the stair-climber, approaches Star, kneels down to look straight at her, gently holds both of Star's hands, and says, "We're not going to ask you 'how' you know Jolene is in trouble."

She lets that statement hang for a moment before she adds, "We want to know 'what' you know."

Star takes her right hand and brushes her bangs back, moves her penetrating gaze from her mother's eyes to her father's eyes for confirmation that he, too, isn't going to question her about "how" she knows what she knows. Tucker understands the meaning of the look on Star's face and nods affirmatively.

Tears continue to form in young Star's eyes as she says, "Jolene is in a strange room. She doesn't know where she is. She can't get out of the room. The only door out of the room is locked. She wants to reach Tank but has no way of doing it. She's sick to her stomach and she thinks she's been drugged. She can't remember anything about what happened or how she got wherever she is, or what the people who locked her in the room want.

"She wants to let Tank know she's in danger."

Tucker pushes the speed dial on his Android cell phone and engages its speaker-phone.

I answer on the second ring, "I was just about to call you. We have a major crisis, Jolene has been kidnapped and a ransom demand has been made by the kidnappers. I need your and Maya's help to work with Powers and me to figure out a strategy to get her back.

"I can tell you right now, if anything happens to Jolene, I'm going to cut his …….."

"Stop. Star and Maya are listening in on the call. We know about Jolene; that was why we were calling you."

I ask immediately, "How can you possibly know that Jolene has been kidnapped? Did they make ransom demands of you, too?"

"No," interjects Maya, "No ransom has been requested of us, but Star has something to tell you."

I stay silent, thinking. I quickly conclude that one of Star's special skills is somehow involved. I've witnessed too many examples of unexplainable things surrounding Star to question the information she might share. Besides, she might be able to help get Jolene back.

The first thing out of Star's mouth makes tears well up in my eyes, "Jolene wants you to know that she loves you. She isn't hurt, but she's sick to her stomach. No one has spoken to her. She has no memory of what happened to her, or where she is."

"Thank you, Star. We'll save her. She'll be all right."

Tucker kneels down to address Star and asks, "Is there anything you know that can help Tank find Jolene?"

Star engages Tucker's eyes, tries to read his thoughts, does so and then moves her attention to Maya. After a few seconds, Star is pretty sure her parents are not going to ask her how she knows what she knows. She says loud enough for me to hear over the speaker phone, "She hears the faint sound of waves crashing against something and smells salt air."

CHAPTER 3 -- THE LAW OF UNINTENDED CONSEQUENCES

1944, Auschwitz. Poland: Dr. Wilhelm Soroson did not share the ideology of the current regime. If the truth had been known, he abhorred politics and never understood the insatiable need for power with which some men were infected. He was a medical scientist under Dr. Joseph Mengele's supervision assigned to Auschwitz, Poland in late 1944.

He knew he didn't have much time left to complete his experiment.   Allied forces were having their way with the allegedly superior German army, and Stalin's Russian army was on their eastern doorstep. Rumors were prevalent that there was a mutiny culminating among the Nazi hierarchy -- the generals no longer respected the Führer.

He selected number *A160092*, a 16-year-old girl, from the thousands of available Jews, for his experiment. She impressed him as one worthy of what he was about to do with her. She was strong compared with others who suffered their fate of a starvation diet in sub-human conditions.   She had dark intelligent eyes recessed in her gaunt face, but seemed to display the foundation of a survival instinct not seen in other incarcerated Jewish teenagers.

He assessed her one more time and concluded she was the one. He couldn't blame her for her current anxiety as she was crying huge tears, wailing in anticipation of what he might do to her. She was tied to a hospital bed, restraints placed across her chest, wrists secured to the bed frame, and ankles wide apart in elevated shackles. In his hand was something she had never seen before in her young life -- some sort of a weapon -- maybe a new Nazi pistol. It was made of shiny metal, with a trigger, and a little bottle-looking thing on top.

"Your name is Marsha Katz, correct?"

She sobbed but shook her head affirmatively. She was looking at a short, pudgy, red-faced man whose fleshy chin oscillated after he stopped moving his head. He was squinting at her as he spoke. "You need to calm down. I am not going to hurt you. In fact, I am saving you from certain death. We will need to keep you alive. It's important that you understand the responsibility you have to humankind."

She had absolutely no idea what he was talking about.

His assignment, along with the other 7,000 Schutzstaffel (SS) at Auschwitz was to learn as much medical science as possible using Jews as guinea pigs. In Block 10, experiments were conducted on prisoners as part of their positive eugenics policy under the direction of Rudolf Höss and Heinrich Himmler.

But Dr. Soroson intended an unsanctioned experiment of his own with the young lady. With the pistol in his right hand and a ten centimeter-long syringe in the other, he began his experimental medical research -- research which he would never know reinforced the law of unintended consequences long after his death.

CHAPTER 4 -- THE THINK TANK

Wiscasset, Maine: One entire twenty-five foot long wall of the library at the Cherokee estate is covered by a heavily-used white-board. Dry-erase colors of blue, red, black, and green cover almost all of the board -- not much of the board is left unused. Powers stands next to one end of the board jotting down thoughts, while I stand at the other end, encouraging others to come up with ideas. Smart phones are used to take digital photos before an idea is erased from the board.

While videoconferencing on one of the 60-inch wide-screen TVs in the room, I listen to a half-dozen inventors and brilliant thinkers from Tucker Cherokee's firm, *Entropy Entrepreneurs,* headquartered in Boston, as they shout over one another with objective and unemotional suggestions.

I look over at Star, who appears to be fascinated with this creative thinking process, the art of controlled chaos. Ram lies quietly by her side.

The level of anxiety in the library is palpable, with fear prevalent and stress rising. Star's brilliant mother, Dr. Maya Li Cherokee, speaks into a headset while researching a law enforcement database on her tablet -- trying to triangulate options about the possible special interest groups with the kind of resources required to kidnap Jolene.

The "think tank" process is dynamic and interactive where the rigidity of logic, mathematics, and science is cross-pollinated with the creativity of art and psychology. Creative juices flow where merging brain power force-multiplies ideas from collected world experiences.

My best friend since childhood, Tucker, prepares a list of plausible motives for Jolene's kidnapping, correlated with the assignment given to me by these assholes. Tucker is especially interested in the history of the dead lawyer and his relationship with former White House residents.

Powers writes in black on the white board in big block letters: NO WARNING ABOUT GOING TO THE POLICE OR FBI!

"Tank," -- Powers is grinding his teeth and suffering from a serious case of too much '*5-Hour Energy*' -- "normally the ransomers threaten to kill the kidnapped victim if the ransomed go to the police. This group doesn't care -- that means something, don't you think?"

I hear Tony, *Entropy Entrepreneur*'s Chief Scientist, yelling through the wide-screen video-conference screen, "That's because these scumbags think they're smarter than law-enforcement. Maybe they are. They don't think there is a risk of Jolene being found."

I ask of anyone that is listening, "Can we track their signal, identify the location of the videocam that is giving us these proof-of-life snippets of Jolene?"

Tucker looks up from his work and says, "Not that we know of, but I have some good contacts at NSA. I'll call them."

Powers writes on the white board:

LAST SEEN IN SALISBURY, MD.

He says to me, "Do you know that Salisbury is on the Eastern shore and is currently the site of a huge anti-poultry-farming protest? Activists have been camped there for weeks."

"Yes, I know. That's why Jolene was there, to protect the company's CEO from militant animal rights activists."

Powers continues writing on the white board:

DO THE PROTESTORS HAVE A LEADER? INVESTIGATE ANIMAL RIGHTS ACTIVISTS!

IS THERE A RELATIONSHIP BETWEEN THE ACTIVISTS AND THE SUICIDE VICTIM?

SEND LUCAS JUSTICE TO SALISBURY TO INVESTIGATE.

The "think tank" attendees pull ideas from the deep dark recesses of their minds and throw concepts out to wide receivers to be lateraled for progress to running backs. A sign over the white board reads: *I never made one of my discoveries through the process of rational thinking." -- Albert Einstein*

Star adds the element of the paranormal when she stands up. Ram rises up on all fours, as if tethered to her. She stares at me and gives me a slight nod. Both Tucker and Maya watch the exchange with anxiety. Powers goes silent and mutes the noise made by the on-going exchanges in the contentious video-conference group.

We all know that Star is sensing something. Whatever it is, it could provide an important clue. I kneel down, bend over and position myself so that Star can whisper in my ear.

She asks, "Can we see Jolene, now?"

"Now?"

She shakes her head up and down. The proof-of-life 10-second streaming webcam is something I suspect I will look forward to everyday as long as this crisis continues. Maybe Star will be able to sense when the best time is to view Jolene each day.

I stand up and say to the entire investigative team, "Listen up! We're going to view the webcam now which allows us to see Jolene. I'm going to put it up on one of the wide-screen TVs so we can view it together. We only have 10 seconds, so be as observant as possible. Maybe something will give us a clue. I'll record it so that we can play it back."

My laptop is already connected to the wide screen TV. I click on my favorites list and pick the website given to me by the kidnappers. An entirely different angle of the large room where Jolene is imprisoned is displayed.

Jolene looks like a fly on a wall. It doesn't look humanly possible to scale a smooth flat wall but that's exactly what she is doing.   She is about eight feet off the floor looking for something to grab onto to get higher on the wall.

The web site goes dark again. The same message as before reads, "You get 10 seconds each day. It's proof of life."

Ten seconds goes by fast!

Tucker notices that I'm paralyzed in thought, stands up and says to everyone, "O.K. let's make a list of observations while they're still fresh in our minds. Powers, will you be kind enough to continue to be our scribe?"

Maya says, "She's unhurt and healthy, no longer drugged. Her survival skills and Marine training have kicked in."

Tucker un-mutes the video-conference and one of the guys in Boston says, "She is looking for a way to escape."

Powers adds, "She's managed to convert her shoes into front-cleat-bearing shoes, probably by using kitchen utensils."

I add, "It is a new angle; they have multiple webcams in the room, yet she hasn't noticed the location of the cameras. She's well trained in the art of identifying and disarming surveillance cameras. They must be state-of-the-art nano-cameras."

Tucker says, "Lighting is perfect.   They're making no attempt to conceal anything from us as it relates to the location of her prison cell.   The kidnappers are either confident or arrogant or both."

Maya says, "The clock on the wall shows the same time as our clocks, so she's probably in the Eastern Time Zone and the video is likely real-time. Maybe it's not pre-recorded."

"Or not," I mention.   "It could be subterfuge, disinformation."

Young Star catches my eye and purses her lips.

My heart fell to my stomach. "What's the matter Star, what is it?"

"We don't want Jolene to try to escape!"

Incredulous at hearing Star's statement, I ask, "What do you mean, Star, that we don't want her to escape?"

"You have to save her, not rescue her."

"I get that. But why don't you want her to escape?"

Star fixes her gaze on me. I love her as if she was my own daughter and she loves me like an uncle. For crying out loud, Ram is my own personal dog -- I gave him to her to protect her. That's how much I love her.

Star continues to fix her eyes intensely on mine -- she doesn't back down. Her eyes provide a window into a universe of emotions. I wish I could read her mind, instead of the other way around.

Finally, Star says, "Jolene is safer where she is than the places an escape would take her. Tank, maybe you should just go ahead and solve the puzzle instead of spending your time trying to find her."

"Puzzle, what puzzle? Do you mean the puzzle about why the bad guys kidnapped Jolene or the suicide-guy puzzle?"

Maya intervenes, "The kidnapping is not really a puzzle, Tank. It's obvious to me that they want you to solve a crime. I suspect that as far as the kidnappers are concerned, the puzzle is the unsolved crime involving the dead White House attorney."

"Star, sweetheart," I continue, "is there anything you haven't shared with me that is important about finding Jolene? Anything at all?"

Star cocks her head, looks pleadingly at me, looks at her mother, and then reaches out to give me a hug around my leg. She says, "Jolene will be very hard to find. You have to save her by solving the puzzle. The only other thing I can tell you is that Jolene wants to hurt the kidnappers real bad. She's had some pretty ugly thoughts."

"If I catch the kidnappers, I'm going to crush them by running over them slowly with the tracks of a fifty ton Caterpillar D9."

The silence in the room in the Cherokee library is deafening. I can hear the hum of the electronic equipment. I can hear katydids and tree frogs outside the well-insulated walls. Not a word is spoken for many long seconds until Tucker finally breaks the silence, "OK, then. Let's focus on the puzzle as well as trying to find out where Jolene is being held hostage."

On the video conference monitor, *Entropy Entrepreneurs'* Chief Scientist, Tony Vinci, says, "The victim in question had very strong ties to the former First Lady at the time of his death. One could speculate that the attorney's death was, and still is, politically motivated."

Maya asks, "What are you saying, Tony, that he might have been murdered to protect the former First Lady from a scandal? Hell, scandal is her middle name. If every time a potential scandal emerged, she murdered someone, the streets of Washington would be littered with corpses."

I respond, "You mean like that Ambassador?"

Tony says, "No. What I'm implying is that the people who are ransoming Jolene in exchange for an investigation into the demise of this victim ... may be politically motivated. Don't forget, the attorney in question was subpoenaed to testify before Congress on his knowledge about alleged wrongdoings of the former First Lady. I bet that a right-wing organization wants us to uncover dirt on the potential future presidential candidate. So, I suspect that the kidnap is politically motivated."

As Tony is speaking, Powers is wiping down the white board to open up a fresh spot to make notes.

Tucker interjects, "Whoever or whatever this person or group is, they are confident that we are going to dig up facts that implicate someone high in the political food chain -- and they think they know the truth. So why don't they just reveal what they know instead of forcing *White Knight* to uncover the information?"

Maya says, "I bet it's fear. The kidnapper is probably more afraid of the wrath of the killers than he or she is of incurring retribution from Tank and Powers."

"And don't forget Ram," I add.

Powers writes on the white board, NO DEADLINE GIVEN. He says, "The victim has been dead for over 20 years. This is the ultimate cold case. They've cleverly manipulated the situation so that the deadline is self-imposed -- an interesting tactic. If they had just hired us, we wouldn't have been motivated to solve the mystery as quickly."

I look over to my best friend since childhood, Tucker, and admit, "Powers and I are damn good personnel security experts and private investigators. We're trained in law enforcement and through *White Knights* are licensed to operate with deadly force around the world. We have a great team of former Special Ops experts who will support this new mission to save Jolene. But I'm too close to the kidnapped person to make unemotional decisions and Powers, here, will leave a path of scorched earth too wide if he leads this mission. Tucker, I know you have your own company to run, but would you consider taking on the role of mission leader? We need your ability to develop an overall strategy, organize resources, coordinate our action, and adjust tactics as the dynamics dictate. We need your level head and the geniuses who surround you to save Jolene."

"OK, OK," Tucker capitulates, "we'll divide and conquer. Instead of concentrating all our resources on finding Jolene, we'll split up. Half of us will work the case and find evidence one way or another that proves or disproves suicide, while the rest of us continue the search for Jolene."

Powers says, "If it's OK with you, Tucker, I'll lead the cold case investigation."

Maya says, "And I'd like to help with the case by providing data analysis and research."

"Hello, out there!   Earth to Starship Tank.   How can we help?" It was Tony Vinci, speaking through an electronic voice synthesizer over the tele video speakers, making him sound like an alien.

It broke the tension.

Tucker says, "Let's return to the ten seconds of video we've just seen, of Jolene. What else did we observe?"

I note, "All we really got to see is her backside. Or am I the only one who noticed her backside?"

No one was dumb enough to admit to Tank that they looked at Jolene's ass. However, Star spoke up, "She is wearing new clothing."

"Good observation, Star. I noticed that, too. This means they bought her clothing, new outfits. They know her clothing size."

Tony says, "It means they expect her to be there for a while and that they're confident we're not going to find her."

CHAPTER 5 – WHERE JOLENE WAS LAST SEEN

Salisbury, Maryland: Lucas drives his late model Jeep Wrangler from Washington, D.C. across the Bay Bridge to Salisbury, on the eastern shore of Maryland. As he arrives at his destination, he notices cars and bikes parked on both sides of the road near the entrance to the headquarters of *Brave Chicken Corporation*, one of the largest poultry product providers in the country. A hundred or so ragged protestors are outside the complex carrying signs, proselytizing their beliefs, and singing rehearsed chants. Lucas grimaces after observing their protest signs. His favorite is *"Chickens are people, too!"* though he thinks that *"Chicken Lives Matter!"* is a close second.

A group of five young college-age protestors block the entrance to the headquarters where a worthless, overweight, and under-trained rent-a-cop guard is posted. The un-armed guard acts intimidated and frightened by the protestors who tease and make fun of him. Lucas gets out of his Jeep, approaches the protestors, and tells them to let him through.

Lucas Justice is not one to be messed with. He is wrapped around the axle way too tight. He is coiled tension just waiting for an opportunity to explode. He trusts no one, likes no one, and only needs a minor excuse to expose his will. Though just five feet, eight inches tall, he is 225 pounds of solid muscle. He looks like a block of granite and carries with him a personality to match. He is not only intimidating-looking, but he is the real deal -- a fighting machine, a former Army Ranger, trained by Powers.

The five protestors are young, and maybe a little high, so Lucas decides to give them a little slack if they act up. The alpha male of the protestors, a tall, lanky, bearded guy with an English accent speaks first: "Cross our picket line at your own risk. You guys are murderers and you torture animals for profit.

26

You guys are lower than whale crap, so you can go to hell. All I have to do is give the protestors here the word and you're toast."

Lucas never smiles, shows no emotion, speaks only if he feels it is necessary, and leverages his body language to communicate. Without saying a word or laying a hand on the young protestor, Lucas communicates volumes. He returns to his Jeep and starts it up, as the protestors wisely make a gap to allow him through.

However, one of the city-dwelling environmentalist protestors with a head full of mush unwisely smashes the back Plexiglas window of the Jeep as it passes through the picket line in front of the entrance to the parking lot. Even before the Jeep comes to a complete stop, Lucas is on the move in pursuit of the college-age kid who is holding a baseball bat. The kid drops the bat, turns and runs into the crowd of fellow protestors for protection, but the crowd couldn't open up fast enough to allow the kid to escape.

Lucas hits the kid hard in the back of the neck with the knuckles on his left hand. The protestor hits the ground like a sack of potatoes. Three male protestors and one female protestor retaliate and land ineffective punches on Lucas as he is scanning the crowd for potential weapons. Out of the corner of his eye he catches the sunlight reflected from a wine bottle flung his way. He ducks just in time, as the empty bottle surprises a non-violent participant nearby, striking him in the nose.

Nine protestors are lying on the ground before the rest of the crowd backs off -- they realize that they are clearly dealing with a well-trained and infinitely more experienced fighter than any of them. Fortunately, though, none of the prostrate protestors is seriously injured. You might say that Lucas has carefully pulled his punches, inflicting no more damage than the threat demanded.

Lucas calmly walks over to the unconscious bat-wielder, turns the dumb kid over, and takes out his wallet briefly to read his identification. He might need to contact the kid's insurance company, or maybe his family. He walks back to the Jeep with purpose at a metered pace, while constantly observing his surroundings. As he passes through the gate, he looks over at the pathetic rent-a-cop guard who then casts his eyes downward with obvious shame and embarrassment.

Lucas parks the Jeep in a visitor's spot near the entrance of the building, gets out, opens the front door, and walks directly to the first floor receptionist's desk.

"Hello, Mr. Justice, here is your visitor's badge. Please, take the elevator to the 5th floor; Mr. Brave's assistant is waiting for you and will escort you to his office."

Mr. Brave's assistant, Lucas would later learn, is a former Miss Maryland in the Miss America pageant. She smiles beautifully at him as he exits the elevator.

Never before had she not had a smile returned; it rattles and confuses her, so she asks him to follow her and just walks away. Lucas follows her and enjoys her very attractive, sexual movements.

Mr. Elliott Brave greets Lucas with an even broader smile than Miss Maryland's. He stands up from behind his clean oversized desk and offers his limp hand to Lucas. Mr. Brave says, "Please, have a seat. That was impressive. I watched the entire event on my security system. I've been watching the protestors and waiting for your arrival. That security guard in the front is worthless. I should fire the firm that provides our guard service."

Lucas nods. He says nothing in response.

Mr. Brave clears his throat and asks, "*White Knight* requested this meeting with me, so why are you here? What happened to Jolene Landrieu? Why are you replacing her? She

28

is very good. My contract with *White Knight* states that you can't replace key personnel without my prior approval. I'm impressed with your skills, but I still need an explanation."

Lucas stares at Elliott Brave for a good ten seconds before he asks, "When was the last time you saw Ms. Landrieu?"

"Mr. Justice," the CEO of *Brave Chicken* condescends, "*White Knight* works for me, not the other way around. Now, answer **my** questions!"

Lucas completely ignores the self-absorbed CEO. "I'd like to view all of your past two weeks' surveillance camera video recordings."

"You have no right or authority to ask to view our surveillance recordings. You're confused about who's in charge here. Get out of my office," Brave blustered, "**now**. I won't tolerate your insubordination."

Lucas leans to the right, pulls a cell phone out of his pocket and touches one number. Five seconds later, Lucas says into the phone, "Mr. Brave just fired us. Do you want to speak with him?" Lucas hands the cell phone over to Elliott Brave, stands up, walks out of the office, and shuts the door behind him. He nods his head to Miss Maryland and stands guard as if he was protecting the entrance to the CEO's office.

Their eyes lock as they both simultaneously hear the unmistakable sound made by helicopter rotors.

The Bell 525 Relentless helicopter with an FBI logo on the side hovers over the *Brave Chicken* headquarters campus. The protesters scramble to escape, as if they are the targets of the intruder. FBI Special Agent Mark Vintage follows five SWAT team members out of the helicopter long before the blades start to decelerate.

I am the last passenger out.

At the front door of the building, *Brave Chicken*'s corporate attorney is waiting, demanding to see a court order or search warrant for whatever the FBI intends to do. Special Agent Vintage hands the attorney a court order co-signed by the Attorney General of the United States to search the premises for evidence in a kidnapping case.

Special Agent Vintage says to the attorney, "The SWAT Team is here to enforce the search warrant. This gentleman, Mr. Tank Alvarez, and his assistant, Mr. Lucas Justice, are under contract with the FBI to assist in the search, since they are intimately familiar with your facility, its security, and your surveillance system. As I understand it, *White Knight Personal Security Services* has recently been fired by *Brave Chicken Corporation;* therefore, there is no conflict of interest with this FBI investigation.

"Now, if you don't mind, we'd like to enter without delay. There is a woman's life at stake here." He nods to the SWAT team which proceeds without resistance into the building, up the stairs to the fifth floor, and to Brave Chicken's CEO's office, where Lucas is still standing at attention.

Lucas wasn't guarding the CEO; he was making sure that Elliott Brave didn't leave his office. Lucas steps aside.

CHAPTER 6 -- TO BE FREE

In an unknown location: The ventilation register on the wall is almost within her reach. "Almost," she thinks, "is only good in hand grenades and horse shoes."

It has taken her fully twenty minutes just to scale eight feet on the sheer drywall using her improvised tree climbing spikes made from steak knives and duct tape. "At least I learned something from watching old MacGyver episodes."

Her left calf is beginning to cramp.

All the ventilation opening is going to do for her is provide a hand and foot hold to climb higher. Her goal is to reach a ceiling joist and climb around the ceiling to see if there is a weakness to this structure, or for something her captors overlooked. This is one time she is grateful for being six feet, one inch tall and only average in the bust department -- she couldn't have kept her balance if she had to lean back even another half an inch.

"Damn, I wish I could reach down and massage the cramp in my calf. A couple more inches now and I'll be able to touch the brass register and see if I can remove it from the opening."

She reaches out and extends her fingers just enough to caress the edge of the metal plate but can't get a good grip.

She falls – and it hurts; it hurts a lot.

Jolene is pretty sure she's dislocated her right shoulder. Somehow, she is going to have to relocate her shoulder joint. She lies there immobile for about five minutes, thinking about the method she is going to employ to get her shoulder in a position to force it back in its socket. If she could crawl to the wall, about three feet away, she could push against the wall with enough force to do it.

Except that, now, she discovers that she has also sprained, or broken, her right ankle. Movement of any kind hurts. She lies there another ten minutes, thinking about her options. "Damn it, I'm a Marine; I can do this."

She rolls on her good shoulder to get into position -- and passes out from the pain.

When she regains consciousness, she finds herself flat on her back. With her left foot, she pushes her damaged body along the smooth bamboo-laminated wooden floor to the wall. It hurts like hell, but she manages to push against the wall with the top of her head. If she could push herself up until her back is against the wall, she'd be in a sitting position.

She wonders if her captors are watching her go through this hell. Are they laughing?

Jolene takes a couple of deep breaths, grabs her right wrist with her left hand, intentionally rolls onto her bad shoulder while pulling on her arm as hard as she can.

She screams from her gut up through her throat like she has never screamed before.

She finds herself in an awkward position, unable to either sit up or roll over without enduring excruciating pain. She also realizes that she was unsuccessful at getting her shoulder back into place.

Jolene begins to cry.

Wiscasset, Maine: Many hundreds of miles away, Maya is trying to console her daughter, Star, who is also crying -- the unexplained pain in Star's right shoulder is excruciating.

CHAPTER 7 -- NOT A WALK IN THE PARK

1945 Death March: It was a cold, wet, windy, overcast, sloppy day. The SS were forcing her and thousands of other holocaust victims out of the Auschwitz encampment to go somewhere else -- she had no idea where. Sixteen-year-old Marsha Katz was healthier and stronger than most of her marching companions, including fourteen year old Viktor Nemath. Viktor was also a "patient" of Dr. Soroson and was taken under Marsha's protective wing as if Marsha was his big sister.

As it turned out, the awful-looking doctor never hurt Marsha. The unusual and intimidating-looking pistol he had in his right hand, it was later explained to her, was something called a "Hingson Peace Gun" -- a new contraption used to provide local anesthesia. She was very grateful that she never felt the injection from the frighteningly long needle. She thought something horrible and painful was going to be done to her, but to her great relief, the opposite occurred. This was extremely unusual conduct, based on all the horror stories she'd heard about the SS doctors. Ever since Dr. Soroson did whatever he did to her, she had been treated gently -- like she was special -- by him. Every day, she would be escorted by an SS guard back to the lab in Block 10 to be interviewed and fed a special meal. No inmate, other than Viktor, was given as much food to eat as Marsha. Dr. Soroson would check her blood pressure, weigh her, check her temperature, listen to her lungs, and give her "special water" which he explained contained dissolved vitamins. Marsha was actually gaining weight instead of losing weight, like everyone else she knew in the camp.

That was true until the SS ordered everyone in the female barracks outside onto the snow covered grounds for a final roll call. Most everyone in the building, young and old, expected this to be their last day. Some expected to be thrown alive into the ovens; some expected to be lined up and shot, and others expected to be gassed. Most of the victims were ready for their death -- it was better than being tortured for science and starved to death. Many were undernourished, diseased and weak, their bodies made grotesque by pain and poor diet.

It wasn't just the female barracks being evacuated; it was the entire camp. Thousands upon thousands of inmates were assembled outside in the cold weather this morning, many without adequate clothing, some shoeless, and almost all too weak for what was being asked of them. The gates to the disgusting place were open.

Marsha saw Viktor as one of the male barracks was being evacuated. The adult males were forced to pull carts filled with camp luggage down the snow-laden roads. Marsha and Viktor gradually migrated toward each other, and eventually Marsha held Viktor's hand as they walked through the gates for an interminably long walk -- and what later would be referred to as a -- "death march."

But Dr. Soroson had given both Marsha and Viktor rubber boots, scarves, gloves, and heavy wool oversized sweaters the day before the scheduled beginning of the camp evacuation. The two children were better prepared to endure the fate of the cruel march than others. Marsha was curious about why Dr. Soroson treated Viktor with the same gentleness as he treated her.

Though Marsha's problems were insignificant compared with the problems others faced, she still had to hide the fact that she felt continuously nauseous, and her breasts were tender and swelling.

CHAPTER 8 -- SOMETHING IS FISHY IN DENMARK

Wiscasset, Maine: "What?" Maya is thinking. "Did I just read this correctly?" She is reading testimony made before the U.S. Senate by a senior U.S. Park Police officer. *"We determined that it was death by suicide, prior to going up and looking at the body."*

"Honey," she yells to Tucker in an adjacent room, "do you know that a homicide investigation was never launched in this case?"

"No," answers Tucker, "I haven't yet read the case material on the thumb drive from Tank's truck. Have you validated the information? How do you know that the autopsy report is the actual report and that it hasn't been tampered with?"

Maya answers, "Most of the information provided on the thumb drive is information that is publicly available; you can download it off the internet. I did a document comparison and confirmed the accuracy. That doesn't mean that the information wasn't tampered with before it was made publicly available, though.

"As you know, *White Knight* has contracts with the FBI and other federal agencies. Powers informed his friend, the former Director of FBI, of Jolene's kidnapping. Powers later influenced some of his contacts in the FBI -- who were former students of his when they were in the military together -- to gather a little background that might not be publicly available on the case. We expect to get feedback soon."

As Tucker is walking into the library where Maya is working, he comments, "You said that 'most' of the data on the thumb drive contained publicly available information. What is on the drive that isn't publicly available?"

"Photos. Photos of the victim at the scene of the 'suicide,' photos of the autopsy, and background information on the law enforcement officer who was first on the scene ... who was intimately involved in the investigation. Powers is currently calling in some chips to validate the accuracy of that information."

Star follows Tucker into the library and smiles at her mother. Maya says, "You look happy today! How's that shoulder?"

Star answers, "It's better now. Dad says it's OK if I have a friend over. Is it OK with you, too? She helps me at the animal rescue shop sometimes. She loves Ram. We're just going to watch a *National Geographic* Special on TV together."

"Sure, sweetheart. It's good to see you smile because you're so pretty when you smile!"

"Thanks, Mom."

Maya says to Tucker after Star leaves the room, "I've been so worried about her ever since this whole thing with Jolene started. I think it has been as hard on her as it has been on Tank. Maybe harder. At least Tank doesn't feel or sense things the way Star does."

Tucker says, "I take it that Star's good mood and painless shoulder are good signs for Jolene, or am I reading too much into it?"

"Who knows? It's impossible to fully understand Star's extrasensory perceptions and correlate meanings with them. But I do think we need to observe her closely.

"We still need a plan, you know, about how to protect Star from herself. She's growing up way too fast and she'll soon be venturing into her teens, where hormones turn angels into demons. Who knows how that's going to affect her special gifts?"

"Do you know a good place where we could hide for a few years?" Tucker jokes.

Maya's cell phone rings. It is Powers.

Maya says, "How's my favorite 'Private Eye' doing?"

Powers answers, "I can't wait to tell Tank that I'm your favorite!"

"Don't let it go to your head."

Powers says, "See if you can locate the whereabouts of the investigating officer for the Park Police. She was the first law enforcement person on the scene."

Maya responds, "I was just reading about her and her testimony before Congress. I'd love to have a chat with her."

Powers quips, "That's the whole idea. But first, we need to find her."

After hanging up from Powers, Maya continues reading reports on the case. She learns that the former First Lady's Secret Service code name was "Evergreed" and that some of the agents referred to her as the FLU for "First Lady Uncensored." Maya also reads that a Secret Service agent once mistakenly spoke to her and said something atrocious to her like, "Good Morning."

Her response was: "Fuck off." After all, he had no right to speak to her even though his job was to take a bullet for her.

But what caught Maya's eye is a report where Evergreed, the FLU, had castigated and berated the former White House attorney in public, stating that "he would never be more than a hick-town lawyer, and wasn't ready for the big time." The report also states, "Agents say that being on Evergreed's detail is the worst duty assignment in the Secret Service. Being assigned to her detail is a form of punishment."

Maya says out loud to no one in particular, "What a sweetheart. She is probably mean enough to have committed this heinous crime."

37

CHAPTER 9 -- GOOD BAD GUYS

At an undisclosed location: The faint sound of something mechanical running, like an air-conditioner compressor, brings her out of her dream state. She can't remember what she was dreaming about, but it had to have been better than the current reality; she is awakening, again, with an awful headache.

Jolene intentionally keeps her eyes closed, endures the wild floating ride, inspects the veins in her eyelids, and tracks a floating yellow ball. She is mesmerized by a drug-induced dizzying experience to which she is being subjected.

She forces her eyes open. Again, she is in bed, disoriented, and nauseous with blurred vision. It feels like "Groundhog Day" to her.

Then it comes back to her -- the fall, the dislocated shoulder, and the twisted ankle. "Why am I not on the floor? How did I get into a bed?"

She tries to focus her eyes to see what is going on around her -- she moves her eyes from side to side to keep from moving her throbbing head. Movement of any kind is painful. What she sees shocks her.

Her arm is in a sling and her ankle is wrapped.

"What the hell?"

Wiscasset, Maine: Powers, Tucker, Maya and the Boston contingent of the *Entropy Entrepreneurs* team all watch the daily ten seconds of live streaming video of Jolene when she has not yet awakened; she is just lying on her bed with her arm in a sling and her ankle wrapped.

Tucker asks, "Observations?"

Powers says, "Jolene's been hurt, but the criminals that hurt her provided medical care. They're on the premises and close by her, watching her."

"Oh my God, Tucker!" Maya exclaims; "can that explain why Star was in such pain last night?" Tucker turns white as a sheet. No one else understands what they are talking about.

"Is it possible," Powers conjectures, "that Jolene fell off the wall, hurt herself, and they gave her medical attention?"

Regaining her composure somewhat, Maya says, "I'd like to believe that. We could certainly rest a little easier knowing they don't have evil intentions for her."

Tony Vinci adds, "At least for as long as they need *White Knight* and company to do their dirty work for them. My observation of the ten-second video is that Jolene has been given a powerful drug again. She's going to wake up and think she's Batman for a few minutes. I don't know if there is a clue there or not, but we might be able to narrow down the list of the kind of drug she is being given."

"What I notice is that the camera perspective is different from the other ten second videos," Powers offers. "They are moving the camera constantly. How are they doing that without Jolene noticing it?"

"Tony," asks Tucker, "What is the state-of-the-art in the science of nano-drone video camera deployment?"

Tony answers, "Can't discuss that, boss."

"Hmmm," respond Powers, Tucker, and Maya.

Tucker says, "OK, but chase it down and determine if it's a clue we need to follow."

"Well, sir," responds Tucker's Chief Scientist, "I already know the answer."

Tucker understands that Tony can't share his knowledge over the telephone. "I'll be down in the Boston office tomorrow. We can discuss it then."

Entropy Entrepreneurs is a Defense Advanced Research Projects Agency (DARPA) contractor with numerous on-going classified projects requiring that *Entropy* maintain a windowless and soundproof Sensitive Compartmented Information Facility (SCIF) where discussions about classified information can be conducted. No cell phones, personal laptops, internet access, tablets, or external communication devices are allowed in. Anything electronic that goes into the SCIF, stays in the SCIF.

Tucker asks, "Any other observations about the 10-second video of Jolene, before we develop a list of action items?"

Maya says, "It looks to me like bottled water, pain medicine, ankle wraps, and other items were left on the night stand."

"These are pretty good bad guys," quips Powers.

Tucker says, "Let's get on with the list of action items required for uncovering the truth about the demise of the dead White House lawyer."

Tony asks, "Isn't there a rock group named Dead Lawyers?"

Powers laughs, "If not, there should be."

Impatiently, Tucker says in a loud and authoritative voice, "Number one: JJ has made arrangements for Maya and Powers to fly to Key West to meet with the retired U.S. Park Police Sergeant Kristen Brown. She was the first law enforcement person on the scene of this alleged suicide. They're scheduled to leave late this afternoon.

"Number two: we've asked the FBI to allow us access to all of their files, including the non-redacted ones, on the case. We won't be able to leave the premises or take photos of the documents, but they've agreed to allow us to view them. I had to call in a few chips to make that happen.

"Number three: we're tracking the whereabouts of the retired chief medical examiner, Dr. Theodore Rich, who performed the autopsy on the dead lawyer, so that we can interview him.

"Number four: the first person to find the deceased in the old Civil War fort, the person who notified the police -- and preceded the Park Police Officer on the scene -- needs to be located and interviewed. His name is Robert Kingsley. JJ is trying to track him down, too.

"Number five: Maya noticed that no fingerprints were found on the handle of the 38-caliber Colt weapon that was alleged to have been used by the White House attorney in his suicide. His fingerprints were only found on the *barrel* of the pistol! Of course, that would be my method of choice for suicide," continues Tucker sarcastically, "hold the gun by the barrel and 'push' the trigger.

"So, next, we need to start creating a list of persons-of-interest -- people who might have had a motive to kill the former White House Counsel."

Tony suggests, "It's hard not to put the former first couple on the list; especially 'Evergreed', the FLU. She had opportunity, means, and motive. Even if she could prove she didn't do it herself, she has to be at the top of the list. She could have contracted the job."

Tucker says, "Good point; they'll remain at the top of the list. In addition, family members should be high on the list of potential candidates based on statistics."

Powers adds, "There may have been many politically-motivated people willing to commit the crime to protect the first family. Who were the people who hitched their future to the political success of the former First Family -- both foreign and domestic? The number of names on that list could be very long."

CHAPTER 10 -- THE ONLY WAY TO KEEP A SECRET IS TO TELL NO ONE

Boston, Massachusetts: Geniuses sometimes come in unusual packages.   Albert Einstein was famous for his wild white unkempt hair. Michelangelo ignored even the most basic tasks of personal hygiene; he very rarely bathed or even changed clothes. He had sometimes gone so long without taking his boots off that when he finally did, the skin came away with the boots.

Tony Vinci is an equally unique genius. His head and upper body are abnormally large. His hands are huge and powerful and his upper arms stretch the threads of his shirt. Anyone who ever shakes hands with him will never want to repeat the painful experience. His legs, however, are dwarf-like.

Though somewhat handsome in a Sicilian sort of way, at four-feet, ten-inches tall and 155 pounds, he is one-of-a-kind. Tony has short-cropped salt and pepper hair, an engaging smile, and a wry sense of humor.

At age 19, Tony Vinci already had five patents pending to his name.   At age 32, he had 76 patents awarded outright, pending, or applied-for.   He was recruited aggressively by *Entropy Entrepreneurs* to be their Chief Scientist and now manages teams of scientists on projects ranging from esoteric basic research for military intelligence, to renewable energy technologies, to developments in pharmaceuticals.

He hears the keypad being used outside the room, then hears the dial being spun, and finally hears the door open. Tucker doesn't greet Tony like he greets anyone else and, of course, he never shakes his hand. It is never "hello" or "good morning" or "how are you?" Instead, this time he says, "Don't you ever take that Outback hat off? Do you take it off when you shower?"

"Good morning to you too, Boss. I don't take showers; I sit in a tub so I don't have to take the hat off."

WHA-CKED   JED O'Dea
(White House Attorney-Counsel Killed)

Tucker asks, "What the hell are you doing, playing video games here in the SCIF?"

Tony is sitting in front of two large computer monitors with superior high resolution graphics -- the best Tucker has ever seen. Tony is also playing with two joy sticks; one in each hand.

Tony says, "Instead of boring you with a *Power Point* presentation which reports the state-of-the art for nano-drones, I thought I'd show you. You're a visual kind of guy, right?"

Tucker asks, "What am I looking at on your monitors?"

"Sit down next to me. You'll figure it out soon enough."

Tony manipulates the joy-sticks while Tucker observes.

Finally, Tucker says, "These are not graphics at all, this is real time video."

"Yup."

"My God, that's Tank. Are you telling me that you have Tank under surveillance using a nano-drone?"

"Yup."

"You flew this thing all the way to Maryland and still have visual?"

"No and yes. I sent it by Fed Ex to Lucas Justice with instructions on how to activate it. The limited battery life prevents long-distance deployment. But yes we still have visual. He launched it last night and watched me fly it right through the front door of *Brave Chicken*'s headquarters the first time he opened it. I've surveyed most of the building but resisted going into the women's restrooms. I do have limits to my depravity."

"That's good to know, but you'll ruin your reputation if that gets out.

"You've demonstrated to me the nano-camera's visual quality and streaming range. How small is the drone?"

Tony smiles and says, "About the size of a large insect; a grasshopper or June bug. A new rare earth metal discovery in battery technology provides the power for this tiny little guy." He points to one on top of the desk, behind a coffee cup, a small white thing.

Tucker asks, "Incredible! How well known is it that this technology has advanced to this state?"

"There's no way to know with certainty. My guess is that around a thousand people know about it today. I figure ten thousand will know three months from now and a hundred thousand will know a year from now. The number of people who know about the state-of-the-art for nano-drones is small enough today to matrix with potential entities which might want to uncover the truth about the cold case we're investigating. But I need better data about the organization or individuals who could be behind Jolene's kidnapping."

"You're a data hog, Tony; you always want more data. And, guess what? I know you. What's the saying, 'it's better to work with the devil you know that the devil you don't know?' I brought you a list; 'It's an interesting compilation of "Who's Who" in the nefarious underworld of special interests. Meet me in my office in thirty minutes and we'll go over the list along with your new assignment."

Tony furls his bushy brow, looks a little puzzled, and asks, "What new assignment?"

Tucker smiles, stands up, and as he is leaving the SCIF says, "Thirty minutes."

Wiscasset, Maine: Maya and Powers create two additional lists. Neither list contains shadow organizations; rather, the lists contain the names of powerful and influential people who might be able to help us solve the two separate mysteries in which we find ourselves engrossed.

The first list contains names of people who might be able and willing to help uncover undisclosed information associated with the death of a White House attorney -- information which is intentionally buried deep in archival vaults under a twenty-year-old court order.

White Knight Personal Security Services has won a government contract to provide personal security services for the Architect of the Capitol, Byron Chism. "Old man Chism" and his equally old friend, Clinton Auclair, Director of the Library of Congress (Librarian of Congress), own a cigar bar in Alexandria, Virginia together. A frequent customer of their *Brown Leaf Cigar Bar* is Gina Goodman, Chairman of the Board of the Smithsonian Institution. The three of them have access to the National Archives and, together, know the contents of every nook and cranny in Washington, D.C.

All three are on the first list.

The second list includes everyone who might have profited from the death of the White House lawyer, even slightly.

Alexandria, Virginia: During its long history, Alexandria has been a tobacco trading post, one of the ten busiest ports in America, a part of the District of Columbia, a Civil War supply center for Union troops, and a street-car suburb for federal workers.

45

WHA-CKED

JED O'Dea

(White House Attorney-Counsel Killed)

The pleasant aroma of a bakery can be enjoyed from inside a vehicle with the windows up as far away as a quarter mile. The tempting smell from a steakhouse attracts customers as it instantly triggers hunger pangs and generates saliva ready to transfer taste enzymes.

For cigar aficionados, the smell that emanates from a high quality cigar trips happy synapses. Before Powers gets within twenty yards of the *Brown Leaf Cigar Bar*, his desire for a *Romeo Y Julieta 1875* is irresistible.

As is his desire for *Glenlivet* on the rocks.

Powers walks straight past the impressive selection of cigars to the bar, orders his favorite cigar and a drink, and waits until one of the owners emerges. He is in no hurry. He watches the depressing nightly news on a cable news channel over the bar until he hears someone behind him boom out with, "Well, if it isn't Senator Powers! How the hell are you? You are a legend around this town. Come join me at my table; I want to hear about your latest adventure. Old men like me have to live vicariously through the lives of people like you."

Powers gets off the bar stool, carries his almost empty glass of Scotch and his treasured cigar over to Ol' Clint's reserved table. Director Auclair is at least 100 pounds overweight, with the buttons on his expensive dress shirt stressed to the max. He breathes heavily just from walking from the table to the bar and back. Powers suspects that Clint's heart works ten times harder than his, just to get through each day. However, he is a jovial guy and achieves his great success in Washington circles due to his pleasant disposition, great repertoire of tasteful jokes, and his perfect memory. Director Auclair could give you a lecture on any topic, whether it be the diet of 14th century Inca Indians in Peru, to the name of a 5th century Pope, to the method used by NASA to store and evaporate liquid oxygen. He also never forgets a Washington scandal. He can still recite for you the name of a former Senator's lady friend or a cabinet member's secret weakness.

Clinton Auclair is a good guy with whom to have a drink and cigar. It is very lucky for Powers that Auclair recognizes and wants to speak with him. Powers always says he'd rather be lucky than good. He is a great believer in luck; the harder he works the luckier he gets.

"So, Senator," Clint asks, "have you had any interesting escapades lately?"

"Please don't call me Senator. That was the worst gig I ever had. I hated that job. Nothing but a bunch of self-important blowhards in there who think that unless you're a lawyer, you are an ignorant fool. Behind closed doors when there is nobody around to record their true character, they are really assholes."

"Rumor has it," Clint says with a wry knowing smile, "that you were most effective at persuading the more stubborn of your brethren to see things your way precisely during those times when there was nobody to record their true character."

Powers smiles and says, "True." He does not elaborate, and Clint senses that he'd better not take that dead-end road with Powers.

Director Auclair changes the subject and asks, "How is business? I understand that *White Knight* is protecting Byron; is that why you are here?"

Powers says, "You don't miss a thing do you, Clint? Yes, I am hoping to catch up with Byron, but I'm not here to protect him; an employee of *White Knight* is shadowing him as we speak. I'm here to pick his brain on another topic."

"Anything I can help with?"

"Possibly, but let's have another drink first. What are you drinking?"

"Wild Turkey 101 on the rocks."

Powers goes to the bar, asks the bartender to refill their glasses, hands him his card, and asks him if he would let the co-owner, Byron Chism, know he is at the *Brown Leaf* commiserating with Director Auclair. Powers notices that the bar population is increasing as the afternoon crawls into evening.

One person, sitting at the bar, seems out of place. Powers notices him but, at first, can't put his finger on how or why he recognizes him.

Powers returns to Auclair's table, places both drinks on the mahogany, and relights his *1875*. Auclair is drawing on a *Gurkha Special Edition,* leans his head back, nose toward the ceiling, blows smoke into the air, and watches it swirl as it is immediately drawn into the ventilation system.

Clint asks, "So, how might I be of assistance to you? Hopefully, it will be exciting; I need some damned excitement in my life."

"Do you recall," starts Powers -- who knows that Auclair recalls everything -- "anything about that White House attorney who committed suicide over twenty years ago?"

A broad smile emerges on Clinton Auclair's rosy face as he peers over his wire-rimmed glasses. He waits for Powers to continue.

"Well, twenty years ago, I was in a different line of business -- Special Operations -- so I didn't pay that much attention to it. What do you recall about it?"

"What I remember," Director Auclair offers, "Is that the FBI investigated it, two Congressional Committees investigated it, and a Senate Sub-committee investigated the case for any wrongdoing, but no one was able to disprove suicide. Now, there were many conspiracy theorists back in the day who believed that there was a White House and FBI cover-up of something nefarious."

Powers asks, "To satisfy my curiosity, where should I go to get the low-down on the case?"

"Powers, you can't bullshit a bull-shitter! You need to give me a little context for your interest in this old story."

Knowing how many projects in the greater Washington, D.C. metropolitan area require secrecy, Powers says, "I'm unable to share with you the reason for my inquiry. Suffice it to say that it may be a matter of life or death."

The expression on Auclair's face is classic; he wishes he could have captured it with a camera. Just as Auclair is about to speak, Powers sees the co-owner and *White Knight* customer, Byron Chism, approach with a big smile on his face.

Byron asks, "Powers, my old friend, are you here on business or did you come to my bar for pleasure?"

"It's a genuine pleasure to be here in your bar. As I enjoy it here, I am fervently wondering why I haven't been here before."

The Architect of the Capitol mentions, "Before I forget, I want to tell you that the officers you have assigned to protect me have been professional, polite, discreet, and conscientious. You employ good people."

"That's good to hear. As long as you remain safe, I know they are doing their job. Any more threats on your life?"

Byron looks around before he shakes his head. Auclair's eyes are wide in surprise. He says, "Here, I am one of your best friends, and you don't share that very important fact with me!"

Powers says to Byron, "I let that cat out of the bag intentionally. You need to keep the people you trust, like Clint here, informed so they can help watch your back. We in the business of personal protection use all the resources we have at our disposal to protect our customers."

49

Clint shakes off the hurt and changes the subject. "Do you know that Powers is reopening the old White House attorney suicide case?"

"Why in the world," Byron says with a frown, "would you be interested in that? You can probably find everything you ever wanted to know about that case on the web." Byron's Hemingway-like face appears to have more facial muscles than the average Joe. He is a short, underweight, frail-looking, white-haired old man of around seventy. However, his intellect emanates from his fragile frame as if he had been sprayed with a protective coating.

"Hell, just contact Forrester. He'll tell you everything you ever wanted to know. He even wrote a screenplay and tried to get a movie made about the case."

Auclair chimes in and says, "I was just about to tell Powers the same thing before you showed up. If there is anything you want to know about that case, just contact Forrester."

Powers' blank expression reveals his lack of knowledge about who "Forrester" is.

Auclair says, "You really were in some other universe twenty years ago! Forrester True was the *Washington Press's* investigative reporter assigned to the case. He was determined to find 'the rest of the story,' as Paul Harvey used to say. He was sure that he was going to uncover the next 'Watergate.'

"What he uncovered was a big fat zero; lots of speculation, innuendos, theories, and fiction, but no facts. Last I heard, Forrester was writing sports columns in a local Salmon, Idaho newspaper. I think Mr. True blogs though; you might find him on social media somewhere."

Powers stands up abruptly, doesn't excuse himself, doesn't speak to either Byron or Clinton, quickly moves to a nearby table occupied by a handsome thirty year-old smoking a *Legends* and reading a two week-old *Washington Times* classified section. Powers reaches over the man's ashtray, grabs his cell phone on the table, pulls the earbud out of the man's ear, and proceeds to search him for other electronics. What he finds instead is a short nosed Beretta 3032 Tomcat. The young man does not resist Powers' assault on his person. A few seconds later, Powers finds what he is looking for -- an eavesdropper. It is a short-range, micro-parabolic-dish, filtered sound-amplifying device with recorder.

The fact that the young man doesn't resist Powers' aggressive treatment of him reveals to Powers that the kid knows who Powers is and that he has been warned not to resist, since he would risk serious injury.

Powers sits down at the table and continues to confiscate anything resembling an electronic device or a weapon. Powers says, "I've been watching you watch me even before you left the bar to take a seat at a table near me. By the look on your face when you lit up that cigar, I'd say it was your first. You coughed two or three times. You don't drink hard stuff either, do you? You haven't taken even one sip of your drink. In the future if you're going to pretend to read a newspaper, you need to move your eyes from left to right and occasionally down the newspaper. You have a lot to learn if you're going to survive in this business. I picked up your tail two blocks before I entered the premises."

The man says nothing.

"Who hired you? Why are you tailing me? How many bones in your right hand do you want me to break to prove to your boss that you were tortured before you broke down and gave me an answer?"

Green eyes stare back at Powers, saying nothing. Powers appraises the guy with new respect. The man shows unusual self-confidence from a face that looks like it never even grew

51

peach fuzz. His dirty blond hair is straight and wears well with his yellow button-down shirt and khaki pants.

Powers leans back in his chair and says, "Maybe you're right. Maybe I won't interrogate you in front of forty witnesses." He lifts the eavesdroppers' phone and punches in a few numbers. A few seconds later he says, "Tank, we have a new lead. He's here with me at the *Brown Leaf* in Alexandria. He's not intimidated by me so I thought you might want the honor of interrogating him to find out what he knows about Jolene's kidnapping."

The blond man's body language changes; he appears more nervous and looks around the room for what Powers suspects is an escape route.

Powers continues, "My gut tells me he's been tailing me to monitor our progress on behalf of the ransomers who kidnapped the love of your life."

The blond man scoots his chair back a few inches. Powers is ready if the blond man chooses to run.

"Hell, Tank, I figure you won't let any rules of fair play get in your way of finding the whereabouts of Jolene."

The blond man looks directly at one of the bar's patrons for help. Powers locks eyes with a distinguished looking grey-haired well-dressed sixty-year-old.

Powers continues, "I'll hold him here until you arrive, but we may need to get Agent Vintage involved. How soon do you think he could get someone from the FBI or the Alexandria City Police here?" Powers listens intently before he ends the call.

He stands up and walks back to the table where Clinton Auclair and Byron Chism are being entertained by the drama. Powers never takes his eyes off the younger man as he hands Byron the Beretta Tomcat and says, "Watch my back; take cell phone photos of the guy I'm going to speak to, and keep the gun for your own protection."

Powers walks up to the distinguished-looking man who locked eyes with him and asks, "How do you know the blond man?" Powers nods in the direction of the nervous eavesdropper.

The distinguished-looking man blusters, "You have no right to get in my face. Who the hell do you think you are?"

"Your response to my question screams of guilt. You know the guy, and you're complicit with felonious kidnapping. I'm under contract with the FBI to help save the life of a kidnapped woman. You are now under my microscope. You just made a bad decision by not cooperating with me."

That is all the blond eavesdropper needs to hear to cause him to bolt. He doesn't head for the door because he would have to cross Powers' path. Instead, he jumps on the bar, rolls over onto the floor, gracefully runs back into the hallway leading to a back parking lot only to be knocked unconscious and fall flat on his face, breaking his nose and pounding his forehead into a concussion. The *White Knight* officer assigned to guard the Architect of the Capitol, Byron Chism, was on the premises when he received this strange call -- someone speaking to him as if he were Tank. Of course, he knew the strange caller was his boss, Powers. The two of them carry the unconscious man out the back door, into the parking lot, and deposit him into the bed of the *White Knight* guard's old Subaru Baja. They cover the bed with the truck's bed apron; Powers takes the keys, nods to his subordinate, and drives away.

Back in the *Brown Leaf*, Clinton Auclair, Director of the Library of Congress, laughs and says, "That was fun. We need to invite Powers here more often."

Oyster Bay, Long Island, New York: Shelby Viking, the former First Lady's campaign manager, uses her affluent father's private mansion to prepare "Evergreed" for the Democratic nomination for President of the United States. At Shelby's request, a tall, handsome, well-mannered servant brings a tray of tea into the room where they are practicing the answers to specific tough questions which are inevitable during the campaign. The servant asks the FLU, "Is there anything else I can get you, Madam?"

She answers, "You can get out of my face. Never speak to me unless I speak to you first."

The servant says nothing, backs away, and looks Shelby in the eye as he leaves. Shelby wants to say something about the rudeness, but decides against putting herself in a position to incur the former First Lady's wrath. Instead, Shelby says, "OK, let's get started. Pretend I'm Chris Wallace of Fox News and I ask, 'You're a big-government advocate. You once said, "It takes a community to raise a child." In your opinion, are there limits to the size of government? Are there any areas where you think the people should be free to make their **own** choices? Are there any areas where the government shouldn't stick its nose into the private lives of the people?'"

"Chris," she answers, "governments, whether federal, state, or local, are necessary to protect good people from bad people. I'm not willing to limit the size of government to achieve the objective of appeasing delusional people. Are you? Do you care that little about the common person that you far right-wing demagogues in your ideological misery would protect debased CEOs of polluting oil giants, but not our vulnerable innocent children from evil?"

Shelby asks FLU as she pretends to interview her, "Why is it that you think it is OK for movie makers, movie stars, and athletes to be in the top one percent of wage earners, but not CEOs?"

"CEOs make their money on the backs of workers, whereas, athletes, actors and actresses, and movie producers earn their income by virtue of their own work. The fact that you would ask a question like that implies you just don't get it -- you're ideologically blind."

Shelby Viking says, "Very good, you'll score well with your constituents with responses like that, but do try to respond with a little less anger."

"But Shelby," responds 'Evergreed', "I **am** angry."

CHAPTER 11 -- ALL WORK AND NO PLAY

Salisbury, Maryland: This is mind-numbing and tedious. I've been at this now for twenty-two hours and I haven't found one second of video with Jolene on it. There is no doubt in my mind that the surveillance cameras' digital recorders have been tampered with.

"Lucas, have you seen any evidence of video splicing?"

There is no response.

"Lucas?"

I look across the room at Lucas and find that he is sound asleep in a sitting position in an uncomfortable metal folding chair. Dammit, I can't blame him; I wish I could fall asleep sitting in a chair. I need to take a walk, get some fresh air, clear my head, and think about my next move. Looking at the clock on the wall, I discover that it is 11:17 PM. I think I'll walk around the Brave Chicken grounds here.

Unconsciously, I pat my side to make sure my 9mm S&W M&P appendage is present. I nod at the night guard at the front desk on my way out of the building, display my day badge, and walk out into the humid and breezy night.

The air is heavy but the temperature is OK. I never cease to enjoy a solitary walk; it stimulates my thinking process. Let's see, what have I learned so far about the whereabouts of Jolene?

Not much.

This is the second time she's been kidnapped because someone wanted to use her to get to me. I wonder if she'll eventually conclude that I'm too much trouble to love.

She's OK, at least. Maybe she is in some pain from her "accident," but she's not being tied to a chair, tortured, or sexually abused. I'll take a little pain over that, for her. The kidnappers or ransomers don't demonstrate the characteristics of sociopaths or people driven by abnormal psychological or mental disorders. They are organized and have prepared a well-thought-out plan. I believe that -- because they have maintained a well-stocked, clean, and healthy environment for her, instead of a dirty basement in an abandoned warehouse or a manufacturing plant -- the kidnappers are not your typical criminals.

The kidnappers must be associated, in some way, with someone or an organization aligned with a federal defense contractor. Otherwise, how would they be using the advanced nano-camera technology to monitor Jolene?

They are well-funded, I suspect. The secret place they are holding Jolene, the number of people assigned to the effort, and the complexity of executing the plan implies that big money is behind this kidnapping.

I suspect that Mr. Brave is involved in the kidnapping of Jolene in some way. What could possibly be his connection? It's hard to imagine a motive. Why would he have the surveillance camera records tampered with? Why eliminate any video recordings of Jolene? Hopefully, Agent Vintage is doing a good job interviewing him. Maybe a lead will come out of it.

Who is the beneficiary of a "successful" outcome resulting from investigating the death of a White House attorney, ruled a suicide over twenty years ago? It is obvious to me that a "successful" outcome for the kidnappers is ... that it's determined that a murder has been committed, and that the murderer or the person who paid for the murder is discovered. So, who benefits from that conclusion?

Sudden movement in the brush fifteen feet away causes me to reflexively pull my 9mm and prepare to defend myself.

The raccoon flees and I return my gun to its holster. I return my thoughts to what I know about the case so far. What should I make of Star's claim of Jolene smelling salt air?

WHA-CKED   JED O'Dea
(White House Attorney-Counsel Killed)

I jump like I've been touched when the sound from my cell phone announces that Powers is calling in.

"How soon can you get here?"

"Where's here?"

"Manassas."

"Why; what's up?"

Powers explains, "I'm interviewing a gentleman who is linked in some way to the kidnappers. I thought you'd want to ask a few questions, yourself."

"I don't have a car here but I might be able to persuade someone to loan me one. I should be there in three and a half hours. Leave him able to speak when I get there, OK?"

"I haven't laid a glove on him."

"Yet."

Manassas, Virginia is not far from Quantico, home to both a Marine base and an FBI training center. Manassas is also the location of a *White Knight* interrogation safe house sometimes used by the FBI and other three-letter agencies, off-the-books. Powers is nursing the thirty year-old blond eavesdropper back to clarity using smelling salts and copious quantities of black coffee. So far, the guy hasn't talked. He vomited an hour ago -- a sign of a head injury -- but seems more lucid, now. Powers says, "You need to rest up a bit before Tank gets here."

The man's eyes show acknowledgement of what Powers just said to him. His eyes also show his fear.

The man finally speaks, "You kidnapped me. That's a felony. My attorney will put you away for a long time."

Powers hands the man his cell phone. He wants the number of his attorney whom he suspects he met at the *Brown Leaf.* "Sure, give him a call!"

The man hesitates.

58

"On the subject of kidnapping," Powers offers, "what is your role in the kidnapping of Jolene Landrieu? You're going to tell us before the night is over anyway, so save yourself some pain and give us the details now."

"I had no role in kidnapping anyone. My assignment was to follow you, record your conversations, and store the recordings in the cloud. Period. I was advised that you are dangerous and not to physically challenge you in any way."

Powers threatens, "If you think I'm dangerous, wait until Tank gets here. It's the love of **his** life whom you helped kidnap for ransom. There will be no limits to his fury."

The man swallows his saliva as he capitulates, "I can give you the website in which the recordings are deposited. I can give you the name of the lawyer you confronted at the cigar bar, and I can cooperate fully ... but I can't tell you where the kidnapped lady is or who, specifically, is responsible -- because I don't know -- so you need to call off Tank. You can't squeeze blood out of a turnip!"

"You're reference to blood is appropriate. It's been my experience that people remember things with much greater clarity, after spending fifteen minutes with Tank."

CHAPTER 12 -- MARGARITAVILLE

Portland, Maine to Key West, Florida: Former Navy fighter pilot, Willie Mays Robinson, and his young co-pilot, who was recently discharged from the Air Force, complete their preflight check-list, pull away from the gate, receive clearance for take-off, and lift off from the Portland, Maine runway in their Bombardier manufactured Learjet 60 on their way to Key West, Florida. The privately owned jet accelerates through the cloud cover into the vast beauty of the troposphere until it levels off at 33,000 feet at a cruise speed of 420 miles per hour, when the co-pilot goes back to see if their only passenger, Dr. Maya Li Cherokee, needs anything.

Maya, however, is engrossed in her review of the Congressional testimony by U.S. Park Police Sergeant Kristen Brown. It amazes Maya that the first law enforcement officer on the scene could have been promoted to sergeant after the numerous errors she made during and shortly after the discovery of the dead White House attorney.

Maya is also a little surprised that JJ located Brown so quickly, and when she was contacted, she was willing to meet with Maya on such short notice. She continues to be amazed by JJ.

Jimmy Jordan, JJ, a five-foot, ten-inch tall, 140-pound wheelchair-bound redneck, was mentored by Tank and Powers after a tragic accident for which Tucker and the two *White Knights* feel some responsibility. With brown eyes and brown hair, JJ is pretty non-descript. He has been through a lot; he was hit by shrapnel which tore through his legs. JJ had third degree burns on the entire right side of his body. He went through fifteen skin grafts and three leg and back operations over a twenty-month period. He can stand and walk ten or fifteen feet on his own with a walker, but otherwise stays in his motorized wheelchair. Tucker and Tony Vinci furnish JJ with every

60

possible state-of-the-art gadget conceivable to make his life as good as possible. Tank originally hired JJ as a *White Knight* employee to answer the phone and perform minor administrative functions. He turned out to have a gold mine's value in added abilities.

What amazes Maya, though, is not JJ's ability to overcome his physical limitations to perform as a valuable contributor to the company, but how he grew intellectually. The once-limited redneck who guarded an abandoned coal mine has grown into a super-sales-person. JJ is one smooth talker. He can sell a ski jacket to a native in a tropical forest, sell a nun birth control pills, or sell a radical Muslim a Bible.

JJ made the arrangements for Maya to meet with Kristen Brown. Powers was originally going to accompany Maya on the trip but something came up. He might be able to make it down if the interview with Maya reveals anything useful to their investigation.

Maya has time on her flight to read portions of a 485-page report prepared by a former White House Independent Counsel which identified numerous instances of systematic alterations in witness accounts, the alteration of many top level reports, and a lack of complete documentation of the original shooting scene. Missing are high quality scene photographs, a videotape of the scene, a detailed description of the scene, diagrams of the location of each item of physical evidence, and the X-rays taken at the autopsy.

The more she reads, the more she realizes just how badly Kristen Brown screwed up the investigation.

Willie announces that they are beginning to make their descent into Key West International Airport. Maya lifts her visor to let the sun in and to peer out at the beautiful turquoise water, white beaches, pastel-colored housing, and boats everywhere. She's never been to Key West, and wonders if she can talk Tucker into coming down for a day of vacation.

Maya deplanes and is met on the tarmac by a pre-arranged limousine that takes her directly to Kristen Browns' home. Willie and the co-pilot wander off to the pilot's cafeteria to await instructions from Maya about the return to Portland.

Maya concludes quickly that she is way overdressed in a long tight-fitting skirt, a white satin blouse and heels. She may be the only person in all of Key West wearing a skirt.

When the limousine turns onto Windsor Street, she realizes Kristen Brown didn't just retire on her Park Police salary. All the homes on the street have to be worth a million dollars or more. The gates to the driveway are open in anticipation of Maya Cherokee's arrival. The limousine driver opens the door for Maya as she gracefully slides her long flawless legs out of the car, stands up with her *Surface* tablet in hand and walks to the front door. Before she reaches for the doorbell, the double front doors open and a woman with a broad warm smile greets her. She is in her late forties, five feet seven inches tall, maybe ten pounds overweight, grey mixed with dirty blond hair, dark eyebrows, and green eyes which match the photograph JJ forwarded to her.

"Please, come in," welcomes Kristen Brown; "this is quite an honor. It's not every day that I get such a famous visitor."

Surprised by the warm welcome, Maya says, "Thank you for your willingness to see me on short notice."

"No problem," continues Ms. Brown; "You're the first former Vice Presidential Candidate and former National Science Advisor to walk through that door. I've had plenty of crank reporters try to track me down, but no one of your caliber. And you're more beautiful in person than you are on TV. You could have been Miss America.

"Where is Senator Powers? I thought he was coming, too."

WHA-CKED   JED O'Dea
(White House Attorney-Counsel Killed)

"Something came up and he couldn't make it."

Retired Sergeant Brown admits, "Too bad; I was looking forward to meeting the most exciting senator to ever be part of the chamber. Would you like something to drink before the interview?"

"Bottled water, please." Maya has learned to accept only drinks from a manufacturer-sealed bottle.

She doesn't comment on the expensive digs or its glamorous location. Instead, she launches right into the interview. First, she asks, "May I record this interview?"

Brown says with a smile on her face, "No. It's my policy not to allow recordings. Sorry."

"OK. My first question is: do you know how I can contact the FBI agent whom you worked with on the case, Agent Richmond?"

"No, I lost contact with him years ago."

Maya's antennae go up. She begins to question the genuineness of the former police officer's answers.

"OK. Do you know how we can find Robert Kingsley, the first person on the scene to discover the deceased?"

"No, I do not."

Maya knows now that the warmth initially presented upon her arrival is an act. She is going to be a hostile witness. There is no longer a reason to be gentle with her inquiry. "Why did you conclude that the death of the White House Counsel was a suicide, and squash any open consideration that foul play was involved?"

Brown parrots a pre-rehearsed response: "The U.S. Park Police investigation was one of seven publicized government investigations concerning the death of the former White House attorney. Thousands of pages from the investigations have been released -- including lab reports, testimony, depositions, and witness interview reports. All seven investigations reached the same conclusion -- that the former White House counsel committed suicide."

"True," agrees Maya; "the key words are 'government investigations.' Maybe a non-government investigation should be conducted. All seven *government* investigators report to the same boss in the White House. This would not be the first time a cover-up was directed from the White House. Now, back to my question -- why did you conclude that it was a suicide without investigating the possibility of his death being a homicide? You could not have known about his supposed clinical depression at the time of the discovery of his death."

"A 38 was in his hand; there was an exit wound on the back of his head; an empty chamber was obvious, and gun powder residue was found on his glasses."

"Sergeant Brown," continues Maya, "Did you jump to a suicide conclusion because you found a suicide note that you have hidden, destroyed, or concealed from the investigation? Did the note implicate the former First Lady? Did you allow your political ideology to get in the way of doing your job?"

Brown leans back and responds, "Dr. Cherokee, for over twenty years I've been defending attacks from many dozens of investigators. Even if your accusation **were** true, why would I suddenly disclose this history-changing information to you? Unless you have some compelling reason you'd like to disclose, I'd like you to leave."

Maya gracefully stands up, thanks her for her hospitality, apologizes if she offended her in any way, and leaves the former police officer's home.

As she is riding back to Key West International Airport, she receives a phone call from her daughter, Star.

"Mom, can I come down to visit with you in Key West?"

Maya responds, "What a great idea! Maybe we can talk daddy into coming down and staying a day or two. Is daddy there with you?"

"Yes." Star hands the phone to her father.

Tucker gets on the phone. "Star is very assertive about this trip. She acts like it is important for the three of us to be together on a short vacation, so I've asked Willie to come back and pick us up. We'll be down tomorrow. You can spend the night at the Ritz Carlton."

"OK. Sounds good to me. I love you for doing this."

"I'd like to take credit but this was initiated by our daughter. I'll call you later tonight."

After she disconnects the phone, the chauffer of the limousine announces to Maya, "You were being observed at the woman's house, and we are now being followed."

Wiscasset, Maine: Star looks extremely relieved after the call. Her body relaxes and her perennial smile returns. Tucker asks, "Are you looking forward to some family time together?"

"I can't wait!" She looks into Tucker's eyes. He is studying his special daughter.

Finally, Star adds, "I didn't want Mom to get on that plane."

Key West Florida: As soon as Maya leaves former officer Kristen Brown's house, Brown makes a phone call. "She's gone, for now. She thinks a non-government investigation should be conducted. I don't know how they're doing it, but our enemy is making the next move through the Cherokees."

"Willie," says the co-pilot, "I'm not feeling so hot. I need to visit the men's room before we start instrument check. Give me a few minutes."

"OK, I understand." Actually, Willie Mays Robinson isn't feeling so hot himself. He feels a little feverish and weak, as though he had just completed a marathon. Beads of perspiration are forming on his forehead, which he attributes to Key West humidity.

The co-pilot returns, looking worse than before he visited the rest room. The two of them complete their preflight instrument check, and continue with their flight as planned.

On their way to 33,000 feet, still on the ascent, Willie Mays Robinson and the co-pilot begin convulsing, lose their vision, hallucinate, and, with excruciating stomach pain, die in their seats. The Learjet 60 became another story in the legend of the Bermuda Triangle.

CHAPTER 13 -- ANOTHER BRICK IN THE WALL

The 1945 Death March: The pathetic old woman in front of Marsha stumbled again, but this time fell flat on her face in the mud. She bent down to help the fragile soul, but was pushed forward by the relentless mass of human tragedy behind her. The SS had a deadline to meet -- to move the prisoners from Auschwitz to the Bergen-Belson concentration camp. Apparently, they didn't care about human losses. In fact, Marsha suspected they wanted people to die on the march. A lot of the girls from her Auschwitz female barracks committed suicide by just walking away. They had been warned by the SS that anyone who walked away got a bullet in the back of the head.

Marsha's feet were killing her; she had been walking twenty five kilometers a day through rain, mud, and snow. She marched with thousands of others who were cold, wet, weak, and ill ... from village to village without food, without rest, and without hope. At least she and Viktor didn't have to make the march in wooden clogs like every other inmate. She witnessed hundreds of bodies on the side of the road during the march and acquired a sad sense that death was normal. She wondered, "Where is God? Why is He allowing such suffering?"

Marsha's constant state of nausea was diagnosed by one of the older women. Marsha was pregnant. She knew that since she never had sex, that she had become pregnant by virtue of one of Dr. Soroson's experiments. She thought about the strange looking gun, the long needle, and her special treatment afterwards. She looked over at Viktor, her cohort, her friend, and asked him what Soroson did to him. Viktor was embarrassed and ashamed, turned bright red, and began to cry. "I am now a girl."

A German soldier yelled at Marsha to pick up the pace. To help her along, he hit her in the back of her head with the butt of his rifle. Young Viktor lost it. He grabbed the rifle from the soldier, turned quickly and emptied the chamber into the soldiers face. Viktor was shot four times by other German soldiers who also managed to hit a couple of marching inmates as collateral damage. Marsha threw herself onto her only friend, Viktor, in abject uncontrolled grief, wailing and sobbing. A German soldier yanked her by her hair, dragged her forward and ordered her to march on. She decided then and there that if she survived and had a baby boy, that she would name him Viktor Soroson.

San Diego, California: More than seventy years later, billionaire Viktor Soroson is considering the next move for his Currency Hedge Fund when he receives a call from his firm's Chief Technology Officer.

"The threats on your life are getting more and more vitriolic. I think you need to take these threats more seriously."

Soroson asks, "What is the threat this time?"

"They threatened to bomb your home. They listed your correct San Diego home address. And they said they'd bomb it whether you are home or not."

Viktor Soroson angrily admonishes, "We've informed the FBI of the threats. They are apparently not willing to do anything. What else do you suggest that we do?"

"I've taken the liberty to contact *White Knight Personal Security Services* to send someone out for you to interview."

"White Knight!   Isn't that God-damned former senator Powers involved with them? I don't want a right-wing capitalist hawk with his nose under our tent. Find another company."

"Yes sir," says the CTO, "But a guy from *White Knight* is scheduled to arrive soon. They're the best in the country -- please, give them a chance."

Viktor disconnects the line and thinks about how he can turn the involvement of *White Knight* to his advantage.

Viktor unlocks his desk drawer and pulls out an Iridium satellite phone with an encryption app. He dials the number for the former First Lady's satellite phone which he'd donated to her campaign. Without introduction or the formality the former First Lady demands from others, Viktor asks, "I have a legal question for you."

She answers, "I answered this phone because I thought you were going to tell me that you contributed more money to my campaign for president, not to ask me for free legal advice."

Viktor retorts, "There is nothing about you that's free except the receipt of vengeful verbal debasement. If I hire *White Knight Personal Security Services*, will that preclude them from ever testifying against us?"

The former First Lady says, "Viktor, take your meds. You have to be fucking kidding me to suggest hiring *them*. Ten minutes after you hire them, there'll be bugs in your office and illegal taps on your phone. You'll have us both wrapped around an axle. There has to be another company you can hire. Stay away from them or our long term plan will be fully exposed."

She hung up.

Viktor muses, "If she only knew my **real** long-term plan."

69

CHAPTER 14 -- BE CAREFUL WHAT YOU WISH FOR

At an unknown location: Jolene massages her swollen ankle while watching *Fox News* which is burned into her wide screen TV.   She hopes to hear something about her kidnapping on national or international cable news, but there is no mention of her.   She wonders if that means Tank has, foolishly, not reported her kidnapping to the FBI.

Jolene is no dummy; she knows that she was kidnapped for a reason which has something to do with Tank.   No doubt, somebody wants Tank to do something he wouldn't normally do, and is being blackmailed to insure her safe return.

On this day, the fifth day of her captivity, Jolene tests her shoulder and ankle and concludes that she has recovered enough from her injury to attempt another escape.

The door into the area where she is being held captive is reinforced solid steel, as is the frame in which it is encased.   The door hinges are on the outside and it feels like it has multiple dead bolts.   The door is not her way out.

She follows the plumbing lines to see if the penetrations into the floor provide an opportunity for escape, but the floor penetrations are surrounded by steel angles.   Jolene looks at the electrical penetrations through the ceiling of the woman-cave area and decides that maybe this is her best shot for an escape.

The chest of drawers in the other room is not nailed to the floor.   She empties it before she drags it through the door to the other room.   Once in position, she climbs on it and determines that she needs another five feet of something on top of the chest to reach the TV cable penetration through the wall high above her, next to the ceiling.   She drags a solid-looking metal kitchen garbage can and places it on top of the chest of drawers.   She knows that she is still roughly two feet short of reaching the cable penetration.

70

"What can I place on top of the garbage can to reach the cable?" She goes into the bathroom, pulls out the vanity stool and arranges the three items until she feels like they, together, are stable. Jolene grabs a steak knife, carefully and cautiously climbs up on the chest of drawers, onto the vanity stool, and then on the kitchen garbage can. It is not as stable as she would like, but it will have to do. Jolene pulls the steak knife out of her pocket and starts sawing on the drywall adjacent to the cable penetration.

On the seventh day of her captivity, she breaks through the outside containment. On the outside of the drywall is insulation. On the other side of the insulation is plywood. On the outside of the plywood is light.

Her excitement at seeing light causes her heart to beat at twice its normal rate. The original opening which she makes to the outside world is small in diameter -- the same as the thickness of the knife's handle. Jolene peers through the opening to see something, anything. All she can see is the sky but she can smell the saltwater. She is, in fact, near or on the ocean. She knows her capturers are watching her; they must not care if she peers outside. "What the hell does that mean?"

She spends another five hours increasing the size of the opening through the plywood with the steak knife. The opening is now two inches in diameter. She still can see nothing but sky. She is frustrated, but determined.

There are no sounds other than the ocean, seagulls, and waves hitting the structure supporting her rooms.

On the eleventh day of captivity, Jolene manages to create an opening large enough to fit her head through, where she finally gets a clear 360-degree view around the place she is being held.

71

WHA-CKED   JED O'Dea
(White House Attorney-Counsel Killed)

Jolene's greatest fears are borne out. Her special room is atop an oil rig in the middle of the ocean. There is no land in sight, in any direction.

There are, however, signs of sharks surrounding the oil rig, feeding on tethered animal carcasses.

Manassas, Virginia: The origin of the name Manassas is Hebrew, where its meaning is "making forgetfulness." But its fame is from the Civil War because in July of 1861 the "Battle of Bull Run," the first major land battle of the Civil War, was fought there.

I arrive at Lake Jackson, near Manassas, at a lake-front house that is probably 60 years old. The road is poorly maintained and it jars my teeth just to get within 100 yards of the place. There are big signs saying **No Trespassing, No Hunting, No Fishing**, and finally two signs to generally discourage even the most authority-averse adventurer -- **Vicious Dog** and **We Shoot Trespassers**. The beat-up exterior badly needs a paint job -- but that's on purpose. Inside the safe house, it is meticulously maintained and well stocked -- not only with food, water, and alcoholic beverages, but with an array of electronics which make it a paradise for us computer nerds.

As I crawl out of my undersized "borrowed" vehicle, I stretch my frame out of its compressed condition and note the musty smell of wet leaves and debris. I enjoy the 100 yard walk from my car to the front door and observe the squirrels chasing each other and the birds warning me not to trespass. I also check the surveillance cameras to make sure they are properly placed and still working. No doubt, Powers knows that I am on the way in.

Powers is standing outside the side door of the safe house. He has a confident smile on his face when he shares, "He'll spill the beans. Our biggest problem is going to be what to do with his soiled britches the second you walk into the basement. I'm pretty sure he won't hold anything back."

I nod at Powers, slowly creep into the house, then walk casually down the steps into the basement, and see the young blond man bound to a chair, eyes wild with fear. I don't change my dour expression, and use my intimidating size to its maximum advantage.

He starts blabbering about how he's told Powers everything he knows, and there's nothing I could do to him to help reveal anything more to find Jolene.

I say nothing.

He continues to speak, almost crying, about his limited role in her kidnapping and how everything is compartmentalized, keeping his exposure to the customer's mission limited. He goes on to say that the lawyer to whom he reports, hired him to only eavesdrop -- nothing else. Then he slips; he relates that he has no knowledge of why the "big guy" wanted to kidnap Jolene.

I hit the blond guy with the open face of my hand.

Powers admits, "You have always been subtle. He'll wake up in a few minutes."

Powers takes out the smelling salts, rubs them under the blond man's nose and brings him around. He blinks his eyes a few times, looks up at me, and screws on an expression that announces volumes. He is ready to talk.

I ask, "What can you tell me about the "big guy"?

The blond man relinquishes, "I understand that he has more money than God."

"What else can you tell me about him?"

The blond man confesses, "I overheard the attorney who hired me say that our client represents a cabal of like-minded people. Honestly, that's all I know."

"Call him. I want to speak with him.

"**NOW.**"

Powers hands the blond man a phone. The blond man asks, "Do you have my phone? I don't remember his phone number. It's in *my* phone call log."

Powers pulls a phone out of his back pocket and asks, "Do you mean this one?"

The blond man nods.

Powers hands the phone to the amateur eavesdropper. The blond man takes the phone, identifies the person he wants to call on his contact list, pushes enter and waits.

I pick the phone up and push speaker phone.

The phone rings until an answering machine announces, "This is Harold Andrews of Andrews, Crosby, and Underwood. Your call is important to me. Please, leave a message and I'll get back with you as soon as practical. Have a good day."

The blond man leaves a message, "Mr. Andrews, this is Richard Kingsley; it is an emergency. Please, return my call as soon as possible. Thank you."

I disconnect the call.

I look at Powers. Powers shakes his head and looks back with an angry expression. I say to the blond eavesdropper, Richard Kingsley, "You're a pretty good little actor, Richard. If I didn't need reliable information from you, I'd pull your head off right now. As it is, I'm going to let Powers maul your hands and feet with a variable speed drill for the next 24 hours until I'm sure you're no longer lying to us."

WHA-CKED   JED O'Dea

(White House Attorney-Counsel Killed)

"Why," I've told you everything I know."

"Except," as I put my hand over his skull like it was a softball, "It seems you forgot to mention that your father was the first person on the scene of the '**suicide**' of the White House attorney."

CHAPTER 15 -- DEDUCTIVE LOGIC

Key West, Florida: Maya wakes up the next morning in a soft King-Sized bed with feather pillows in a comfortably cool Ritz-Carlton honeymoon suite. She smiles when the fog of waking lifts and she remembers that Tucker and Star are going to join her in Key West for a couple of days of rest and relaxation.

She looks at the clock, and to her surprise she has slept until 8:45 AM. She needs her morning coffee before she can think clearly. She uses the room coffeemaker for her first cup. It is never good coffee when she makes her own in the room, but it does give her a needed jolt of caffeine.

While the coffee is brewing, she turns on the TV to listen to cable news. The usual talking heads are discussing the merits of Putin's latest geopolitical moves, and the pros and cons of giving illegal immigrants driver's licenses.

Her cell phone rings, startling her as she simultaneously reads across the ticker tape news alert on the bottom of the TV screen, "......debris from private jet found twenty miles east southeast of Miami."

A knot forms in Maya's stomach. She reaches for her cell phone and answers, "Hi, Love."

"Hi, sweetheart."

The tone of his voice told her all she needed to know.

"Our Lear crashed in the Atlantic. I called Willie's wife. That was a tough conversation. It is impossible to console someone who has just learned that her husband has died."

Maya starts to sob and can't talk any longer. Then she sighs, "Let me call you back later when I regain my composure."

Tucker quickly yells, "Maya! Maya! Before you hang up, you need to hear about something."

"OK?"

"There are guards outside your hotel room door. Don't be shocked or surprised. I don't want to see you use your hand-to-hand combat and surviving-an-armed-violent-encounter training on a friendly."

Maya suddenly regains her composure and asks, "Tucker, what's going on? Why do I need to be guarded?"

"It's just a precaution. I ordered it last night even before the aircraft tragedy. I called JJ and he sent officers from the Miami office of *White Knight* down to your hotel. Powers and Tank know about it and agreed with the precaution. Until I know that the jet tragedy was an accident and not sabotage with you as the target -- I'm going to take extra precautions."

"Do you have some reason to believe that the downing of the Learjet was intended for me?" Maya says incredulously.

Tucker hesitates.

"Tucker, what are you not telling me?"

Tucker hesitates further, but eventually shares, "Think about it, Maya. You were supposed to be on that flight immediately after you met with the former U.S. Park Police person who is a solid lead for you in your investigation of the death of the White House lawyer. And ...." his voice sounds unsure as to how to proceed.

"And what?"

"And Star was determined that you not be on that flight."

Maya suddenly remembers that the limousine chauffeur suspected that they were being followed from the Kristen Brown estate to Key West International. She was probably observed going into the private aircraft terminal.

Maya deduces, "If your logic holds up and the Learjet was sabotaged, maybe they think I'm dead."

"Possibly. But I don't want to count on it."

"Tucker," Maya expresses with heartfelt concern, "Do you really think Star could have a premonition accurate and compelling enough to know that I was in danger?"

"No way of knowing, but I'm not a strong believer in coincidences."

"So, what now?"

"Stay where you are. Don't even go down to the gym. Have your meals catered by the hotel. I'll call you after I sort things out and speak with the team. And, honey ... I'm *so* glad you weren't on that flight. I love you and I'm very grateful for Star's premonition."

Manassas, Virginia: The blond man, Richard Kingsley asks, "How did you know?"

I answer, "I didn't. It was a guess. The first man on the scene of the alleged suicide's last name was Kingsley. You were eavesdropping with electronics on Powers' conversation in the *Brown Leaf* on that very subject. It wasn't exactly a giant leap of investigative genius. It is now more important than ever that you tell me the truth. My patience with you is just about at an end!"

Powers is smiling. "I remember well that last time I heard you say that. Wasn't that the time you introduced a mercenary assassin to Ram? Ooo-wee that was a mess to clean up." Knowing full well the answer to his next question, Powers asks, "You did bring my favorite military-trained attack dog -- Ram -- with you?"

I reach out, pick Richard up off the floor by his neck with one hand and whistle for Ram. Sure enough, Powers was right, the blond guy soils his britches as he is trying to speak, but can't until I let go.

"I was recruited by that lawyer you met in the bar, Harold Andrews. He knew who I was, and knew that I wanted to learn if the death of the White House attorney was why my father died in a 'freak accident.' I always wondered if there was a relationship between his being at the wrong place at the wrong time and the accident."

I ask, "Your father is dead?"

"Yes, he died almost twenty years ago in a collision with an eighteen wheeler."

"I'm sorry for your loss."

"I was just short of eleven when it happened."

"This may sound cold to you, but I'm trying to prevent the death of someone I love. As sad as I am about your situation, I am still going to squeeze out every piece of knowledge you have on the kidnapping of Jolene."

My anger is reaching a crescendo; I am about to break and he knows it. "Now, for the last time, what do you know?"

"Harold said that if I get involved, not only do I have a chance to find out the truth about my father's death, but I might be able to make serious money while doing it. He said the pool of funds from this client was as close to infinite as it gets.

"I don't really care so much about the money, so if I can help you recover Jolene, I will. I think I have a better chance by aligning myself with you for finding out the truth, than I do working for Andrews."

I say, "Call him again. I want to visit with him tonight."

Richard, the blond, looks around, "Ram isn't here, is he?"

I repeat my instructions, "Call Harold Andrews again."

WHA-CKED   JED O'Dea
(White House Attorney-Counsel Killed)

While Richard is seeing if Harold answers the phone this time, Powers leans over to me and whispers, "The kid needs to go to the hospital, get his concussion treated, get his nose realigned, and he needs a change of clothes. He smells like urine … plus."

I answer, "After we pay a visit to the attorney who hired him."

"Actually, he lives only about ten miles from here."

I look at Powers quizzically and just grunt "Huh?"

He holds his hands out, palms up and fakes innocence, "Hey, that's why we're partners. I uncover stuff."

CHAPTER 16 -- EVIL

Washington, D.C. and San Diego, California: Viktor
Soroson's satellite phone rings, and the ring tone assigned to the
former First Lady … it's Darth Vader's theme song. He
answers, "I take it you learned of my new 501(c)(3) shadow
company against which your campaign manager can withdraw
funds."

"Yes," she answers without thanking him, "But I called to
tell you that I have read the chapter in your manifesto entitled,
'*Approach to Accelerate the Achievement of a One-World
Government.*' It's quite creative and ingenious. I fully
understand how you intend to bring the European Union, India,
and the Peoples Republic of China into the fold, but I'm anxious
to read the section which describes how you intend to get the
United States to agree to the concept."

His laugh is genuine -- he honestly has trouble regaining his
composure -- but he finally says, "My little squirrel, that's where
you come in ….. but first we have to get you elected as President
of the United States of America. As a corporate member of
standing with *The Council on Foreign Relations,* I have been
very successful at influencing council policy towards our goals,
without fully disclosing our power-sharing end game.

"When you become president, we'll leverage your position
to change the world order forever."

Salisbury, Maryland: "When was the last time you saw
Jolene, Mr. Brave?" asks Special Agent Vintage.

The *Brave Chicken* board room is outfitted with a polished light-reflecting twenty-foot long mahogany conference table with wood-accented high-back leather executive chairs and floor-to-ceiling tinted double-paned windows which overlook a man-made lake spraying geyser-like fountains.

Elliott Brave looks over at his lawyer for approval to speak. His attorney nods his head and the Brave Chicken CEO answers, "Two days before you rained down on me and served me a search warrant; it was around 11:30 AM. She was speaking with one of the animal rights protestors -- trying to talk some sense into them, I suspect."

Vintage asks, "Could you identify the protestor with whom she was speaking?"

Brave gives a quick side glance towards his lawyer and answers, "No. Only that he was shorter than she was, white, and fairly young; I'd say he was less than 25 years old. But I couldn't pick him out of a line-up."

"Brave Chicken has surveillance cameras around the campus, here, correct?"

"Yes."

"Do they record 24/7?"

The attorney speaks up and contentiously reprimands, "There is no way Mr. Brave can know with certainty that all surveillance cameras were operating properly at the time of Jolene Landrieu's abduction, if, in fact, she was abducted on Brave Chicken property."

Agent Vintage is not distracted and asks, "If the surveillance cameras were recording properly, were they intended to record 24/7?"

The lawyer arrogantly asks, "Where are we going with this line of questioning, Agent Vintage?"

Mark Vintage smiles and condescends, "Isn't it obvious? We'd like to see **all** the video so we can observe Ms. Landrieu with the protestor so we can interview him. Your defensiveness in the light of such mundane questioning makes it appear as though you are guilty of something. What are you hiding?"

"This interview is over. Unless you are charging my client with something, we'd like to ask you to leave the premises."

"Your failure to willingly cooperate in this kidnapping investigation is going to bite you in the ass. You just ratcheted up the pressure the FBI is going to apply to Brave Chicken. You're in big trouble, men; everyone gets shit on them in a shit storm." Agent Vintage packs up his voice recorder, papers, clipboard, and heads for the exit.

The Special Agent walks down the hall, into the stairwell, down three flights of stairs, and into a spare room being used for storing janitorial supplies. Lucas Justice is still reviewing surveillance recordings.

"Anything new, Lucas?"

"Nothing from the video cameras, but I've heard from Tank. He and Powers are working a lead. Also, Tucker and Maya Cherokee's corporate jet went suspiciously into the drink after she interviewed former Park Police, Sergeant Kristen Brown. We must be getting close to something; we've hit a damn hornet's nest."

Vintage agrees, "Mr. Brave is guilty of something if not complicit with the kidnapping of Jolene. We need to raise the intensity of our investigation and look under their skirt. Something is definitely not kosher here."

Special Agent Mark Vintage's cell phone vibrates. He looks at the number of the caller; it's his boss.

"Yes, Sir."

"Mark, you need to get your ass back here. I have a new assignment for you. This came down from the seventh floor. We have a hostage rescue mission; we need you in El Paso." He hangs up on Agent Vintage.

Mark stares at the phone. He looks at Lucas and warns, "There must be some powerful people involved with this kidnapping case, Lucas, for them to have me removed so quickly from this case. I hope you and Tank don't get cremated when all the dust settles. Stay vigilant."

With that, Mark Vintage calls the FBI helicopter pilots on-call and instructs them to prepare to return to Quantico. He asks "Lucas, do you need a lift somewhere?"

"No, I have a job to do here; I've decided to take the initiative and investigate another potential person-of-interest."

New York City, New York: "It's time to end the male dominance of corporations, government, the military, Wall Street, and Hollywood. Women have been pushed down to a second-citizen level since the beginning of time. Though females evolved more quickly than males, females have been dominated by males, and not because of their biggest organ -- their brain -- but because of their proclivity for violence."

The former First Lady continues, "As president, I will issue an Executive Order to mandate that 55% of all Congressional seats be filled by women, to match the national population."

"Whoa!" exclaims the former president ... simultaneously with the orals coach.

"This speech is supposed to be funny; it's too close to the truth about how you really feel," admonishes the former president.

The First Lady responds, "If I want any crap from you, I'll squeeze your head."

"Ooh," jokes the former president, "That sounds like fun."

"Not that head," she retorts.

The orals coach from *Saturday Night Live* says, "Madam First Lady, you have deviated substantially from the script. While we appreciate your impromptu and surreptitious improvements, we do need to be more humorous to entertain the viewers, so we'd appreciate a little more conformity."

Shelby Viking, the First Lady's campaign manager advises, "Alienating potential male voters is not a good thing. I suggest that you tone down the anti-male rhetoric."

The First Lady says, "O.K. But I do like the part of the script that says "It's about time we have a First Significant Other in the White House, to entertain state guests. He'll like having to spend all his time escorting the wives of State visitors from around the world. Don't blame me for the consequences of what he does with those women."

"That wasn't in the script," announces the orals coach.

"Well it should be."

The former president teases his wife, "Maybe you can make a joke about the renewed investigation into the death of our former White House Counsel who was your partner in your old law firm. I understand that the investigation has been reopened."

"Go fuck yourself. Why in the world would you bring that up?"

"Because it's true. Rumor on the street is that a new non-government-funded team of researchers is dredging up the cold

case.   I understand that Maya Cherokee is on the warpath.
You'd better take it seriously."

"That bitch!" screams the former First Lady; "Why would
she be playing private investigator when she's a fucking
scientist? She is prejudiced in favor of big business which is a
keystone of the foundation of conservatism. She sees business
as the provider of jobs, health benefits, income for families, and
in many cases on-the-job training, instead of business as evil like
it really is."

"I don't know," answers the former president, "But you
better watch your back. I've set an investigation of my own in
motion, about her motives."

"Well, I'm not intimidated by her and I'll squash her ability
to uncover anything. I've already been exonerated from any
wrongdoing -- twenty years ago!   There's nothing more to
discover."

The former president just smiles and capitulates, "Sure, my
love; whatever you say."

CHAPTER 17 -- MISSING IN ACTION

Clifton, Virginia: My borrowed vehicle has its bright lights on as it is blasting at unnatural speeds around sharp turns in rural Virginia. Clifton, a quaint town with a population of 282, was originally the home of a Civil-War-era train station and is now an upscale community in Fairfax County with beautiful million-dollar homes on multiple acres shared with horse farms and well-manicured property. Even at 2:00 in the morning, there is more traffic than seems reasonable.

"Powers," I say, "we want to arrive there in one piece. Don't you think we need to appreciate the winding road a little more?"

"I enjoy practicing my aggressive driving skills when the mission dictates. When was the last time you experienced a real driver behind the wheel? Besides, we're almost there."

"Kingsley," I ask, "you OK back there?"

The blond man answers fearfully, "I am thinking about what would happen to me if we have an accident. Me, having one arm handcuffed to the back seat and all."

Powers says, "You would probably die when the car caught fire."

Kingsley sighs fitfully and squirms.

I caution, "Slow down and find a place to pull over. Kid, hand me those night vision binoculars I placed in the back seat next to you."

It is pitch black -- no street lights, and lots of distance between houses.

As I peer through the night goggles, I search first for surveillance cameras, then motion detectors, guard dogs, and evidence of security barriers. I find nothing that concerns me.

"Odd," I say to Powers, "this mansion is unprotected."

Powers answers, "There is no sign of life, either."

"Richard," I order, "hand me the other glasses back there, the thermal scope."

I take the scope and survey the property. I see no heat-producing bodies of any kind -- neither people nor animals.

"OK," I say to Powers; "we might as well drive up the driveway."

"Uh, Tank," Powers responds questioningly; "You might have noticed the steel gate in front of the driveway."

"A minor problem."

I get out of the car, walk over to the gate and inspect the gate opening mechanism. Like most security gates, it is electro-mechanically-operated. I climb over the eight foot high gate to the other side. I quickly find the gearbox and its electric motor's switch, take out my continuity link and energize the motor; the gate begins its opening sequence.

I wave Powers through, get into the passenger seat, and ride up the driveway to the garage.

Powers asks, "What, do you carry that thing with you wherever you go?"

"It comes in handy."

The large Victorian-looking house has no security lighting, no lights inside or outside, no night lights, and no flood light.

I ask, "Richard, have you been here before?"

"No; we always met in the city."

Powers asks, "Tank, my radar suspects a trap. Does yours pick up anything?"

I say, "The storm door to the garage is not fully closed." I walk to the door and test it. The hardwood door inside of the storm door is open. I peer into the garage. It's empty.

"Richard," I order, "go up to the front door and ring the doorbell. Announce your presence."

Richard tentatively does as he was told. As he steps up to the front door, he slips and falls awkwardly to the ground on his right elbow on warm slimy liquid.

"Awggghh." Richard is covered in blood.

None of it is his.

Following, along with me, Powers chides, "As they say, 'and the plot thickens.'"

CHAPTER 18 -- STUFF HAPPENS

Key West, Florida: The warm breeze blowing through the open balcony sliding-glass doors overlooking a turquoise sea from a spacious top-floor hotel suite reminds her that she is living the Key West Chamber of Commerce dream. But claustrophobia has grabbed her and sucked the oxygen from the air she is trying to breathe. Her lungs are struggling as she reacts to a sense of restlessness with irritability, boredom and impatience. Maya is sick and tired of being stuck in a hotel room.

"I think I know how Jolene must feel. I feel like *I* am being kidnapped and held hostage. "

Still straining for air, she picks up her cell phone with shaking hands and calls Tucker. "Here I am in paradise, and I'm stuck in a hotel room guarded by a *White Knight*. I have to get out of here; I have cabin fever."

"OK, sweetheart, I understand. Open the front door, lean out and ask the *White Knight* guard to speak to me on the phone."

She carries the phone with her, releases the lock and cracks the door open. The guard is standing with his face directly on the other side of the door, vigilant and alert. She hands the cell phone through the door opening into the hands of the guard. She notices another guard by the exit sign at the end of the hallway.

The guard says, "Yes, sir." A few seconds go by and he repeats again, "Yes, sir."

The guard hands the phone back to Maya and nods his head to her.

She asks Tucker, "You want to enlighten me?"

"I know you will want to go back and re-interview Kristen Bro vn and follow that thread. I told your guard that I want three

White Knights protecting you at all times. I'm also going to call Powers to see if he can go down and support your investigation.

"And sweetheart, I did a little digging into the distant background of Sergeant Brown. Her birth certificate shows that her full name is Kirsche von Braun. She is the great granddaughter of the famous rocket scientist, Werner von Braun."

"Hmmm," Maya responds pensively; "I don't know what to do with that piece to the puzzle, but somehow, I think it is an important piece. It will certainly make the interview more interesting."

Tucker empathizes, "I know you have cabin fever and I understand your need to get out of the hotel room, but I sure wish you would wait for Powers to show up before you try to speak with Sergeant Brown again. Don't forget, the loss of Willie and the Lear might have been intended for you, after you spoke with her."

"Hopefully, I'll be able to speak with Powers sometime today and establish a short term plan of action. In the meantime, I'd like to perform a little surveillance on Kristen Brown ... er von Braun."

On his satellite phone, the hired surveillance expert says, "Dr. Cherokee is returning to Winsor Street to watch Kristen Brown. She'll find nothing, nor will she uncover any leads. What do you want me to do?"

The mission chief answers, "Nothing, just keep track of her. Hopefully, she'll lure her husband down and we'll find a way for both of them to have an unfortunate accident."

"The person she's luring down here is more likely to be Powers. Do you have a plan if he shows up?"

"Yes, back off and just observe and listen. Don't try anything stupid with Powers."

Boston, Massachusetts: Tucker "herded the cats" to participate in a conference call, so that he could assess our progress, reassess priorities, and adjust action items. He announces, "Roll Call!

"Tank?"

"Here."

"Powers?"

"Here."

"Tony?"

"I'm on."

"Lucas?"

"Yo."

"Maya is with me on this call so let's review our progress. Let's start with our status on finding Jolene."

I explode, **"We're nowhere, people -- no fucking progress!"**

The expression of my anger shuts the conversation down. No one speaks. "I swear, I'm going to jam the kidnapper's nose into his brain when I catch up with him."

I regain my composure. "Each ten second video shows that Jolene is OK. After she cut a hole in the wall and peered outside, she seems to have given up. She acts like there is no hope of escape. She just sits around and watches TV. That's not like Jolene; she's a fighter, so whatever she saw out there has to be damned discouraging. Anybody have any ideas?"

Tony theorizes, "Picking up on what Star said about her smelling salt air and hearing waves crashing, she could be on a ship in the middle of the ocean, somewhere."

"Good thought, Tony," says Tucker, "let's start studying satellite photos of possible locations nearest to Salisbury.

"And Tony, how are we coming with that matrix you are building which compares the people who know about nano-drones with potential shadow organizations?"

Tony answers, "No one sticks out as a solid candidate, yet."

"Are you focused on the organizations on the National Crime Investigation Center watch list?"

Tony answers, "Yes, sir; so far I've investigated thirty-eight potential organizations. None of them have solid ties to the nano-drone surveillance technology."

Tucker says, "Let's broaden your search to include international organizations. I'll get you an expanded list.

"And I've decided to give this mission a name. The mission is named 'WHA-CKED' for 'White House Attorney-Counsel Killed.' The name also refers to the mental state of the people who kidnapped Jolene. As well as their future condition.

"Stating the obvious, the key to finding Jolene is to find the people behind her abduction. We've interrogated Richard Kingsley, interviewed Kristen Brown, and Agent Vincent interviewed Elliott Brave. What we have learned is that the group holding Jolene acts like they are inside our camp. The downing of the Lear, the disappearance of -- and possible death of -- the attorney Harold Andrews, and the inability to find Kristen Brown after Maya's interview with her implies that our team is being watched and our communications are compromised. I suggest that we communicate only by encrypted satellite phones from this point forward. Assume that they are even listening to **this** conversation."

Maya adds, "It might not be the people holding Jolene who are surveilling us and listening to our conversations; it might be the party linked to the death of the White House attorney."

Tucker concludes, "Either way, I think the use of encrypted satellite phones from this point forward is a necessary precaution to take. Let's stop this discussion now and I'll call each of you individually beginning twenty-four hours from now, after you have activated your phones.

"Lucas, I'll start with you, tomorrow around 1330."

"OK." This is all I ever expect to hear from the laconic Lucas Justice.

Key West, Florida: On his satellite phone, the hired surveillance expert announces, "They're going dark. How do you want me to proceed?"

The mission chief concludes, "We'll need to break the weakest link."

The surveillance expert asks, "Who might that be?"

"That's not your concern; I'll take care of it."

CHAPTER 19 -- THE HEIDI

On the oil platform, Heidi, in the middle of the ocean:
"Twenty-three, twenty-four, twenty-five. Whew! I used to be
able to do forty pushups without breaking a sweat." Jolene has
reached the point where she speaks to herself just to hear a
voice; she is about to scream from loneliness. This solitary
confinement without windows feels worse than being in prison.
At least people on death row get an hour a day outside and can
speak to the guards.

She screams in frustration, "Tank, where the hell are you? I
thought you loved me! You're an asshole for not saving me."

The isolation and claustrophobia are literally driving her
crazy. Though she could watch TV or movies, the inability to
talk to another person during her incarceration is maddening.
She starts jogging from room to room; she thinks she'll do 4000
laps today.

In her madness she thinks she hears something out of the
ordinary. She runs to the TV and turns the cable news channel
off so she can listen more intently. "Yes," she prays out loud,
"Tank is here to save me. That's a helicopter." She climbs her
makeshift stand and sticks her head outside.

"Yes, Yes, Yes!"

The helicopter is landing on the top of the platform. "Of
course, the oil rig has to have a helicopter pad."

Her heart is beating at 130 beats a minute. She hears the
thump of the helicopter and the deceleration of the blades. She
waits at the steel door with extreme relief and excitement. She
can hear footfalls coming up a ladder which must be right
outside the door.

She hears the sound of a bar being lifted off the front of her
door. The deadbolts are disengaged one at time -- she counts to

three -- and she hears voices but can't make out the words. She holds her breath.

The door opens.

Her heart sinks to an unimaginable depth.

Four armed men with Beretta machine pistols walk through the door. A fifth man -- obviously the leader -- follows them in. He is forty-five years old or so, roughly her height, with blond hair, blue eyes, no eyebrows, and wire-rimmed glasses.

"Jolene, my dear, I hope you find these accommodations tolerable," he articulates with a barely discernable German accent. "I see that you have recovered from your awful fall."

Jolene does not respond, but her body language demonstrates her emotional letdown. Her disappointment that Tank has not come to save her throws her into a deep depression.

"I apologize for having to bring these soldiers with me, but I am well aware of your hand-to-hand combat skills, and know that I would be no match for you.

"My name is Gunter Korf. I represent a consortium of companies with a common interest. The member companies represent some of the largest corporations in the world. In fact, they normally compete with each other and despise each other. So you can imagine that their common interest must be very special indeed.

"We want to reveal the truth about the goings-on of a truly diabolical group who own shell corporations responsible for many murders, which has a long-term ruthless goal with unimaginable consequences. The leaders of the evil group suffer from mentally-blocked logic -- some call it 'groupthink' -- where they cannot process information which conflicts with their ideological predispositions. That's all I'm willing to share with you at this time.

WHA-CKED
(White House Attorney-Counsel Killed)

JED O'Dea

"The mission that we've given your lover, Tank, and his *White Knight* team is to investigate the twenty-year-old death of a White House attorney. The results of Tank's investigation will reveal much to the world. His successful disclosure will also result in your safe release. We are extremely confident in Tank and his team, especially in view of his relationship with Powers and Tucker and Maya Cherokee, along with the resources which *Entropy Entrepreneurs*, Tucker Cherokee's firm, brings to the table. Collectively, we have no doubt about their ultimate success. By kidnapping you for ransom we think we've accelerated the conclusion of the investigation by months, if not years.

"To demonstrate good faith, I'm providing you with a satellite phone, pre-programmed for you to speak with Tank at will. I may give you some hints to pass along to Tank from time to time, to help him succeed.

"You can tell him that you are on an abandoned oil-rig in the middle of the ocean. It will make no difference; he will not find you. And in the highly unlikely event that he does, his finding you will result in your death because this flat of yours is rigged to kill you if intruders pass a certain barrier. It's fail-proof.

"Now, do you need anything?"

"Fresh air. Would you allow me to go out on the platform with you for a few minutes?"

"Sure, but I must warn you, if you attempt to jump, the fall will kill you. We are eighty feet above the ocean. If you survive, it would only be for a few moments. We maintain this as a shark feeding ground."

Jolene pleads, "OK. I just need to get outside and breathe fresh air and see the sun."

Korf nods to the guards, and the six of them walk through the door, down the steel ladder, and finally onto the helipad.

Jolene is surprised at the wind velocity; it must be twenty miles per hour and much cooler than she anticipated. In less than a minute she is freezing and ready to return to the warmth of her "flat," as Korf refers to it. One thing that doesn't surprise her is the view -- there's no sign of land in any direction, only rough seas.

The soldiers never lower their pistol muzzles, never let their guard down, and never let her within fifteen feet of Gunter Korf. All six of them return to Jolene's jail cell.

Gunter hands the satellite phone to one of the soldiers who, in turn, walks it over to Jolene. Another soldier places an envelope on the kitchen table. The third and fourth soldiers place boxes inside the front door.

"The envelope has Tank's phone number and the first clue or hint to help him along. The boxes contain supplies. We don't want you to go hungry. There are fresh fruit and vegetables in there.

"Goodbye, Ms. Landrieu; I will return."

The men back out of the room, close the door, fasten the dead bolts, and bar the door. She looks at the clock. The whole visit took only thirty minutes.

She opens the envelope even before the helicopter blades begin to accelerate.

There is a phone number on the sheet. Under the number is a short statement:

"Follow the money."

CHAPTER 20 -- THE INVESTIGATION

Key West, Florida: "Powers," asks Maya, "are you working with me to solve the mystery of the dead White House lawyer or not? You've been chasing the whereabouts of Jolene with Tank instead of collecting information and interviewing people like Sergeant Brown who, by the way, seems to have disappeared off the face of the earth ... immediately after she called someone to have me crashed and drowned in the Lear."

"Time out, Maya," Powers responds through his satellite phone; "We're a team. And part of the team includes the deep *White Knight* bench and the *White Knight* network of contacts. So while I was out risking my life in the field and you were living the good life in paradise and Margaritaville, the bench made progress. JJ has located Theodore Rich, the Chief Medical Examiner on the case. Can you pull yourself away from the Mai-Tais and join me in Baton Rouge, Louisiana to interview him?"

Maya smiles through the entire bantering exchange, "What time do I need to arrive?"

"JJ set the interview up for 2:00 PM Central Time. Let me know your arrival time and I'll pick you up at the airport. And Maya, be sure that at least one of the *White Knight* officers guarding you travels with you. Otherwise, Tucker will fit me for a body bag."

Powers and Maya disconnect. Less than ten seconds after he hangs up, he receives a call on his cell phone. It is Clinton Auclair, Director of the Library of Congress and co-owner of the *Brown Leaf.*

"Powers, my fascinating friend, I enjoyed the entertainment you provided at the *Brown Leaf* the other night. Can you come back? It's boring here without you."

"It will be my pleasure. I'll try not to disrupt your business next time. Did you lose any customers after the incident with the blond man?"

"Au contraire," retorts the Director; "The *Brown Leaf* is the talk of the town. Listen, I have some information for you."

"Stop right there and let me call you back on a safe line."

Powers' response makes Auclair's day; the intrigue is exciting to him and a joyous feeling that makes him feel alive makes him shiver all over. Clint's phone rings; he answers, "Is this connection more suitable for you?"

"Thanks for your understanding, Clint. What's on your mind? What information do you have for me that you said you wanted to share?"

"I found Forrester True, the *Washington Press* investigative reporter Byron and I mentioned to you when you were performing your hard-ass act in the *Brown Leaf.* He is the most knowledgeable person in the world about the White House Counsel's alleged suicide. True is in Pasco, Washington working for the *Tri-City Herald.*

"I not only found his location -- I spoke with him and told him to expect contact from you. He knows who you are, and it makes him nervous that you want to meet with him. I can understand that -- excitement and trouble follow you like a shadow."

Wiscasset, Maine and Key West, Florida: "It's time, Maya," Tucker says over the satellite phone. "It's finally time to grant Star her wish. This could be a very positive first step for her development for the long-term. It will provide our daughter with meaning in her life, and it will demonstrate to her our trust and confidence in her."

Maya responds, "I'm so afraid for her; she's still so young. Tucker, she's only twelve. It's way too early for her to do this."

Tucker states, "She may never have a more important chance than now. Think about it -- she'll finally see the good that can come from the cross she bears. Star and I will meet you in Baton Rouge. Maybe the three of us can go together to New Orleans for a couple of days afterwards and have fun."

"OK, but we better give Powers a clue about what we're doing."

Baton Rouge, Louisiana: Tiger paws are painted on the sidewalk leading to the front door. The front door is painted gold, framed in purple. Baton Rouge is Louisiana State University territory, and old-man Rich is apparently eaten-up with it. He answers the door wearing an LSU sweatshirt and an LSU baseball cap. Dr. Theodore Rich is stooped over and looks much older to Maya than the recent photos made him appear. She immediately suspects that he is ill, possibly suffering from a debilitating affliction.

"Well, well," Dr. Rich says to the group standing outside his front door, "Please come in. I am truly honored to have a former U.S. Senator in my presence," he looks over his reading glasses, "not to mention the most beautiful woman to ever pass through this door ... my dear late-wife notwithstanding."

With some effort, he leans his old body over further, saying "And who is this pretty young lady?"

WHA-CKED

(White House Attorney-Counsel Killed)

"This is my daughter, Star, and," she graciously swung her arm over as if she were a dancer, palm up, "this is my husband, Tucker. I'm sorry for the intrusion by so many of us, but my husband and daughter wanted to join me to tour Baton Rouge. Hopefully we'll get to see the LSU campus."

Dr. Theodore Rich grows a good two inches taller as he suggests, "Maybe I can give you a tour of the campus myself."

Maya graciously responds, "That would be wonderful."

"Please, let us sit in my study; I have room for all of us in there." Dr. Rich leads the four visitors to his study which contains wall-to-wall, floor-to-ceiling bookshelves organized by areas of forensic science on three walls. The fourth wall is graced with a bay window overlooking a garden of beautiful red and yellow roses.

After everyone is seated, Dr. Rich offers, "Before we get started with the history lesson, would anyone like something to drink?" Everyone thanks Dr. Rich but declines the offer. He continues, "I have a play room in the house where my grandchildren, when they were younger, entertained themselves. There are dolls and toys there; would you like to play there, Star, while we talk business?"

Dr. Rich casually and comfortably looks directly into Star's captivating eyes. His facial expression changes; he suddenly feels overwhelmed with uncontrolled grief and begins to weep.

They all remain quiet for what seems to be forever, but is actually less than a minute.

"I'm sorry," says Theodore Rich as he pulls out his handkerchief and dabs the tears in his eyes, "for my loss of emotional control. I've been that way ever since I started taking these damned chemotherapy drugs. I failed my 250,000-mile checkup."

Star breaks the awkward situation with "I'd love to see your grandchildren's play room."

He smiles; "It's down the hall, second door on the left; the door is open -- you'll figure out quickly which room it is."

"Come on sweetheart, I'll help you find the playroom." Tucker and Star leave the study while Powers and Maya stay with Dr. Rich. Tucker turns back on his way out and says, "I'll be right back."

The playroom is happy with yellow walls covered with colorful photos of hot air balloons, butterflies, Minnie Mouse, and clowns with huge shoes. There are stuffed animals, worn old dolls, and many children's books. The room has fresh red and yellow roses in a vase that give the room an incredibly fresh smell.

Tucker inquires, "What was that really about?"

Star answers, "He'll never tell you the truth."

Tucker waits.

"Bad people have threatened to torture and kill his children and grandchildren if he talks. When he looked at me, he saw his own grandchildren when they were younger. He'd much rather just die now than have anything happen to his family."

Tucker asks, "Can you do it from here?"

She closes her eyes and concentrates. She opens her eyes and smiles at her daddy. Tucker smiles back gently, leaves the playroom and returns to the study.

Maya is doing her best at small talk with the good doctor until Tucker returns. As Tucker walks into the study, Dr. Rich is describing last week's winning LSU drive for a touchdown.

Tucker announces, "OK, I think we have Star all settled into the playroom."

Maya starts the interrogation by asking, "Dr. Rich, as the medical examiner who performed the autopsy on the White House attorney in question, did you take X-rays of the deceased?"

"Yes, of course; what kind of medical examiner would I be if I hadn't followed protocol?"

Maya continues, "Do you know what happened to the X-Rays? There are no records of them having been taken at the time of the autopsy."

Dr. Rich answers, "No, I'm afraid I don't. After all, it has been over twenty years."

Powers asks, "Did the X-Ray photos show any bullet fragments?"

Dr. Rich's eyes look downward as he answers, "No."

Powers and Maya say nothing but stare accusingly at Dr. Rich.

Maya then asks, "Witnesses at the scene claimed that there were no exit wounds visible. Can you explain how that might be possible?"

"The fatal entrance wound was in the posterior oropharynx. There was a soft palate tissue defect with powder debris in the same area. There was an irregular wound measuring one and one quarter by one inch measured three inches from the top of the head, on the midline with good alignment between the entrance and the exit wounds. This was an entrance and exit defect configuration."

Powers asks, "Could someone have shoved a gun into his mouth and caused the same entrance and exit wounds? I understand that the only fingerprints of the deceased found on the Colt were discovered on the barrel of the gun."

Dr. Rich takes a deep breath, and repeats a well-rehearsed line, "The victim revealed no other wounds or trauma other than to the head, and there was only evidence of the gunshot wound. My conclusion was that this was a self-inflicted wound.

"The textured handle grip area of the revolver was not the type of surface which facilitates development of identifiable latent fingerprints."

Maya asks, "You used the old fingerprint powder method instead of using more modern fingerprinting techniques that were available at the time, like cyanoacrylate fuming, laser, and forensic lighting techniques. Why?"

"Transferable substances like sweat, oils or other substances are required to leave latent prints as well as having a surface that is receptive to capture the latent prints. A clean, smooth, flat surface is most receptive for transfer of any substance from the hands."

Tucker interrupts Dr. Rich, "So far, you have parroted to us the information that was presented in your forensic report. Based on the conjecture presented by many others, and based on any post-autopsy information you've entertained over the past twenty years, do you have any doubts about the conclusion you reached?"

"Conspiracy theories are plentiful and easy to find, especially by enemies of the president and First Lady. Based on the evidence collected and presented, I believe the correct conclusion was reached. I do, however, as a Monday-morning quarterback, wish that I had recommended that an investigation about a potential homicide be conducted in order to validate my conclusions."

Tucker is driving an SUV around the LSU campus with Powers riding shotgun and Maya and Star in the back seat. Star, being a precocious child, understands the significance that her response to questions about this investigation could have on her own life. She also understands that her response is potentially going to affect not only the rest of her life, but the lives of many others. But in spite of the importance of her answers to the questions they want to ask, the three adults in the car have not yet asked her a single one. They wait patiently for her to speak when she is ready -- no sooner.

Star worries that if she says what she learned from reading Dr. Rich's thoughts, it may result in the murder of one or more of Dr. Rich's family members.

She remains silent.

The name that repeatedly emanated from Dr. Theodore Rich's thoughts, which Star received, was Viktor Soroson.

Washington, D.C.: Earlier today, I spoke with Jolene -- for over two hours. It was an emotional experience for both of us. I clumsily blurted out how much I love her and how hard I am working to find and rescue her. She told me how relieved she was to be able talk to me, how important that it was for her sanity, and how much safer it made her feel.

After I hung up from that first call from Jolene, I called my partner Powers, on my sat phone, to update him with the developments and to discuss how we were going to run *White Knights'* day-to-day business with both of us fully invested in saving Jolene.

Next, I called Tucker to share the new developments and determine the impact on our overall strategy. We evaluated the new information, modified our list of action items, made new assignments, and re-assessed our need for new personnel resources. Last, but not least, at Tucker's direction, I called Tony Vinci, *Entropy Entrepreneurs'* Chief Scientist.

"Tony, I spoke with Jolene today. She's OK. It was a wonderful call, though I'm afraid I got a bit emotional. The thing is, she has been given a satellite phone programmed to speak with me any time she wants to talk, which I suspect and hope will be often. She tells me that she is in the middle of the ocean on an oil rig, and that the hostage-takers don't care that we know that. Tony, there can't be that many oil rigs in the world; we should be able to determine where she is. The head kidnapper is a German, named Gunter Korf. Why would he offer up his name? Does that name mean anything to you? Powers, Maya, and Tucker couldn't connect any dots. What do you think is really going on here, Tony? Any ideas?"

"Nothing that immediately jumps out at me. Let me explore all the oil rig possibilities and narrow them down. I'll throw in the potential German ownership factor and see what pops up. No doubt you've given the name to your FBI contacts; yes?"

I ask, "Where can I find Jimmy Ma?"

I heard clicks on keyboards on the other end of the phone. Tony finally answers, "He's on 'H' Street between 5th and 6th street, Northwest, Washington, D.C."

"Washington's Chinatown; how do you know that?"

"What! You didn't like my answer?"

"You GPS track your own employees' whereabouts?"

"Only Jimmy Ma. He's too damn valuable and equally unpredictable. So one night when we found him passed out on the floor of a bar in a rough Anacostia area in Washington, we inserted a chip in his ass. It probably feels like a mole to him."

I ask, "Do you have the exact coordinates?"

WHA-CKED
(White House Attorney-Counsel Killed)

JED O'Dea

Chinatown, Washington, D.C.: Jimmy Ma is bleeding from an artistic-looking shallow one inch long knife wound on his neck; his back is pressed up against a wall, and a sharp six-inch Ka-bar knife is still up against his throat. An irate man of Chinese heritage with no eyebrows is yelling at Jimmy at the top of his lungs, his nose pressed against Jimmy's nose. The odor from the man's breath alone might kill him.

Two armed men surround their apoplectic boss, ready to dispose of Jimmy's carcass if the need arises. Jimmy says, "I don't understand a word that you are saying. I don't speak Mandarin or any other Chinese dialect. I'm an American. If you're going to yell at me, yell at me in English."

The Chinese boss steps back, nods at one of the armed men who proceeds to punch Jimmy as hard as he can, in the stomach. Jimmy doubles over and falls to the floor gasping for air as the boss begins to kick him repeatedly in the side of his chest, while screaming, "You cheat at 'Go;' no one can always win. You cheat. I teach you a lesson."

Jimmy closes his eyes tightly and prepares for the next blow. Instead, the screamer throws himself on top of Jimmy; as do both the armed body guards.

They don't move; they are just dead weight on top of him. Jimmy finally opens his eyes and looks around and says, "Oh. Hi, Tank!"

I look down at the pathetic display of human debris, "Let's get your trouble-magnet ass out of here before these goons wake up." I ask, "So, how much money did you win from this guy? Did you cheat at the ancient Chinese game of 'Go?'"

"Tank, that hurts. You know me; I wouldn't do anything like that. There's no way to cheat at 'Go' anyway; it's like chess. I'm just good."

I escort Jimmy down a flight of stairs and out onto "H" street, through the "fresh" air that smells of ginger, fried pork and soy sauce, and into a taxi.

"The Mayflower Hotel on Connecticut."

Washington, D.C.: Jimmy asks, "How did you find me?"

"I could smell you; it's the smell of trouble."

"Seriously, Tank; how did you find me?"

"I found you because I was looking for you; it's the business I'm in. What you should be saying is 'thanks for saving my sorry ass.'"

"OK, thanks for saving my sorry ass. Why are you looking for me?"

"Because someone instructed me to 'follow the money.' Who would you look for if those were your instructions?"

"Tank, you know you'll need to get Tucker's and Tony's approval for me to leave my current consulting assignment with the U.S. Treasury before I can help you."

I just look at Jimmy like he is an alien.

"OK, that was sort of stupid for me to mention. Of course you've talked with Tucker."

"Jimmy, I know of no one who would enjoy this new assignment more than you; have fun with it."

WHA-CKED
(White House Attorney-Counsel Killed)

JED O'Dea

I pay the driver, get out of the taxi, and proceed to walk with Jimmy into the Mayflower Hotel lobby where we stand long enough to watch the taxi which dropped us off pull away, and head for another part of the city.

"Follow me." I escort him to an apartment building three blocks from the Mayflower Hotel. As we meander through the streets, I continuously survey the area to make sure the taxi that brought us to the Mayflower doesn't follow us to our real destination. After all, the taxi driver could be in the Chinese boss' pocket.

I use my key to pass through the front door of the apartment and invite Jimmy in as if he actually had a choice. Though the hallway in the building is empty, two surveillance cameras are recording our movements. Jimmy stands in front of an elevator, assuming that we are going to take it to an upper level apartment. I gently grab his elbow and encourage him to follow me to the stairway.

We go down into the basement where the lighting is poor and the dreary atmosphere even less impressive. We come to an unmarked door with a card reader. I slide my card through the reader and open the door into an entranceway containing another door. I place my thumb on the biometric reader and proceed to open the door into a brightly lit room with multiple computer stations.

Lucas Justice is sitting in front of one of the monitors. "Hi, Lucas. I brought our friend Jimmy Ma here to perform his magic."

Jimmy Ma says with theatrical exuberance, "Hi, Lucas."

Lucas grunts but says nothing.

I show Jimmy his work space which contains three computers and six monitors. One of the state-of-the-art computers is tied to a high speed line with access to a supercomputer located in Fredericksburg, Virginia. The space reserved for Jimmy contains its own Keurig coffeemaker.

"There's plenty of food in the kitchen. I want you to be comfortable. You need to wash up, clean your knife wound, and change out of your bloody shirt and jeans. There are some extra clothes in the bedroom. After you've completed your assignment we'll get you to a doctor to see if you've cracked a few ribs as side effects resulting from cheating at 'Go'."

"I don't cheat.

"What's my new job? What is it you want me to do?"

"I want you to follow the money. Who is paying for Jolene's stay at the five-star oil rig, and who is paying for the disappearance of people associated with the death of the White House attorney? And, finally, look for anything suspicious in the financial transactions of Brave Chicken Corporation. My gut tells me that they have something to do with Jolene's abduction.

"Search the financial history for anything suspicious about Kirsche von Braun and her alias, Kristen Brown, of the U.S. Park Police, plus Harold Andrews of *Andrews, Crosby, and Underwood*, plus Dr. Theodore Rich, former Chief Medical Examiner, plus Elliott Brave, CEO of Brave Chicken Corporation, plus Agent Brian Richmond, FBI Agent-in-charge of the investigation into the death of the White House Counsel."

Jimmy says sarcastically, "Oh, is that all? What do you want me to do tomorrow?"

Lucas adds, "I'd add Miss Maryland to the list. I intend to pay her a little visit and investigate her relationship with Elliot Brave. I suspect there are skeletons in that closet."

"Jimmy," I mention, "when you're done with that, I want to know who has contributed money to the former First Lady's campaign, to her 'charitable foundations,' and any of her undisclosed off-shore funds.

"After that, I want to know anything you can find about Gunter Korf.

"My buddy Lucas, here, has agreed to keep you company. In the event that you elect to go back to Chinatown to play 'Go,' you'll have to go through him to get out of this basement."

Lucas looks over at Jimmy; Lucas' granite face muscles almost form a smile.

CHAPTER 21 -- A DEFINING MOMENT

New Orleans, Louisiana: Star is devouring her first-ever crawfish Po-Boy in the outdoor café on Bourbon Street called *LeBayou Restaurant*. She watches the costumed freaks go by, co-mingled with iPhone camera-happy tourists.

Star is also reading the thoughts of her parents during this lunch experience at an outdoor table. Her mother Maya is worried about Star's happiness. "How can my special Indigo child with the burden of mystic skills achieve happiness? What should I do about it? Maybe we should return to Wanaka, New Zealand."

Star's dad is worried about how she will handle the stress associated with the dilemma in which she finds herself. "How can I assure my daughter that the grandchildren of Dr. Rich will not be hurt if she discloses the information embedded in his private thoughts? Hell, how can I assure myself that they'll be safe? How do I protect Star? How is Star going to wrestle with the moral dilemma of choosing between helping Jolene and the safety of Dr. Rich's grandchildren? How can she pursue her life dream to be a U.S. Fish and Wildlife law enforcement investigator and be happy?"

Actually, Star is very happy; happy that both her parents are worried about her and not just interested in learning about the thoughts which are trapped in Dr. Rich's head.

Tucker's sat phone rings. He listens intently to the person speaking on the other end. His eyes dart between Maya and Star. His face looks sad; his body language goes negative. Finally, he disconnects the call and returns the phone to its case.

"That was Powers. Dr. Theodore Rich is dead; he committed suicide. The suicide note states that he didn't want to go through the pain of cancer."

113

Star read the thoughts of both her parents: "Or risk the lives of his grandchildren."

"Viktor Soroson."

Both Maya and Tucker simultaneously say, "Who?"

"Viktor Soroson," repeated Star, "is the person who was in Dr. Rich's thoughts, yesterday. He was afraid of the man; he thought that he's a monster. He thought words about Soroson that you won't let me repeat."

San Diego, California: He moves his pawn into place with arrogant confidence that he is only three moves away from putting his opponent in check-mate. Though he is a chess master and can plan nine moves ahead, he is sometimes vulnerable to other equally aggressive players -- he has less acuity as a defensive chess player. It will take his opponent, who is nine thousand miles away, some time to make his next move.

Viktor Soroson leaves the computer monitor showing the chess game and moves to a wide-screen monitor which displays fifteen icons. Each icon represents one of his shell corporations or one of his 501(c)(3) tax-free enterprises. He clicks on the icon entitled WWB, LLC. Several folders are arranged alphabetically -- he clicks the "progress report" folder. A new file is in the folder; it is from Ahmed Mohammad and named "Trojan Horse." The report includes the line "Sixty-seven trained and armed 'refugees' crossed the border today." A second line in the report states, "Three hired by *Rheinmetall* to work in warehouse." And third lines states "Unable to locate Herr Korf."

Soroson thought, "Two out of three ain't bad."

Marsha Katz's experiences before Viktor was born laid a foundation of cynicism that she felt compelled to share -- it was her way of protecting him from evil. She taught her child about the ugliness of mankind. There were 7,000 SS soldiers at Auschwitz; the holocaust wasn't horror just conducted by a few -- it was a fundamental flaw in "all Germans." The death march from Auschwitz concentration camp to the Bergen-Belson concentration camp resulted in the death of 38,000 men, women, and children. Marsha was one of the "lucky ones." Liberation by the Soviet Red Army's 322nd Rifle Division was a joyous moment -- that is, until she was gang-raped by drunken Russian soldiers when she was four months pregnant.

Soroson's bitter mother explained to him from the front porch of their Tel Aviv home that his father, Wilhelm Soroson, was convicted of war-crime murders in April of 1947 by the Supreme National Tribunal, and hung by his neck until dead.

His mother either lied to him, or she did not know the truth. Viktor spent a fortune to track down and get a DNA sample from a family member of his long dead father. His research concluded that Viktor was not related to Dr. Wilhelm Soroson.

"Who was my father?" he asked himself many times. "I'm damned well going to find out!"

Viktor Soroson thought that, like his chess match, his master plan is only a few moves from achieving its execution goals -- a plan whose genesis is almost as old as he is. A plan that was formulated the first time his mother told him the horror stories of her incarceration in a concentraion camp, and the inhuman things done to people simply because they were Jews. He is determined to get even. After that, he intends to win; he's not going to settle for just getting even.

CHAPTER 22 -- YOU DON'T KNOW WHAT YOU DON'T KNOW

Salt Lake City, Utah to Pasco, Washington: A storm around Chicago creates chaos all around the country, including the delay of a flight on the Canadair CRJ 100 from Salt Lake City, Utah, to Pasco, Washington. Some of the passengers on the delayed flight spend the extra two hours working on their laptops; others read newspapers or magazines, and still others spend the time drinking in the concourse's nearest sports bar.

One of the reasons Maya hates to fly commercial airlines is not because she is a snob or spoiled; it's because of the gawkers. One would think that she had won life's lottery. To some extent she has, but there is a cross to bear when you're breathtakingly beautiful. People stare, gawk, whisper to each other, sit too close, and come up to her to ask when her next movie will be released. The problem is further complicated when she travels with Star, because she reads the minds of passing men when they observe her mother.

Star has had to grow up way too fast. Maya learned to travel with an iPod for Star so that music competed with Star's tendency for mind-reading.

Finally, the packed flight is finished boarding. Powers had never even heard of Pasco until yesterday. "I can't figure it out. What the hell goes on in Pasco that fills airline seats?"

Maya, sitting in the isle seat opposite Powers answers, "Pasco is the primary airport servicing Hanford."

Powers looks at Maya with a blank stare.

"Hanford was part of the Manhanttan Project in World War II where we manufactured plutonium for "Fat Man," the hydrogen bomb dropped on Nakasaki. It's also the site where plutonium was manufactured for another 60,000 nuclear weapons.

116

"As National Science Advisor, I got very familiar with all the technologies proposed to clean up the legacy waste byproducts of weapons production. In the 1940s we had no idea what the hell we were doing when it came to nuclear waste. So now, we are spending more tax dollars on cleaning the place up than we ever spent on making plutonium.

"It's also an agricultural center for Burlington Northern, Boise Cascade, and Brave Chicken."

"Brave Chicken?"

"Maybe it's not a coincidence that Forrester True is here. We'll have to ask him about that."

Powers notices that the four seats in the row behind them are occupied with loud, laughing, twenty-something men who were a little too intoxicated. He turns around and makes eye contact with each of the four passengers in an attempt to dampen their loud and inappropriate jokes about Maya. His stare doesn't intimidate them. Each man pulls $20 out of his wallet and passes it to one of the four. A bet of some sort is on.

Thirty minutes into the flight at an altitude of 35,000 feet, the man directly behind Maya reaches around and firmly grabs Maya's left breast. The three other men erupt in uncontrolled laughter and high-five each other.

Maya calmly places her left hand over the man's hand on her breast and holds it there for a good three seconds, causing the three men to rejoice even more, before she takes her right hand and grabs his wrist.

She dislocates his thumb first, before she breaks his index finger. His scream fills the cabin.

Powers doesn't give the other three an opportunity to help their friend. He jams his extended fingers into the throat of the man on the other side of the aisle from the womanizer, pinches a nerve in the shoulder of the window-side passenger, and head-butts the last guy as he tries to stand up and defend the others.

WHA-CKED   JED O'Dea
(White House Attorney-Counsel Killed)

The entire episode took fifteen seconds.

Explaining the episode to the TSA agents who boarded the plane in Pasco was another story.

Richland, Washington: Though the air is dry and cool in Eastern Washington, Forrester True is perspiring. The blacklisted former *Washington Press* investigative reporter, now merely a sports reporter for the *Tri-Cities Herald*, is unaccustomed to being the one investigated. The brightly clothed umbrella table outside the Hanford House restaurant allows the four of them a perfect view of the Columbia River.

"Senator Powers and National Science Advisor Cherokee, I have no idea what is going on with your investigation into the death of the White House attorney, but suffice it to say that I am pleased that the case has been reopened. I truly believe that foul play was involved in his death and want to believe that your re-investigation is, to some extent, an exoneration and vindication of all the time and effort I put in to the investigation. I bucked the pressure exerted on the *Press* to drop the investigation, and it cost me my career. That means ... I will do anything to help you."

Powers asks, "Why are you so nervous? We're just here to learn what you know. And **please** don't call me Senator."

"Uh, your reputation precedes you. It makes me nervous being around someone who could kill me with his bare hands."

"Well, then you need to be nervous around this beautiful woman, Maya. She is also well-trained in hand-to-hand combat."

118

Maya adds without cracking a smile, "Trained by the best. It comes in handy from time to time."

"Mom, I need to go to the bathroom." This was code for, "We need to talk."

Maya politely smiles, offers her apologies to the two men, and then excuses herself and Star from the table. Mother and daughter wander naturally and casually through the hotel doors in the direction of the Ladies' Room, while Powers makes small talk with Forrester True. Once out of earshot, Maya asks Star, "What's up? What's going on in the man's head?"

"Mr. True is an alcoholic. He doesn't know how he's going to make it through the interview without a drink. I think that is why he is sweating and is so nervous."

"You know, Star, you're becoming even more of a treasure! You're very good at what you do."

Star smiles and says, "Thanks, Mom."

Maya walks over to the hotel bartender and requests a waiter or waitress to provide drink service to their table.

The waiter appears at their outdoor table just as Maya and Star are returning. Forrester orders a double Martini.

An hour later, Forrester True is slurring his words, but providing valuable information about the death of the White House Counsel.

"I interviewed Robert Kingsley before his untimely death. You may remember, he was the first person on the scene after the White House Counsel's death. He emphatically said that there was no gun in the attorney's hand when he found him. The gun was placed there afterwards. The FBI put great pressure on him to change his testimony. Why?"

Powers asks the reporter, "What is your theory?"

Forrester True acts paranoid, looks around, and lowers his voice, "Because the FBI is involved in the cover-up."

Powers then asks, "What is your theory about why the FBI would cover up a homicide?"

Forrester True took a deep breath, "Because the Director of the FBI instructed them to cover it up."

"And what is your theory about why the Director of the FBI would instruct his agents to cover up a homicide?"

Forrester is definitely getting uncomfortable with Powers' line of questioning: "Excuse me; I've hit my high level switch and need to head to the Men's room." He stands up and leaves for the hotel restroom.

Maya and Powers look at Star.

"He intends to slip away and not come back." Powers stands up and follows him into the hotel, to make sure that Forrester doesn't bolt.

Maya smiles at Star and asks, "Anything else in his head that might be important?"

Star says, "He's afraid you might think he is a con.., consp…, conspir…"

"Conspiracy?"

"Yes, a conspiracy theory … ist."

"A conspiracy theorist!"

"That's it, whatever that means."

Maya asks, "Any other important words in his head?"

"Yes. He thought the words 'First Lady' many times."

Powers returns with Forrester True in tow. Powers asks the question a second time, "What is your theory about why the Director of the FBI would instruct his agents to cover up a homicide?"

Forrester answers, "Because his boss directed him to cover up the murder of the White House attorney."

"Are you suggesting that the Attorney General of the United States, the number one law enforcement officer in the country, ordered the Director of the FBI to cover up the murder of the White House Counsel?"

"No, sir," responds Forrester, "I'm suggesting that his boss, the President of the United States, ordered the cover-up."

Boston, Massachusetts: "Tucker," says his office assistant in his *Entropy Entrepreneurs* office in Boston, "the Lloyds of London insurance adjuster is on the line. He wants to speak with you about your claim for the downed Learjet."

"Sure; patch him through."

"Mr. Cherokee," states the Lloyds adjuster, "we want to let you know that we are delaying the processing of your claim pending completion of forensics on the Lear and an autopsy of the pilots."

Tucker asks, "Is there a statute of limitations on the claim, if the Lear is never recovered and, therefore, an autopsy of the pilots is impossible?"

The adjuster is silent for ten full seconds, and then says slowly "Mr. Cherokee, have you not received a call from the NTSB?"

"No," Tucker responds, "not recently; why?"

"Because they found your Learjet yesterday and pulled it up from the seabed this morning. Before they brought it up, they sent scuba divers down to extract the pilots. The autopsy reports should be available before the close of business today."

Tucker is pissed, but maintains his composure; "Thank you for your initiative to call and advise me of the developments." Then, Tucker disconnects the line.

He pensively considers the ramifications of the call. The National Transportation Safety Board is keeping him out of the loop until they complete their investigation. "What does that imply? It can mean they suspect foul play, or it can mean that they suspect the pilots were intoxicated when the jet took off."

Tucker continues his thought, "Or it can mean that someone high up in the NTSB is compromised. Whoever organized and orchestrated the downing of the Learjet on such short notice, in hopes of murdering Maya, could just as easily manipulate the outcome of the NTSB report. Who might gain from a manipulated report? The people guilty of attempted murder, of course."

Tucker's contemplation is interrupted when someone nearby clears their throat. Tucker looks toward the doorway to see the undistinguished-looking Chief Scientist, Tony Vinci.

"Sorry, boss, for the interruption. Is this a good time?"

"What do you have for me, Tony?"

"First, as you requested, I cross-referenced the people with knowledge about nano-drones with well-funded potential international organizations which may be interested in influencing our next presidential election. I came up with only three candidates. One of the organizations is German, another is Israeli, and the third is an American tax-exempt company."

"Great job, Tony. Can you get me a 10-K financial report on all three companies? Are annual reports available? Would you please get that information to Jimmy Ma?"

"Already done. You need to look at the report on the American company first; you will find it interesting reading."

Tucker walks behind his desk and opens the file Tony gave him on the American company. The photo on the inside jacket is of the Chairman of the Board. Tucker stares at the photograph of the billionaire philanthropist Viktor Soroson.

"So that's what a monster looks like.

"Tony, do you have a nano-drone ready for deployment?"

CHAPTER 23 -- BOUGHT AND PAID FOR

Annapolis, Maryland: The blond man, Richard Kingsley, and I have been on a stake-out now for more than twelve hours in a five year old Ford Expedition outfitted by *White Knight* for extended surveillances. The windows are tinted and bullet-proof. Two hidden pan-tilt-zoom cameras are mounted on the frame and linked to monitors inside the cab. Infrared cameras and night vision telescopes are standard issue for all our surveillance SUVs. I thought about how useful it would be if Tony could outfit the vehicle with nano-drones. Maybe that isn't too far-fetched.

In Tucker and Maya's search for people with motive to sabotage their Learjet, they discovered an abnormal alliance between Sergeant Kristen Brown and the former FBI agent-in-charge of the investigation into the White House attorney's death, Brian Richmond. In fact, former Agent Richmond had boarded a flight to Key West from Baltimore-Washington International Airport during the time when Maya was interviewing Sergeant Brown. Records uncovered by the resourceful Tucker revealed that phone calls were made between Brown and Richmond on the very day the jet crashed.

I was voted to be the best person to interview him.

"Kingsley." He jumps as if I had thrown a firecracker in his face; "Pull up about fifty yards or so, out of line-of-sight from the house. I need to stretch and move my legs for a couple of minutes. You stay in the car and monitor the fixed camera so that there is no gap in our surveillance. You can get some time to stretch when I return to the cab. Let's take a maximum of five minutes each."

When Kingsley stops the Expedition, I get out and stretch, do a couple of pushups, jog ten yards and back, and reach for the sky. A mosquito bites me on the back on my neck; I reach back to smack it, and scratch the bite. It isn't a mosquito; it is a tranquilizer dart. I pull it out, knowing that if they used the right dosage, I'll be out soon and won't wake up for at least fifteen minutes.

My vision is beginning to blur; I turn to see a man with the tranquilizer gun standing next to the man I am trying to stake-out, Brian Richmond. Former FBI agent Richmond reaches for his concealed 38-caliber H&K. I see, as I am beginning to lose consciousness, that Kingsley is frozen, unable to react.

I do the only thing I can think to do. I say as loudly as I can before I blank out, "Bad, Bad."

Ram flies out of the Expedition like he was shot out of a cannon. He first goes for the man with the tranquilizer gun -- his throat is gone before he has time to react.

Kingsley has no training in close combat and is no match for Richmond, so he just tackles him before Richmond can get his weapon into firing position. He hits Kingsley in the side of the head with the butt of the gun, rolls over, and gets into position to fire ... just before he is thrashed by a 100-pound fighting machine, teeth-first.

As I regain consciousness, I see that the Maryland State police have me handcuffed to a cruiser and that Kingsley in the back seat of another cruiser. Ram is sitting next to me, splattered with blood. I look around to see a medical examiner surveying the condition of the two bodies. I make eye contact with Ram, "Thirty-eight black." Ram is gone like a rocket, before the troopers can react. I couldn't take the chance that they'd put Ram down for the murder of the former FBI agent.

PART II

CHAPTER 24 -- RULES OF ENGAGEMENT

Frankfurt, Germany: Gunter Korf sits in the lobby on the 49th floor of Frankfurt's CommerzBank Tower, waiting to be called into the Board Meeting. The Forbes' Top 40 revenue-producing companies in the Federal Republic of Germany have formed an organization similar to the U.S. Chamber of Commerce called The Deutsche Chamber. However, there is an enormous difference between the two entities; The Deutsche Chamber is an unsanctioned secret organization designed to ensure Germany's continued economic superiority in the European Union. The organization's primary charter, as voted on by its members, is to protect Germany's industrial complex from predatory entities and its jealous enemies worldwide.

A serious-looking middle-aged woman with short-cropped blond hair opens the doors to the Board Room and says to Gunter Korf, "They're ready for your progress report."

The floor-to-ceiling windows overlooking Frankfurt's brightly lit skyline are covered by thick-lined curtains, designed to assure complete secrecy, damp out sound, and prevent industrial espionage from rogue nations.

Gunter walks to the head of the table, nods to the Chairman, and then asks the meeting administrator "Is the file loaded?"

She nods her head, "Yes."

Gunter Korf opens his presentation with, "Members of the Board, what you are seeing on the screen is an unmanned aircraft video recording of ISIS warriors pretending to be refugees crossing the border into Germany through Austria. It is estimated that there are now 125,000 ISIS soldiers in the homeland. More are on their way. They are organized by this man ... whose picture is now on the screen before you -- an Iranian named Ahmed Mohammad. Ahmed is not an ideological Islamist. His activities are not sanctioned by the Iranian cleric. He is purely a mercenary with a beautiful mansion in the Canary Islands.

"You might ask, 'Who or what organization is funding Ahmed Mohammad? What is their long term goal? Why is this happening in Germany instead of France, the United States, or Israel?'

"The photo on the next slide is of the American billionaire, Viktor Soroson. He's an émigré from Israel who previously immigrated to Israel from Hungary with his mother, a holocaust victim, when he was a small child. He is also the son of one of Auschwitz's war criminals, a medical doctor who enjoyed experimenting on inmates in the name of science. This man, Soroson, hates the Aryan race; he thinks that anyone even remotely German needs to be erased; this billionaire wants to employ his own version of eugenics. If he could find a way to do it, he would lead a genocidal war against all of Germany. It's the root cause of his motivation to fund our demise."

Korf pauses to let the statement sink in with his audience. Many members are uncomfortable with Korf's presentation, and had begun shifting around in their plush seats.

"This Board," continues Gunter Korf, "correctly voted 'yes' on a motion to remove Soroson -- as a threat to Germany, with the condition that his removal must not, in any way, come back on this organization; his removal must not have our fingerprints on it."

All heads around the table shake in agreement.

"Suffice it to say then," Korf continues, "that to protect the Members of the Board, and to provide you with plausible deniability, I will not go into the details of the operation. The plan is for Mr. Soroson to ultimately pay for his many past crimes within the U.S. prison system. I'd like to assure all of you that your investment in this operation will pay great dividends, and you will be satisfied with the return on your investment.

"The next photo presented here is of Jolene Landrieu. She is key to our success. By 'employing' her, I've **energized** the best investigative company in America, *White Knight Personal Security Services,* to reveal Soroson's criminal activities and ensure his incarceration."

"Thank you, Herr Korf," says the Chairman of the Board; "NATO is politically and bureaucratically limited in how it can protect Germany, mostly military defense. Member nations must be essentially unanimous in their support for military action. The European Union has its advantages as it relates to commercial trade, yes. But it is unable to organize itself to protect the union from outside forces -- ruthless predators -- nation states that manipulate currency, countries that subsidize the manufacturing of products, entities that extort other nations in times of natural crisis, and nations which steal trade secrets and intellectual property.

"Herr Korf, your job is much like the U.S. Chairman of the Joint Chiefs of Staff. We need your strategic and tactical genius. We need an offense, not just a defense. However, our funds are finite. We're financially strapped, and we would like you to bring the current mission to a close as fast as practical without jeopardizing the mission objectives. Are we clear?"

"No," says Gunter Korf; "we're not clear at all. Keep the Euros flowing. If we fail to stop the attack on Germany, you'll look back and ask yourselves why it was so damned important for you to make your quarterly projections. Maybe you forgot about the intelligence I shared with you during our last little get-together. Don't forget the consequences of the worst case scenario if our enemy succeeds."

CHAPTER 25 -- GUILTY BY ASSOCIATION

Washington, D.C.: "My husband tells me that the there's a right wing group out there trying to dredge up a bunch of conspiratorial bullshit surrounding the death of my law partner twenty years ago," says the former First Lady. "It sounds to me like my Republican attackers are trying to make his suicide look like a murder. Their next move will be to make me look like I had a motive, like I'm the murderer. Damn, my enemies are getting desperate. But in a way, that's good news.

"Viktor, is there anything you're not telling me about who might be behind the investigation, and why that bitch, Maya Cherokee, is involved? Damn it, Viktor, don't keep me in the dark."

Soroson answers, "Did you have a brief lapse in memory? Did you forget the one with whom you are speaking? Don't speak to me like I'm one of your mindless groupies who would vote for you even if you were an axe-murderer; you can't even come close to repaying me the debt -- financial *or* political -- which you owe me. I could put an end to your political future tomorrow, so treat me with the respect I've earned, and quit pretending that you don't know what's going on, while you're so shamelessly full of yourself."

"Viktor," the former first lady retorted, "Cut the bullshit; I'm your only pathway to being the future Ambassador to Germany. If I don't win, you don't win; we need each other. Now, please, fill me in on the recent developments surrounding the renewed investigation into the suicide of my law partner and White House Counsel. How soon do you think it will be, before the press picks up on the reopening of that awful wound?"

"Nice try," responded Soroson; "I will not allow you to trap me into implicating myself in any way, with current events. All I know is what I read in the newspapers, and that is -- a Learjet 60, registered to *Entropy Entrepreneurs*, Tucker Cherokee's firm, went into the Atlantic Ocean near Miami. I also read that Tank Alvarez, co-owner of *White Knights Personal Security Services* and close friends with Maya and Tucker Cherokee, has been arrested for the murder of former FBI Agent Brian Richmond, the FBI Agent-in-Charge of the investigation into the death of that White House attorney."

The former First Lady says, "You're fucking kidding me!"

"No. And add to it, I read that Dr. Theodore Rich, the Chief Medical Examiner for your ex-partner's 'suicide' case, committed suicide himself, this week."

"Please, tell me that you had nothing to do with any of these new developments. Some news reporter is going to connect the dots and wave a mic in my face any moment now, asking for comments."

Viktor smiles and says, "I read about all of this in the paper."

The former First Lady knew it would be useless to ask him again to answer her question.

Salisbury, Maryland: Elliot Brave didn't reach his level on the corporate ladder by being indecisive, but this time, he couldn't make up his mind. Should he be worried that his assistant, Miss Maryland, might have turned on him, after she was interviewed by the FBI, or should he be worried about her wellbeing? It wasn't like her to miss a workday without calling in -- much less, two days in a row.

"Jesus," he says to himself, "She knows everything. If she talks, we're toast."

Annapolis, Maryland: I wish I could say that this is the first time that I've been hauled into jail by the police, but "this is not my first rodeo."   Normally, however, the cops release me after I show them my credentials, but then again, I've never been accused of murder before.   The Maryland State Highway Patrol placed both Richard Kingsley and me in the same ten by ten foot Annapolis jail cell.

Clear thinking has not yet fully returned to me, and I really need to get my stuff together pretty damn soon.   The drug from that tranquilizer gun has kept me in a dysfunctional funk for hours.

Finally the fog feels like it's lifting, so I call out to a guard, "I want my phone call. Now."

He takes his damn time, but finally I am handed a cell phone. I call Lucas who picks up on the second ring.

"Justice."

"Call Powers and our lawyer, Sam Pearson, and have them bail me and Kingsley out of this Annapolis jail; I'm being given extended stay service here at the Maryland taxpayers' expense.

"Second, pick up Ram. Do you know where to find his GPS transmitter frequency on the computer server? If not, call Tony or Tucker.

"They've impounded our number-three DC surveillance Expedition. My sat phone is still on the front seat and I need it - - Jolene will call in and I won't be there to answer it. She'll panic."

Lucas says, "She has a right to; you're in jail."

I let that slide and ask, "Would you hand the phone to Jimmy?"

After a few seconds, Jimmy Ma says, "Did I hear that correctly; you're in jail? Ha! And you say I'm always the one in trouble."

"Have you made any progress?"

"Damn right I've made progress. Tank, I've never seen so much money changing hands. The GDP of half the nations of the world pale in comparison to the amount of money that has been moved in and out of Switzerland and the Cayman Islands by these guys."

"I don't have much time before they shut me down, here, so cut to the chase. Who's funding the kidnap and ransom of Jolene?"

Jimmy Ma says, "I don't know."

"Wrong answer, Jimmy. What do you know?"

"The shell game going on with these transactions is impressive. Whoever is running these operations is good.

"Before they take your phone away from you, you need to know that a very small fraction of the money crossing wires (only hundreds of thousands) landed in the breadbasket of former FBI Agent Brian Richmond. I believe that he is the guy who you went to Annapolis to visit; is that right?"

"That's why we have a love-hate relationship. Get that information to our *White Knight* lawyer. Lucas knows how to reach him."

The guard tells me, "Time's up, big guy."

I hand the phone to Kingsley and say to the guard, "The law says he gets a call too, right?" The guard grunts.

Richard Kingsley looks at me like he is confused. I figure he doesn't know who to call so I give him a number and tell him to put the call on speakerphone.

"Hello, this is Tucker Cherokee."

I say to the blond man, Richard Kingsley, "Tell him what happened."

Richard gives Tucker a blow-by-blow description of the event in front of the home of former FBI agent Brian Richmond.

Not surprisingly, Tucker's first question is not, "How is Tank?" or "Is Powers aware of the situation?" or "What can I do for you?" No, his first question is: "Is Ram OK? Do you know where he is?"

Leash laws are strictly enforced by the animal control department of the city of Annapolis. In his twelve year career, the director of the department had never received a call directly from Chief of Police from the City of Annapolis, or the Chief of the Maryland State Highway Patrol -- much less a call from each of them on the same day.

He had also never before heard an All-Points-Bulletin put out on a dog. One hundred and thirty-one law enforcement officers are on the look-out for a 100-pound German shepherd that is extremely dangerous and had already killed two former FBI agents. The instructions are: shoot to kill.

Sitting on the floor inside the Ford Expedition, Tank's satellite phone rings for the third time in the last half hour.

CHAPTER 26 – SOROSON'S FISCHER MEN

Detroit, Michigan: A Jell-O-like fog in his head suppresses his ability to move, even to open his eyes. Rook tries to recall his dream, but it's just out of reach. Some people remember their dreams every morning when they awaken, but not the Rook, and it pisses him off. And it's the first thing he has to do, now, every morning. Just like yesterday, he stands over the toilet, angry that his prostate is enlarged and that he never remembers his dreams.

Even when he was in the big house, the Rook could remember his sweet dreams; back then, it was the best part of every day for him … but he hasn't had a dream, good or bad, in many years. He suspects that there is no doubt some deep-rooted psychological reason -- something he is sure he doesn't really want to learn.

He hears a familiar sound, the sound of his phone vibrating on the wooden night stand, and he immediately leaps to answer it, his thing still hanging out, waiting to finish the business it started. Though he is sure the phone only vibrated once, he fails to reach it in time to answer it.

It is their code. He looks at the screen on his smart phone: "Private number."

The Rook knows what this means; he has a new assignment. Rook leads a group of hardened criminals, turned mercenary, whom their employer calls the Fischer Men after the famous master chess player, Bobby Fischer. Though each member of the group is paid handsomely, each would gladly work for peanuts as faithful soldiers for their benefactor -- whoever the hell he is.

The Rook was on death row twenty-seven years ago for the murder of a cashier in an armed robbery gone badly. That was until a team of lawyers from a charitable organization called the "Minority Civil Liberties Union" first got him a "stay of execution." Fifteen months after the "stay," the Rook was released from prison based on technicalities that only lawyers and judges understood. Upon his release, he was offered employment by a virtual company called VJC, LLC. Originally, Rook had no boss, no physical contact with his employer, and no supervisor. Initially, he was requested -- by way of notes slid under his apartment door -- to perform simple tasks. As he proved himself to his unknown benefactor, tasks and assignments increased in complexity until he was "promoted" to leader of a group of six ex-cons like himself -- all found guilty of capital crimes. The group of men had many other things in common; each had been convicted of murder; none had close family ties or children; none had been rehabilitated; none were of Aryan heritage, and all had avoided the death penalty or life in prison because of an unknown benefactor.

Though the Fischer Men are congenital failures, each one is smart enough to know that nothing is free and that they have a debt to pay -- a debt that they are more than happy to repay to an unknown benefactor -- for their lives, their freedom, and their good-paying jobs. The members of the Fischer Men know each other only by their assigned nicknames. Rook is the oldest and is most respected for his ability to stay in rock hard shape. His washboard stomach is the result of 500 sit-ups every day for more than 25 years.

The Bishop is thin, wiry, and wears thick-lensed black-framed glasses. He is best known for his quickness and lightning fast reflexes -- especially with a knife.

Queenie is mis-named; he should be named "Monster" at six feet four inches tall and 475 pounds. Queenie wears a perpetual smile that belies his real temperament.

Pawn is anything but a pawn. He is small, insecure to the point that he pads his package, but by far the most dangerous person on the team.

WHA-CKED   JED O'Dea
(White House Attorney-Counsel Killed)

Horse looks like a computer nerd, dresses obnoxiously to cover a body covered with moles, always wears a baseball cap with an overly long bill turned backwards, and carries a simpleton's facial expression. But Horse is a brilliant thief with refined skills in disarming electronic alarm systems.

The Kingster is a soldier; he follows orders, does what he is told, never deviates from the plan, and always completes his mission. He has no redeeming features and would blend into any crowd if it were not for his head-to-toe display of hundreds of tattoos.

Detroit's public library system has deteriorated over the last few years, though it still provides free computer access and internet service. Years ago, a librarian taught the Rook how to use the computer to access internet search engines. This time he uses Yahoo, types in the web address and a password texted to him earlier this morning on his iPhone.

On the designated web site, there is a folder entitled "Rook." Rook opens the folder to find one file. He opens the file and reads it and blurts out loud in the quiet public library, "Holy Fuck!"

CHAPTER 27 -- BAIL

Annapolis, Maryland: I am lying on a hard cot in my cell wondering what is taking our corporate attorney so damn long to bail us out of jail. He fully understands that, as of this moment, his contract with *White Knight* is in jeopardy. The longer he takes to do the job for which we pay him a handsome retainer, the greater the risk is that I'll fire him. If I have to eat another garbage meal that the State of Maryland feeds us, I think I'll force-feed it to Sam Pearson. He's gotten us out of some real jams in the past, but he is definitely falling on his ugly face on this one.

I hear the door between our one-star jail cells back here and the police headquarters' administrative area unlock, and I find myself a little hopeful that Sam has finally done his magic and posted our bail. Three guards walk down the hall and stop in front of our cell. Richard stands up, like I do, as we prepare for processing out of the cell. I begin to think about what we have to do to get the surveillance-outfitted Expedition out of impoundment so that I can get my sat phone back.

One of the guards says, "Richard Kingsley, bail has been posted and you're free to go after you've been processed. I'll escort you to the administration department where conditions will be set for your release."

Richard looks into my eyes and shrugs his shoulders as I watch the blond man walk through the cell door into the hallway.

"Mr. Jorge Alvarez," continues the fat guard with a smirk on his face, "we'll escort you to the visitor's room where you can have a conversation with your attorney who is here to see you. But first, we must restrain you in handcuffs and shackles."

I can't believe what I'm hearing. Maybe it's a good thing that they are restraining me; otherwise, I might strangle Sam. Two guards stand on either side of me with nightsticks and

Tasers in their hands, while a third guard puts shackles on my legs and handcuffs on my wrists. I hate the shackles, since they make me walk like a duck with a load in its pants.

I'm escorted to a room with shaded Plexiglas walls where Sam and another lawyer, a partner in his firm, are waiting to speak to me. The guard pulls out a chair for me, and places another handcuff on me which tethers me to the steel table, bolted to the floor.

I'm not smiling, and I know my face is flush with anger. I ask, "Why am I still in here, Sam? What the fuck is going on?"

His hands are shaking, his brown eyes are not engaging mine and his face is colorless. He takes a deep breath, smooths his goatee with his right hand and says, "The State of Maryland is charging you with the murder of former FBI agent Brian Richmond and a former FBI agent Derrick Dominick. The State has determined that you are not to be released on bail, pending your hearing which is scheduled in four days. They believe that you are a flight risk. I spoke directly with the State Attorney General and he is adamant about pressing murder charges on you. I submitted an appeal for a waiver with the judge assigned to your case, and he is equally adamant that you need to stay in jail until your Grand Jury hearing.

"Tank, I'm doing everything within the law that I can to get you out, but the AG and the judge are in lock-down -- something else is going on here and I intend to find out what. In the meantime, I'm trying to get your case moved to another jurisdiction, maybe even into federal court, to get you out from under the thumb screws being applied in this case."

I restrain my anger; "Tell Powers and Tucker about the situation. I suspect that there is a connection between my treatment by the State of Maryland and the case I am investigating. A source of mine discovered that some serious money was transferred to the now-deceased former FBI agent;

he was the agent-in-charge of the investigation of the dead White House Counsel.

"Also, since I was shot by a tranquilizer gun in a public area by a former FBI agent whom I was watching, then he knew I was investigating the cold case. That act alone makes it highly likely that he is complicit with the cover-up of the death of the White House lawyer. Get that information to the team, and maybe that will help expedite the release of Jolene. And use that information to get me the hell out of here. I can't save Jolene from the inside of a jail cell and that, my friend, is probably why somebody is keeping me here."

Beads of sweat start to pour off Sam's forehead; an uncontrollable twitch is vibrating on the left side of his face, and he's acting like he's on "speed," unable to sit still.

I ask, "OK, Sam; what else?"

"The actual murder of the two FBI agents was performed by Ram under your order. Ram is missing. The police consider Ram a dangerous animal and are currently hunting for him, with orders to shoot to kill."

Sam continued, "I petitioned to get the order reversed, but without success."

I explode with rage; the guards come in and Taser me into submission. The pain is excruciating, but nothing like the pain I would feel if anything happened to Ram.

The instruction "Thirty-eight Black" meant only one thing to Ram: Find the nearest culvert and wait. Five blocks later, and fifteen minutes after he received this instruction from Tank, he finds a culvert running under a driveway. He's been there, now, more than five hours -- waiting.   He is hungry, but waits as instructed.   A Maine Coon cat comes within fifty feet of Ram before smelling him; Ram resists the instinctive temptation to chase the cat.   A raccoon which uses the culvert in its normal route takes one look at Ram, and scoots away as fast as possible.

Ram waits.

Lucas secures a *White Knight* Jeep Wrangler, stops to pick up a bag of Purina Dog Chow, some beef jerky treats, and a plastic bowl to hold water, and heads to Annapolis.   As expected, he gets caught up in the Route 50, Washington, D.C. area traffic -- big time, as they say.   He listens to the news about the murder of two former FBI agents and learns that they have a person of interest in custody for ordering his attack dog to maul the two men.   He also hears on the news that a man-hunt is on for a German shepherd responsible for the "vicious and bloody slaughter" of the agents.   People in Annapolis are warned on the breaking news to stay indoors until the dog is found.

Lucas looks at his GPS tracker: there are three and a half miles to go.   Lucas is as hard as nails; his history as a Special Forces combat soldier placed him in danger repeatedly, against men who could have been Lucifer himself.   In situations where most men would panic, some would cry, and others would run, Lucas had stood his ground fearlessly.   However, though he admits this to no one, he is afraid of Ram.   There is something about Ram which embodies the savagery of nature.   Ram looks you dead in the eye -- and what you see clearly is that Ram has zero fear.

Lucas knows that Ram senses Lucas' fear and distrusts him, maybe, as a potential enemy.   God knows Lucas does not want to be Ram's enemy.

After another eight minutes of stop-and-go driving, the GPS indicates that Lucas is getting close to Ram.   He stops the Jeep, turns the ignition off, grabs some beef jerky … and his Beretta, just in case. Lucas was informed that the instruction "thirty-eight Black" meant that Ram was likely to be hiding in a culvert. Lucas finds the culvert within a minute, takes out his flashlight, and looks inside. Ram is lying on his stomach, vigilant, and ready to strike. Even though Ram knows Lucas, Ram will not move until he hears another instruction.

"Thorgon!" This made-up word, given to Lucas when he was given the GPS signal frequency, releases Ram from his prior instruction. Ram stands up and leaps, with his tail wagging, in Lucas' direction. Lucas could have sworn that he actually saw Ram smile.

Lucas says, "Come on, Ram; I bet you're hungry. I've got some dog chow for you." Lucas and Ram head for the Jeep, which is only twenty yards away from the culvert.

As Lucas places his hand on the passenger side door handle, a man yells, "Stop right there or I'll shoot! Annapolis City Police. I've called for backup. Turn that dog over to me right now; that dog is dangerous to the public and is wanted for mauling two men."

The cop is young; Lucas judges that he may have a year of experience out of the police academy under his belt. If the young cop bags the dog, this could possibly result in some serious kudos for him -- or maybe it should result in Cujos! Lucas is pretty sure the kid is nervous, trigger happy, and scared to death.

"Officer, Sir," responds Lucas, "you must be mistaken; this is my dog. Does he act like a mad killer dog to you?"

"His markings are an exact match; it's him."

About that time, a backup cruiser pulls up to the curb with lights flashing. A more senior but more out-of-shape officer steps out of his police cruiser and says, "Put the gun down Barry; let's make sure it's the right dog before you fire your weapon. You know how much paperwork discharging your weapon will cause, not to mention an Internal Affairs investigation!"

Barry lowers his weapon, but never holsters it or puts the safety back on. The senior officer pulls out a photo of Ram and walks toward him. Lucas instructs, "Sit," and to Lucas' surprise, Ram sits, obediently.

Lucas repeats, "Does this dog act like a vicious killer?"

The cop answers, "Let me see your driver's license and registration."

Lucas hands the cop his driver's license, walks to the passenger side door, opens it, rummages through the glove box, and finds the registration. With the passenger side door open, Lucas says to Ram, "Get in."

He did.

The cop says, "Hold on, Mr. Justice -- I like that name by the way -- I did not give you permission to put the dog in the vehicle, now ask him to get back out. Lucas pretends to give Ram new instructions and says something that sounded like gibberish to Ram's ear.

Ram does not get out of the Jeep. It was, in fact, gibberish.

The cop says to the kid, "Well, look here, Barry; what a coincidence. This Jeep is registered to the same company that the guy arrested for murder of the FBI agents works for!"

As Barry, the not-quite-there cop, is bringing his weapon up, the fat senior cop is reaching for his standard-issue weapon.

Reflexively, not actually thinking about it, Lucas grabs the young cop's wrist, twists it until it breaks and throws an elbow into the bridge of the senior cop's nose. Both Annapolis City policemen are disarmed and writhing in pain within five seconds of the young officer's initial movement. Lucas grabs his license and registration back from the older policeman, handcuffs the two of them to each other, grabs both of the officers' radios, and jumps into the Jeep.

He thinks, "What the fuck did I just do?"

At forty-one, he is one of the youngest State Attorneys General in the nation. He is ambitious, and is aiming at moving into higher politics -- maybe even a run for the Governorship of Maryland. He is a damn good prosecuting attorney and fights hard for justice. He is considered tough, but fair. He is a handsome family man and works hard for his favorite charity, *Wounded Warriors*. He is driving home, trying to get there in time to attend his son's soccer match, when he hears and feels the unmistakable vibration caused when a tire goes flat.

This is not going to go well with his wife and kids with whom he promised he would attend the soccer match. Nor will it go well for the expensive suit he is wearing. He pulls over, thinking that his tires are fairly new and, well, he likely caught a nail. He pulls out his cell phone, calls his wife, and, to his surprise, has to leave her a message.

He opens the hatch of his Volvo XC-60, opens the floor cover to access the spare tire, and stands back. There, on top of the tire, is a strange placard: "WARNING!"

The sign was professionally made. He turns it over. It reads, "DO NOT RELEASE TANK ALVAREZ"!

The AG's cell phone rings; it is his wife. She says, "We didn't make it to the soccer game. The Honda Pilot has a flat tire. I thought tires were supposed to last longer than 12,000 miles! Anyway, I've called AAA to come help us."

"Wait a minute; are the kids with you?"

Alarmed, she answers, "Yes."

"Are you near anyplace, anywhere you can mix with pedestrians and hold out until I get there?"

"You're scaring me; what's going on?"

The AG answers, "Just get out of there before the pretend-AAA guys get there. Hurry. Keep the phone connection open. "

She is on the move, getting the kids out of the car when she asks, "Pretend?"

He arrives at a nearby *Sheetz* store in a State Patrol Car in fifteen minutes. Everyone is OK. The AG and the police reach the Pilot, open the hatch to the spare tire and view a new sign: "WARNING!"

He turns it over: "GO TO YOUR SON'S SOCCER MATCH."

The young AG decides, after discovering that both flat tires had bullet penetrations, he'd hold Tank Alvarez without bail until he figures out who is threatening his family.

I am still fuming, thinking about what Jolene must be going through, wishing I could hold her in my arms, thinking about Ram, about what might happen to him, and thinking about retiring from this business. God knows, I no longer do this for the money. Maybe I'll sell my controlling interest of *White Knight* to Powers or Tucker.

There's nothing to do in this jail cell but think. Someone powerful is controlling my destiny. Why? I'm in the middle of a war between two factions. One wants me to discover the truth about the death of the White House attorney and the other powerful entity is trying to stop me. I wonder what Jimmy Ma has learned. I wonder how Powers and Maya made out, interviewing the former Washington Press Investigative reporter.

The door between the administrative area and the jail cells opens, breaking the vacuum created when the door is sealed. The same three guards who escorted me to meet with my lawyer earlier today are escorting a giant man to his cell. Ugly is a relative term, but this guy would look ugly to his mother. He is so obese that he can't walk straight ahead; he has to waddle back and forth, left then right at forty-five degree angles, just to move forward. His thighs rubbing together sound like fingernails scraping down a chalkboard. He has hair in all the wrong places; one eye is dilated; his nose points in multiple directions; he has tiny ears with large earlobes, an uneven mouth, and he looks like he could eat an apple through a picket fence.

Just looking at him makes my teeth hurt. Hell, my hairy butt is prettier than his face.

And then to my horror, the guards open my cell door and push this smiling monster of a man in. One of the guards says, "OK, Queenie; this is your home away from home."

And I had thought things couldn't get worse.

Lucas is a law-abiding citizen and, in general, respects law enforcement officers. He knows that he has just fucked up, royally. He is unsure what to do, but one thing he is sure of -- he needs to ditch the Jeep. He stops behind an office complex and parks at the far end of the parking lot, under a tree, and out of the line-of-sight of passing cars. He feeds Ram, to keep the hungry beast from chewing on Lucas' right arm for nourishment. He finally resorts to placing the call that everyone at *White Knight* makes when they get into trouble and need a way out.

He calls Powers.

Powers doesn't answer. Lucas remembers that Powers is probably on a flight back from Pasco, Washington after his interview with the reporter.

Lucas considers his options, waits until the sun sets, and everyone in the office building has rushed home or gone to their favorite watering hole. He even waits until the cleaning crew has completed their tasks and left the premises.

One vehicle is left in the parking lot. It's a Chevy Silverado with a company logo on the driver's side door which looks like a surveyor's transit.

Should he or shouldn't he?

He calls Powers again. No answer again, so he calls Jimmy Ma. "Jimmy, I won't be returning tonight with Ram. Are you OK?"

"I'm doing much better than you are. I think it's a damn good idea that you stay away for more than just tonight."

Lucas patiently waits for Jimmy to continue.

"You are now a YouTube star, you dummy. The cops had a video camera on the dashboard of their cruiser. You were caught in action. Damn, you're fast! I suggest that you turn yourself in before you get into any more trouble. You and Tank are in deep kimchi."

Lucas says, "Thanks for the heads-up, Jimmy. Any developments on your end?"

"Many, many developments. So many that I'm afraid to stay here; any moment, now, someone is going to walk in here and chain me to the bumper of their SUV and drive to San Francisco."

"I thought you were the best; I thought they couldn't follow a thread back to you."

Jimmy answers, "I hope I'm as good as I think I am. If I'm not, I'm probably dead already."

"Do you know how to get to the Manassas safe house?"

"No," but I do know a safe place to hide here in D.C."

"Where?"

"I'm afraid that if I say where, it will no longer be safe."

They hang up. Lucas decides that he should turn himself in to the police, but not until he delivers Ram to his home in Wiscasset, Maine.

And not until after he finishes his investigation.

Lucas and Ram are crossing the Chesapeake Bay Bridge in the Silverado on their way to the Eastern Shore when Powers finally returns Lucas' call.

There are no niceties from Powers, no "hello," "how are you" or "what happened?"

The first words out of his mouth are, "We'll discuss why you screwed up later. What's your current plan?"

Lucas answers, "To deliver Ram to his home, and complete my investigation of *Brave Chicken* on the way."

"You're going to drive all the way to Maine and expect not to be detected, arrested, and crucified?"

Lucas asks, "What do you suggest?"

"I suggest that we contact Tucker. He's *amazingly* resourceful. He and Maya will do almost anything to make sure that Ram sticks around to protect Star."

CHAPTER 28 -- THE MURDER CONDUCTOR

On the abandoned oil platform, Heidi, in the middle of the ocean: Jolene watches cable news, non-stop, after learning that Tank was arrested for ordering Ram to maul two former FBI agents. She knows that one of the victims was the FBI agent-in-charge of the investigation which took place over twenty years ago, the investigation into the death of the Deputy White House attorney.

She wonders what went wrong, and why Tank's investigation got him into the mess he's in. She feels guilty about the fact that Tank is in jail after trying to save her, and that Ram could end up losing his life because of her. She is frustrated, helpless and angry.

She wonders who has Tank's satellite phone. Could she speak with Powers or someone at *White Knight* who has the phone? She calls again, but no one picks up.

As she does every day, she climbs atop her precariously arranged ladder to stick her head outside and breathe fresh air. The weather today is gray and frigid.

The satellite phone's ringtone "Du Weibt Ich Weib" erupts. She can't believe it rang when she is least able to reach it. It repeatedly plays the stupid phone tune until she climbs down to it and says, "Yes, Yes, I'm here!"

"My dear Jolene," says Gunter Korf, "I know you are there, and I know you will not be leaving your little flat any time soon. It seems that your boyfriend is no longer able to pursue his mission. If he gets life in prison, then you get life on the Heidi in solitary confinement.

"However, it seems that the rest of the investigative team is making progress, so there is hope for you yet. But the team has disturbed a hornet's nest which has forced my enemy, a chess master in his own right, to make some very aggressive moves.

But this is not a game we can lose. He will be surprised when some new chess pieces show up on the board."

Boston, Massachusetts: Two *White Knight* agents are waiting at the gate in Logan Airport for Maya, Star and their boss, Powers, to provide both escort and guard services. A driver is waiting outside the terminal in a reinforced Durango with bullet-proof windows. The crew makes their way through the Callahan tunnel into downtown Boston and on up to *Entropy Entrepreneurs'* Headquarters.

Tucker Cherokee, Chief Executive Officer of *Entropy Entrepreneurs*, is waiting in the main conference room with Tony Vinci, Chief Scientist, and three very special guests who will surprise and delight Powers, Maya, and Star.

Tucker's assistant sticks her head meerkat-like into the conference room and announces, "They're here!" Star comes running into the conference room with her arms spread wide yelling "Daddy, Daddy," but stops suddenly before she reaches Tucker and says, "Uncle Ray? Oh, boy! What are you doing here? Did you bring Al with you?"

Ray is not really Star's uncle but he has always been treated like he is. Retired General Ray LaSalle and Tucker had teamed up on a couple of life-threatening escapades which bonded them forever as friends. Ray and his best buddy, Al, retired to Trinidad to live the good life. Al is one of Ram's pups, given to him by Star when she was ten years old.

Maya enters the room next, and before she can give Ray a hug, she is distracted by her former boss, sitting at the table. Former President of the United States of America, Winston

Allen, stands up and extends his hand out to Maya who rushes to him, throws her arms around him, and gives him a big hug -- something she'd never done when she was his National Science Advisor. President Allen actually blushes. Maya says, "My God, what are you doing here?" Then, she shakes herself and quickly goes over to give Ray LaSalle a hug, too.

Ray says, "That alone was worth coming all the way up here from Trinidad. Wow!"

The third special guest shakes hands with Powers and nods his head deferentially to Maya. Damian LaTorre was the FBI Director during the Allen Administration and maintains an excellent relationship with the current Director of the FBI, who calls on LaTorre frequently for advice and counsel.

After about fifteen minutes of chit-chat and catching up with each other, Tucker finally announces, "Let's continue these discussions tonight over dinner. Three other people are going to call in, two of whom I'd like Star to speak with briefly before we excuse her from all this boring stuff." Tucker gives Star a wink; Star rolls her eyes.

Tucker enters the conference call number and password, and finally he enters the PIN number. The first person to call in is Jimmy Ma. Jimmy is dumbstruck after Tucker introduces him to everyone on the phone. Tucker asks Jimmy, "Where are you calling in from, Jimmy?"

"Ah, … Washington, D.C."

"Are you in the D.C. safe house?"

"Sir, I'm not sure there are any more safe houses left, but, no, I am in hiding."

The call was interrupted with "Mockingbird here."

Tucker says, "I don't want to know where *you* are and most of the people around this table don't want to know *who* you are, so we'll just use your code name, Mockingbird. What I *do* want to know -- before we drill down and get into the details of our investigations -- is: how is Ram doing? Star is in the room, so please give her a status report."

"Ram is healthy, getting his exercise, well-fed, and seems to enjoy our current location. He's here; I'll put my phone on speaker so he can hear Star's voice."

"Ram, I miss you!" says Star. Ram barks twice -- the first time he's made a sound since Lucas picked him up. Lucas takes the phone off speaker just as the final person comes on-line.

"This is Jolene."

Maya, Star, Powers, and Tony all yell simultaneously: "Jolene!!" Star blurts out, "Are you home?"

Jolene says, "No, but the man who took me hostage wants to help us complete our mission and uncover the truth about the deceased White House lawyer, so he agreed to let me make this call. I was able to talk with Tucker earlier today, which is how I knew about it."

Powers asks, "Are you OK, health-wise?"

"Yes."

Tucker introduces all the attendees to Jolene, and asks Star to excuse herself and visit with his assistant -- another of Star's best friends.

"We have a long list of things to cover today. The goal of the meeting is to develop a strategy to get Jolene back, get Tank out of jail, collect all the information we can on the death of the White House Counsel, discover who tried to kill Maya by crashing the Lear, clear Lucas Justice and Ram from any charges, and find out who kidnapped Jolene."

Though he works for Tucker, Jimmy interrupts: "And don't forget to come up with a strategy to keep me alive after I tell you the information I uncovered."

Tony quips, "Not high on the list, Jimmy." Everyone laughs except Jimmy.

"Let's start with Tank. What do we know so far?"

Powers opens with, "I got a complete debrief from Richard Kingsley who was with Tank on the stakeout of the former FBI agent, Brian Richmond. Richmond wouldn't meet with Tank, so the two of them thought they'd act like paparazzi and see if they could catch him off guard. Little did they suspect that Richmond was lying in wait for an opportunity to return the favor! Once Tank passed out from the tranquilizer dart, Kingsley suspected that they were going to tie Tank up and ask questions of their own -- like who his customer was. They probably would have beaten him to a pulp thinking he wasn't telling the truth about not knowing.

"The curious part of all of this is not that he was arrested -- after all, the police found Tank on the scene with two dead men. The curious part is that he is being held without bail. The evidence is that he was assaulted by the agents with the tranquilizer gun, that he is a registered Private Investigator with impeccable credentials, and he's famous worldwide for saving the lives of dignitaries. Yet, he is in jail without bail. We need to check out the judge and AG to understand what's going on." Powers continues, "Maybe I should have a talk with them."

Maya says, "Just what we need -- for you to land in jail, too."

Winston Allen speaks up for the first time: "I know the Governor. I'll give him a call and see if he is willing to investigate the conduct of his AG."

Tucker asks, "Anyone else have an idea about what to do for Tank?"

Ray LaSalle speaks up and asks, "Who are the best defense lawyers in the country? Retain them. Or retain someone who has the judge's ear, someone he trusts."

Tucker says, "I'll take that action item."

"This is Lucas Justice." Lucas rarely spoke, so it shocked Powers that he would jump in. "Jolene, you were abducted in front of Brave Chicken's Headquarters in Salisbury, Maryland, right?"

Jolene answers, "Yes, to the best of my recollection. The drug they gave me still has that part of my memory blacked out."

Lucas continues, "I was in the CEO's office of Brave Chicken, when FBI agent Mark Vintage served him a warrant to search the facility, primarily to seize surveillance camera video. In less than twenty-four hours, Mark Vintage was pulled off the case by his boss and sent to El Paso, Texas.

"Director LaTorre," continues Lucas, "Is there a way for you to find out who pulled Agent Vintage off the case? That thread may lead us to the group which masterminded Jolene's kidnapping."

Jolene adds, "My kidnapper is a German named Gunter Korf. He claims that he represents a group, if that is any help."

Former FBI Diector Damien LaTorre responds to Lucas by saying, "I'll see what I can find out."

Tony Vinci clears his throat and states, "Jolene, I think I know where you are and the name of the group that is holding you hostage."

BEEP! BEEP! BEEP! BEEP!

It's the fire alarm. The fire plan is for everyone to leave the room, calmly take the steps down to the first floor, exit and meet at a designated area so that the company emergency response officer can count heads and make sure that no one is left in the building.

That is protocol.

BEEP! BEEP! BEEP! BEEP!

The Secret Service detail assigned to former president Winston Allen throws protocol to the wind, moves him quickly out of the conference room -- he is not seen again on this day.

BEEP! BEEP! BEEP! BEEP!

Powers says to Tucker, "I don't trust this at all. Don't go outside; stay here. We need to lock-down."

Maya rushes out of the conference room in search of Star. Tucker's assistant is holding Star's hand, walking in the direction of the stairway.

"Stop!" yells Maya, "Bring Star into the conference room, please."

The assistant brings Star into the room.

Powers says to all, "This is my world. Everyone stays in the conference room. Lock down and I'll guard outside just in case the fire alarm is fake. Tucker, are the weapons still in the same place?"

Tucker nods his head, "Yes."

"Code?"

"6672."

Powers locks the team in the conference room, goes to the hidden supply cabinet, punches in the access code and opens the gun safe.

Powers is now armed and *very* dangerous.

The smoke bomb is released on a floor seven levels above *Entropy Entrepreneurs*. "Horse" releases the bomb directly under a smoke detector in an empty office space. Pawn and Kingster are waiting on the roof across the street with rifles. When Powers and Maya leave the building, they will use their sharpshooting skills. If one of them misses, it is Horse's responsibility to finish the job.

Powers waits. He feels it in his gut that someone will emerge on their floor to perform whatever dastardly deed was planned.

Neither Powers nor Maya leaves the building. Pawn says to Horse through his earbud, "Negative visual contact with targets."

The Kingster says, "Ditto, here."

Pawn says, "Implement the back-up plan. Be careful. We're not dealing with a virgin here."

Horse carefully wanders down seven floors, step by step. He is carrying a tear gas canister. The door to the *Entropy Entrepreneurs* floor is locked. A key card or a fob is required to access the floor from the other levels. Horse had stolen a fob yesterday; he is prepared. He cracks the door open, activates the tear gas and throws it into the hallway before he puts his gas mask on. Horse waits a full forty-five seconds before he reopens the door from the stairway and walks down the hall.

Horse doesn't see it coming.

When Horse awakes, he is looking into the face of Lucifer's wrath. Powers is going to learn everything Horse knows, and a few things Horse would probably make up just to avoid the pain.

What Powers doesn't expect Horse to know is who killed Pawn and the Kingster across the street, using a 50-caliber sniper rifle.

CHAPTER 29 -- WRONGHEADED

Washington, D.C.: After spending thirty five minutes getting make-up applied, her hair done, and rehearsing her lines, the former First Lady is ready for her Sunday morning talk show interview.

The host greets her warmly, thanks her profusely for making herself available for the interview and extols all her accomplishments in her career as a public servant. The host goes on to lob her slow-pitch underhanded softball questions. "Why do you want to be president? Don't you think it is time for a woman president? What will you do for the poor? How do you intend to deal with global warming? What is your plan to deal with undocumented immigrant children?"

She knocks every question out of the ball park. The interview is going to strengthen her poll numbers. She is feeling great.

Until the host asks, "We have it on good authority that the death of your former law partner -- who was also your husband's Deputy White House Counsel -- has been reopened, and that there are people related to the original case ... ruled as a suicide ... and people investigating the case today ...who are either dying or are having their lives threatened. Do you have any comment that you would like to make to our audience about this?"

Viewers who recorded the interview and could rewind and replay it, observed her eyes slightly narrow, her gaze harden, her facial muscles tighten, and her fake smile look even more fake. There was just enough silence in the interview for the host to become uncomfortable. He begins to speak just as she starts to answer the question.

"It is still painful for me to recall the news of his suicide. He was a friend, a good attorney, someone you could trust, and we still miss him. I encourage the investigators to pursue complete understanding of his death. All of us close to him want to know the real reason for his suicide."

San Diego, California: Viktor Soroson uses his remote to turn the TV off. He can't take any more of the interview. He sits thinking about his next move. It's time to begin phase one of his three phase plan. He pulls out his encrypted satellite phone and contacts Ahmed Mohammed.

"Ahmed, my friend, is everything in place? It's time to flip the switch. Start the snowball rolling on Operation Avalanche. When the mission is complete, you will discover the funds I promised you in your Cayman Islands account … with just a little bonus."

"Yes, sir, everything is in place and I'm excited about our chances for success. I will use the money you promise me to promote our theocratic ideology."

"You offend me with your bull, Ahmed. We both know you are an atheist."

CHAPTER 30 -- PERSEVERANCE

Ocean City, Maryland: Lucas has very little experience at throwing a Frisbee, but he gets the hang of it. It is something that helps him bond with Ram. The ocean is too cold for Lucas' liking but it doesn't seem to bother Ram, as he jumps into the water after the Frisbee and brings it back. On this, their second day in Ocean City, Maryland, Lucas finally sees what he came here for. He sees Miss Maryland walking the beach, mostly looking down for seashells and sand crabs. She doesn't see Lucas until it is too late.

She turns a full 360 degrees as if searching for someone, anyone, who might be able to help her. She is frightened, but she knows it is useless to run or ignore him.

Boston, Massachusetts: Tony Vinci was very disappointed that the fire alarm drama interrupted the progress meeting his boss, Tucker, was running. He wanted people like former president Winston Allen and former Director of the FBI, Damian LaTorre to hear about his scientific discoveries and the new information that he was about to drop on everybody. He thought that well-connected people like Allen and LaTorre would spread the word about Tony and *Entropy Entrepreneurs,* resulting in even more work and more interesting and exciting new things to investigate.

He settles for asking to have a meeting with Tucker; he tells Tucker it is pretty important.

Twenty minutes later, Tucker walks into Tony's office with Maya and Ray LaSalle afoot. Tucker says, "OK, my resident genius, let's have it. If you say, it's important, it probably is."

Tucker remains standing; with his nervous energy, he leans against the wall and looks at the wide screen in Tony's office. Maya and Ray settle into office chairs to view the screen as if they were going to watch a new thriller movie.

Tony elevates his pneumatic chair as he announces, "Actually, I have three important things to cover. The first is that we have learned who the likely entity is which kidnapped Jolene. That information led to identifying her location.

"Tucker, you handed me a list which was compiled by you, Powers, and Maya in the first few days after Jolene's kidnapping. I was able to cross-reference this list with German organizations known to contribute to senatorial and presidential campaigns in the United States. That action narrowed the list down to just nine groups. I compared the nine organizations with likely companies that had financial interest in oil drilling. That narrowed the group down to five companies, and groups which the five companies might be a part of.

"Then I spoke with Jimmy Ma and compared his research in money transfers with my list and bingo, all five companies belong to a group called The Deutsche Chamber. All five companies are in the Top 40 of revenue generators in Germany.

"This leads to knowing the whereabouts of Jolene. There is only one oil platform currently not in production that is co-owned by a German consortium and Royal Dutch Shell. It's out-of-commission due to a case of sabotage. Lloyds of London are not paying the cost of repair because sabotage is excluded from the coverage. They are expected to settle the dispute in court sometime within the next eighteen months."

All eyes are on Tony; some of them are getting angry that he hasn't told them yet where she is. Finally, Tony pulls up a satellite photo of the oil platform in the North Atlantic, seventy-five kilometers north of Scotland.

Tucker, Maya, and Ray bolt out of Tony's office to call various people that might be able to use the good news to help save Jolene.

Tony is yelling out to anyone who would listen, "Jolene told Tank that the platform is booby-trapped so we need to be careful with this knowledge. I'd do more investigation if I were you, before you launch a rescue party."

Tony thought, "I guess they didn't want to hear about the other two important things."

Ocean City, Maryland: "Impressive looking dog," Miss Maryland says nervously.

Lucas answers, "He's much more impressive than he looks.

"Good, Good," Lucas says to Ram. Ram wanders over next to Miss Maryland and waits to be petted. She does, and Ram then walks back over to Lucas.

While gesturing with her hands she asks, "So, why are you here? What do you want from me?"

"Neither Agent Vincent nor Tank Alvarez got a chance to interview you. You were too low on their priority list. You're on my list, instead."

"What do you want to know?"

"First, why are men following you?"

She answers, "This may sound egocentric to you, but men have been following me since I was a teenager. I don't notice it anymore."

"There are two men following you, and they have been, since you left your beachfront home. If you count me and Ram, four men have been following you. But the other two are not friendlies."

"And you and Ram are?"

"I suspect we are friendlier than they are. Do you have any idea who might hire someone to follow you and why?"

"Sure, Elliott would; he's had me followed before."

Lucas asked, "Why?"

"Elliott pays the mortgage on my ocean front property even though the deed is in my name."

"That's not why he's having you followed though, is it? He probably now has photos of you walking on the beach with me. Does that put you in danger?"

"It's doubtful."

Lucas continues, "What is he hiding?"

"Me, for one." She throws her head back, her long blond hair catching the cool ocean breeze and she shivers. "Can we continue this discussion someplace a little warmer? There's a coffee shop, *Grinding Halt*, two blocks from here."

They walk north on the beach until she points to a sandy walkway which leads toward the street. She says with some concern, "You'll need a leash for Ram, or you won't be allowed to bring him inside the coffee shop."

Lucas stays silent. The three of them walk into the coffee shop. Lucas walks over to a table, looks at Ram and instructs, "Stay." He proceeds to the counter and orders coffee. The manager of the coffee shop advises Lucas that he can't keep "the dog" in the shop.

"OK. But you'll have to tell him, yourself. And good luck with that."

Addressing Miss Maryland, "I see your friends are across the street, still following you."

161

"Or you."

"Or both of us."

Ram rises up, moves his snout onto Lucas' lap, and makes a sound. The sound was not a bark, nor was it a growl. Somehow, he conveys the idea that Lucas needs to get on the move. Ram doesn't head for the front door -- he heads through the kitchen and out the back screen door. Lucas and Ram are long gone by the time the four police cruisers pull up to the coffee shop and secure the area. They take Miss Maryland to the Ocean City police station for questioning. The police want to know why she is harboring fugitives. The two men following Miss Maryland wait patiently across the street from the police station.

Annapolis, Maryland: I am about to confront my roommate about his hygiene problems when the door from the access control gate opens and the three amigo policemen come to the cell door carrying shackles and handcuffs. I am hoping and praying that the restraints are for Queenie and that, maybe, the cops would remove him permanently from my presence.

But, as recent luck would have it, the shackles are for me.

The guards escort me to the visitor's room as they tease me about how long I am going to be jailed. My grand jury hearing was once again moved out in time to who-knows-when.

As I enter the guarded visitor's room, I witness the last person I ever expect to visit me here in an Annapolis jail. "Ray," I happily exclaim in a gleeful tone, "what a surprise. Wow, you came all the way from Trinidad to see me? What a great friend! You look great." Actually, he didn't look so good

but I didn't know what else to say.   I probably blushed at
General Ray LaSalle seeing me in shackles and handcuffs.

Ray explains, "I'm here as a messenger to pass information
to you, to offer my assistance, and the assistance of former FBI
director, Damian LaTorre. The Director, by the way, is also
waiting in the lobby to meet with you after we're through
talking.

"First, let me give you some good news.   We've identified
Jolene's location."

"Fantastic.   Is a team being put together to save her?   When
is the extraction date? Is Powers leading the team?"

Ray says, "Slow down, Tank.   When I say 'we' identified
the location of Jolene, I mean Tony Vinci located the site of the
deep water oil platform in the North Atlantic above Scotland
where she is probably being held captive.   As you recall, Jolene
said the place was booby-trapped and that if we try to save her,
she may be the victim.   Powers and Tony are investigating the
potential methods that could be used to prevent our rescue, so
they won't develop a team or strategy until they understand the
trap, and until the method for defusing the trap is fool-proof.
One of us will keep you apprised as the mission to save Jolene
evolves.

"A second piece of information that this messenger, me, is
sharing with you is that *Entropy Entrepreneurs* was attacked
during an impromptu meeting when we -- Tucker, Maya,
Powers, Winston Allen, Director LaTorre, Tony and me -- were
meeting to discuss progress on saving Jolene and exploring the
ransom assignment dictated to you by the kidnappers.   The
attack was crudely planned, but might have been effective if
Powers hadn't smelled a rat.   Their team of killers was trying to
flush Powers and Maya out of the building where sharpshooters
were positioned to take them out.   Incredibly, the two
sharpshooters were ultimately assassinated by snipers

themselves by an unknown party. There's a lot more going on here than meets the eye.

"A third killer was captured and interrogated by Powers. As you are well aware, Powers is very persuasive. What he learned from the guy whom Powers calls Horse face is that there are three more members of their killer team. One of them has the assignment of threatening the Maryland Attorney General and the Judge assigned to your case to keep you in jail.

"Another member of the killer team is assigned to make sure you are damaged to the point that you can no longer pursue your investigative efforts. All the members of the killer team have nicknames taken from chess pieces. The guy Powers interviewed was named Horse. He told Powers that the Queen is assigned to take care of you."

I understand immediately that Queenie is the killer assigned to eliminate me as a threat to whoever seems threatened. I ask Ray, "Who's behind these guys? What did Powers learn in his interrogation of Horse about where the orders are coming from?"

Ray says, "Nothing. His orders come down from the killer team's leader, a man they call Rook. Rook gets his orders from an unknown benefactor who paid for all of the lawyers that got them off of death row and who secured their freedom."

"Well," I say, "Thanks for the heads-up; you probably just saved my life. I was planning to sleep sometime in the next couple of days, but I think I'll skip that pleasure."

Ray says, "Now, I would like a favor from you."

General LaSalle has never asked me for anything.

"Promise me that when you get out of here that I can be a part of your mission to rescue Jolene."

I start thinking about trying to talk him out of it and telling him that he is much too old and physically unable to contribute in a meaningful way to such a dangerous mission, but when I look into his eyes, I capitulate, "Sure, welcome to our next mission."

I change the subject and ask, "So how is Algorithm doing? Has he grown up to be as good a protector and companion to you as Ram has been to Star?"

I watch Ray's eyes light up, "Al is fabulous; I could tell you stories all day. The one thing I can tell you is that he is a great guard dog -- absolutely no one bothers me. I have a sign on the gate in front of my property that warns people about Al. The sign deters few, but when they see him and hear his ferocious bark, they evaporate into thin air. Crime doesn't happen on my property. He is a clone of his father, Ram."

"Time's up, asshole," says the jail guard, "you have ten minutes, max, with your second visitor."

I shake hands with Ray -- and he leaves a yellow Post-It-Note in my hand as he leaves. I don't look at it, just in case the guards are watching.

When FBI Director Damien LaTorre is escorted into the visitor room, I thank him for coming by and doing whatever he is doing on my behalf. "It is much appreciated."

"Tank, I have no doubt that you are innocent of murder. I will do anything I can to help you; after all, you saved my ass in the past and I owe you.

"What I'm doing is trying to discover why the Maryland Attorney General and the Maryland Criminal Judge are so adamant that you be held without bail. We smell a rat. Former president Winston Allen contacted the Governor of Maryland and pressed him to disclose the logic for holding you. The Governor was unsuccessful at persuading the AG or the judge to alter their position. This is consistent with the information Powers squeezed out of the guy he interrogated. The odor of injustice has gotten so redolent that Winston and I presented evidence to the decision makers about a possible conspiracy to murder you, Maya, and Powers.

"Still, we were not able to persuade the AG or the judge to change their positions."

I conclude, "They're being threatened like Powers said, aren't they? Much like I am being threatened with ransom to investigate the death of the White House attorney."

"That's our conclusion, too, so we worked with your *White Knight* attorney to get your case moved to Federal court."

I say, "Great news. What's your estimate on when that will that happen?"

"It'll take a couple of days."

I think about a couple of more days with Queenie and conclude that I am going to have to take care of business tonight.

"Thanks for everything, Damian."

Damian adds, "One more thing. Promise me that when you put together a team for the mission to rescue Jolene that you will include me on that team."

Hmmm.

When I am escorted back to my cell, I find Queenie still there, his perpetual Cheshire-cat-like smile bellying his felonious intent. We don't speak to each other; rather, we are sizing each other up anew.

I take the time to look at the yellow Post-It-Note which Ray handed me. Written on the paper is, "If anything happens to me, I would like you to be the executor of my will. Safe deposit box key is in Al's collar."

Hmmm.

Boston, Massachusetts: Tucker is considering his priorities after the debacle that followed the fake fire alarm test, the attack on *Entropy Entrepreneur*'s offices, the potential attempted murder of his wife, Maya, his partner Powers, and whatever other mayhem the team of killers were planning to perpetrate. His first priority is the safety of Maya and Star.

Déjà vu all over again.

He concludes that he needs to get Ram back to help protect his loved ones. He calls Lucas' cell phone number but has to leave a message. "Lucas, this is Tucker; we need to coordinate the safe return of Ram to Star. Give me a call ASAP."

Tucker walks around his office hallways until he finds Maya and Star talking with Tucker's administrative assistant. Tucker says, "Ah, just the people I wanted to catch up with."

Maya recognizes the tone in Tucker's voice; Star recognizes even more.

Tucker asks, "What do you two think about a trip to our vacation home in Wanaka?"

"What did I tell you?" Maya says to Star, "didn't I predict this? I know my husband way too well.

"Honey, I can't interview people who need to be interviewed for the safe release of Jolene ... from New Zealand."

Star adds, "Daddy, that didn't work when we tried it the last time. Remember?"

"OK," capitulates Tucker, "at least I hope you agree, Maya, to return home and allow me to double the security detail there."

Star asks, "Aren't you coming with us?"

"I want to," answers Tucker as he gives both of them a hug, "but Powers and I have something we have to do first."

167

Washington, D.C.:   Powers and Tucker grab an early shuttle from Boston's Logan to Washington Reagan National. Two *White Knight* security officers greet them and escort their bosses to the Washington, D.C. safe house where Jimmy Ma and Lucas Justice were previously residing.   The safe house is secure, but empty as expected.

Thirty minutes later, two other *White Knight* officers enter the safe house after passing the biometric access control barriers -- with Jimmy Ma, insecure and hesitant as always.

Jimmy asks, "How do you guys always know where to find me? Am I tagged or something?"

No one answers his question.

Finally, Jimmy says, "Hi, Boss. I kind of knew you'd show up. Do I have some super-information to share with you!"

"Share it, please. I'm getting a little tired of my wife's life being threatened, not to mention my friend Powers here."

"Let me show you instead."   Jimmy boots up the computer linked to a Cray supercomputer.   "Look at this." Tucker and Powers look over Jimmy's shoulder at a 60-inch monitor. Neither Tucker nor Powers understand what they are seeing -- just a bunch of alpha-numeric lists, Greek symbols, and Roman numerals embedded in code.

Jimmy Ma continues, "I found fifteen different charitable tax-free 501(c)(3) accounts, fourteen of which routed funds from Phoenix to Hong Kong. From Hong Kong to Belize. From Belize to Abu Dhabi. And finally Abu Dhabi to Atlanta. All fourteen accounts have three letter names like WWD or GHR; they empty into nine new accounts which are political action committees, news media slush funds, and foundations that fund the presidential campaign of the former First Lady."

Powers adds, "And the former First Lady is the one with a motive in the death of the White House Counsel."

"It gets better," smiles Jimmy Ma.

Neither Powers nor Tucker could think of how it could get better.

Jimmy continues, "The fifteenth account winds up in an account in Detroit. There is only one signatory to the account, Duke Dillinger."

Tucker and Powers looked at each other quizzically, neither recognizing the name.

"Ole Duke," Jimmy says, "is on the FBI Criminal Justice Information System, and spent about four years on death row until he was released on a technicality."

"Let me guess," interjects Powers, "He goes by a nickname that is a chess piece."

"Right you are. The Rook."

Tucker furrows his brow, walks around the room, scratches his chin with his left hand, screws up his face and finally asks, "Who would fund the former First Lady and a team of killers? For what purpose?"

Jimmy Ma excitedly announces, "I thought you'd never ask. Have you ever heard of the billionaire, Viktor Soroson?"

Ocean City, Maryland: Lucas suspects that since the Ocean City police had caught him and Ram at the *Grinding Halt,* that a concerned citizen must have recognized them on TV as fugitives and called it in. He assumes, therefore, that their stolen van has also been compromised.

They need a new ride.

Lucas has previously scoped out Miss Maryland's beachfront home and noticed a Mercedes ML 350 SUV with tinted windows in the garage. It would be perfect for Ram. He figured it was a thirty-minute walk south on the beach to reach her place. Despite the cold wind, it would be a pleasant enough walk with Ram.

"Dammit," thinks Lucas as he spots a bicycle cop headed north, about a hundred yards away. These bad-ass fugitives, Lucas and Ram, have been spotted and the young cop has pulled his radio to share his discovery. Lucas has a choice to make: either surrender, which would put Ram at risk of being killed by an overzealous police officer, or dig an even deeper hole with law enforcement.

Lucas decides his chances of survival are better in confronting the police than in reporting to Tank that he'd let someone kill Ram. Lucas walks south as casually as possible, at a metered pace, not acting like he is guilty of anything. When Lucas reaches a point within five yards of the policeman, the cop says, "Stop right there."

Lucas takes two more steps forward and the cop starts to pull his weapon of choice, a Taser. Lucas is six feet away when the cop realizes that Ram is in mid-air, flying towards him, traveling at what seems to him like Mach 1. The poor cop's forearm was in Ram's jaws before he could react.

"Stop! Stop," Lucas says. To Lucas' and the cop's relief, Ram stops before he tears the man's arm off. In the meantime, Lucas has recovered the Taser and the cop's radio. He flings the radio as far as he can towards the beach, into the beach grass. Then, he says, "I'm going to borrow your bike; sorry."

WHA-CKED   JED O'Dea
(White House Attorney-Counsel Killed)

Lucas starts pedaling as fast as he can south, in the hopes of reaching Miss Maryland's home before he becomes a blip on more policemen's radar screens. Lucas is wondering how he is going to avoid being tracked, knowing full well his tire tracks in the sand will be easy to follow. He rides as close to the ocean as possible, hoping that the tide is coming in so it would cover his tracks. Though Lucas is struggling mightily to maximize his speed, Ram is effortlessly jogging to the pace.

He sees it first in the bike's rearview mirror. "Damn," he says out loud. A jeep is closing in on him, and he knows he isn't going to make it to Miss Maryland's house. Since he has no better plan, he turns right, due west, away from the ocean, in the direction of a sand knoll. He turns and looks back in the direction of the Jeep -- it has no police markings on it.

Lucas wonders, "If it's not the police, then who is it?" He jumps off the bike, dives behind the knoll, rolls to one side, pulls his 40-caliber German Luger and prepares for battle. Ram lies down low, by his side.

The Jeep is flashing its lights off and on and comes to a sliding stop ten yards from Lucas' position. The Jeep is occupied by the two men whom he'd previously seen following Miss Maryland. One of them yells out, "Lucas Justice, please, jump in. We've been instructed to escort you to Carmen's house."

Lucas has no idea who Carmen is. Seconds later, the same man yells, "The woman you were with at the coffee shop has asked us to bring you to her."

"Oh," thought Lucas; "Miss Maryland's first name is Carmen?" Lucas yells out, "Why?"

"I have no idea. I just follow orders."

That statement had a lot of corollary meanings to it -- too many meanings for Lucas to instantly assess.

WHA-CKED

(White House Attorney-Counsel Killed)

With a Taser in one hand, an H&K in the other, and Ram alongside ... he thought that he could handle whatever might happen after jumping into the Jeep with the two unknowns.

Five minutes later, Lucas and Ram are comfortably in Miss Maryland's SUV headed north in the direction of Delaware. Carmen, Miss Maryland, is driving -- with the two bodyguards following in the Jeep behind them.

Lucas asks, "Why? Why are you helping us?"

"It's complicated. We have plenty of time to discuss it. Where are we going; where do you want us to take you?"

"Wiscasset, Maine."

"You're kidding, right?"

CHAPTER 31 -- PHASE ONE

Caracas, Venezuela: He moves his knight into position and intentionally leaves his king vulnerable. Soroson is baiting his Russian chess opponent and anticipates Yuri's next move -- a move which would put Soroson's king in check. As Viktor expects, his opponent does, in fact, take the bait. Now it is Viktor's turn to move, and he places his bishop in a position to protect the king ... and waits for his opponent to make his next move. Viktor is making moves to make it look to his opponent as though he were on the defense, which is anything but the case.

But his chess match with the Russia master is kid's play compared with the other game he is playing. He can plan nine moves ahead in chess, but he's been planning twelve to fifteen moves ahead in his three decades-long geo-political game. He is getting close to the equivalent of check-mate in the big game, so his latest "super move" requires him to transfer all his billions of dollars off-shore, relocating his headquarters to Caracas, Venezuela where there is no extradition treaty with the U.S. He must also short-sell German company stocks, short-sell European insurance companies, and place orders for currency swaps. He estimates that he will earn $300 million tax-free dollars in the next few days as a result of these moves. It is tax-free because he dodges federal income tax. Taxes are for the "little people" who can't afford tax lawyers. He already owes the US Treasury over a billion dollars; what's a few tens of millions more?

The part of the "super move" which includes shorting insurance stocks is a move that, years ago, he taught Usama bin Laden ... who acted on what his mentor, Soroson, taught him. Usama short-sold U.S. insurance company stocks just days before UBL's masterpiece -- the 9/11-attack on the New York World Trade Center. But Soroson's current "Phase One"

173

planned attack on Germany would be even bigger than bin Laden's attack on the U.S.

Germany: Volkswagen's manufacturing techniques have evolved over time to use robots to perform complicated welding and assembly tasks. Very sophisticated software, protected vigilantly from industrial espionage, represents the brains of the manufacturing business of the world's largest automobile manufacturer. So when the brains grow a tumor -- Soroson-sponsored malware -- the entire manufacturing capability of Volkswagen, Audi, and Porsche comes to a screeching halt. VW's Wolfsburg plant and Audi's Ingolstadt plant together employ over a hundred thousand people who are now just standing around being unproductive until a fix can be invented. Volkswagen's bottom line suffers with the compounding problem of both decreased revenue due to its loss of production, and the increase in production cost per automobile. Stock prices fall precipitously ... and ultimately, Volkswagen must lay off workers. Unemployment in Germany rises and the economic stability of the European Union is threatened. This act of economic terrorism is only the first of many planned by Soroson in 'Phase One' of his three phase plan.

Rheinmetall, a Dusseldorf manufacturer of ammunition, discovers that they are missing thousands of rounds of 40 x 53mm airburst munitions -- DM131s -- used in their extremely accurate and effective automatic grenade launchers. With a maximum range of 2,400 yards and a GPS programmable Infrared target finder, the grenade launcher is on every jihadist's wish list.

On the same day that Volkswagen's auto manufacturing capabilities are compromised, an insider attack empties Rheinmetall's warehouse, slaughters their amateurish security guards, and uses the stolen grenade launchers to level their warehouse at its conclusion.

One hundred and twelve terrorist attacks are then made on German companies using the stolen grenade launchers and Rheinmetall munitions. BASF's polyalkylene glycol-based lubricant plant in Ludwigshafen will likely burn for weeks. Its pipelines in Stade that supply natural gas, oil, and other products through the transportation hub will take months to reopen.

Bayer Healthcare Pharmaceuticals' headquarters in Berlin is severely damaged from grenade attacks, with its senior management either dead or in critical care.

Lufthansa Technik AG maintains their worldwide fleet of airliners in Hamburg. The company's critical inventory of spare parts is stored in five lightly guarded warehouses. Forty-three grenade launches successfully level the warehouses before the jihadists are killed by Hamburg police. Lufthansa's fleet of Boeing 747s, Boeing 777s and Airbus 380s are down for weeks until new parts can be secured.

The attacks on German industry are going to have a serious impact on the nation's economy -- an economy which all of Europe depends upon as the strongest link, the foundation for success for the entire European Union. Only one of the Soroson-financed attacks on the first day of this organized chaos fails. The plan to collapse the Elbe Crossing is unsuccessful. The stock value of Switzerland's Zurich Insurance Group, the largest insurer of German industry in all of Europe, falls like a rock. The faster it falls, the more money Soroson makes, as he had shorted the stock. In fact, he makes enough in one day to pay for his entire investment in the now-complete "Phase One."

CHAPTER 32 -- NEAR-DEATH EXPERIENCE

Annapolis, Maryland: I am lying on my cot in the cell, breathing through my mouth to keep from smelling Queenie, my 475-pound plus-sized cellmate. We all require sleep, some of us more than others. Powers taught me how to fight sleep, how to stay awake and vigilant at a time when my body needs sleep the most. There is no way that I can afford to sleep, knowing that Queenie is probably waiting for the moment I fall asleep to make his move.

I wonder how Queenie managed to get himself into my holding cell -- there were others into which he could have been deposited. It all comes down to money, I suspect.

I've got to get this impending confrontation over with, because I need my beauty sleep. But I don't have a plan; I can't just go over to him and start pounding on him without provocation. Or can I? I close my eyes to concentrate on a plan. It feels real good to have my eyes closed. I feel a little dizzy, disoriented, and weak. I startle myself as every muscle in my body jerks from a smooth swan dive into sleep … and the accompanying instant wake-up a millisecond later; it's the kind of feeling I've experienced when I almost fell asleep driving.

I have to do what Powers taught me to do to keep from falling asleep, so I jump off the cot and start to do jumping jacks, pushups, sit-ups, and running-in-place.

My cell mate and apparent adversary says with a frozen fake smile painted on his face, "What da fuck are you doing? I can't fucking sleep with you acting like a fool. Stop it!"

"Have you ever executed a sit-up? Is it physically possible for you to do a sit-up with all that blubber around your carcass? Are your arms long enough to do a push up? You'd have to be the strongest man on earth to do a pull up. You ever try it?"

WHA-CKED JED O'Dea
(White House Attorney-Counsel Killed)

My 475-pound cellmate, grunts, farts, and negotiates the wall and cot frame to get into a position where he can try to stand up from his lying position. It is a well-rehearsed eight-to-ten-step process which, at times, looks like it defies physics. The ugly man out-weighs me by over a hundred and fifty pounds and in the close quarters of this confined cell, he might actually have a fighting advantage over me. We'll see.

Once he reaches his full standing position -- I wonder later why I let this happen -- he says, "You calling me fat, you Spic?"

I say, "You know, I find that the very people who condemn bigotry are among the most bigoted. No, I'm not calling you fat; I'm calling you disgustingly obese."

He wastes no time and takes a swing at me with his catcher's-mitt-sized right fist while he pushes a hard plastic shank in the direction of my gut.

Queenie is surprisingly quick, agile, and strong for a pile of blubber -- but not quick enough. The right fist he throws in my direction isn't even close to connecting with my jaw, but the shank almost reaches its target before I chop his wrist -- and the sharp hard-plastic shank clicks as it hits the floor.

He grabs me with both arms, squeezing me in a bear hug grasp, and drives hard with his mammoth legs into the cell wall. I would have had a better chance at stopping a Mack truck than resisting the pile drive from Queenie. My head hits the block wall hard; I see stars, feel dizzy, and nearly black out -- it's a damned good thing I have a thick skull.

But during the half-second when I was almost blacking out, Queenie continued driving me, this time to the floor where I hit my head a second time, just as hard. I regain consciousness a couple of seconds later, but it is too late; Queenie has thrown his 475 pounds on me, stomach first, over my face.

It's obvious to me, now, that he intends to smother me. I'm a pretty strong guy myself but I can't bench press this "Jabba the

177

Hut" off of me so I do what any trained close-combat fighter does without a weapon -- I hit his testicles with every ounce of strength that I have left.

Queenie is apparently experienced at this; he is wearing a protective cup. I'm not sure, but I think I broke my knuckles. If I could have screamed in pain, I would have, but I can't even breathe. Powers never taught be how to fight an amorphous pile of fat trying to smother me. So, I do the next thing I could think to do in this situation; I bite his blubber as hard as I could until the blood is oozing onto my face.

It didn't seem to faze him.

My lungs are starting to burn and I begin to feel dizzy. I can no longer think straight. I worry about what will happen to Jolene if I die right here and now.

Fortunately for me, Queenie makes a tactical mistake -- he reaches for the shank on the floor. This shifts his mass ever so slightly and allows me enough leverage to roll him over and grab a breath of wonderful air.

Very few things ever felt as good as that breath.

But I know I don't have time to enjoy breathing; I have to move. Queenie has the shank in his fat paw, but he can't get on his feet in time -- too many steps in the process. I kick the fat man in the face, stomp on his hand, throw an elbow into his throat, and kick him into unconsciousness.

After all the fighting, yelling, and banging around, one would expect a guard to have been alerted to the scuffle, but no one shows up. I bang on the cell bars and yell, "Medic, Medic, Medic!" The three musketeer guards enter and ask, "What happened in here?"

"I think this obese clown had a heart attack. Who could blame his heart for giving out?"

CHAPTER 33 -- INADMISSIBLE EVIDENCE

Washington, D.C.: The nano-drone is in place. It took Tony Vinci days to maneuver the nano-drone into position inside the former First Lady's current residence.

Her security detail is in the process of performing a room sweep to locate potential listening devices. Tony has to move the nano-drone outside the room during the sweep, only to move it back into place when the sweep is complete and the security detail is convinced that the room is clean. He tries not to the think about the consequences of getting caught planting a bug in her office. But, the nano-drone is back in position when it records the conversation between the former First Lady and Viktor Soroson after she carelessly put the call in her office on speaker phone.

First Lady: *Viktor, we need to talk.*

Soroson: *Is the call secure? Did you call on the encrypted satellite phone?*

First Lady: *Of course.*

Soroson: *Are you alone?*

First Lady: *Again, of course.*

Soroson: *Are you in the safe room, the room designed in accordance with specifications for a secure compartmentalized information facility? The room I paid for?*

First Lady: *God damn it, Viktor, yes. Now can we get on with it? This is ridiculous.*

Soroson: *You have proven yourself to be unreliable with top secret information, so I assume you are even less reliable with merely confidential information. Now what do you want?*

179

Frankfurt, Germany: The Chairman of the Board of the Deutsche Chamber summons Gunter Korf to his office. The Chairman states, "We have been viciously attacked by ISIS. I know damn well that Soroson is behind this. It has his fingerprints all over it. They attacked Volkswagen, Bayer, Rheinmetall, Deutsch Bank, and BASF. You are feckless and you failed to prevent the very situation we predicted and hired you to stop. You are, hereby, relieved of constraints. You no longer have rules of engagement. We'll deal with the enemy in our own way. Just kill that mother fucker, Soroson, and **anyone** who may be able to link us to his death."

North Atlantic Ocean: Jolene is startled when her satellite phone rings -- a very unusual event. She hopes it is Tank, but instead, it is Gunter Korf.

"Fraulein Landrieu, it is with great regret that I inform you that the deadline for the completion of the investigation into the death of the White House attorney has passed."

"I was unaware that there was a deadline."

"I have a new assignment for your Tankster. His new assignment is simple. He is to assassinate the hideous billionaire, Viktor Soroson. If he is successful, I will release you without harm. If he attempts to rescue you instead, I will see to it that you both die a painful death."

San Diego, California: The U.S. Government has suspected Viktor Soroson of criminal wrongdoing for many years. He is suspected by the Treasury to owe in excess of a billion dollars in back taxes. He has been suspected of insider trading by the Security and Exchange Commission and for illegal currency manipulation. So when the FBI receives a tip from a former FBI director, of Soroson's financial complicity with the attacks on German industry, a judge grants the FBI an arrest warrant.

The FBI mobilizes a SWAT team within hours of the warrant grant, cuts off access to the Soroson estate, and descends on the property in full tactical gear. The newly hired security firm is immediately overwhelmed by the team. No shot is fired, as the firm understands the situation.

Though the Soroson mansion is fully furnished, it is obviously abandoned. In fact, through interrogation of the security firm, the FBI learns that the estate was abandoned just before the ISIS attacks on Germany began.

CHAPTER 34 -- STRANGE BEDFELLOWS

St. Petersburg, Russia: Governments around the world have tried, in vain, to keep secret: irresponsible actions they wish they had not taken, tactical mistakes, plans they consider to be in the nations' best interest, technologies that give them a military edge, failed experiments, embarrassing mistakes, intelligence on alleged allies, events that have had unpleasant and unintended consequences, illegal activities, indiscretions, lapses in moral judgement, and even, in some instances, evil intent. These secrets are stored in the bowels of such locations as the Pentagon in Arlington, Virginia; the Louvre, in Paris, France; in hidden vaults inside "The Great Wall of China" along the border with Mongolia; CIA Headquarters, in Langley, Virginia; the Kremlin in Moscow, Russia; and in The Vauxhall Cross Building, in London, United Kingdom.

But it is the content in a subterranean secret vault camouflaged as a bomb shelter excavated three stories below the foundation of St. Isaac's Cathedral in St. Petersburg, Russia that interests Viktor Soroson. The keeper of that vault, Russian Orthodox Priest, Yuri Prociv, is also GRU -- Main Intelligence Directorate of the General Staff of the Armed Forces of the Russian Federation -- and his only job is to protect the contents of the vault from falling into the hands of outsiders.

Yuri understands that the information he protects is both a geopolitical time bomb with an infinite number of repercussions, and a potential scientific treasure chest. Never in the chronicles of human history had more experiments on live humans been conducted than the medical experiments in the concentration camps like Auschwitz. When the Soviet Red Army, 322nd Rifle Division overran Auschwitz and freed the remaining inmates, the Soviets discovered that the Nazis had destroyed all the records of what went on there to avoid further retribution.

WHA-CKED   JED O'Dea
(White House Attorney-Counsel Killed)

Or … that is what the Red Army told the Allied Forces. What really happened was that all of the records were collected by the Red Army and transported back to Moscow under Stalin's direction. The Soviets wanted to know what was in the records that might give them a military advantage over the British, French, Canadians, and the Americans. Eventually, after careful scrutiny in the hapless search for weapons research information, Stalin had the records hidden in the vault in St. Petersburg.

Yuri's job has been that of the archivist, with the ability to recall and present details of research on any experimental subject. He has spent the better part of his life, reading, categorizing, coding, cataloging, and in later years, bar-coding the data. He has read everything. Seven years ago, he began scanning the data into a secure data-base.

Yuri feels like he has spent his entire life on a meaningless mission. No one has expressed interest in the contents of the secret vault in more than two decades. That is … until he reads on Saint-Petersburg.com about the eccentric American billionaire, Viktor Soroson who also shares Yuri's proclivity for chess. What intrigues him is his last name. Yuri remembers reading in the secret files about the Auschwitz researcher, Dr. Wilhelm Soroson, and his unsanctioned but recorded experiments. Yuri reads on the virtual newspaper that Viktor's mother was a holocaust survivor. "Is it possible," wonders Yuri Prociv, "that Viktor Soroson is who I think he might be?"

Yuri smells an opportunity to become wealthy beyond his dreams. At his age, Yuri knows he has too few opportunities left to live the good life.

Yuri has too little to do in his Priest role, so he plays a lot of chess. He joined chess clubs and plays other equally skilled players. Over the last fifteen years, he had played against other chess-obsessed fanatics and computers. It took him almost two years before he was able to play against Viktor Soroson.

Yuri is impressed with Soroson's aggressive style of chess, but sees vulnerability in his being weak defensively. Yuri intentionally makes a questionable move and loses his first match against the American.

Yuri proposes a re-match and a wager. If Yuri wins, Soroson would deposit a hundred million rubles into a foreign account Soroson would set up for Prociv. If Soroson wins, Yuri would provide to Viktor evidence about who his father might be. Soroson agrees to the wager, on the condition that he would first have an opportunity to validate the authenticity of the documents. He'll deposit half in the joint account which requires both their signatures, with the ability to withdraw it within five days of viewing the documents, and the other half when the documents are authenticated.

It is now Yuri's chess move.

CHAPTER 35 -- GUARD RAILS ARE DOWN

Boston, Massachusetts: In a universe where time is warped, light bends, and gravitational shock waves ripple the ethereal fabric of space and time, it should be no surprise that chaos manifests itself in his daily life. Tucker contemplates relativity as it relates to his lifestyle of choice. Today, like almost every day, he forces ten pounds of business into a five pound bag. He wishes that he could take a sabbatical, escape from his day job, and spend a hundred percent of his time helping Tank find and rescue Jolene. But as CEO of *Entropy Entrepreneurs*, he has a fiduciary responsibility to stockholders, irrevocable contractual obligations to customers, and a moral commitment to keep his staff employed.

And then, there are his unspoken commitments to his country. Today is one of those days in which he questions his own sanity.

"Did I really need to stick my scrawny little neck under this self-imposed guillotine?"

Tucker is just about to make a phone call which he is dreading when he is interrupted by his executive assistant announcing over the intercom that he has an incoming "blue" to "red" call. A "blue" call is a good news call; a 'red' call is a bad news call. 'Blue' to 'red' means that it could go either way.

"Hello, how can I help you?"

The Lloyd's of London Insurance Company agent answers, "Sir, I'm processing the claim made by *Entropy Entrepreneurs* on your corporate Bombardier Challenger Learjet which went down in the Atlantic Ocean between Miami, Florida and Grand Bahama Island.

"Excellent, what additional information do you need from me? "

"Have you been informed of the results of the autopsy of your two pilots?"

"No." Tucker responds with some irritation. He expected to hear autopsy results directly from the investigator, not the insurance agent.

"Well, the conclusion of the medical examiner is that there was no pilot error. Lloyd's of London, therefore, will pay your claim in full in compliance with the insurance policy obligation to *Entropy Entrepreneurs*. Of course, there is a large deductible, but I'm sure you know that."

As Tucker is speaking with the Lloyd's of London agent, he hears his assistant announce another "blue" to "red" call from the NTSB investigator-in-charge.

"Thank you for the call. I don't mean to be rude, but can I call you back? The NTSB investigator is on the other line."

Tucker respectfully terminates his call with Lloyds and takes the call from the NTSB. "This is Tucker Cherokee. How can I help you?"

"Sir, I'm the investigator-in-charge of the downing of *Entropy Entrepreneurs'* Bombardier Learjet 60. I need to inform you that we've completed the autopsy of your pilot Willie Mays Robinson and his copilot. Sir, they were poisoned."

Rage overwhelms Tucker, "Someone is going to fucking pay for attempting to kill my wife."

Ocean City, Maryland to Rehoboth Beach, Delaware: The drive north on Ocean Highway from Ocean City, Maryland is fortunately uneventful. Lucas breathes a slight sigh of relief when he sees the "Welcome to Delaware" sign. He looks back to observe the two Miss Maryland bodyguards in the Jeep still dutifully following behind them.

Carmen doesn't notice Lucas slipping his cell phone out of his jean pocket to check his messages. In fact, she is talking non-stop ... and has been for fifteen minutes about minutiae, gibberish, and otherwise meaningless little bits of worthless information.

She asks, "Did you know that the State of Delaware is named after a German American named Baron De La Warr who employed "scorched earth" tactics against the Native Americans, the Powhatans?"

She shifts conversational gears, "Do you think that the constant cycle of ocean tides can be used to develop perpetual motion machines?"

It doesn't stop there, "I think it is odd that the Chinese men in the Xuan dynasty lowered their testicles into boiling water as a birth control method. Wouldn't that kind of ruin the moment?"

She is obviously a nervous talker. She keeps going on and on, but Lucas tunes her out as he looks at his phone messages.

"Do you think Preparation A through G were laboratory failures?"

"Damn," he says out loud, "I missed a call from Tucker Cherokee. He has never called me before. He is the best friend of my boss, Tank, and a close partner-in-crime, so to speak, with my other boss, Powers. Damn, damn, damn."

Lucas checks his text messages. One is from Powers, "CALL IN. I MEAN NOW!" Lucas looks up to see that Carmen is saying something to him but he can't focus on what she is saying. None of the three people that

187

demanded his immediate response compared in urgency to the fourth demand. He is frozen at the sight of Ram in the back seat making eye contact with him.

Lucas orders, "Pull over as soon as possible. No, pull over right now."

"Why?"

"Ram made eye contact with me. I've heard rumors about that. Pull over now."

As former Miss Maryland puts on her blinker and pulls over onto the narrow gravel shoulder with the shadow Jeep pulling over right behind her, she states, "You're afraid of Ram, aren't you?"

Lucas admits, as he is opening the passenger side door, "I was, until a couple of days ago. Now, it's about respect."

He lets Ram out of the car so that Ram can do his business and says to Carmen, "This is not just a dog; Ram may be the best trained dog in the entire world. If he receives a command, he responds immediately. But when he gives a command, he expects the same kind of response. It's a mutual respect thing."

Ram returns, jumps back into the Mercedes, and waits for Lucas and Carmen to return to their seats. Lucas looks east out across the sand dunes at the beauty of the Atlantic Ocean, "Not bad, Eh?"

Carmen pulls out onto Coastal Highway and continues north with Little Assawornan Bay on the left and the Atlantic Ocean on the right. Lucas pushes a single digit on his cell phone and waits for Powers to pick up which he does before it rings twice.

"You're AWOL, son!"

"No, sir. I am on a mission. I am...."

Powers interrupts, "I know where you are. Did you forget that Ram is still wearing his collar with a GPS transmitter?"

"No sir."

"Well, keep going the route you're on and stop when you get to Rehoboth Aircrafters. You should be there in another twenty minutes." Powers hangs up.

Lucas tells Carmen, "You may not have to take me all the way to Wiscasset, Maine after all." They pass through Bethany Beach and squeeze between Indian River Bay and the ocean until they reach Rehoboth Beach. Four miles later they are at the tiny airport, staring at Powers and Tucker Cherokee standing next to an impressive Agusta Westland 109S Grand helicopter with two Pratt & Whitney 735-horsepower Turboshaft engines.

With his tail wagging, Ram leaps out of the SUV onto the tarmac and runs in the direction of Powers and Tucker and then playfully runs back and forth between them.

"Well, well," says Powers who stares with obvious admiration at the beautiful former Miss Maryland as she gracefully slinks her long, tanned, and firm athletic-looking legs out of the Mercedes. She stands erect and walks in the direction of Powers and Tucker, swinging her hips as if she were strutting down a modeling ramp, shaking her head so her hair falls back behind her and displays her perfect hour-glass-shaped physique.

Tucker says jokingly to Powers, "Stop drooling, the slobber on your chin is unbecoming."

Tucker stands with a happy smile on his face as she approaches him instead of Powers and says, "You must be the famous Mr. Cherokee. Hi, I'm Carmen."

"Pleased to meet you. Did you have anything to do with saving Ram from the Maryland police?"

"Yes," she brags, "I managed to help these two dogs escape from the manhunt, excuse me, dog hunt. They owe me, big time."

Lucas adds, "Carmen here is one of the last people to see Jolene before she was kidnapped. She is the executive assistant to Elliott Brave, CEO of *Brave Chicken*."

"Well, I'm impressed."

"Actually," adds Carmen, "I haven't been completely forthcoming with your super sleuth friend, Mr. Lucas Justice, here. I'm actually a little more than just an Executive Assistant to Elliott Brave. My full name is Carmen Brave and I'm Vice President of Operations for *Brave Chicken Corporation*."

Annapolis, Maryland: I hear the pneumatic airlock to the cell block open. Three emergency medical technicians rush to my cell and stare at the monster lying on the cell floor. All three look up at me without saying a word. I know what they are thinking, "How the hell are we supposed to get Queenie's dead weight on a stretcher, out the cell door and into an ambulance?"

I shrug; not my problem.

I don't notice at first, but when the EMTs came in, so did my lawyer, Sam Pearson. He is wearing a smile which is alive and contagious. A thrill overwhelms me -- I know I am free.

As we are walking down the front steps of the Annapolis courthouse ninety minutes later, Sam says, "Your bail is set at one million dollars. Your friend, Tucker Cherokee, posted bail for you. Tank," he says, making sure I am paying attention, "You can't leave the country until your grand jury hearing is over, which may take three to six weeks to schedule."

I don't react at first.

"Tank," he repeats, "You can't go on a mission to save Jolene. Do you understand?"

I don't. I get into his Jaguar, not even thinking about anything except how I am going to rescue Jolene from the deep water oil platform north of Scotland.

"Tank, do you understand?"

I don't. I refuse to understand.

I'm not paying much attention to where Sam is taking me. He repeats, "Tank, you need to organize and develop mission plans from the operation center, but you can't lead the mission. Do you understand?"

I don't.

Finally, Sam gives up and says, "We're here."

I shake myself out of a funk and ask, "Where is here?"

My door is opened from the outside as if I am getting valet service. It turns out, I am.

The valet looks a lot like Lucas Justice. Apparently, I am being escorted to an Augusta Westland 109S Grand helicopter.

CHAPTER 36 -- HELP WANTED

Alexandria, Virginia: He walks with purpose, ignoring the nasty drizzle, as he parades down Duke Street in Old Town Alexandria. The young blond man, Richard Kingsley, is on a mission to restore his own self-esteem, to learn why his father died after being the first on the scene of a supposed crime, and to help solve a two-decades-old mystery. He is trying to track down the lawyer Harold Andrews, of *Andrews, Crosby, and Underwood*, who hired him to eavesdrop on Powers at the *Brown Leaf Cigar Bar,* and who then promptly disappeared when the going got tough. Harold Andrews hadn't been seen or heard from in a week, and didn't show up in court for a civil case which he was litigating. Richard has been unable to find Andrews' family members or loved ones -- the blond man is feeling incompetent.

So when he gets a text from a number he doesn't recognize, and he's invited to appear at the *Brown Leaf Cigar Bar* at 10:00 in the morning on a weekday, he feels optimistic -- for some reason -- that he is about to catch a break.

Richard's hair is matted; ringlets of rainwater drip off his nose and earlobes as he reaches for the front door knob of the cigar bar. The door is locked, so he bangs on it hard to make sure someone hears him -- and someone does. The guy answering the door is the same guy who tackled him in the kitchen the last time he was here. He's a *White Knight* who works for Powers and Tank ... and if Richard remembers correctly, he is protecting one of the old guys who owns this bar. The big, tough-looking bodyguard says, "Follow me."

Richard follows him through a door in the back of the bar, past wine racks, past a storage area with kegs of beer, past a temperature and moisture-controlled room filled with premium cigars, to a flight of stairs which leads up to the second floor.

The *White Knight* guard opens an ordinary-looking door, revealing a cigar-smoke-filled room with a large mahogany table stacked with old leather-bound books, important-looking papers, and three very old-looking people. The guard turns to stand at attention by the door, and pats his side-arm to make sure that Richard notices that he is 'packing' -- just in case he is planning to cause trouble.

None of the seniors stand up, but one of them says, "Please, Mr. Kingsley, sit down; we have a lot to talk with you about. Can we get you a towel or something? You look soaked to the bone. By the way, I'm Gina Goodman." She sweeps her arm around the room and says, "This gentleman here is the esteemed Byron Chism, and that trouble-maker over there is Clint Auclair. These two old men own this bar as a hobby. They have pretty prestigious day-jobs, as do I." Ms. Goodman stands up and leans on her cane, a cane she does not need for health reasons.

"But we're not here to impress you with our bureaucrat credentials; we're here to impart information which," she can't restrain a sly smile, "let's just say, we've stumbled across."

Byron Chism interjects, "You may not remember us when you caught the interest of Senator Powers the last time you were here, but we couldn't help but notice you."

Richard looks down at his wet tennis shoes and says, "I hope Powers and I didn't damage your bar when I tried to escape out the back."

Clinton Auclair hands Richard a dry tablecloth and says, "Son, you know they've invented a new contraption called an umbrella; they're quite useful. You should try one sometime."

"Well," continues Gina Goodman, the Chairman of the Board for the Smithsonian Institution, "My colleagues and I are very curious people. In fact, we love a good political mystery. So when Powers said he was investigating a twenty-year-old crime, Clint and Byron couldn't contain themselves and immediately requested that we convene our little private mystery-solving club. There's not much that goes on in this town that gets past the three of us.

"So, we collected a few clues that may be useful in your investigations. We've sent Powers a package by courier that he should receive tonight or tomorrow."

Byron says, "We sent another package to a washed-out investigative reporter in Pasco, Washington, which contains information likely to make the nightly news before too long."

The huge and jovial Clinton Auclair mentions, "But we ran across two items of information to which we thought only you should be privy." Director Auclair hands two envelopes to Richard Kingsley.

"We're depending on you," continues Auclair, "to follow the threads that are contained in these envelopes. You may not see it at first, but the pieces of information in these two envelopes are connected. Chasing the leads down is a young man's task, but we think you have motive enough to pursue the mysteries."

Gina Goodman states, "Our 'club' has a little fund set aside to help you find clues and follow leads."

Richard stares at the two envelopes, trying to understand the motives of these three seemingly powerful Washington insiders.

As if reading his mind, Byron Chism says, "You're probably wondering why we picked you and what we want in return."

Richard looks into Byron's bloodshot eyes with anticipation.

"You must call in every two days at exactly 10:00 AM Eastern Daylight Time with a progress report. No report, no expense money. The phone number is in one of the envelopes.

"As far as why we chose you -- that will become evident as you begin to collect clues."

"Wally," Byron says to his bodyguard, "will you please escort Mr. Kingsley to the door? And Wally, please give him one of the umbrellas out of our 'lost and found' collection."

After Richard Kingsley leaves the *Brown Leaf Cigar Bar* and wanders off to read the contents of the two envelopes in private, Gina Goodman makes the requisite phone call and says to the person on the other end, "Yes, sir; though he is not yet ready for prime time as an investigator, the seed has been planted."

CHAPTER 37 -- CONTACT

North Atlantic Ocean: She is jogging in place, and has been for thirty-five minutes. Her blond ponytail waives back and forth rhythmically like a windshield wiper while she bounces freely in her halter top. Her muscular legs glisten from the perspiration, though her chest heaves slowly as if she were merely walking casually.

Gunter Korf watches Jolene through the eyes of the nanocamera lens with admiration. It is too damned bad that he has to make this next call.

But he has to.

He picks up his satellite phone and makes the call. He watches her mask-like facial expression come alive.

Jolene is excited the second she hears the phone. She says out loud, "Maybe it's Tank."

It wasn't.

"Time is up sweetheart. Or should I say sweat-heart."

She doesn't take the bait.

"Your man has a deadline. Either he completes his new assignment within the next five days or you're toast -- burnt toast to be exact. I've altered the restrictions on your satellite phone. You can call directly to anyone you want. I'd suggest that you call Powers first. Here, I'll give you the number." He does just that, and hangs up.

She immediately calls the number she was given by Korf, and Powers picks up on the third ring. "Whoever this is, I can't talk right now because I'm piloting an aircraft. Please call back."

Loudly and anxiously she hollers, "It's Jolene!"

WHA-CKED   JED O'Dea
(White House Attorney-Counsel Killed)

Sometimes Powers can be just a little too cool. I'm sitting in the back of the Agusta 109S helicopter when Powers yells back to me dryly and without cracking a smile, "Call's for you."

Slowly, I manage to navigate my way to the co-pilot's seat and ask, "What call?"

Powers nods down toward the satellite phone lying on the floor between us. I pick it up, "Hello, how can I help you?"

Jolene screams with joy, "Oh my God, Tank, it's you, you're safe, and you're with Powers, does that mean that you are on the way to get me? It's so heavenly wonderful to hear your voice. I miss you so much. How'd you get out of jail? Where are you?"

I love hearing her voice so much that I am content just to let her ramble on, without answering a single question.

"What's the plan, Tank? My captor says you have only five more days. I've got to get out of here." A couple of seconds pass, and then she says, "Are you still there?"

I don't know exactly what happened to me. It's like I had no self-control, no discipline, and no way to stop myself from blurting it out.

"Jolene, you're the love of my life, the one who brings me joy. Will you marry me?"

Falls Church, Virginia: Richard Kingsley is sitting in his day-job cubicle where he enters mind-numbing data into a computer for an insurance company. It is as safe a place as any to open and read the contents of the two envelopes, except that his office co-workers keep talking to him about totally unimportant trivia. He wants badly to tell them to shut up and leave him alone, but he endures more commiseration about why the Redskins couldn't tackle a five-year-old, for all the millions they are paid.

Finally, he is left alone to break the seal on the first envelope. It contains roughly twenty five sheets of recently-copied paper with dates on them from the 1990s. The first few pages are on FBI letterhead and stamped *For Official Use Only*. Richard doesn't know what this means, but he gets the gist of its contents quickly. It is a report from the FBI Internal Affairs Unit on an investigation into the conduct of the now deceased -- by the jaws of Ram -- Brian Richmond. He was the Agent-in-Charge of the investigation of the death of the White House attorney, and the man whom Richard witnessed foolishly attack Tank.

The report states that the charge of misconduct by Agent Richmond was centered on the pressure he had put on one Robert Kingsley, Richard's father, to change his testimony.

"Holy cow!" Richard says out loud. The report is signed by the then-head of the Internal Affairs investigation, Harold Andrews, the very man who hired him to eavesdrop on Powers and the man who is now missing.

He muses, "All of this on just the first page! These papers are going to be an interesting read."

On page three, the blond man reads that a Federal District Judge ordered that five of the ten crime-scene Polaroid photographs taken by the FBI at the scene of the alleged suicide be released. One of these photos Richard has seen before; it was a photo that was previously leaked by the White House to Reuters News Service of the dark blue steel revolver lying near the White House Counsel's hand.

Richard's father had insisted that there had been no gun near the White House Counsel's body when he was first on the scene. Richard thought, "Why would someone plant a weapon at the scene unless he was murdered elsewhere and moved to the old Civil War Park?"

The copies of the other four Polaroid photos taken, he suspected, have never before been seen outside the Hoover FBI Building. They show a second wound -- on the neck of the deceased attorney.

Richard had heard rumors and conspiracy theories surrounding the potential murder of the White House attorney, but hadn't seen evidence as compelling as the papers he is currently holding in his hands that supported these theories.

Richard contemplates, "What should I do with this information? This is the kind of stuff Tank and Powers are looking for, to save Jolene. I need to get this information to them immediately."

On pages seven through ten of the document, the FBI's electronic forensic experts provide an analysis of data which had previously been in the memory on the White House Counsel's pager, before it was erased.

Richard wonders, "Why would they erase a pager message from the former First Lady? It would only be natural that she would page him. It must have been threatening. Hmmm."

Next, Richard reviews a memorandum prepared by the Secret Service which states that the White House Counsel's body was actually found in his own car.

"Why would a Secret Service agent tell a story like that if it wasn't true? What would be the motive of the agent to lie about something like that? I wonder where he is today."

"Boo!"

Richard practically jumps out of his skin; his heart starts beating at ninety miles per hour. He says, "Melody, damn it, you scared the piss out of me."

Melody, a co-worker, responds, "I've been standing here for at least two minutes. You didn't even look up. Whatever you're reading -- I've never seen you so engrossed. What is it?"

Richard has a serious crush on Melody, a vivacious, fun-loving, cheerful, intelligent, and fresh-looking girl five years his junior. She has auburn hair, auburn eyelashes a little too long, a pixie-looking nose, a dimple on the right side of her face when she smiles, and a mouth a little too large for her petite face. And then there were her other assets, the kind which make it difficult for him to raise his eyes to meet hers.

He lowers his voice, whispering to her in a conspiratorial manner, "It is top secret stuff. I can only show it to you in my apartment over a glass of Pinot Grigio."

To his amazement, she smiles, bats her eyelashes, cocks her head a little, looks him straight in the eyes, and says, "OK. When?"

Richard has been trying to get a date with Melody for months. This is the first time she has accepted. He isn't going to lose this chance. He'll read the rest of the documents later.

Annapolis, Maryland: The young Maryland Attorney General is disheveled, slumped on a hard chair, driving his once-manicured fingernails through his hair, scratching his scalp until it bleeds. It is the third straight day in the noisy room without changing clothes or washing up. His eyes are bloodshot from crying openly and shamelessly. He probably hasn't eaten 500 calories a day, recently, and is at risk of dehydrating.

WHA-CKED   JED O'Dea
(White House Attorney-Counsel Killed)

His seven year old son looks so fragile and vulnerable in the intensive care hospital bed, with tubes and wires keeping him alive; this the third day that he has been in a coma.

There are witnesses who saw what happened. His son was chasing a soccer ball across a lightly-traveled residential street -- he'd done it a hundred times before. This time an old Chevy Silverado without plates which was parked in front of a house fifty yards away accelerated and hit his son, and then sped away at a high speed. The truck had been stolen, and was found a couple of blocks away. No prints other than the owners' were found.

The AG knew what happened. He had no control over the release of Tank from jail, but his blackmailer didn't care; he had followed through with his threat. If it is the last thing he ever does, the AG swears to himself, he is going to bring the asshole who hurt his son to justice.

CHAPTER 38 -- THE FIRST ENVELOPE

Falls Church, Virginia: Richard Kingsley is running down the sidelines, trying to outrun the cornerback in the championship game. He launches himself, feet off the ground, horizontal with the field of play, his arms extend to the maximum, to catch the pass which just grazes his fingertips. It turns out that it isn't a football; it is a hand grenade. It explodes and thousands of rabid bats fly out, attacking his genitals -- until he wakes up.

His head hurts, but his bladder hurts even more. He wants to crawl out of bed, but the bright sun blasting through the window is blocking him, pushing him back, and irradiating him with what feels like megawatts of visible and ultraviolet light.

With one eye half-open, he crawls to the edge of his bed. He rolls off the bed onto the floor onto two empty bottles of Santa Margarita Pinot Grigio, a pair of panties, and a bra with extra-large cups.

Then he remembers last night with Melody. He painfully rolls his head to look over to the opposite side of the bed, opens both eyes, and sees her sitting up in bed with the reading light stilled turned on from the night stand. She has a sheet over her legs and hips, leaving her upper body delightfully exposed … and she's wearing a pleasant but studious expression on her face.

"Good morning, stud."

"Good morning. You sure know how to make a man feel good about himself."

"Hey," she quips; "I had a good time last night."

Richard Kingsley can't hold it anymore and moves urgently to the bathroom almost tripping over their clothes, scattered haphazardly around the bedroom along with half-empty cardboard containers of Chinese food and, unbelievably, a third empty wine bottle. No wonder he has a headache.

He finishes reducing the pressure in his bladder, washes his hands, brushes his teeth, combs his hair, looks in the mirror at his bloodshot eyes, and makes himself as presentable as possible.

When he returns to the bedroom, she is no longer there. He wanders into the kitchen to find her looking for coffee filters for the coffee maker. She is as naked as he is, and she apparently feels very comfortable being that way -- totally uninhibited. He thinks that he could sure get used to being around her all the time.

"You know," she says, "the stuff in that envelope you are reading at the office is very interesting. I assume you are related to Robert Kingsley."

Richard turns bright red, "You shouldn't have read that without asking me first. It's private and confidential."

"How could I resist, after what you said in the office about it being secret." She grabs his hand, pulls him in the direction of the bedroom, and continues, "Come on, let's read the stuff in the envelope in bed together while the coffee is perking."

Richard is torn between being angry with her and appreciating her infectiously pleasant tone-of-voice. The wine doesn't seem to have affected her at all. They crawl back in bed together, sit side by side, naked as jay birds, and begin reading material he hadn't yet finished reading, in the envelope. She reads out loud, "*A New York City detective, a forensic scientist for the City of New York, and a former head of the New York State Crime Lab conducted an investigation of the case of the White House Counsel, on behalf of the New York Journalism Center.*

"*The investigators concluded that homicide should not have been ruled out in this case, that the position of the corpse was totally inconsistent with suicide, and that the White House Counsel's hands were not on the pistol's handgrip when it was fired.   The three investigators noted that they had never witnessed a weapon or gun positioned in a suicide victim's hand in such an unusual way.'*

"The investigators documented that the White House attorney's body could have been in contact with one or more carpets prior to his death, yet the carpet in the trunk of the alleged suicide victim's car had not been analyzed to see whether he had been carried to the park in the trunk of his own car.

"The investigators concluded that the force of the gun's discharge probably knocked the White House Counsel's glasses off, however it was 'inconceivable' that the glasses could have traveled 13 feet through thick plant growth to the site where they were claimed to be found.   The investigators concluded that it was a high probability that the scene had been tampered with.

"The same investigators concluded that the lack of blood and brain tissue at the site implied that the victim was placed at the scene."

Melody puts the papers down, slides the sheets back, and walks into the kitchen while asking Richard how he likes his coffee. He answers, and as she is pouring his coffee she yells out, "How are you related to Robert?"

"He was my father."

She becomes quiet; only the sound of a spoon clinking against ceramic in the kitchen could be heard. She shuffles in, still naked, with a cup of coffee in each hand, pursed lips, and a tear rolling down her left cheek.

"I'm so sorry. I really had no business reading your private papers. I just thought you were investigating something interesting, and that we could be make-believe private investigators together. It sounded like fun. I'm so sorry."

Richard takes the coffee cup she extends to him and says, "It's OK. I can see that you're genuinely sorry. Maybe we can investigate this case together as real private investigators."

"So, let me get this straight." Melody talks while gesturing animatedly with her hands. "Your dad discovered the body of the White House attorney. He didn't see the gun that they're talking about in the papers we're reading. The FBI put pressure on him to change his testimony to admit he had seen the gun, to align with the suicide story they were telling. Then, this independent team of experts concluded that the scene had been tampered with, and your dad is killed in a vehicle accident shortly thereafter. Do I have it right, so far?"

Richard is drinking his coffee, and shakes his head up and down.

"Then, out of the blue, all these years later, someone gives you this envelope full of proof that the White House attorney was murdered and, maybe, that it's likely your dad was murdered, too.

"Don't you think that's odd? Someone wants you to do something. What is it they want you to do?"

"People want me to make this stuff public because *they can't*, for reasons that I don't yet understand -- it's no doubt political."

"Well, let's read the rest of the material in the envelope."

They crawl back into bed, sit side by side, and she reads, *"A ton of documents were removed from the White House Counsel's office by the First Lady's chief of staff, and were taken to the private residence within the White House. Fifty-four pages from those documents were released. A set of billing records which had been under subpoena for two years finally appeared right after the documents were removed from White House Counsel's office, with the First Lady's fingerprints on them."*

Melody asks, "So, who ordered the office looting?"

WHA-CKED   JED O'Dea
(White House Attorney-Counsel Killed)

"The President was on camera with Larry King at the time of the office looting, but the First Lady was on the phone from Little Rock, Arkansas to someone at the White House only moments before the theft took place."

Melody adds, "No wonder the people who gave you this information didn't want to be the ones to disclose it. They didn't want to end up like the White House attorney and, maybe," she says gently and sadly, lightly touching his face, "like your dad."

"I want to know the truth about my dad's death. I want to know what really happened."

She finally sips her coffee and then holds his hand. Neither of them speaks for a few moments; they're both deep in thought. Finally, Melody asks, "What's in the second envelope?"

"I don't know for sure, except that it has some correlation with the contents of the first envelope."

He looks over at his new friend, "What do you think? Should we risk getting ourselves even further sucked into the quicksand of this mystery?"

She smiles, "You know what, handsome? You haven't even kissed me this morning."

They crawl close together again and embrace; the second envelope will just have to wait.

CHAPTER 39 -- STRATEGIES

Caracas, Venezuela: The German-hating Soroson has been referred to as an "economic war criminal" by a number of financial magazines around the world.

He is a master at manipulating currencies.

"The Man who Broke the Bank of England," once dumped 10 billion Pounds Sterling to force the devaluation of the currency for his own gain, resulting in a billion dollars in personal profit. It is estimated that he once made another billion dollars by betting against the Japanese Yen.

He believes that he can collapse Germany's economy by destroying the Euro. The attack on German industries in Phase One seriously weakened the European Union, because it is Germany which provides the economic engine of the EU in world competition. The Euro is vulnerable. Phase Two is underway, as Soroson sells twelve billion Euros in the shadow of the attack on Germany and drives the Euro down to its lowest value since its inception. He hedged his bet by buying Chinese Yuan and U.S. dollars.

Soroson says out loud, but to himself, "There is more than one way to skin a cat. Those hateful Anglos are on the ropes."

Annapolis, Maryland to Wiscasset, Maine: Lucas is calm, shows no emotion, and hides the fact that his anger meter has pegged out. He is flabbergasted. Carmen Brave has hidden from him who she is and the role she plays at *Brave Chicken Corporation* for two days, but willingly opens up and discloses it to Tucker within minutes of meeting him. "What is that all about?"

Surprising him even more, she asks if she can come with them in the helicopter, telling her bodyguards to return her Mercedes back to Ocean City. She sits down right next to Lucas, with their hips touching, as they fly to Annapolis to pick up Tank. The mixed signals are confusing him.

But on the flight from Annapolis to Wiscasset, Maine, while Tank is on the phone with Jolene, and while Tucker is having a bonding moment with Ram, Lucas leans over to the stunning former Miss Maryland and says, "You owe me an explanation."

Nobody ever touches Lucas. His demeanor and body language discourage it; his granite-like body and humorless expression don't invite contact. But she touches him gently on his hard face with the tips of her soft fingers on his lips. Her touch conjures up a feeling in him he's never previously experienced. She leans over, her hot breath whispering into his ear and says, "I didn't think Tucker would have let me in the helicopter with you if I was merely an executive assistant. I wanted to come with you; not just because I need your protection, but because I like being with you."

Lucas wants to believe every word that she says, but the cynic in him considers whether or not he is being conned and manipulated. He suspects her motives, but decides to play along … just in case her move toward him is genuine. Instead of returning the affection, though, he says, "What is it that you want me to protect you *from*? I need to understand the threat in order to protect you."

She stares into his cold gray eyes with her warm baby-blues, purses her lips, and changes her facial expression from one of someone infatuated with her companion, to an expression of serious consternation. But her hip never leaves contact with Lucas, and her ample breasts are pressed against Lucas' elbow.

Lucas tries desperately to listen to her words, and to ignore his heart pounding against the ribs in his chest.

"It is a very long story. My father runs *Brave Chicken Corporation* efficiently, but he has no vision for the financial growth of the company. Stockholders were calling for his head, and the Board of Directors was asking for his resignation. I'm on the board because my dad gave me enough stock to be considered a major stockholder. At the Board meeting in which they wanted to fire him, I spoke up for the first time *ever* and shared with the Board an idea for growth that my father was about to propose.

"No one was more surprised than my father, but the idea staved off the mutiny. I explained how we planned to turn animal fats, which were then a Brave Chicken disposal expense, into a profit center by converting animal fats into biodiesel fuel."

Lucas looks at Carmen Brave with renewed admiration. He has no technical understanding of what she is talking about, but decides to believe her.

"My dad," she continues, "gave me carte blanche to make my biodiesel idea happen. So I structured a deal to provide feed material to a biodiesel plant commissioned by the Chinese near Salisbury with a condition attached to it -- that we would **also** sell them chicken at a fixed, negotiated rate."

Lucas' eyes start to glaze over, so she shifts to the bottom line.

"Brave Chicken couldn't keep its end of the bargain, and it was later determined that my deal was illegal; it wasn't approved by the State Department. The Chinese want me to boil in liquid methane, and my father is trying his very damned best to keep the Feds from finding out about the illegal deal I got us into.

"You can imagine the panic he felt when the FBI showed up with a warrant to search our records."

Lucas asks, "What does any of this have to do with Jolene's kidnapping at Brave Chicken's Headquarters?"

Carmen looks Lucas straight in the eye, bats her too-long eyelashes, and answers, "To the best of my knowledge, nothing."

Lucas stays silent because he doesn't buy it; he just doesn't believe in coincidences.

Wiscasset, Maine: "OK, kids," Powers says over the aircraft intercom; "we're about to land on the Cherokee helipad."

But Powers couldn't land because Star is standing in the center of the helipad with a trance-like pose, staring up at the lights beaming down from the helicopter.

"Tucker," Powers yells loudly over the sounds of the helicopter rotors, "you might want to see this!"

Tucker unbuckles his seat belt, maneuvers forward to replace Tank in the co-pilot's seat and sees Star, still standing in the middle of the helipad, the wind produced by the rotor blades blowing her hair away from her face, and her nightgown pressed tightly against her little body.

Tucker orders, "Use the backup landing spot."

Powers begins to lift higher and maneuver the Agusta 109S to the alternative helipad until Maya, in her bathrobe, rushes out onto the first pad to embrace Star and carry her off.

Powers gently sets the aircraft down and shuts down the Pratt & Whitney turbines. As the blades decelerate, the doors fly open and the eclectic passengers begin to file out -- Tucker is first.

He runs over to Star and Maya and says, "Star, baby, are you all right? What was that all about?"

Maya is standing behind Star with her hands on Star's shoulders and concern in her eyes. Suddenly, Star rushes toward the helicopter.

Ram has followed Tucker out; the reunion with Star is not only joyous for both of them but for all who watch.

Maya says to Tucker, "We apparently have a new development in Star. She says she has no memory of standing in the center of the helipad. It's the second time this week that she has done something like sleep-walking."

The fifteen-foot dining room table in the Cherokee mansion is covered with Chef-Rhino-prepared dishes. Carmen didn't realize how hungry she was until she sat down in front of shrimp tarts, sausage won-ton cups, to-die-for crab dip, and brie-berry bruschetta.

"Rhino, my man, this is a great spread, as always -- and this coffee is absolutely superb," I remark. "After several days of consuming food that tasted like cardboard, at the behest of the State of Maryland, you have no idea how good everything tastes. I bet I dropped down to my fighting weight of 310 while I was in there."

Powers jokes, "You drink all the coffee you want; I compliment Maya and Tucker on their taste in Scotch."

Carmen asks, "You don't fly that machine out there after you drink that stuff, do you?"

211

Powers responds, "Stuff! You call Glenlivet **stuff**? Good God, woman, Lucas is going have to teach you some manners."

The crowd around the dining room table in the Cherokee mansion laughs and teases one another for ten minutes before Maya says, "I'm sorry but I'm tired and it's late. Please, feel free to stay and commiserate as long as you like, but I'm bushed. I've been working the last couple of days with Tony Vinci on a scientific snipe hunt, and he can wear your brain to a frazzle if you try to keep up with him."

I react, "I always thought it was you who wore people's brains to a frazzle. You two must be into something pretty heavy. What are you up to?"

"There is no Reader's Digest version, Tank; it would take longer to explain than I have the energy for, tonight. Would you accept a rain check on the subject? All I can say is that it could help you find the answer to the mystery surrounding the death of the White House attorney."

"Before you retire for the night," I ask, "Is it OK if the rest of us stay here for another half hour or so, to discuss the mission details? We're going after Jolene and we have to formulate a plan."

"Sure, but if I were you, I'd include Tony in your plan. I think he has some ideas about how to identify and disarm whatever it is that might harm Jolene if you trip a wire or cross a laser or something.

"And Lucas," Maya continues, "you and Miss Brave are welcome to spend the night in the bedrooms in the guest house. You know where it is. Make yourself at home." Maya stands up while all the hardened, rough men around the table, who are normally insensitive to etiquette, actually stand up with her. She asks, "Tucker, do you need anything from me before I retire for the night?" A slight smile emerges on her beautiful face as she adds, "besides that!"

Everyone laughs and thanks Maya for her hospitality, as she sashays off to bed and they settle back into their seats.

I look over at Tucker and ask, "So what **are** Maya and Tony up to?"

Tucker answers, "I gave them an assignment. They're working it. I don't want to steal their thunder. I think they'll announce a discovery in the next few days. All I can say is that it is radical."

Hmmm.

"OK, we'll get out of your hair in a little bit, Tucker. I've been sitting in a cell for days with nothing to do but think … with the little exception of a few minutes of absolute terror when I thought I might suffocate. Anyway, here's my plan."

Powers, Lucas, Carmen and Tucker listen to the framework of my mission strategy, with Powers and Tucker contributing tactical suggestions. Thirty minutes later, I conclude that the approach is feasible. All I need is some input from Tony and we'll be good to go. I offer Powers the chance to join me and stay at my summer home on the river. I am not sure that I want to stay there alone, as it is going to be painfully empty without Jolene.

CHAPTER 40 -- IT'S ABOUT DAMNED TIME

Wiscasset, Maine: Lucas and an exhausted Carmen walk down the driveway to the four-bedroom guest house. As they are walking, Carmen asks, "Where did Maya and Tucker get all their money? They are so young. Did they inherit it? I thought my dad was wealthy, but he can't hold a candle to the Cherokees."

The laconic Lucas answers, "They earned it."

Carmen looks around and adds, "They have a lot of security around here, lots of people armed and patrolling the property. Why? What are they afraid of?"

As Lucas is opening the front door to the guest house, he answers, "Bad people." He flips the lights on and escorts her to one of the bedrooms, shows her where the toiletries are and says, as he is leaving, "Call me if you need anything. Typically, the Cherokees think of everything. I generally wake up at 0600 and make coffee."

Lucas shuts Carmen's bedroom door and picks a bedroom adjacent to hers and begins to undress. He places his Beretta under his pillow, removes his sheathed Ka-Bar knife from his belt, and realizes just how badly he needs a shower. He wonders for the first time if his body odor has been offensive to Carmen -- it bothers him even more, now that he actually gives a damn about her feelings.

Each of the bedrooms in the Cherokee guest house is designed to be a master bedroom -- each with its own bathroom. He wanders in and starts the shower, removes the packaging from the bar of Irish Spring soap, searches and finds some shampoo on the counter, and enters the hot shower. The water feels superb as it removes sand, salt, dirt, sweat, and probably some German shepherd-related odors. Unexpectedly, he hears a gentle tap on the shower door. His first reaction is to position himself for hand-to-hand combat ... but, an instant later, he realizes it might be Carmen. He cracks the shower door only to observe a completely naked Miss Maryland.

"Come on in; there's room for both of us." Lucas glances at her beautiful smiling face occasionally, but is nearly fixated on her perfectly flawless body. As she enters the shower, she presses her chest against his and gives him a kiss on his lips. He pulls her tight against his rock hard body and kisses her firmly, with passion he's never before experienced.

He has no control over his erection; there is no way he can keep it from also becoming rock hard. She says, "Hold on just a second," as she leaves the shower stall for a couple of moments ... and returns with a travel-sized bottle of hand lotion. She smiles at him while she opens the bottle, pours some lotion into her hands, and begins to spread the lotion up and down on his rock hard manhood.

Lucas puts his hands around her waist, picks her up like she is a feather, and allows her to wrap her legs around him. He then places his hands around her firm buttocks and gently, with her guidance, enters her. He leans their bodies against the shower tiles to give them leverage for movement. They both struggle to control their passion and move as slowly as the situation allows. Carmen can feel the strong hand on her lower back helping her maximize contact with her most important features ... until ... she starts to joyously gasp, groan, and make sounds too unique to describe. That's all he needs to hear, to let loose and writhe ecstatically with her all over him, skin-on-skin in shuddering bliss. They wash each other, towel off, dry and brush her hair, and climb into bed together. She places her head on his chest and quickly falls asleep. They don't say a word to each other after the shower experience. He lies there, on his back -- getting hard again -- and wonders where this relationship is going. He wonders where he wants it go.

215

CHAPTER 41 -- THE LAST BREAKFAST

Wiscasset, Maine: I look over at the clock; it flashes 0615. I didn't want to get out of my bed because it felt so damned good. Those jail cots weren't designed for comfort.

I can smell Jolene even though she isn't in the house -- it brings me some comfort, but it also motivates me to move. It's time to save Jolene, dammit!

I swing my extra-large frame into a sitting position, reach over and grab my blue jeans from the back of the Lazy-boy, put on my 4x flannel shirt, white sox, and 16 DD moccasins.

It is good to be home. Everyone should spend a couple of days incarcerated to appreciate freedom. I wander half-awake into the kitchen. The Keurig's power light is on, so I grab a K-cup, pop it into in the coffee-maker, and wait for my extra-bold cup to fill up.

I don't hear Powers moving around ... which surprises me, because he always wakes up early. As I sip my coffee and smell its aroma, I call out for Powers. He doesn't answer. So I put myself into Powers' shoes. I concentrate: "Where would I go if I woke up in the house early with nothing to do? Ah, of course." I open the basement door and start down the stairs. Even over the wonderful smell of coffee, I can whiff the unmistakable odor of machine oil.

On the breakdown bench, Powers is cleaning weapons for the mission. He has cleaned his 4-inch-barrel Chiappa Rhino 357 Magnum Revolver with rubber grips, the two 650-rounds-per-minute M-4 carbines, a semi-automatic 12-gauge Mossberg shotgun, six 40-caliber Sig Sauer P226s with 12 round clips, and three 16-ounce ESEE-5 knives with quarter-inch thick blades. Lying on a sheet on the floor is a grenade launcher, some smoke bombs, three four-point grapple hooks attached to coils of rope, and a Mossberg MVP 300-caliber bolt-action patrol rifle. Still in the open walk-in safe are three separately-packaged bars of C-4 plastic explosive, an acetylene torch, three pairs of night vision goggles, several tactical flashlights, and enough ammunition to fight a small war.

I jokingly say, "Thanks for cleaning the weapons I'm going to carry on the mission; what are you going to take?"

Powers says, "While you are sleeping the day away, your fiancé is rotting away in prison. Let's get a move on. We only have a couple of hours before the team heads out to Edinburgh, Scotland.

"Ray LaSalle and Damian LaTorre left for London this morning to solicit some additional help from the Brits. I understand that former president Winston Allen made a few phone calls. Tucker and Maya are on their way over here now, to provide some additional intelligence and to give you something that Maya is keeping secret. That could be damn near anything."

Powers stands up straight, his scarred and wrinkled face serious, and sticks his face over next to mine when he asks, "Tank, is there any way I can talk you out of going? You know you can't skip bail, right?"

I shrug my shoulders, lift the palms of my hands up and say, "Who's going to tell the judge I left the country?"

"Probably the British News Network. Ok, so at least you'd better call Tony Vinci. He may have something up his sleeve."

"I'm going upstairs to cook us something to eat. We're going to have to have a high-protein, high-carb meal before we head out."

"Don't bother. Chef Rhino begged Tucker to let him come over with them."

"It sure is good to have friends."

The intrusion alarm sounds, informing me that a vehicle has passed into my driveway. I look over at the closed-circuit TV monitor to see Maya's Tesla pulling up. At just the same time, my cell phone rings; it is Tony Vinci.

"Yeah Tony, what you got for me?"

Tony answers, "Me."

"Why would I want you?"

Tony answers, "You need me to go on the mission with you."

"You," I laugh; "No offense, Tony, but you're not exactly the best person for a special operations mission where speed and hand-to-hand combat might be required; I'll have to save your ass."

Tony answers, "Maybe you didn't hear me correctly. What I said was you **need** me. I didn't say that I want to go."

"OK, I'll take the bait."

"How are you going to disarm the booby traps? It seems to me that you might like to know what the traps are, before you risk everyone's life."

"I'm listening, but hold on while I let your boss in the front door."

I keep the phone at my ear with my right hand while I open the front door to let in Maya who kisses my left cheek, Tucker who pats my back, Chef Rhino who carries in groceries, and Star who brings in her shadow, Ram. I put the phone on speaker.

"OK, Tony," I say; "Tucker, Maya and Star are listening."

Tony says, "Hi, Star. Can you read my mind from 300 miles away?"

Star frowns, looks away, and shakes her head.

"That's a good thing, because I was thinking some bad things about Tank."

I say, "Be careful, Tony. Ram's also listening."

Tony says, "Oh, no! Ram, I was just kidding."

218

Everyone laughs, and Tony continues, "You **need** me on the mission because I can commandeer Joy, my nano-drone. Depending on the wind velocity, if you can get me within a half-mile of the oil rig, she can give it a thorough inspection in about 45 minutes. Not only can she visually inspect it, but she can audibly listen for machinery, and she can sniff for chemicals and explosives."

Powers comes up through the basement door, wiping his hands on a towel he brought up with him and says, loud enough for Tony to hear, "Haven't you left yet? I don't want to have to wait on you."

"Actually, I'm at Logan Airport with three of your *White Knights*. With your permission, I'll get on the same flight with these guys to Heathrow, and then continue on up to Edinburgh."

Powers and I say "OK," simultaneously.

Tony says, "I wasn't asking for permission from you two guys. I was asking my boss for permission."

Tucker says, "What's the status of the patent application which you and Maya are working on?"

"I'll have it ready for Maya to review by the time we land in London."

Tucker asks, "Have you manufactured a back-up for the drone you nicknamed Joy?"

"Uh," Tony mumbles; "Uh, she's actually on assignment, sir."

"On assignment, Tony?"

"Yes, sir."

"We'll talk more about that when you return. Last question: if something happens to you while *you're* on assignment, does Maya know everything about how the thing you're patenting works?"

Maya answers, "Yes. Tony and I both know **how** it works. But I know **why** it works."

Tucker says, "OK, Tony; go on your first mission."

Chef Rhino calls out, "Breakfast is ready!"

We all move to the buffet-style meal, except for Powers and Star.

Star is glaring at Powers.

Powers is standing with his hands on his hips with a "what am I going to do with you?" expression on his weathered face.

Maya, Tucker, Rhino, and I know what is going on; Star is reading something in Powers' thoughts that he doesn't want her to know. Finally, Star speaks and says, "Uncle Powers, I think you have to tell Tank."

Then I say, "Yes, and you need to tell me now. Star's already let the cat out of the bag."

Powers says, "OK. Well, my daughter, Sonja, is going to meet us in Edinburgh."

Chef Rhino hollers out from the kitchen again: "Come and get it. Breakfast is ready." I'm no dummy; I am the first up and into the kitchen to get in line for the biscuits and gravy, sausage, monkey bread, bacon, ambrosia … and omelets made to each person's preference. He knows that I prefer everything in mine.

As I complete my fabulous meal, Maya floats over to my spot in the dining room and asks, "Can we have a private conversation?"

"Whoa," I think; "this is a first." So I stand up, look over at Tucker quizzically, and follow Maya into another room. Tucker doesn't appear fazed at all, which means that he already knows what is up.

Maya hands me a little wrapped package with a tiny bow on top. She says, "Take this with you. You'll need this when you get to the oil platform. Don't doubt me on this; you'll thank me later."

I take the package and thank her. What else could I do?

CHAPTER 42 -- THE SECOND ENVELOPE

Falls Church, Virginia: Richard breaks the seal on the second envelope. This time he and Melody are dressed and sitting together in a booth at an IHOP sharing pancakes. The second envelope contains three times as many pages as the first envelope. It also contains a key housed in a jewel case labeled *"BB&T Alexandria, Box 2141."*

While taking a napkin to the corners of her Angelina-Jolie mouth, Melody says, "That branch of BB&T is not too far from here. Come on; let's go. This is exciting!" She starts to grab her pocketbook and rise before Richard says, "Slow down, road runner; I think we need to give these papers a cursory look first, just to make sure that we don't have instructions about what to do with the contents of this -- probably -- safe deposit box. At least, let's categorize the subject of each document."

Melody resigns herself to remain in her seat. They look over the first set of papers that are held together by a black metal binder clip. The cover page is a 1995 legal document on *Executive Branch of the United States* stationary with blacked out or redacted words which refer to an attachment entitled "Worst Case Scenario and Methods of Mitigating Consequences." A quick scan of the eleven pages reveals that the document has something to do with the former First Lady.

Melody says, "She's guilty of something. I can't wait to dig through the rest of these pages."

Richard takes a Post-It-Note and places it on the clipped pages and marks it "First Lady." Richard surveys the second set of papers containing roughly 75 pages in a half-inch binder, which has a colorful cover sheet -- it features a satellite photo of Earth taken from the space station, with a title in large bold letters: *"One World Government."* On the blank inside first page of the document in cursive handwriting is this: "To the First Lady," and "From VS, the Queen-Maker." Richard positions his left hand to hold the manuscript and flips through it quickly, covering the entire binder's contents in less than two minutes; he concludes that it is too intellectually heavy to read while breakfasting in IHOP. Melody asks, "Who do you think the Queen-Maker is?"

Richard says, "I don't know. I guess that's part of our assignment."

The third document is a twenty-page Confidential FBI report on the activities of the Minority Civil Liberties Union. As he quickly scans the report in search of its relevance to his new assignment, his eye catches the name "Robert Kingsley" towards the end of the report. He whispers as he reads, *"Fingerprints of one of the released prisoners were found at the scene of the traffic death of Robert Kingsley."*

Richard Kingsley is paralyzed, deep in thought. This piece of information is the first solid evidence he's seen to correlate the traffic accident with malfeasance. This is exciting to him, and he suddenly feels mission-bound to follow this thread.

But the fourth document -- which is only two pages long and stapled together -- shocks him even more. It is a pair of black-and-white photocopies of two 8- by 10-inch photos of the former First Lady in embarrassingly compromising situations.

Melody turns bright red. Richard immediately looks around to see if anyone was looking over his shoulder who might have accidentally viewed the photo.

Richard looks at Melody, who averts her glance, and says, "We'll leave these in the safe deposit box when we go to BB&T in Alexandria. This is too damned dangerous to carry around. There are people on both sides of the political aisle who would kill for these. Let's go."

WHA-CKED   JED O'Dea
(White House Attorney-Counsel Killed)

    St. Petersburg, Russia: Yuri's next chess move against his opponent, Viktor Soroson, is a weak pawn move one space up … which doesn't appear to be a tactical move at all.

CHAPTER 43 -- THE PLAN

St. Andrews, Scotland: A halogen light is perfectly positioned behind General Ray LaSalle's right shoulder as he occupies a comfortable high-backed chair designed for manuscript readers.   Three other similar chairs are equally spaced around a three-meter mahogany coffee table.   Damian LaTorre, the prior U.S. administration's Director of the FBI, sits in one of the chairs assessing MI-5 Agent, Stone Garry, who sits in a second chair.   Member for the House of Lords Randolph Randolph IV sits in the remaining chair in a small private study rented for the day at the Fairmont in St. Andrews, Scotland, gazing pompously at the rest of the gathering.

General Ray LaSalle speaks first. "Thank you for making the long trip from London to meet with us here in St. Andrews. We truly appreciate the effort you've made to meet with us."

Lord Randolph, an overweight and unduly respected member of the House of Lords says, "It isn't often that I get a call from a former U.S. President. Winston Allen is well respected by us British, so when he asked us to meet with you here, we considered it an honor.

"Having said that" ... the arrogant Lord Randolph steals a glance at Agent Garry ... "how is it that we can be of help to you Yanks?"

LaTorre, masking his contempt for the "Lord" says, "First, you need to understand that our mission is not a U.S. Government-sponsored mission; it is a private mission to save a kidnapped woman being held hostage on a German-owned oil platform by thugs in international waters off the coast here in Scotland."

Agent Stone Garry admits, "We know the rig about which you are speaking. It's about seventy-five kilometers off our coast. We refer to it as the 'Heidi' deep-water oil platform.

"Why," asks Ray, "has the 'Heidi' found its way onto MI-5's radar screen?"

Stone answers, "Everything is on our radar screen, General. At one time there was a lot of activity up there and we were concerned that it could be used to launch a mission against the United Kingdom. We're still a little paranoid when it comes to German activity near our mainland."

Ray LaSalle continues, "We need access to a sea-worthy vessel from which we can launch our mission. All it really needs to have is a helipad."

Stone asks, "What size helipad; how big a vessel?"

"I don't know," says Ray; "what do you have which we can borrow?"

"You've got to be bloody kidding!" interjects Lord Randolph. "We will not be seen as attacking sovereign German property; that would be viewed as an act of war, for God's sake."

Ray LaSalle looks over at LaTorre and says, "Damian, what did you say the next mission was, for the unmarked and unlisted MI-5 Westland WG-13 Super Lynx helicopter sitting on the tarmac at Menwith Hill Air Base?"

Agent Garry looks over at Lord Randolph, who has no idea what the two Americans are talking about. He returns his attention to the Americans and asks with renewed respect, "Are you two Yanks also going to tell us what barge you want us to supply you, and where it is located, too?"

LaTorre says, "Inverness."

"I'm impressed. What's the quid pro quo?"

Though Ray already knows what the MI-5 agent wants, he asks, "What is it that you want? We might be able to help out."

Stone looks over at the pompous stuffed-shirt member of the House of Lords and says, "Lord Randolph, in order to provide you reasonable deniability, I'll step outside with the Yanks and discuss the terms and conditions of our deal."

Lord Randolph says, "As long as you don't place us in an international jam, I'll stay out of it."

Stone, Ray and Damian step outside the meeting room and into the hall. Stone cocks his head in the direction of the room, smirks, and says, "I find most of the members of the House of Lords cowards, much like your American senators.

"We can't talk out here in the open; follow me."

Stone opens a door to the stairway and the three go down two flights of stairs into the sub-basement. He leads their way into a room where the huge hotel furnace is rumbling. Agent Stone Garry then says, "There is no way anyone can overhear our conversation in here."

The MI-5 agent proceeds to explain to the two Americans what he wants. It *was* what the two men suspected he wanted. A deal is struck.

They climb back up the two flights of stairs and re-enter the meeting room to find that Lord Randolph is involved in a conversation with an attractive five foot, one inch tall, 115 pound, 35-year-old, short-haired brown-eyed blonde.

Neither Ray nor Damian appears at all surprised. Stone Garry, however, is shocked speechless, apoplectic. He looks over at the two American men with absolute amazement and asks, "You knew exactly what I wanted, in advance of arriving here?"

Ray shrugs his shoulders and Damian just smiles.

Again, Lord Randolph has no idea that he is speaking with the world's most-feared sniper, much less that Sonja McLeod is an Israeli Mossad agent whose current assignments include the assassination of top ISIS and al-Qaida leaders.

Powers had learned of his daughter's existence only a few years ago, and he has tried hard since then to make up for lost time. Powers and Sonja ultimately bonded, and now watch each other's backs. Sonja is in Scotland for exactly that reason -- to watch her Dad's back. She didn't show up to take on a new assignment on behalf of the Brits.

There isn't a person in the espionage business who hasn't seen photographs of the petite Sonja McLeod. Nor is there a spy in the universe who isn't fearful that Israel has decided that their time was up, and instructed this famous sniper to take them out. Stone knows that his time isn't up, or he would never see her -- he would just suddenly cease to exist after a high velocity 50-caliber bullet smashed through his head like Gallagher smashes a watermelon. She is deadly from 1,800 meters, over one and one-eighth miles.

Only minutes before seeing Sonja McLeod, Agent Stone Garry had asked the Americans if they could help MI-5 take out an organizer who is hell-bent on rekindling the old Irish Republican Army. He is damned sure that it is no coincidence that the pretty little blond is here.

He looks over at Ray and says, "The barge will be towed north, up Moray Firth and out into the North Atlantic to a spot about five kilometers from the oil platform.

"Your team should pull up to the main gate at Menwith Hill at 0500 sharp and ask for the American Commander. He'll take you to the Lynx helicopter which must leave the base before daylight.

"You haven't asked for a pilot, so I assume that you already have one. The chopper will be fully fueled, but you don't have enough for the round trip, so we'll store fuel on the barge. It'll take the barge sixteen hours before it will drop anchor at its destination."

Agent Garry says with some reluctance, "You probably already have all the intelligence you need, but just in case you don't know, this oil platform has a special sensor signature. Be careful."

With that, Stone Garry and Lord Randolph leave the room. As they are making their way out, you could hear Lord Randolph ask, "What the bloody hell is going on?"

Caracas, Venezuela: In his Caracas mansion, Viktor Soroson concentrates on the electronic chess board displayed on his 75-inch flat screen TV. He thinks, "What a stupid move, Yuri. Too stupid; what the devil are you up to?" But Viktor can't resist and moves his queen into position and says, "Check, you old fool!"

Wiscasset, Maine: Lucas sleeps very little, while Carmen sleeps like a baby. Usually, Lucas is one of those lucky people who can sleep soundly anytime, anywhere, in any position, and wake up in an instant if he senses something or feels threatened. It is a gift he hasn't appreciated until last night. Lucas has never previously fallen in love, but knows instinctively that it is happening to him now -- and he doesn't like it. He doesn't like the feeling of vulnerability; he prides himself at being invulnerable -- he is a warrior, after all!

His smart phone vibrates and buzzes. It's a text from JJ, the *White Knight* office administrator in charge of assignments. He thinks, "I don't want a new assignment unless it is to help Tank rescue Jolene."

As number three in the corporate chain-of-command, Lucas is crushed to learn that his new assignment is not to join in the rescue mission, but rather to stay put and run all of *White Knight's* business operations while Tank and Powers are out of the country. This job, usually performed by Powers, now requires Lucas to resolve conflicts which come up on their twenty to thirty active contracts. *White Knight Personal Security Services* provides hundreds of security officers across the globe to customers who are, sometimes, uncooperative prima-donna-types. Conflict resolution skills are also required when *White Knight* officers use force in the execution of their protective role, sometimes considered over-the-top by local law enforcement officials. Since Lucas is still wanted in the State of Maryland for incapacitating a couple of overzealous cops whom he suspected were about to kill Ram, he is uncomfortable with his new temporary role.

His second assignment is to protect the Cherokees from an outside threat. According to the report attached to the message, this threat is from the same group which had tried to kill Powers and Maya at the *Entropy Entrepreneurs'* offices in Boston.

Protecting Carmen is not on JJ's list of new assignments.

But it is Lucas' number one self-imposed priority.

Powers' satellite phone ringtone sounds; it is Jolene. He takes the phone off his belt, and while he continues eating his high-protein breakfast, he hands the phone to me.

I say, "Hi, sweetheart. You OK this morning?"

"While it's not morning here, I'm OK in knowing you're on your way. What's the plan?"

I first tell her she is beautiful and amberdelic. This is a made-up code word we use to provide an eavesdropper with disinformation. This is a precaution I use just in case the kidnappers are overhearing our conversation with their nano-cameras. Then, I tell her an absolute bullshit story about the plan and add that we won't be there for another week, which is also absolute BS. She screams and hollers and yells at me, to make it sound realistic. She finally says that at least there is some light at the end of the tunnel.

"Tank," she reminds me, "Korf told me that I was 'toast.' And then she adds, 'burnt toast, to be exact.' Does that provide a clue about his booby traps here?"

I think about it for a minute and ask, "Have you smelled propane, kerosene, oil, natural gas, or gasoline around there anywhere? Have you heard a generator running or figured out what provides the electricity?"

She answers, "Yes, there is a generator that pretty much runs constantly, but I can't tell you the fuel source. I haven't smelled anything."

I respond, "It is an oil rig, after all, so my guess is there is a large oil storage tank used to run the generator, and a possible source of an explosion that could burn pretty hot for enough time to burn all of us to a crisp.

"I'll get Tony to study that when he deploys Joy."

"Who?"

"Uh, … never mind."

"Tank," Jolene asks with some trepidation in her voice, "Were you serious last night when you asked me to marry you? I mean, after all these years and after all we've been through, what happened that prompted you to propose, now?"

"Why? Are you thinking about saying 'No'?"

She laughs her infectious Dolly-Parton laugh and says, "No, of course not."

I say, "It's because I had an epiphany and realized how stupid it was of me not to have asked sooner. I guess I've gotten so wrapped up in my work and our adventures that I lost sight of what is most important to me -- you."

There is no response.

"Jolene, honey, are you there? Jolene? Hello?"

Silence -- this can't be good.

The urgency to save Jolene just made a quantum leap upward.

The team works efficiently with little discussion, preparing for a long trip to Scotland and points north.

Harrogate, United Kingdom: While Powers -- with one of the *White Knights* and a USAF pilot -- is checking out the unmarked Westland Super Lynx helicopter, I am going over the details of the mission with the entire team. Tony Vinci swept the meeting room at The Cold Cotes hotel in Harrogate before we began our mission in-brief. The entire rescue team consists of two over-the-hill guys (Ray and Damian), Tony -- the dwarf who is unable to run more than a half-a-mile-an-hour, an Israeli sniper whose value is questionable on this particular mission, three well-trained former Special Forces soldiers, and Powers -- who is invaluable on any mission.

And, of course, me.

The execution of the mission itself is simple, and we expect no resistance. The complication is discovering the lethality of the booby traps.

"Tony," I ask, "What are our options if the wind velocity is too high for you to control Joy?"

"I brought a few other tools with me. Tank, the kidnappers are limited out here in the middle of the North Atlantic, especially if they're trying to respond to our rescue remotely. They can blow up the Heidi, kill us with weapons of mass destruction -- like chemical and biological weapons -- use various forms of radiation, like microwaves or gamma radiation, or trap us in there so we can't get out.

"For them to blow us up -- the most likely scenario in my opinion -- they'll need explosives and an igniter. I borrowed a mobile nuclear quadrupole resonance sniffer that can detect parts per quadrillion of energetics from The Organic Semiconductor Centre, here, at the University of St Andrews. The nose of a sniffer dog is still the best detection system for explosives, but we didn't bring Ram. The technology is based on Flir's Fido technology, but rather than using fluorescence to detect explosives, they focus on using laser light from fluorescent polymers."

"Stop, Tony. You're not sharing information with Maya; you're talking to old leathernecks, soldiers, and bodyguards, so cut to the chase."

Tony says, "OK. We'll be able to determine if there are explosives on the oil rig."

I ask, "How close do we need to get to the oil rig for this method to be effective."

Tony says, "We need to get within roughly twenty feet of the explosives, wherever they are located on the oil platform. Your officers will have to take the sniffers and walk around the entire oil complex to rule out -- or to find -- the explosives."

233

"What other tools do you have for us?"

"I brought our own Fido X3. It starts from cold in five minutes and has a battery that lasts about eight hours. I also brought a Berkeley Nucleonics gamma survey radiation meter."

I ask, "What could go wrong with this mission, Tony? What's the worst case scenario?"

Tony answers, "We don't know what we don't know."

"As a precaution," and I look over a Sonja McLeod, "Sonja has agreed to set up on top of The Heidi platform with the tools of her trade in the event we are approached by an enemy."

"If Tony and Joy, Tony's drone, determine that the oil platform is clean, we'll land on the helipad with the Lynx after dropping Sonja into position on the parapet.

"If the oil platform is determined not to be clean, we'll scale the oil rig using our grapples to climb the structure from a Rigid Inflatable Boat -- our 'RIB.'

"We'll all meet at the entrance door to Jolene's prison cell. We'll survey the situation and find our way in.

"Ray and Damian, I'm depending on you to maintain contact with MI-5. They'll be the first to know if the assholes are headed in our direction.

"Any questions?"

Sonja raises her hand. I nod in her direction. She asks, "What are the rules of engagement?"

I smile and answer, "Engage the enemy; no friendlies, please. Notify me if you have a reason to take a shot; we'll keep our communication headsets active. The earphone isolates the sound in the ear so nothing can be heard from the outside.

"And Sonja, please wear your Kevlar vest."

"Any other questions? If not, let's hit it."

WHA-CKED

JED O'Dea

(White House Attorney-Counsel Killed)

The rescue team files out of the Cold Coats meeting room, each hauling the gear they need to execute their role in the mission. We wear heavy coats, special gloves, ski hats and goggles as we climb into two waiting Land Rovers. The ride to Menwith Hill is uneventful, as each member of the team is lost in their own thoughts.

The seven rescuers file into the WG-13 Lynx helicopter to join Powers who has completed his preflight checklist and is ready to "rock and roll." Sonja approaches the cockpit and sits in the copilot's seat, fastens her seatbelt, and stoically says, "I'd give you a hug, but I'm afraid others might misunderstand our relationship."

"Bullshit. Give me a hug."

She does.

"My commanding officer doesn't know I'm here. I'm on 'R and R.'"

Powers says, "I'm glad you came." He looks over at his daughter and says, "But, your CO *does* know that you're here, and has sanctioned your mission."

North Atlantic Ocean: The blackness of the night flight from Menwith Hill to the anchored barge -- rigged with an oversized helipad -- in the cold wintry North Atlantic gives way to a gray, drizzly overcast day. The barge is rocking five degrees or so from side to side in a harmonic and rhythmic motion, but Powers lands the helicopter gently without a problem.

I climb down to the barge deck, hauling my ninety-pound backpack, and say, "Lovely day out here. This is a great vacation spot.   Everything the Chamber of Commerce promised."

Damian adds, "Where's the rum bar?"

Two of the White Knight security officers, both former Army Rangers, help the physically-handicapped Tony Vinci off the chopper.   All eight of us hurriedly find our way to the living quarters and mess area of the barge.

After everyone sheds their wet overcoats and locates their gear in a safe spot, Sonja leans over and whispers into her dad's ear, "This is no normal barge. I'm a little surprised the Brits would let us use this vessel."

Powers answers, "You think? Doesn't every barge have five-foot-wide screen monitors in the mess hall displaying radar, sonar, and satellite visuals? A barge doesn't have a power plant either. This barge is a ship camouflaged as 'just a barge.' Good cover, don't you think?"

Looking out at the distant oil platform, Sonja says, "I didn't appreciate just how big an oil platform was. That thing is huge."

Powers looks at Sonja and says, "The parapet is 160 feet off the surface of the ocean. Are you going to be OK with that?"

"I'm most worried about staying warm. If my hands get too cold, I'm less effective."

Tony has climbed up on a step-ladder and is looking out a port-hole, acting dejected. I walk over to him and ask, "The weather is too harsh for Joy isn't it?"

Tony shakes his head in the affirmative. I say, "Let's go talk to the captain of this little high-tech barge."

Powers is already in conversation with Captain Spaulding of the *Kenda Rose* surveillance ship when we arrive. Powers introduces Tony and me to the young thirty-something captain who has grown a red beard to look older than he really is, but his youthful green eyes give him away.

I ask, "With all this fancy technology on board, you probably can predict if the wind velocity will be a little lower this afternoon. We can't launch a tool we have in this ferocious gale-force wind."

Tony looks on anxiously, waiting until Spaulding laughs and says, "My, my. You blokes should know that today is a mild breeze compared with the usual wind conditions here. I'd say you caught a break. Don't expect an improvement later today. Look for it to get worse."

Powers says, "OK, Tank; it's time for the four of you to explore the target from the bottom up. Though the seas are choppy, you can still take the RIB.

"Captain, can you tell the tug to take us to within a couple hundred yards of the monster oil platform and let our boys do the rest?"

"No, I'm afraid that I can't," answers the captain; "my instructions are to not allow any Brit within five kilometers of the German oil platform, in case a video or satellite photo captures us invading their space -- it would cause an international ruckus."

Powers looks at me and says, "You better get going. You all brought insulated suits, right?"

I answer, "Yeah, we did."

Captain Spaulding adds, "I hope you guys understand that they feed the sharks from there, so try to stay in the boat."

The Rigid Inflatable Boat has a small outboard motor to propel us through an uncooperative cold ocean swelling ten feet every few seconds. The 40 degree Fahrenheit water splashes constantly in my face, chilling me to the bone. Five kilometers felt like a thousand miles. I look over at my *White Knight* warriors to see each of them smiling -- they are in their element.

PART III

CHAPTER 44 -- THE MISSION

North Atlantic Ocean: The hostage rescue team includes me as Knight Alpha, and three hand-picked former-Special-Forces warriors, Knights Bravo, Charlie, and Delta. All four of us have been trained by Powers.   Knight Charlie is surveying the monster structure using the gamma detector while Knight Delta is holding the explosives detector.   We circle the massive structure twice to take measurements, adding thirty minutes to our mission.

"Powers," I ask over the earpiece, "do you or Tony know of any reason based on our findings why we shouldn't climb?"

Powers answers, "Go for it, big guy."

We position ourselves under a ladder normally used by a larger watercraft. I throw the grapple up about fifteen feet above my head and luckily hook the ladder on the first try. I take a deep breath and will myself to overcome my self-doubts about my arm strength and start climbing the rope, pulling my 320 pounds up.   I mutter through clenched teeth, "I've really got to lose some weight."

Fortunately, my will to save Jolene and the adrenaline of the moment overcome my self-doubts. When I reach the bottom rung of the ladder, I still have to do a pull-up to get myself onto the ladder. I pull my gear up, and prepare to help Knight Beta. He is wiry, weighs half what I weigh, but is burdened with carrying the acetylene torch and tank. I reach down and help pull him up. "I'm going to search the rig for Jolene while you help pull up Knight Charlie."

I continue up the ladder, staying vigilant, looking for signs of potential trip wires, or land mines, or anything that remotely looks like a booby trap. "This place reminds me of an aircraft carrier. There are an infinite number of hiding place for traps." After surveying the first level, I have discovered nothing out of the ordinary. There is a boiler and a large oil storage tank that could be used to launch a fireball, but there is nothing remotely like a bomb or igniter. The oil-fired electric generator is running on this first level; its oil gage indicates that the oil tank is 70 percent full.

"Powers," I ask, "what do you think about turning the electricity off? The booby traps could require power for initiation."

Powers and Tony are talking over each other to answer the question but the answers are the same, "No, turning the power off could just as easily trigger the trap in a fail-safe mode."

The only other unusual item on the first level is a two-inch-diameter steel cable that runs through the center of the structure. One end of the cable is attached to a ten ton dead weight with the other end attached to who-knows-what below the water level. I don't know enough about oil drilling to know one way or the other if that is normal.

So I go on up to the second level. This level contains storage of what looks like a million parts for the equipment that is required to drill thousands of feet underwater and thousands of feet more into the seabed. This level also contains a machine shop, air compressors, a locker room, a first aid station, and rooms filled with workers' gear. Forty-five minutes later, I decide to go to the third level. This level contains the control room. There are probably thirty monitors and hundreds of instruments to measure pressure, temperature, voltage, depth, amperage, volumes, and liquid levels.

I wander up to the fourth level where the kitchen, mess hall, and residences are located. I suspect that this is the level where Jolene is being held. I check every room, every door, and every closet. Some of the doors are locked but none of the locks are impenetrable; Powers taught us how to pick locks very well.

It takes me a solid hour to go through the residence level, even with the help of the other three knights. No Jolene.

We carefully climb the stairs up to the fifth level. The helipad occupies the majority of this level. We spend fifteen minutes surveying the fifth level for trip wires, switches, or anything that could trigger an explosion. Nothing.

I suddenly had a big fear. "What if Tony was wrong and this is not the oil platform where Jolene is being held?"

I persevere and climb to the sixth level. This level contains the office complex, with desk-top computers, copiers, printers, offices, conference rooms and a visitor's guest house -- a guest house with a newly-installed steel door. The door has a steel bar across it, secured by steel angle-iron cradles on either side. If you were trapped inside, there is no way to get out through that door.

I check the door for a wire but find none. I pull my Glock and use the butt to signal Jolene, if she is inside. I tap in Morse code, "Tank".

She taps back, "Help." My heart races; we have found her!

The four of us smile in unison but I'm sure my smile is broader than the other Knights. I told Knight Delta to tell Powers it is about time he did something. "Come and get us."

Knight Bravo and I lift the steel bar out of the angles and place it on the floor. I push the handle to open the door, but it doesn't budge. I look at the dead-bolt and lock arrangement, and unlock three of them. I still can't open the door. The fourth lock requires a lock pick. Before I even ask for a pick set, Bravo has unpacked it and handed it to me.

We try for ten minutes but can't pick the lock. Knight Bravo asks, "Do you want the torch?"

Instead, I tap the code out on the door again, this time saying: "Stand back -- C4"

She taps back, "Roger that."

Knight Charlie places the C4 on the outside hinges and tapes the RF igniter to the explosives. We all go down a level and stand outside on the helipad. I nod, and Knight Charlie pushes the button.

The noise is incredible. It frightens me that we might have under-estimated it's explosive force, and that maybe we had hurt Jolene.

I run hard up the stairs and through the frame where the steel door had been, moments earlier. I run right into her arms. She tackles me like a linebacker and holds onto me like a pit bull.

But it isn't Jolene.

I release a primal scream at the crying forty-something woman with stringy and matted grayish hair, "Where is Jolene, damn it. I want to know where she is right this fucking second!" When the cowering woman finally speaks, it's in English with a thick German accent. "You are Mr. Tank?"

I nod my head.

"I am a prisoner here. I am instructed to give you a message from Gunter Korf."

Again, I nod.

"You should have followed your orders! Neither you, nor your woman, are of value to him any longer. Auf Wiedersehen."

I can't contain my rage; I throw tables, chairs, chests of drawers, bed frames, kitchen utensils and anything not tied down against the prison walls. I recognize the layout as the rooms in which Jolene was imprisoned. I'm too fucking late.

I ask, "How long have you been in this prison?"

She answers, "Four days."

I look to the team and say, "OK, let's give it a thorough going-over, before we abandon this God-forsaken structure."

North Atlantic Ocean: The wind is gusting between 15 and 45 miles per hour. Powers is struggling to keep the big Super Lynx helicopter in control. He tries three times before he finally sets the chopper down.

That's when all hell breaks loose. A load-cell on the deck of the helipad trips two programmed devices and signals the kidnappers that their facility has been compromised.

As Sonja McLeod, General LaSalle, and former FBI Director Damian LaTorre are stepping down from the helicopter, the intolerably loud foreign sound of a mechanical monster attacks their ears. It is a screeching sound of metal on metal; the entire oil platform structure vibrates. The high-frequency, high-decibel sound obscures the roar of the pre-programmed ultra-high pressure water jet -- normally used to cut steel -- which sweeps across the center of the helipad at about five feet off the deck. The 70,000 psi waterjet cuts across Damian LaTorre and slices him in half at the upper chest level.

Sonja sees it coming, throws the heavy shoulder harness containing her sniper rifle to the deck, and intentionally knocks Ray down -- the deadly water jet sweeps just over their heads. Powers lifts the water-jet-damaged Lynx helicopter off the helipad before it is totally un-flyable.

The gamma meter in Knight Charlie's backpack starts screaming. I know what it means immediately. All of us had

242

been through CBRNE or Chemical, Biological, Radiation, Nuclear, and Explosive training. I ask, "What's it reading?"

Knight Charlie says, "25 Rads per hour."

The other three of us say in unison, "Fuck." Knight Beta adds, "We don't have long."

As if on cue, Ray LaSalle says -- while lying on the deck -- "I just got a call from Captain Spaulding. We're about to have visitors."

Sonja crawls over to a point where she is out of range of the waterjet's arc, and drags her heavy gear up the stairs to the sixth level, and then on up to the parapet where she pulls out her sniper rifle and starts getting into her job-focused mental zone.

Ray LaSalle crawls out of the range of the water jet, rolls to the stairway and goes down the stairs to the lower levels. He speaks into his headphone and says, "Searching for the source of radiation."

I say, "The closer you get, the more danger you are in!"

"I'm an old man. Do you have another idea? I'm certainly open to any ideas."

I say, "Keep the line open."

I hear Tony yelling into my earbud, "Turn the fucking generator off; the waterjet will stop, then Powers can land and all of you can escape with minimal radiation exposure. But the longer you stay there the greater you are at risk."

Ray hears Tony, too. He decides with greater urgency to reach the first level anyway. He is only on the fourth level; he has to hustle.

Captain Spaulding contacts Ray who is wearing his headset and says, "I have a message for you from MI-5 Agent Stone Garry. He told me to advise you that the German owners of the oil platform are two minutes away."

Ray isn't sure if he can move any faster with his 70 year-old heart. He's made it to the third level.

In my earbud, I hear Sonja say, "Incoming in sight."

I ask, "How many?"

Sonja says, "One."

Powers says, "I'm a sitting duck. I can't hover here forever."

Ray says, "I'm now on level two."

I ask Powers, "Do you have the grenade launcher on board?"

"Yes."

"We may want to use it the minute you touch down."

"Roger that."

Sonja says, "Closing rapidly. Looks like a CH53-G."

North Atlantic Ocean: Gunter Korf has flown in from the Faroe Islands. He was expecting the attempt to save Jolene by her support group but believed it would be a week from now. His employer will not be happy about the new development. He has to be aggressive; desperate people, after all, do desperate things.

North Atlantic Ocean: "I made it," says General Ray LaSalle; "I'm standing in front of the generator. I don't see an on-off button. How do I turn this damn thing off?"

Tony says, "Ray, is there a digital control panel in view?"

"Not that I see."

"Is there a lift up cover anywhere?"

"Yes, it looks like a circuit breaker cover."

"Good. Lift it up and flip the switch at the very top."

"Tony, I'm a little dizzy. I'm having a little trouble focusing."

"No problem, we can feel our way through it. Flip the switch that is on the very top; you can do it with your eyes closed, Ray. You can do it."

Suffering under the dog of agony, Ray does it.

The killer waterjet stops.

The gamma radiation, however, doesn't stop.

I ask, "Ray, what do you see down there that could be the source of this radiation?"

Ray answers, "A basket filled with pellets lifted out of the sea. Whatever tripped the device, it was pulled up from its submerged location."

Knight Beta says, "I'm guessing Cobalt-60 or Cesium-137 in terminal quantities."

Powers lands for a second time on the helipad and says, "Get on-board everybody, and I mean now!"

The three Knights, the female prisoner, and I rush to reach the Lynx. We bag the nauseating remains of Damian LaTorre's severed corpse and jump into the helicopter. Missing are Sonja McLeod and Ray LaSalle.

In his earbud he hears Sonja say, "Twenty seconds out. Yes or No?"

North Atlantic Ocean: Korf says to the passenger, "Lock onto the Lynx. Ready the Hellfires."

North Atlantic Ocean: Sonja says over the com, "The incoming has Hellfires. Taking my first shot." And she did.

Ray sees the basket, suspended at the end of the steel cable, and concludes that he can actually reach it, and dump it back into the sea if he can just keep his strength. His nose is bleeding; he has begun to vomit, and his skin feels like it is on fire. The basket is loosely sitting in a bucket. It doesn't appear to be tied or bolted down. If he could reach it, he could push it out of the bucket back into the sea.

A 50-caliber bullet traveling at a high velocity can penetrate most barriers including windshields of many aircraft. The German-manufactured CH53-G is no exception.

The windshield shatters from the first round, and the pilot is suddenly exposed to the elements, as is Korf. He says, "Launch."

The first Hellfire missile launches in the direction of the monster oil platform, but without a specific target. It hits the first level and explodes the oil storage tank.

Ray LaSalle is evaporated from the explosion that results in a fireball which burns everything on the first level.

That is … except for the radioactive Co-60 and Cs-137 source pellets. The metal pellets didn't burn or melt.

Sonja focuses on the closing helicopter; through her telescopic sight, she can actually see Gunter Korf in the copilot's seat. She fires, and watches his head explode; brain matter splatters all over the pilot … who turns the helicopter around and heads back in the direction of the Shetland Islands.

Powers waits for Sonja to scurry down from the seventh level and jump into the cabin of the Lynx before he takes off for the *Kenda Rose* and ultimately, he suspects, back to Royal Air Force Harrogate in North Yorkshire.

All of us are silent on the flight back to the barge. An aura of anger envelopes me and no one, not even Powers, dares to make eye contact with me. My jaws are clenched, my thoughts criminal, and I downshift into a low gear. I've never before felt hate like this.

Jolene is now in more danger than before the failed rescue. We have all lost a great friend in Ray LaSalle. And the former Director of the FBI has been sacrificed for nothing.

I recall Star telling me, "You have to save her, not rescue her."

This is the worst day of my life.

Then it hits me.

CHAPTER 45 -- AFTER ALL, WHAT ARE FRIENDS FOR?

Over the North Atlantic Ocean: I think my clearest when I'm under pressure; it's a gift. I say to Powers, "Can you get Maxwell Smart on the com?"

Powers asks, "Are you referring to the MI-5 guy, Agent Stone Garry?"

"That very one."

Powers says over his Bose A20 aviation Bluetooth headset, "Powers here, Captain Spaulding, please, come in; over."

Kenda Rose's Captain Spaulding doesn't answer the communications request; Tony Vinci answers instead. "The German CH53-G has landed at the following GPS coordinates." Tony proceeds to call the exact latitude and longitude numbers. "I highly recommend landing at the little Tingwall Airport. I've viewed real time satellite photos of the tiny Foula Island location using the high tech stuff on this barge. I've viewed the thermal images, UV signature, and believe it is relatively unoccupied. The pilot of the German helicopter had to make an emergency landing. They're unprotected, Tank. I bet the pilot of that helicopter knows where Jolene is."

I ask, "Let me speak with Captain Spaulding for a moment."

"Uh, he's asleep at the moment."

I say, "So that's how you took over the technology on the boat. Has agent Garry called in? I need his support."

Tony asks, "What do you need? I might be able to help since I hacked into their data base here."

"Tony, you're in deep kimchi. They'll haul your ass in for spying."

Tony says, "As I see it, I led you into a trap, told you that the oil platform was where Jolene was held prisoner, and got our friends Ray and Damian killed. I think I can stick my neck out a little."

"OK. MI-5 was watching the oil platform and the Germans for a reason. What's on or near Foula Island that could be similar to that oil platform? Is there another one nearby or another German-owned structure in the area?"

Tony says, "I'm a step ahead of you. Foula is a bleak little island twenty miles west of Walls in Shetland. On the main Shetland Island is the Sullom Voe Oil Terminal which is the main terminal in the area fed by pipeline from many of the billion-dollar deep sea oil platforms. One of the platforms resides in the Schiehallion oilfield. Schiehallion was discovered in 1993, with the semi-submersible drilling rig Ocean Alliance, while it was exploring the deep waters of the Shetland Trough in the northwest Atlantic. Schiehallion lies in 400m of water and it extends across four blocks operated by BP, and a fifth operated by Amerada Hess. In all, six oil companies are involved in the licenses.

"They have an outpost on the west side of Shetland Island where there is a training facility. The oil drillers use it to test construction materials. They do salt-spray tests and corrosion experiments with composite materials. According to the real time satellite photos, it's got three Jeep Wranglers and one Land Rover parked there."

"You're kidding me, right? You really know all this already?"

"I've been looking at this information ever since the CH53 helicopter took off from the Faroe Islands. Wait a minute; Captain Spaulding is stirring. I need to put him back to sleep."

During the silence while waiting for Tony to take care of the poor captain, Powers says, "Eight minutes until we reach the Foula airstrip where the downed German bad guys are ready to ambush us. We need to ready the troops."

I pick up the intercom and say, "All right guys, check your weapons. Here's the plan."

Over the North Atlantic Ocean: Foula has a grand population of 38 fishermen, sheep farmers, and at least one, no-doubt-armed German pilot who has just crash-landed his helicopter. The German CH53-G helicopter is occupying the limited space on the airfield which includes a couple of small prefabricated aircraft hangars big enough to store Piper Cubs.

I tell Powers, "No sense in getting too close. Drop me off about a quarter mile away without landing; I'll rappel down. You return to the *Kenda Rose*, refuel, drop off our Fraulein passenger, load the Gatling gun, arm the rocket launcher, and bring back Tony Vinci with Joy, his nano-drone, plus Sonja with her rifle and night-vision scope.

"By the time you get back here, I expect to know where Jolene is being held." I turn and address the team: "Let's take inventory; I don't want to jump out of this warm and comfortable chopper and realize that we forgot something.

"40-caliber Sig Sauer P226 with six 12-round clips?"

"Check."

"Silencerco Osprey 40-caliber Suppressor Pistol?"

"Check."

"ESEE-5 knife?"

"Check."

"Brick House Headset"

"Check"

"Tactical Sleeveless holster"

"Check."

"UC3.400 Tactical Flashlights?"

"Check."

"ATN PS-15 night vison goggles?"

"Check."

"Odin-31thermal weapons sight?"

"Check."

"OK, then, let's open the doors, and when we get within fifty feet of the ground I'll go. See you in a couple of hours or so. Keep the communications devices on."

Knight Beta asks, for all of them, for at least the fourth time: "Are you sure you want to do this alone?"

I smile and start my descent, without answering. I don't want anyone to witness what I am about to do. I am damn well going to learn where Jolene is being held captive, before it is too late.

Foula Island: I think, "What would I do if I were the downed German helicopter pilot? He surely has heard our Super Lynx beating the air, nearby. The few people who live on this island must also have heard the German's emergency night landing. What would I do? I'd either ask for help in leaving the island or, if I thought someone was tracking me down, I'd try to steal a plane and fly my ass off this island."

As surreptitiously as a man of my size is able to move, I hustle in the direction of the airfield's hangars. The rocky landscape underfoot benefits my attempt at stealth. I pull my thermal vision sight and search the airfield for activity. The German helicopter's engines are still hot, and glow brightly through the scope. There is also a thermal shadow of a small man near the chopper. I put the scope down, pull my night vision goggles on, and spot green light through a hangar door. I have a decision to make. Check the small man near the helicopter or investigate the hangar. If the pilot was able to start a small plane and fly it out of here, I have failed. If the small man is the German pilot, well, I'll be able to find him on this small rock of an island.

I try to hear if something mechanical is going on in the hangar, but all I can hear is the drone of crashing waves on the rocks. I take almost twenty minutes to go the last fifty yards, in order to maintain the advantage of surprise and to constantly monitor my surroundings.

I pull my silenced P226 and make sure that my six-inch tactical knife is comfortably loose in its sheath. I silently approach a back door to the enclosed hangar, slowly turn the door knob, and crack the door open about an inch. Fortunately, the hinges are well oiled and the door opens silently. An overhead fluorescent light is on inside, but no activity is obvious. I wait in silence for two minutes, listening for sounds of movement -- a shuffling of shoes on the concrete floor, human breathing, or the chambering of a weapon.

I sense it before I hear it -- movement just inside the door, not more than six feet away. He comes around on my right through the door opening, swinging a crowbar, at lightning speed. Instead of using the Sig on him, I instinctively block the crowbar thrust by using my right forearm at his wrist, and pull the tactical knife with my left hand.

The 40-caliber Sig Sauer falls to the floor. The first cut is into his left thigh.

He screams.

While he is screaming, I butt his nose with my big hard forehead. He falls backwards onto the floor, his head bounces off the concrete, but he is still able to roll to one side, lamely picks up a wrench left on the hangar floor, and throw it at me; it isn't close.

I take a step in his direction.

He has a panicked look on his face -- a look I've seen many times when my opponent realizes that they cannot win a close combat fight. He lunges for my Sig. Just as his hand reaches the gun, his arm fully extended, I step on his forearm with all my weight and kick the side of his head with my booted right foot. I lean over, and using both hands, grab the man by the jacket around the collar and stomach, lift him off the floor, and deposit him on a tool-covered workbench.

I estimate that I have roughly five minutes to prepare him for his interrogation before he will regain consciousness. I am a real believer that people spill the beans a little sooner when they are naked and vulnerable than if they are fully dressed and comfortable.

This outmatched helicopter pilot is freezing when he wakes up. His head feels like someone kicked the hell out of him. His leg, where he was stabbed, is in excruciating pain. He can't move -- he is tied down tight with rope and duct tape. He is also embarrassed, as he is lying on his back, with his cold-shriveled genitals fully exposed, and his lily white, hairless, and mole-covered body shivering.

I don't want him to bleed out. I want him to stay alive long enough to tell me where they are keeping Jolene ... so I put a tourniquet on his bleeding left leg.

I ask, "Sprecken ze English, Herr pilot?"

He doesn't answer.

I say in German, "What do you have to gain by resisting my interrogation? Just answer my fucking questions. I have no beef with you other than that you tried to ruin my day with that crowbar. I can get over that. And you can return to life as an uber helicopter chauffeur -- we can both be happy."

He answers in English, "I am Gunter Korf."

"Whoa," I blurt out. "I didn't see that coming. I thought your brains were hanging around in the interior of your helicopter. Of course, our sharpshooter didn't know what you looked like, and apparently shot the wrong guy. If you weren't in the passenger seat of the helicopter, then you were flying the machine. Who was shot?"

"Just a mercenary whom I hired to support my mission."

I ask, "So why didn't you get him to do all of your nasty dirty work? Why did you tag me for all of your ugly work?"

I hear something outside the hangar. Before Gunter can answer the question, I hit him square in the jaw with a left, to silence him. He lies unconscious on the bench as I listen to feet shuffling outside the back door. I am expecting the small man whom I saw near the downed German helicopter to show up, sooner or later. What I didn't expect is for the shuffling outside to sound like three or maybe four other people.

I pick up the night vision goggles and place them on my head in the ready position. I reach over and flip the light switch off; the interior of the hangar goes pitch black. I flip the goggles down. It is an unfair advantage -- the only way to go into combat.

They are whispering to each other outside the entrance door to the hangar. Two of them move away from that door, in the direction of the big hangar door. One of the amateurs who stays near the back door actually turns his flashlight on before he attempts to enter.

The door cracks open a little.

The barrel of a shotgun pokes through the opening. I grab the barrel and lift it straight up; it discharges. With a little assistance from yours truly, the recoiling gun stock knocks the shooter to the ground. I stomp on his right hand to keep him from attacking me, and look for the luckless intruder's associates. One is high-tailing it away from the back door as fast as possible. Two others are running towards me, yelling and screaming, "Henry, are you all right? Are you shot?" They round the corner, and I easily grab the weapons out of their hands before they even realize that I'm there.

One is a woman; one is a boy whom I suspect is the small man I had previously seen near the downed German helicopter.

"I'm OK," the shotgun-toting local says. "I'm OK. Except for a crushed hand, I'm OK."

The fortyish woman with a weather-worn face finally looks at me, and says, "My God, soldier, why are you here? Why are you in our hangar, and what do you want? We're a poor sheep-farming and fishing community here. We don't normally have crime of any kind on this island. What would a Special Forces soldier like you want with us? Damn, you're a big bloke! It's obvious that you could have killed my husband if you wanted to, so what is it you want?"

The husband says, "Maybe if you shut up for a second, he'll have a chance to tell us."

She takes a breath long enough for me to speak. "A helicopter made an emergency landing at your air strip, here."

"Yes, we saw it," she says; "were you on it?"

"Mom," says the boy; "will you give this man a chance to tell us?"

I take the chance that I might be able to finish a sentence: "The pilot of the helicopter kidnapped a close friend of mine and is holding her against her will. I tracked him down, here in your airplane hangar. I have him tied to a bench and intend to learn from him -- using any means at my disposal -- the location of the love of my life. I was about to question him when you decided to investigate what was going on, here.

"What I want from you is the temporary use of the hangar. It won't take me long, and I'll clean up the mess afterwards. If you could stand guard so that no one else interrupts me, I'd appreciate that, as a sign of your hospitality."

They are thinking. To help them along, I stand the weapons against the wall. I have at least ten different lethal weapons within reach. The alternatives to supporting my activities soon don't appear very attractive to them.

The woman says, "We have a propane torch in the shop if that will help speed up the ...." She hesitates, and uses her fingers to make quotation marks and then continues, "to help speed up the interrogation."

Foula Island: Korf doesn't last long. The missus sends her husband and boy home to get us some food, and gleefully cranks up the torch using her spark lighter. She goes straight for Gunter's genitals with the 3,000 degree flame, and suffers real disappointment when he confesses to everything -- including the whereabouts of Jolene -- after only her first burn. She places a steel plate behind his ear and begins melting his earlobe. She also promises him that she will help by burning off every mole on his disgusting body. It is evident to the Korf-man that she is going to have a good time at his expense if he doesn't answer my questions immediately.

Korf discloses that Jolene is being held prisoner on an abandoned oil rig 300 miles away, owned by a French conglomerate. The oil platform is permanently abandoned, meaning that Jolene will eventually starve to death. They believe that, after the White House Counsel mission was ordered canceled by the Deutsch Chamber, she is only a liability. Korf also admits that the rig is unguarded.

"What is your end game?"

The sadistic female sheep farmer says, "Answer his question or I'll melt a hole in the head of your pathetically little penis."

I grab the torch from the demented lady before she succeeds in her sick quest. He screams in relief and understands that I'm the only thing stopping the sadistic crazy lady from cutting him into pieces. Gunter Korf is now clay in my hands.

"My customer wants Viktor Soroson dead and the former First Lady discredited and ruined, so that she cannot be elected president."

I ask, "Are you certain that they are guilty of the murder of the White House attorney?"

"No, but my client has good reason to believe the two of them are complicit in some way. We were hoping that your investigation would prove it."

"It would have been cheaper, safer, and easier if you had just hired us."

"My customer wanted to be anonymous. Now please, sir, stop this sadistic woman from torturing me."

"My second question is ...." I hesitate as she cranks up a welding machine and welds a chain link to a plate on one side of his neck, and then starts welding the other end of the chain to the same plate on the other side of his neck. I'm pretty sure this guy is never going to leave this island. I finish my question, "What were Richard Kingsley's and the attorney Harold Andrews' roles in all this?"

The chain is tight across his neck, but he could still speak. He asks, "Who?"

I think that his answer to my question is genuine. He apparently didn't have anything to do with hiring the two people who were spying on Powers at the *Brown Leaf Cigar Bar.*

She doesn't believe him. She keeps on torching him long after he passes out in pain.

Gunter Korf has met his match. I couldn't watch after she pulled out a drill. He kidnapped Jolene and though he hadn't hurt Jolene to the best of my knowledge, I suspect that he plans to let her die when their mission was over. He deserves his just reward.

I pick up all the weapons and leave the hangar. It is time for Powers to pick me up to fly to the coast of Aberdeen, Scotland.

If it had only been that simple.

Foula Island: "Powers," I ask, "are you on the way back here or are you sitting at a poker table somewhere, drinking Scotch?"

"I love flying this thing after I've drunk a little Scotch. You're in Norway, right?"

"ETA?" I ask.

"Another 25 minutes."

"Loaded?"

"Everyone volunteered. Even Gatling!" There is no weapon more awesome than a fully-equipped 50-caliber Gatling gun.

Foula Island: They slide out of the sea like reptiles -- killers in the night with only one purpose in mind. Little do they know that they're too late. Orders are orders, though -- they had to provide proof of the kill. The death squad quickly locates Gunter Korf; he is already dead -- killed in the most grotesque of ways. The hired killers take photos of his tortured body, use a pipe cutter to remove his thumb, place it in a Ziploc bag, and head back out the hangar door. Mother Sickwoman is hiding from the new intruders, but accidentally knocks over some tools, revealing her location. She is shot through the heart three times.

I sense the sound of the silencer shots; it's more like a metaphysical experience. I pull my thermal scope out of my BDU pants pocket and lie low, weapon safeties off.

There are four of them. They move effortlessly, quickly, and smoothly toward the water. I hear Powers' helicopter approaching -- timing is everything. The four rubber-suiters react to the sound of the Lynx helicopter. It is obvious that they feel threatened, and are prepared to fight.

"Powers," I say over the com, "I'd wander south a little before landing. There are four Special Forces folks here ready to take you on, since they heard your approach. There must be a ship nearby; check it out."

Powers answers, "Tank, I'm still ten minutes out. There is no way they could have heard me."

"Fuck," I say to myself; "This little island with only 38 -- or rather 37 -- residents has suddenly become a focal point with an international flavor. And I'm out here in the middle of the landing strip totally vulnerable to thermal imaging. I've got to find cover."

The helicopter gunship overhead begins strafing the island with 50-caliber rounds. Fortunately for me, the gunship targets the four men on the beach, trying to reach the water. All four are torn to hamburger meat before the gunship explodes from a hellfire missile launched from the fast attack boat waiting for the return of the Special Forces unit.

The debris from the exploding helicopter falls all around me; a piece of hot metal brushes against me. I roll away from it just in time to avoid another piece of the debris, this one weighing at least 300 pounds, which lands on the spot where I was.

Then there is absolute darkness and silence. I don't move; I hardly breathe, and I wait there in the weeds for Powers to arrive.

I think to myself, "What the hell is going on? I'm missing something."

Over the North Atlantic Ocean: On the way to the Elgin PUQ oil platform, 150 miles off Aberdeen on Scotland's east coast, Powers receives a call from MI-5 agent Stone Garry.

"My condolences, Powers, for the loss of your friends, Ray LaSalle and Damian LaTorre; they were good people and conducted themselves professionally."

I look at Powers and can tell that his antennae are alerted, just as mine are, sensing that this Brit is trying to manipulate the situation to his advantage in some way.

I ask, "Stone," do you have anything to do with the battle that just raged on Foula Island?"

"Yes," he answers; "I was monitoring your progress, tracking the activities on the *Kenda Rose* that we loaned to you for your mission; I witnessed the refueling and takeoff of the WG-13 Lynx helicopter we loaned to you, and monitored the communications between you two.

"And what thanks do I get? You incapacitate the *Kenda Rose*'s captain, commit cyber theft of top secret data, and run off to attack a French-owned oil platform. You are trying your bloody damn best to start an international crisis."

I interrupt Stone and ask again, "Was that a British helicopter that exploded over Foula? Who were the Special Forces men who were killed on that little island?"

Stone dismisses my question. "What's important is that they know you are coming. They want you dead, Tank. They don't care one way or the other about Jolene anymore, but they want you, Powers, and Maya Cherokee dead. They think you three know something that implicates the people who funded Gunter Korf's operation. You're flying into a trap. So, I thought you guys could use a little … heads-up, as you say."

On the Elgin PUQ: She had always wondered what she would do if it happened. The electricity goes out and it becomes pitch black in her oil rig condo. She has no flashlight, no lighters or matches, no cell phone light, no lap-top computer which could be used to light her surroundings, no candles, no nothing.

After about thirty minutes of lying on her back on her bed, she feels her other senses sharpen. She hears new sounds, feel new vibrations, and smells new odors. Were the sounds really new, or does she just sense them now that she is effectively blind?

Jolene decides that the sounds, the vibrations, and the smells are new. Something is going down. She decides that she needs to stay close to her only weapon -- a four-inch steak knife.

261

On the Elgin PUQ: The six mercenaries on the French
energy giant's oil platform have learned that Gunter Korf's
attempt to eliminate Tank Alvarez and Powers has failed. They
have further learned that Korf made an emergency landing on a
small island and that he was subsequently killed. With their
boss dead, that leaves the second-in-command, Konrad
Schneiderer, as the mission leader. Their customer, The
Deutsche Chamber, made their assignment clear: "Assume that
Korf revealed their secret and eliminate **anyone** who may have
learned of that secret. And since they will be trying to save the
hostage, stay close and ambush the entire crew which might
come to save her."

After cutting the electricity to the oil platform, Schneiderer
stays up top with a heat-seeking, shoulder-fired 105mm RPG-29
launcher and five rockets. Three of his underlings stand nearby,
vigilantly surveying the sky and the ocean with night-vision
binoculars and long rifles. Two mercenaries go down below
with high illumination tactical flashlights to find a place to sleep.
The team rotates shifts, in the event that this mission might last
longer than eighteen hours.

It doesn't.

The mercenary on the west side of the platform sees it first
and says, "Commander, incoming at nine o'clock."

Schneiderer speaks through his headset to the other
professional soldier on deck, "Go down and muster the others.
Return and ready the RPGs."

"Yes, sir."

"I hear it now, Commander; it may be an armed UAV."

Schneiderer grabs a rocket, leans down into firing position, and waits for the drone to get within range.

On the North Sea: The Royal Navy's Echo class ship displaces 3740 metric tons and supports a helipad on which the rescue team's Lynx helicopter sits.   Powers, Sonja, and I watch them launch the General Atomics MQ-9 Reaper Unmanned Air Vehicle equipped with 500 pound laser guided Hellfire missiles and anti-interceptors, and it quickly passes overhead.

The three of us are sitting on top of the rolling sea in a Seamagine Hydrospace Aurora-3C.

But not for long.

The launch of the Reaper is our signal to dive.   The dual 40kW direct-current electric powerhouses with venturi-shaped thrusters push us to submerge with Sonja piloting the mini submarine; we navigate with our GPS guidance system to the oil platform.

On the Elgin PUQ: The six mercenaries on the top deck are watching the RF distance monitor as the drone closes in to within 300 meters.

"You know," says the perspiring second-in-command, "some UAVs are equipped with Hellfires."

Schneiderer says, "No way they'll fire at us, as long as the lady down below is alive."

"Is she?"

"I don't know. We've been instructed to have no contact with her.

"If we fire a rocket at them and take down the drone, then we will have provoked someone with a 17-million-dollar toy. I don't know who these guys are, but they probably have the financial capability to out-gun us. We don't want to poke them in the eyes. Let's watch the UAV and see how close it gets."

It gets close enough for the six mercenaries to see the intimidating Hellfire missiles under the Reaper MQ-9's wings.

"Sir," says one of the mercenaries, "I think the Hellfire lasers have locked in on us!"

Schneiderer says, "Launch, now."

The UAV has circled to within only 150 yards; well within the RPG-29's range. The mercenaries do not know that the UAV is equipped with an Israeli-supplied anti-rocket interceptor which activates immediately upon sensing the incoming rocket. It explodes the first RPG rocket before it reaches the Reaper.

"Mutterficker," says Schneiderer, "we're up against more than a tiny band of American independent rescuers. I've never seen an RPG rocket intercepted before."

The UAV circles the Elgin PUQ repeatedly without incident as a diversion until we reach the rig in the mini-submarine. Powers and I climb onto the platform as Sonja stays onboard as the pilot of the submersible. It takes me a good ten minutes to reach the upper platform where the six mercenaries are preoccupied with the UAV. Powers is not far behind me.

I aim my laser-sighted 40-caliber Sig Sauer P226 at the chest of the guy who is their apparent leader.

His second-in-command says, "Uh, sir ... I think we've been compromised."

Schneiderer seems confused. The subordinate nods his head in the direction of his commander's chest.

Schneiderer sees the laser dot on his chest and looks in my direction. Though I am shielded behind a steel I-beam, he recognizes where I'm located. Then a second dot appears on his chest.

The second-in-command spins and fires his Ruger SR45 in Powers' direction. It is time to open fire. I put a 40-caliber round into the shooter's throat, causing his head to drop as if he were a ragdoll. This human blood-geyser collapses in a heap with body appendages projecting at unusual angles.

Schneiderer throws himself to the deck and rolls behind a storage locker; the remaining four mercenaries split up and dive away haphazardly in different directions. They don't have ear buds or headsets and, as a result, cannot communicate. Their response to our assault is to fire their weapons.

One of the men unloads his only magazine from his AR-12 semi-automatic. Powers puts a hollow point round into his thigh, dropping him like he'd been tackled by a linebacker. Once down, Powers finishes him off with a round into his left eye. It was not exactly where he was aiming, but it would do.

A third mercenary circles around behind my position with his 9mm Glock, but I am able to shield myself from the attack behind the steel structure. Then he tries to attack me with a knife. Before he can thrust it in my direction, I put two rounds into his forehead.

The fourth mercenary doesn't have a weapon, and has no idea who he is dealing with when he tries to work on Powers from behind. It's comical; no contest. His neck breaks before he hits the deck.

The fifth mercenary is good. He isn't carrying a pistol, but he somehow comes out from the shadows and inserts his Kaybar into my vest. It provides enough resistance for me to throw a 500-horsepower elbow into his throat. The sound he makes with a fractured wind pipe reminds me of an old Buick with a bad muffler which I once owned.

Schneiderer is the last man standing; he has three laser dots on his forehead. We both turn to see Sonja holding one of the H&Ks. Powers says, "I thought you were going to stay in the sub!" She just smiles at her dad.

I hope that this remaining private-military guy will surrender; I want to interrogate him.

He does.

Powers controls Schneiderer and binds him with plastic tie fasteners around his wrists while Sonja massages his ear canal with the barrel of her black Sig. Powers then radios the captain of the Echo to have Knight Beta fly the British Lynx helicopter to the Elgin oil platform along with Knight Delta.

While Powers is directing mission traffic, I calmly lift the restrained Schneiderer off the deck by his jacket collar with my right hand and leave his feet dangling helplessly trying to find ground. I stick my big angry face a millimeter from his -- we could smell each other's breath. I used my other hand to pull my six-inch tactical blade and touched its tip into the puffy flesh under the bag of his right eye.

I engage my four-wheel-drive attitude and ask, "Where is Jolene?"

The rent-a-soldier says, "The Schlampe is on Level C, Corridor C3, Room C21."

The man hits the deck with a dull kerrump.

I take out my flashlight and cautiously enter the stairwell to the lower levels. There could be more mercenaries below deck, so I vigilantly take a cautious approach. I find Room C21 within four minutes and stare at the door imprisoning her.

I yell out loud, "Jolene, are you behind this door? Are you OK?"

She answers, "Thank God! It's you!" We talk loudly enough to communicate through the steel door while I survey for a bomb. I am fearful that the door is booby trapped like the first oil platform we were on earlier today … fearful that something terrible might result from my opening this heavy door.

The door is barred. After a thorough inspection, I lift the bar and open the door. Cold stale air escapes quickly, followed by a joyous, but tearful, Jolene.

She's a lot stronger than she looks. I'm not sure that I could have broken away from the bear hug she had on me. But, of course, I don't want to -- I hope that she never lets go.

I kiss her salty tears away, run my hands through her hair, and repeatedly say, "I love you." She is shaking from the cold and she's an emotional wreck -- laughing while crying.

Then I remember.

I fumble for the package which Maya had given me, stuffed into one of my shirt pockets. I gently roll over out of the hug and get down on one knee, open the package, and say, "Will you marry me?"

The diamond is too big, but the ring size is perfect. Jolene can't stop crying long enough to say yes, so she shakes her head up and down. Then she reaches up and wipes the tear running down **my** cheek.

CHAPTER 46 -- TMI

Alexandria, Virginia: After practicing their delivery in front of a mirror, Richard Kingsley and his new friend, Melody, dress professionally and walk into the BB&T branch in Alexandria, trying their best not to act nervous. They ask to see a bank Vice President; Richard presents him the key, and then asks for access to the safe deposit box. The banker looks into his records and says, "Yes, Mr. Kingsley, this safe deposit box is registered in your name. Please, follow me."

Richard and Melody exchange glances, both of them wondering how the safe deposit box came to be registered in his name. The banker uses the two keys to pull the box out and then brings the box down, sets it on a table and leaves them alone to examine the contents.

Richard takes a deep breath before he flips the box top back to view the contents. The box contains only one thing, a Ziploc bag. In the Ziploc bag is a gun -- a dark blue- steel revolver.

Richard says to Melody, "Do you realize what we have here? I bet that this is the gun the FBI claimed was at the scene of the death of the White House attorney -- the gun my father claimed wasn't there when he arrived first at the scene.   Why isn't this gun with the FBI? The chain of custody has obviously been broken!

"I have to call in to the 'three manipulators' at 10:00 A.M. I need some answers."

Caracas, Venezuela and St. Petersburg, Russia: Twenty-two chess moves later, Yuri Prociv and Viktor Soroson agree that they have reached a stalemate; neither chess master has won. A stalemate is a lot like a tie in soccer -- very unsatisfying.

As a famous philosopher once said, "It's a lot like kissing your sister."

Soroson Skypes with Prociv and asks, "How much will it cost me to buy the information I want from you?"

Yuri Prociv gets excited, his heart rate accelerates, and his semi-crippled hands begin to shake. He doesn't want to leave a lot of money on the table so he counters, "How much is it worth to you?"

Soroson is an experienced negotiator, "Not a damn thing unless I can validate the authenticity of the documents. A lot, if they are authentic, and conclusive."

"Trust is a difficult commodity to obtain. There is no way for us to trust each other. So, to that end, I will agree to a joint account where you deposit five million dollars in rubles. You can arrange it so I don't have access to the account until you authorize access. You arrange and pay for my travel expenses to Caracas and I'll bring the originals to you. Of course, I'll keep a photocopy of the documents here.

"But you have to promise me that you will pay me, regardless of what you discover in these documents.

"There's an old but wise saying, Viktor: 'Be careful what you wish for.'"

Wiscasset, Maine: Lucas invites Carmen out to dinner at the best restaurant in town. It is their first real date. Lucas organizes a surprise for Carmen ... by inviting other esteemed guests to join them.

It is still relatively early in the evening; remnants of daylight linger, and they are the first to enter the restaurant which is just opening for the evening meal. Lucas orders a local dark beer while Carmen orders some hot tea.

Carmen asks, "Do you know the origin of the word, Wiscasset? It sounds like it might have an American Indian origin."

"I'm told that it means 'coming out of the harbor but you don't see where.'"

Lucas recognizes the trouble before she does. Five tough-looking oriental guys walk in and fix their gaze on the two of them. Lucas mentions to Carmen, "What do think the odds are that the Chinese mafia would show up here in an out-of-the-way Wiscasset, Maine restaurant where you just happen to be having supper? Ten to the minus something, right? You need to figure out a way to move around behind me. I will protect you."

The leader of the hit squad nods to a soldier who then locks the entrance door. He says something in Mandarin to another soldier, who disappears into the kitchen. Lucas thinks, "Good, four adversaries is better than five."

The obvious leader of the group walks towards the table where Lucas and Carmen are sitting, and says in unaccented English to Carmen while maintaining eye contact with Lucas, "You are quite resourceful, Miss Brave. We lost you for a few days, but you had to know that eventually we'd find you. We will punish you for your indiscretions, but you do have a chance to redeem yourself, and save the life of your father. Just come with me; your body guard here can't save you from your past sins. As they say, 'that bell has been rung, it can't be un-rung.'"

A restaurant patron is banging on the front door to the restaurant, asking to be let in. The leader yells again to one of his gang, in Mandarin. There is a little scuffle at the front door but it is over quickly.

The leader then says to Lucas, "Mr. Carmen Brave Bodyguard, you didn't sign up for this. You probably had no idea what you were getting into when you decided to guard Ms. Brave."

Lucas smiles and says, "Back at you."

The leader of the Chinese gang asks, "What do you mean, 'back at you'?"

Lucas says with an uncharacteristically broad smile, "You probably had no idea what **you** were getting into."

"You aren't that good, Mr. Bodyguard."

Standing right behind the Chinaman, I announce, "Yes, he is." The leader looks around for his team. Powers, standing by my side, says "If you're looking for your muscle, they're taking a nap." Sonja has her 40-caliber Sig Sauer P226 aimed in the leader's direction while Jolene has her Smith and Wesson Military and Police 9mm pistol to guard their flank.

The Chinese strong man addresses Carmen: "Goodbye. For now." He backs away slowly, moving too near me for his own good, and with quick sleight-of-hand, reaches into his pocket for who-knows-what. I grab his wrist with one hand and his throat with the other. The Chinese martial arts expert tries some sort of well-practiced kick move, only to have it blocked immediately by Powers, and the barrel of Sonja's Sig is suddenly wedged against his temple.

I ask Powers, "How do say 'dumber than a box of rocks' in Mandarin?"

"He may be dumb, but he's damned dangerous."

I look at Lucas and Carmen and ask, "Sending this hood on his way isn't going to put an end to it, is it?"

Carmen shakes her head.

"What will put an end to him or someone like him from coming around?"

"I'm a 'dead woman walking' until Brave Chicken Corporation honors an illegal bad deal I got them into," Carmen answers.

"The only people I know who could help you with a business problem like that are likely to walk through that door in the next few minutes. In the meantime we'll provide you with protection.

"Did you hear that, Kung Fu or Fuk Yu or whatever your name is? Miss Brave is now under tight security. Tell your dynasty bosses that we'll contact somebody soon. Now leave before my friend's daughter puts a new vent hole in the side of your head. Here, we'll even help you drag your Keystone Cops out into the street."

Powers, Lucas, Sonja, Jolene and I drag the four other Chinese Mafiosos out into the cold, and suggest that they drive south for the next month or so.

Sonja leans close to Powers, "Wedged under his shirt collar." Powers smiles and nods his approval that Sonja had planted a tracker on the Chinese enforcer.

As we walk back into the restaurant, the classic Cossack-looking proprietor has her arms across her chest with an angry expression on her face. I say 'she,' but I've never been completely sure. Maybe if she shaved more often, she'd look more feminine.

She says, "Why is it that the only time we have any kind of trouble in this restaurant, it's because you or that partner-in-crime of yours bless us with your presence?"

Powers answers before I do: "You must lead a boring life, then, if we're your only excitement. Just for you, we'll try to come here more often."

Her -- I assume -- eyes brighten, her expression changes and her facial muscles transform into a facsimile of a smile; she is looking past me. "Mr. and Mrs. Cherokee, I'm **so** glad to see you. Please, let me take your outerwear and secure it in our coat closet. And may I take your hats?"

Maya and Star ignore the proprietor and instead go to Sonja and Jolene, to give each of them big hugs.

Three tables have been pushed together, and the nine diners are sitting around with multiple conversations going on simultaneously. Jolene is talking to Maya, Sonja, and Star about the upcoming wedding. Lucas is talking to Tank about whether or not the judge learned about his leaving the country. Powers

and Tucker are talking about when and where Ray LaSalle and
Damian LaTorre's memorial services were going to take place.

Until my phone rings.

St. Petersburg, Russia: The musty smell of mold fills the
underground bunker. Yuri has explained to his superiors many
times that the rooms containing all of these old artifacts need to
be climate controlled -- at least to reduce the humidity. He
might as well have been talking to a brick wall.

The Wilhelm Soroson reports are marginally legible, but to
some extent that reinforces their authenticity. He allows the files
to air-dry before he places them in large envelopes. He
ultimately places the bags in a Halliburton case and rolls the
combination lock number wheels to lock it. Yuri has never been
out of Eastern Europe, and is both excited and apprehensive to
have a chance to travel to Venezuela. Most of his apprehension
is about getting caught with a fake Lithuanian passport sent to
him by overnight mail from Viktor Soroson. However, the
passport appears to be an excellent forgery.

Yuri is also apprehensive about how Viktor might react
when he reads the files his namesake drafted seventy years ago.
He clearly understands that he has just stepped out onto a very
slippery slope.

Washington, D.C. and Wiscasset, Maine: "OK, this is
what I want. I want Tucker to give me a raise, I want my own

chauffer, and I want a date with Maya's sister. You can make that happen, right?"

Jimmy Ma is too excited to wait for an answer. "You see, I tracked back to the source of funds for the 'chess pieces' who tried to kill your entire team in Boston. I know who pays the leader of the Fischer Men."

"Fishermen! What the hell are you talking about, Jimmy?" At the mention of the word "fishermen," I notice that all conversation at the table goes silent. Apparently, I'm the last one to know what Jimmy is talking about. I put my phone on speaker, "Jimmy, you're on speaker. Do you want to ask Tucker for that raise real-time, and do you want to ask Maya to set you up on a date with her sister … in person?"

Jimmy stutters, "Well, uh, if I had a choice, I'd rather have that date with Maya's sister than the raise -- but the chauffer is non-negotiable."

I ask impatiently, "Spill it, Jimmy, what do you have?"

"I not only know who funds the Fischer Men; I also know how to give them an assignment, pretending to be their benefactor. Don't you agree that's worth a date with Suzanne?"

Tucker speaks calmly but authoritatively, "Cut the crap, Jimmy. Who is trying to kill Maya and Powers?"

"You already know that Viktor Sorenson funds the guy called Rook and the rest of the Fischer Men who, by the way, are named after the chess master Bobby Fischer. You also know, from my previous fine work, that he funds the former First Lady's presidential campaign, but what I can now prove is that the Rook was paid by Soroson to cover-up the murder of the White House Counsel. Their relationship goes back at least two decades. That's why I called Tank and not you, boss."

Powers asks, "Cover-up the murder, not execute the murder? How could you discover that through just the tracking of money?"

"Powers, if I tell you all my secrets, I won't be so valuable to you guys."

Tucker asks, "Do you know where Soroson is, now, by tracking the money transfers?"

There is silence for a few seconds as Jimmy is thinking about how he might best leverage the information. Finally, it is Maya who broke the silence, as she winks at Tucker.

"I can put in a good word for you with Suzanne."

"Really! He's in Caracas, Venezuela.

"And I've got more."

"You're getting a lot closer to that chauffer you're lobbying for," I tease.

"Mr. Soroson did not escape to Caracas alone. He has a protégé, a lover, a Jonestown cool-aid-drinking follower with him who supports his megalomaniacal ambitions. It's the glue that ties everything together with a neat little bow. This person had motive, opportunity, and means to pull off the murder of the White House Counsel."

"Jimmy," Maya asks, "you're not suggesting that, uh, someone involved with the cover-up of the murder of the White House attorney is in Caracas with Soroson, are you?"

"Bingo! Can you give me Suzanne's phone number now?"

The people at the table are excited and animated in their discussion about what all the information Jimmy Ma delivered meant. Tucker wants to put an end to the Fischer Men and is discussing with Jolene how to trap the killers. Powers and Maya are strategizing about solving the mystery surrounding the death of the White House lawyer. I am talking to Lucas and Carmen about how the former First Lady fits into all this.

One by one, the conversations become subdued and finally stop. All eyes are on Star. She has that aura about her; she is in a zone, concentrating on Sonja.

All eyes move to watch Sonja, who knows about Star's special skills.

"OK, OK" Sonja confesses, "I took out the two Fischer Men in Boston who were attempting to assassinate my father and Maya."

Wiscasset, Maine: My phone rings, again.

The implication that Sonja knew that Powers was in danger from the Fischer Men, ahead of anyone else at the table, screams volumes. There are too many questions needing answers for the people in the restaurant to quickly process.

My phone rings a second time.

Finally, I answer the phone; "Yeah."

"Hello, is this Tank?"

"Yes."

"Tank, this is Richard Kingsley. Hey, I'm glad you made it out of jail."

"Richard, this isn't a good time. Can you call me back at some other time?"

"Tank. Don't hang up. I have important information I need to share with you about the death of the White House lawyer and my father."

"Richard," I admit, "I really don't give a flying, ah, pig about who killed the White House Counsel twenty years ago anymore. I've got my lady back and don't need to solve the crime to support some radical asshole's political agenda."

The people sitting with me at the table begin to fret, to look at me agitatedly and questioningly, so I put my phone on speaker.

"OK Richard, what's new?   What have you discovered? You're on speaker."

"The White House Counsel had a second wound in his neck not disclosed by the autopsy. He was moved to the scene of the alleged and staged suicide. I have the gun that was placed at the scene to make it look like a suicide … and the former First Lady was being blackmailed. I have a copy of the blackmail photo."

We are all processing the new information when Maya asks, "You have the gun? How could you come to possess something which should be locked up in an FBI evidence locker?"

"Yes, I have the gun. It's currently in a safe deposit box. As to how I have it, well, because someone chose me as the next target, I guess. Do you have any idea who that might be? The old mystery enthusiasts at the *Brown Leaf Cigar Bar* have been most prolific with information on this case; a little too prolific."

I start to say something, but Maya jumps in again and says, "You need to get that gun to Tony Vinci in Boston somehow."

Tucker stops Maya before she discloses any more information, "You need protection, as I suspect there are people who don't want you to learn how your father was killed, or the details about what he knew of the death of the White House lawyer. We need to provide you with an escort to our labs at *Entropy Entrepreneurs.*"

"Richard," I add, "you are not calling from a secure phone. Can you find your way to the place where we first met? We'll provide you protection and escort you under armed guard to the safe deposit box, and then on to the lab. Be there eighteen hours from now. Stay low. Is anyone else aware of the information you just shared with us?"

"Yes, the three people previously at the cigar bar … and my lady friend, Melody."

"Melody who? We need to check her out."

"Uh," Richard realizes with embarrassment that he doesn't know her last name. "Oh, damn. You don't suspect….." He lets it fade, and goes on to say "I'll be more careful and reach the rendezvous point alone."

I repeat, "Eighteen hours from now.   Synchronize your watch with mine."

We disconnect the line.

I look at Tucker, "OK, my friend, what do you know that I don't, that's so important to protect Richard and secure the gun?"

Before Tucker could answer, Maya says, "Tucker, the patent application has been submitted.   Disclosure of the description of the patent will not endanger the value of the discovery.   Besides that, the unpatented trade secrets are locked away according to *Entropy Entrepreneur* protocols."

"Sweetheart," says Tucker gently, "It wasn't that long ago when a colleague of ours was murdered because he partially disclosed benign information over a dinner in a restaurant just like this."

Tucker looks me in the eye, "Later, in a different environment."

And that was that. For now.

CHAPTER 47 -- THE MANIFESTO

Caracas, Venezuela: *We must curtail American sovereignty in order to create a one world government committed to proportionally equalizing world resources. Energy is not the province of a short list of economic powerhouse nations; energy resources belong to all of the people on earth. We must defeat America first, before we can share the earth's resources. But, we cannot defeat America militarily. We cannot defeat America by going door to door. To defeat American sovereignty, we must kill it from within; we must plant a malignancy that will weaken its resolve -- one brick at a time."*

Viktor Soroson continues to write his manifesto in his derisive manuscript, his Godless bible: *"Insofar as there are collective interests that transcend state boundaries, America must become subservient to international bodies, under international law, in a borderless world. America must have its own Federal Reserve subordinate to the World Bank and International Monetary Fund."*

Viktor feels a slight pain in his chest and realizes he hasn't taken his medicine. He speaks loudly, "My Dear, would you bring me my pills?"

His "Dear" is twenty-seven years younger than Viktor, and probably 40 years younger in health, but is dedicated to Viktor Soroson as if he were her God. She is his mentee, student, groupie, lover, worshipper and ideological follower. He recognizes his own mortality but believes that his mission, his ideology, his Godless religion is immortal. His follower is in her late forties, five feet seven inches tall, maybe ten pounds overweight, grey mixed with dirty blond hair, and green eyes.

The billionaire initiated a plan over thirty years ago to cultivate someone to follow in his ideological footsteps. His lady is helping him to draft his manifesto. She supports his multi-generational plan to fund causes to advance his one-world

279

government philosophy. She believes in his "philanthropic" activities to bring the unfairly wealthy down to the same level as the pathetic, downtrodden, disadvantaged and poor people of the world.

Both Soroson and his lady-follower view him as a messianic figure. She enjoys hearing his megalomaniacal comments like his famous quote, *"I admit that I operate under an exaggerated view of my self-importance; I believe that I am some kind of god"* or *"I carry some messianic fantasies within me, which I feel that I occasionally have under control."*

She brings him his pills with a bottle of water. After he takes his heart medicine, she gets down on her knees and kisses his hand. She would, and has, done anything he has asked of her over the past two decades. To suit her mentor, her god, her messiah, she wears a classic French-maid costume including a black with white trim one-piece dress with a full skirt above her knees, white half-apron with lace, a ruffled headpiece, long fishnet stockings, long black socks with white ribbons, a white lace garter, and high heels. She wears pearls which Viktor gave her, and carries a feather-duster. And she wears no underwear, to show off her pronounced genital features. She is totally **whacked**, as crazy as bat-shit.

Whimsically, Viktor muses about how lucky he has been to have found her. She is the only person on earth whom he trusts to ensure his legacy. That's why he allows her to manage his philanthropic contributions; she has Carte Blanche access to millions of his billions.

He continues to write: *"As expected, the decadent citizens of America have grown to accept less and less freedom and less sovereignty in order to maintain peace with soft and comfortable prosperity. A majority of the American people are now willing to vote for a candidate whose political platform espouses government control of their lives. The candidates for president of the United States which we have funded and cultivated are now positioned to advance the cause of a one-world government.*

Highly educated Master-race elitists feel or need to feel superior to others. They believe that they are more intelligent than others, and want to distance themselves from the common people, or their prejudiced vision of the common people, whom they distain. They need to believe that they are aristocrats, a universe apart from those incapable of making the correct decisions in life. If someone disagrees with a German elitist, it is because that person is hateful, ignorant, selfish or unenlightened; there is no possibility that it is because the elitist is wrong. The highly educated elite feel compelled to make decisions for those obviously incapable of making sound decisions. I have observed that the highly educated elite genuinely believe that those who have not had the benefit of exposure to superior thinking cannot possibly comprehend the concepts of macroeconomics, advanced social paradigms, and enlightenment. The German elite are prejudiced against those who do not share their position of superiority. The very people who vociferously condemn bigotry in others are among the most bigoted. To this we must put an end."

He stops writing and decides to check cable news to see how bad things are going in Germany. He wants to hear that the country is beginning to collapse and that the people of Germany are suffering from the attack on German industry and the attack on European currency. After thirty minutes of surfing through English-speaking news networks, he calls on his lady, French-maid, student, confidant, and partner. He calls-out, "My dear, would you get Ahmed Mohammad on the line for me? I think it's time to begin Phase Three."

The immigration officer at Simon Bolivar International Airport is dutifully checking his passport for authenticity. He scans the document with a UV light, furrows his forehead, and looks at Yuri Prociv suspiciously. The officer observes a small sixtyish man with a grey and white goatee dressed in a black cassock, black pants, and a clerical collar. He asks the Russian Orthodox Priest something in Spanish. Yuri responds in Russian.

The officer stares into Yuri's eyes and says in English, "Why, Father, did you come to Venezuela? What is the purpose of your visit?"

"I'm here to visit a very old man who asked for me personally to perform his last rights."

The officer stamps his Lithuanian passport and Yuri Prociv proceeds through immigration control with his carry-on Halliburton briefcase into the overcrowded, hot, humid, and odorous walkway, then down to the baggage claim area where he is accosted by sensory overload. Nothing is like Russia. He feels like he has been transported to a parallel universe, as the culture, the people, and the ambience are too dissimilar to be on the same planet.

He walks slowly and deliberately in the direction of ground transportation with the intention of finding an exit to get some fresh air and make cell phone contact with Viktor Soroson, but before he reaches the exit, three men in suits stop directly before him. One of them says in English, "Father Prociv, please come with us. Your chess opponent is expecting you."

Yuri nods acceptance of the situation, but feels his heartbeat accelerate in anxiety. He is escorted to a waiting Mercedes limousine with tinted windows where he is treated by his newfound bodyguards with gentleness and courtesy. Two of the men ride with him in the limousine while one follows behind in a black Land Rover.

The ride from the airport to his destination seems interminable, as he views the squalor, the congestion, the poverty, and the misery which hapless Venezuelans have inherited. Yuri feels a chill run down his spine as they look back at the tinted glass with hate and envy in their eyes. He is pleased when they finally reach Viktor's mansion in LaLagunita. The limo stops under a canopy; his back door opens for him, and a smiling man who must be Soroson's butler says, "Father Prociv, welcome to the Soroson Estate. I will escort you to your room where you can freshen up before you meet with the host."

The butler's body language stiffens, and his smile becomes less genuine when he asks, "Did you bring the important documents for which Mr. Soroson is waiting?"

"Well, well, Yuri, you appear in person just as you do on Skype -- quite the well-executed cover."

"Cover?" asks Yuri.

"Please, don't insult me," responds Viktor; "I do my homework. I needed to know in advance of depositing funds in your name and in advance of your visit whether or not it was even remotely possible that you could have access to the documents you claimed to have there in the vault."

"So then," Yuri recovers, "you must know that the documents are authentic and exceedingly valuable to you. You'll learn your true heritage -- whose sperm was used to impregnate your mother."

Viktor starts to hyperventilate, sweat appears on his forehead as he asks, "You must already know. Who is my father?"

"Dear Viktor," Yuri says in a condescending tone, "you need to read the documents yourself in a private setting. It is unfair to you that I just blurt it out. I don't think you'll trust my answer unless you read the report by your namesake, Dr. Wilhelm Soroson."

Yuri Prociv spins the wheels to unlock the Halliburton briefcase which contain the treasured documents for Viktor Soroson.

All four of their hands shake in trepidation as the transfer is completed.

CHAPTER 48 -- THE PIECES START TO FIT

Alexandria, Virginia: The Chairman of the Board for the Smithsonian Institution and leader of the Washington Mystery Club, Gina Goodman, sits at the conference table on the second floor of the *Brown Leaf Cigar Bar* impatiently waiting for the 10:00 AM call from their protégé investigator, Richard Kingsley. It is 10:03 when the Washington Mystery Club co-conspirator Clinton Auclair, Director of the Library of Congress says, "Stop fretting, Gina; he'll call. He's young and doesn't yet appreciate the importance of being on time. Maybe he'll make a good president someday."

The phone rings and Byron Chism, Architect of the Capitol, pushes the console button on the speaker phone. "Good Morning."

A nervous-sounding Richard Kingsley responds with a shaky and tentative voice, "Good Morning. I'm sorry for being a few minutes late, but I'm ready to give you my report.

"But first, I need to understand the motive of your little group for revealing such potentially explosive information to me. The evidence in the envelopes and safe deposit box is extraordinary, but it's the kind of stuff that can get me killed. Who all knows about the contents and who knows that I now have it? Do I need to watch my back?"

"Richard, this is Gina Goodman. Two other people on our end know about the contents: the person who gave the 'stuff' -- as you say -- to us, to make it available to the investigation, and his confidante. I can't tell you who they are, but suffice it to say, they are on your side and are no risk to you."

"OK, but it makes me very nervous to have this information. I guess it will eventually lead us to the answer to the mystery about who killed my father.

"I need some expense money so that I can travel to Boston to have tests done by *Entropy Entrepreneurs* on the item from the safe deposit box. The primary new development on my side is that *Entropy Entrepreneurs* think they have some special ability to garner new information useful to solve the mystery of the death of the White House attorney."

Byron Chism says, "Richard, you might want to track down the person who took the photographs. I'd follow that thread."

"How in the world am I going to do that?"

"Take a little bit closer look at the photos."

Clint Auclair speaks up and says, "If you see Powers while you're up there, tell him he may have a target on *his* back."

Wiscasset, Maine: "Dr. Cherokee," says the guard at the front gate of the Cherokee Estate over the intercom, "this is Marcus, I'm on-duty today. Uh, are you expecting a delivery today? Star and Ram are up front here and there is a van coming up the driveway. My first order of business, of course, is to protect Star, but I wanted to check with you first, in the event you are expecting anything."

"No, we're not expecting anything. Please have one of the other guards bring Star back immediately, and I'll be on my way out to meet them. Stay vigilant; pull the other *White Knights* up to the gate and also notify Lucas immediately."

Marcus takes the safety off his Colt and walks out of the guard house to meet the on-coming van. As Maya requested, a second guard approaches Star, "Come on Princess, let's go back to the house while Marcus checks out this van."

Ram growls at the guard, bares his teeth, and makes it clear that he better not take another step in Star's direction. Star says to the guard, "It's OK; this delivery is for me."

Maya runs from the house to find out what is going on and yells loud enough for Star to hear, "What are you doing? Come here; you don't know who is in that van."

Star smiles at her mother, "Yes, I do."

The van stops at the gate. Marcus instructs loudly, "Stop and state your business." His Colt is at the ready.

The man driving the van answers, "I have a special delivery for a Miss Star Cherokee. I'm with the Wounded Warriors K-9 unit. The late General Ray LaSalle requested that we deliver his German shepherd, Algorithm LaSalle, to Miss Cherokee as a condition of his generous gift from his estate to the Wounded Warriors. May I get out and open the back doors to the van?"

"Stay put for a moment until I get authorization."

Marcus backs away from the van, maintains eye contact with the driver until he reaches the gate where Maya, Star, and Ram are standing -- just on the other side.

Marcus inquires, "Dr. Cherokee, do you authorize this delivery?"

"Have him bring the dog out. Let's see if it's really Al."

Marcus gives the driver a thumbs-up. The delivery driver gets out of the van cautiously with his hands held high to display submission, goes to the back of the van, opens the back door, disconnects the leash from the van hook and invites Al to jump down. Al pulls the leash tight and drags the driver to the gate, with his tail wagging as he barks excitedly. Star and Ram run over to meet them.

Maya asks the driver, "What receipt documents do we have to sign?"

287

WHA-CKED   JED O'Dea
(White House Attorney-Counsel Killed)

The Pentagon: A mind is a terrible thing to waste. Sometimes I feel like that expression was written by someone who knows me too well.   After I hear the story about Ray LaSalle's dog being delivered to Star in Wiscasset, I remember that Ray told me that a key was hidden in Al's collar.   That was just a few days ago -- back when I was vacationing in Annapolis at the Maryland taxpayers' expense -- but it seems like a lifetime ago.

I call Lucas and ask him to retrieve the key and have a White Knight run it over to me.   Powers, Jolene and I catch a flight from Portland to Reagan National and catch the Blue Line to the Pentagon station.   Powers has made all the necessary calls to assure our smooth acceptance, albeit with escort, to the second floor South East Ring 'D' branch of the Navy Federal Credit Union.   The key goes to a locker, not a safe deposit box, much like a mail box at a post office.   I open the box, and it contains two items: an envelope and a DVD in a plastic case.

The envelope contains a "Last Will and Testament" and a letter addressed to me.   I open the letter and read it out load to Jolene and Powers.

"Dear Tank, thank you for your willingness to be executor of my will.   By the time you read this, I will already have suffered through my terminal cancer."

I look up at Powers and Jolene and say, "Ah.   That explains Ray's high interest in joining the mission to rescue Jolene.   He didn't want to die of cancer."   I read on:

"As many of you suspected, I used my infamous algorithms to benefit the nation by predicting outcomes of domestic and international events.   I'm proud to have served my country in that way. As you also know, I developed another algorithm for personal use to predict financial futures resulting in an embarrassingly large financial net worth with no family other than you guys to leave it to. You will see in my will that I have left my estate's financial holdings to the Wounded Warriors K-9 Unit. I left Al to Star, my Trinidad Estate to you and Powers as a White Knight holding, and my most treasured possession to *Entropy Entrepreneurs*, my algorithms. It is my belief that Tucker, Maya, and Tony are way smarter than me and can continue my legacy.

"One special note for you is that on the DVD is an algorithm I prepared to help you solve the mystery of the death of the White House Counsel. Please give this to Tony and have him run it; if it was not suicide, the person who most probably committed the murder will surprise you."

Boston, Massachusetts: After we leave the Pentagon, Powers and I charter a flight in a Bombardier Challenger from Manassas Regional Airport to Logan International Airport in order for the two of us to guard and escort a very nervous Richard Kingsley. He is anxious to turn the blue metal Colt "hot potato" over to Tony Vinci to apply a new forensic technology developed by *Entropy Entrepreneurs*.

Maya Cherokee and Tony Vinci are in Tony's office when we arrive. Richard eagerly hands the bagged pistol over to Tony as if it were diseased.

I ask Maya and Tony, "Can you two explain to us in layman terms why you wanted this gun so badly and what you expect to discover?"

Tony answers immodestly, "Maya is a genius and two geniuses are better than one genius. We've taken the greatest forensic discovery since fingerprinting, DNA profiling, from a molecular level to a subatomic level."

Maya adds, "We combined that technology with the DNA software refined by Tony to untangle commingled genetic evidence. Together, these interwoven technologies have resulted in a quantum leap for DNA profiling."

"Additionally," Tony continues, "We've learned to apply nanoparticles to bond with a complex cocktail of compounds present in fingermark residues to identify fingerprints not found with classic fingerprinting methodologies."

Maya espouses, "We're excited about the chance of identifying new fingerprints and new DNA information on the gun left at the scene."

Jolene asks, "How long will this take?"

Tony looks at his watch, "We should have our new data within an hour. After that, it could take anywhere from minutes to days to correlate the new data with the FBI fingerprint and DNA databases."

Annapolis, Maryland: Queenie has spent three days handcuffed to a reinforced oversized hospital bed recovering from his concussion, broken ribs, back contusions, and the ten fractured bones in his right hand. Upon release from the hospital, Queenie is quite surprised to get his belongings back from the police and to hear that he is free to go, that the State of Maryland has determined that they don't have enough evidence to keep him in jail for his original crime.

WHA-CKED
JED O'Dea
(White House Attorney-Counsel Killed)

Queenie makes a bee-line to the nearest fast food restaurant, orders three triple-decker hamburgers and a diet drink, and sits at a corner table. Two minutes later, he calls Rook for instructions.

Rook answers the phone on the first ring, "Where are you?"

"I'm out. Next stop?"

"Boston. Rent a van without windows and drive up. Call again, same time tomorrow." Rook hangs up.

The call took fifteen seconds. The Fischer Men have a rule - - never talk on a phone for more than thirty seconds.

Queenie goes back to the counter and orders two large fries to carry with him to a rental car location three blocks down the street. Queenie seldom walks three blocks; at 475 pounds, it is difficult to go that far without creating a rash on the insides of his thighs. The noise alone made by the sound of cloth on cloth rasping against each other with each step is irritating to him.

And it keeps him from hearing someone coming up from behind; someone with an X26P Taser. There is no warning; the shock and surprise magnify the torturous sensation Queenie feels when the electric gun makes contact with the lard on his back. He screams with pain.

The small man with the Taser also has a 33-inch composite wood Louisville Slugger with him. The Hispanic Taser operator says, "You scream like a little girl, fat man. Now, get in this van that's pulling up -- get in the back."

"Fuck you," responds Queenie as he makes an attempt to grab hold of the small man who still has the Taser in his hand. The second hit makes Queenie shake like a bowl of Jell-O and cry out loud.

The small man says, "Now, get in the fucking van." Queenie doesn't move fast enough, so the small man swings the bat square across Queenie's extra-large ass.

Queenie falls to the floor of the van. The door is shut behind him, and the small man climbs into the passenger's seat with his Taser charged and ready. The van drives into an empty warehouse two miles away in an industrial complex.

291

Inside the warehouse the small man says, "Roll out, fat man, or I'll turn the voltage up on this thing. I like how you sing falsetto."

With some difficulty, Queenie manages to move his body a few inches at a time to the edge of the van floor, and eventually rolls out onto the concrete floor of the warehouse with a splat and a swoosh as the air is exhausted from his lungs.

The State of Maryland's Attorney General, who had resigned his position two days earlier, stood over the huge killer, next to the Taser operator. The AG says, "Thanks, Freddy; I appreciate what you're doing for me, but I don't want the police to be involved with what I am about to do, so I'll take it from here."

Freddy, the off-duty Hispanic police officer says, "OK, but this guy could be dangerous if he manages to get his hands on you, so please don't get within arm's length of the guy. You want the Taser?"

"No. It could be traced back to you if something goes wrong. I brought my own weapons. I'll take responsibility for what happens here."

Queenie rolls to one side and begins his often-practiced procedure for getting onto his feet. As he turns his back on Queenie and begins walking to his vehicle, the ex-AG says to Freddy, "You better be going now." The off-duty Maryland State Trooper leaves as requested in the van. The warehouse door shuts behind them leaving the AG alone with the "Fischer Men" killer, Queenie.

"Queenie," the AG asks, "Do you know who I am?"

"No. What have I ever done to you?"

The AG ignored the question, "I'm the guy who arranged for your release out of jail today. Say 'thank you, sir.'"

Queenie says, "I don't think that I am really thankful -- at this moment -- to be out of jail."

"You got that right. Do you know that I'm an expert marksman with a crossbow?"

292

WHA-CKED

JED O'Dea

(White House Attorney-Counsel Killed)

Queenie says, "So what? Just what is it you want from me?"

"It's simple. I want to know who was blackmailing me to make sure Tank Alvarez stayed in jail until you killed him. Since I failed to keep Tank in jail and you failed to kill him, my son is lying in a coma with his little body broken.

"I want to know who ran over my son with a truck. Which of your murderous buddies did that to him?" The warehouse can't contain the suffocating emotional steam which is emanating from the AG in his hatred for Queenie -- it's as though all of the oxygen has been sucked out of the air.

"I'm going to put the first arrow into one of your thighs. It will pass even through your tree-trunk-size thighs, with the arrowhead on one side and the feather on the other. If I don't get an answer, I'll put the second arrow through your other thigh. You'll really start losing blood when I put an arrow through the fat of your stomach from left to right. I won't hit any vital organ but it will hurt like hell.

"I want to know who did this to my son and I want you to make arrangements for the two of us to meet that 'dead man walking.'

"Now, so that you know I'm serious, here comes the first arrow -- hold your thighs still for me, okay? Do you have a preference, right or left?"

The ex-AG opens the trunk of his car and pulls out a Wicked Ridge Invader G3 Crossbow and a carbon arrow with blazer vanes. The Crossbow cocks and Queenie says, "Wait." The ex-AG doesn't.

Queenie screams ... and reaches his highest musical notes yet.

293

WHA-CKED
JED O'Dea

(White House Attorney-Counsel Killed)

Boston, Massachusetts: Powers asks me, while we are sitting in the *Entropy Entrepreneurs* conference room, "Did you read the article in the *Boston Globe* on the quote, 'mysterious deaths' of both the former Director of the FBI, Damian LaTorre, and the famous Pentagon guru General Ray LaSalle? The press is fishing for why they both died while visiting Scotland. Sooner or later, the truth is going to come out ... and they will discover that you've skipped bail."

Jolene responds before I have a chance, "I think it is wonderful that they will be buried in Arlington on the same day. I am surprised to learn that Director LaTorre was in financial stress.   Apparently, he made bad commodity and futures investments. He was, however, smart enough to have a huge accidental death policy that'll keep his family secure."

"Hmmm."

"Both those men died to save me and they did so as soldiers. I'm so proud to have known them." Her eyes tear up and she decides to stop speaking, just as Maya and Tucker walk into the conference room.

Maya says, "Tony's on his way up to share the finding of our forensic discoveries on the gun found at the scene of the White House lawyer's death. We need to start thinking about what we're going to do with this information. There is no way this stuff will hold up in a court of law."

Tony Vinci waddles into the conference room with Tucker standing by his side. Tony uses the three-step stool to make his way into a conference room chair. He looks around the room to see Powers, Maya, me, Jolene, Tucker, and Richard Kingsley.

He explains, "The science behind 'how' we reached the conclusions remains proprietary; the 'what' is not. The good news is that we discovered new prints on the gun. The bad news is that we found fifteen new prints on the gun. The gun is, after all, a 102-year-old 38-caliber Army Colt Special. It's been handled by a few people. We're lucky that we only got fifteen new prints. We've only identified seven of the new prints, but among them are the prints of the White House Counsel, the Park Police officer Brown, and one Duke Dillinger."

Powers says, "The Rook?"

"Correct.

"The new DNA technology that we have trademarked *Hyper Profiling* provides some pretty exciting results. Can you believe that we were able to identify 138 discreet DNA types that have touched the gun and left enough residue for separation? Unlike the original forensic results, we found DNA type DQ alpha 2,5 -- the White House attorney's DNA -- on the gun handle, not just the barrel. We identified one other new DNA type from the national database that was cross-matrixed with the short list of people involved in the investigation -- the FBI investigator-in-charge, Brian Richmond.

"Finally, last but by no means least, we put all this information into Ray LaSalle's algorithm and it provided us with scenario probabilities. The probability that the White House Counsel committed suicide or, stated differently, was not murdered is 38 percent. The probability that he was murdered elsewhere and transported to the Civil War Park is 47 percent, and the chance that he was killed in the White House and transported to the site of the 'alleged suicide' is 3.5 percent."

I ask, "Does Ray's algorithm list the people most likely to have murdered the White House Counsel?"

"Yes," answers Tony. "The people most likely to have either murdered the guy or contracted to have the guy murdered include the following in order of highest probability: Viktor Soroson, the former First Lady's Chief of Staff, the late FBI agent-in-charge, the first civilian on the scene Robert Kingsley, the former First Lady herself, followed by the first law enforcement officer on the scene, Sergeant Kristen Brown."

Richard Kingsley speaks out, "Did you say that my father was high on the list of suspects in the death of the attorney? That's preposterous."

295

"Sorry, Richard," answers Tony; it's just the way it turned out. Ray also ran an algorithm on the death of your father. The computer agrees with you -- the output concluded that there was a 73.5 percent probability that your father's auto accident was no accident. It goes further to list Viktor Soroson, by way of Rook, to be the most probable murderers."

Maya adds, "None of this new data is admissible in a court of law but we're at least homing in on the truth. We have other technologies -- don't we, Tony -- to actually convert theory to fact in this case?"

Tony answers nervously, "Yes." He doesn't want anyone to know that it was his boss' idea to use one of the nano-drones for illegal surveillance.

CHAPTER 49 -- CONSPIRACY CONFIRMED

Berlin, Germany: The Bundestag is in session when phase three of Soroson's master plan begins. The German Parliament Police rush in to protect key cabinet members and escort them to an underground bunker where the Chancellor is already secured.

They all watch the news stories on **Kabel Deutschland as their nation is under attack by radical Islamists.** A devastating explosion kills 83 civilians and wounds 113 at the Mall of Berlin in Leipzinger Plavetz.

Thirty-five children and 21 teachers are killed by a suicide-vested six-year-old at the Bavarian International School in Haimhausen.

Attacks are made across the country during well attended soccer matches, in grocery stores, in hotels, and hospitals. All in all, tens of thousands of German civilians are killed or seriously wounded. War has been declared on Germany; it's a war partially funded and planned by atheist, Viktor Soroson. His Trojan horse plan to embed radicalized Islamists disguised as refugees to facilitate a German caliphate is working.

His life-long goal of revenge against the Master Race is coming to fruition. The end justifies the means. The enemy of his enemy is the pursuit of the caliphate and his friend.

Caracas, Venezuela: For more than two hours, estate servants heard sounds continuously coming from Viktor Soroson's study. The butler checks on him, but is rudely dismissed and asked to leave him alone. "If I need you, I'll call for you."

Even his lady friend, student, lover, and ideological partner could not console Viktor Soroson. She is summarily dismissed. However, Viktor does ask for Yuri Prociv to come to his study, but Yuri refuses to place himself in danger while Viktor is in his current state of mind.

Crystal glass is all over the terrazzo, along with champagne and expensive wine. An empty bottle of Scotch sits on his desk. The totally inebriated Viktor Soroson is taking his wrath out on this office; it has become his punching bag. He is constantly yelling at the top of his lungs, screaming at demons of his own making, and exercising verbal Judo on a now-smashed wide screen TV.

"How can this be?

"I must hate myself.

"I'm the very monster I pursue.

"Yuri, you fucking asshole, come in here and tell me the truth. Tell me this is a big lie. Tell me my entire life ambition is to find a way to kill decedents of my ancestors.

"Yuri, I'm going to torture your petulant ass. I'm going to cut your little nuts off and make you eat them. I'm going to tell the Russian mafia to make you suffer a long and protracted death.

"Where's my gun? Where is my God damn gun?"

The gun shot is heard in every corner of the Soroson estate.

Caracas, Venezuela: The Policia Tecnica Judicial arrive after the estate butler calls Venezuelan Guardia Nacional to inform them of Viktor Soroson's suicide.

WHA-CKED
JED O'Dea

(White House Attorney-Counsel Killed)

After sealing the study crime scene and performing a thorough investigation, the police zero their interviews in on Yuri Prociv and Soroson's lady; neither of whom speaks much Spanish. The two of them are forced to stay in the estate library until an English-speaking investigator arrives.

They do not know each other and have never spoken previously. She is dressed in an outrageous costume resembling a street whore. He is dressed in his usual Russian Orthodox priest clothing. The dichotomy is almost comical. The investigator notices that neither persons-of-interest is shedding a tear, and neither seems emotionally upset -- the room feels cold -- in an otherwise hot and humid library.

After ten or so stressful minutes the lady says, "I understand you played chess with Vik. You must be good; he only played against chess masters."

Yuri nods his head affirmatively.

She continues in an accusatory tone, "You're the priest from Russia who gave him the papers which drove him mad, yes?"

Yuri looks more closely at the woman dressed like a prostitute and responds, "And you are?"

"I am," she catches herself and continues, "I was his wife; I'm Ingrid Soroson."

Yuri can't contain his shock and disbelief, the expression on his face shows total incredulity.

She continues, "As an obedient wife, I dressed in costumes to please him. Today, I'm dressed as a prostitute. He requested that I alter my costumes daily depending on his mood. Tomorrow, I was supposed to dress up as a Catholic school girl. I guess there is no need for that now.

"It was a small thing, actually, to please him in that way."

The door to the library opens and a new investigator arrives who speaks English. He says as he enters, "Well, well; who do we have here? You, father, are the Lithuanian Yuri Prociv according to our passport office. Am I correct?"

Yuri nods his head.

The investigator looks Mrs. Soroson up and down and makes a calculated comment, "And you are his whore?"

Her answer is cool, and smooth, surprisingly calm. "Sometimes. Sometimes I'm his French Maid; at other times his mother, but always his wife."

The investigator has a renewed respect for the lady in front of him and says, "My condolences for your loss, Mrs. Soroson, but I must add, you do not appear to grieve for the death of your husband, no?"

"I'll not show a public lack of dignity; Vik would not have approved. I'll grieve in private."

Neither the inspector, nor Yuri, believes a word of it. What they both sense is pure evil.

The inspector asks, "Mrs. Soroson, why do you think your husband would commit suicide, if that is in fact what happened?"

She answers, "Father Prociv here gave my husband papers that drove him mad, drove him to drink, and then finally to stick a gun under his chin."

"And what did the papers contain that would drive him to commit suicide?"

She looks over at Yuri, engages his eyes, does not look at the investigator and answers, "The papers are still on his desk; you can read them yourself, but the fake priest here who just killed the golden goose can probably answer your question."

The investigator looks at Yuri with a little more suspicion and asks, "Fake priest?"

Yuri answers, "I'm a Russian Orthodox Priest serving at St. Isaac's Cathedral in Saint Petersburg, Russia. I discovered a

(White House Attorney-Counsel Killed)

JED O'Dea

document that described an experiment performed by Dr. Wilhelm Soroson on Viktor Soroson's mother, Marsha Katz, in 1944. Viktor and I played long-distance chess electronically, so I became familiar with his passion to learn who his real father was; he was interested in his genealogy. At some risk to myself, I brought the documentation to him."

Ingrid Soroson interrupts, "Don't pretend that you brought this document to him out of the goodness of your heart."

Yuri continues, unfazed, "Dr. Wilhelm Soroson impregnated young Marsha Katz with sperm from the cryogenically stored contents of the sperm bank. The Third Reich was at the end of its run. The impregnation was unauthorized."

"Please," says the inspector, "Get to the point."

"Marsha Katz was impregnated with the sperm from the Führer. Viktor Soroson was the son of Marsha Katz and Adolph Hitler!

Victor was devastated to learn he was the son of the very man who promoted the evil concept of Aryan superiority, the Master Race -- the very thing he spent his lifetime fighting."

CHAPTER 50 -- GUILTY AS CHARGED

Boston, Massachusetts: "Let's have another toast to that damn Sam!" I am on my fourth Sam Adams while celebrating the good news I received from our lawyer, Sam Pearson -- celebrating with Jolene, Powers, and Richard.

Powers asks, "Which Sam are we toasting, Sam Pearson or Sam Adams?"

"Yes." We laugh at the lame joke as if it were hysterical.

Jolene asks, "Did Pearson provide specifics as to why they dropped the case against you?"

"Only that new evidence presented to the Maryland Attorney General convinced him, not only of my innocence, but also of the innocence of Ram and Lucas. We're all in the clear."

Sometimes I get creeped out when events occur that seem paranormal to me. I've never quite felt comfortable, as an example, with Star's specials gifts. It runs chills down my spine when Jolene asks me a question about something I was just about to tell her. The call I am receiving from the Maryland AG while talking about him is one of those events which transcend science and logic, that challenge metaphysics, and the time and space continuum. I hold my hand up to the noisy table.

"Tank Alvarez, I am the man who held you in the Annapolis City jail without bail for the murder of former FBI agent Brian Richmond."

"Yes sir, and thank you for relinquishing and ultimately dropping charges."

"Technically, I didn't do that, but I did persuade Judge Mayer to drop the charges as I resigned my post as the State of Maryland Attorney General a few days ago. I resigned because I failed to execute my oath of office and denied you justice. I was being blackmailed, and I've learned that you, too, were being blackmailed by someone. I don't believe in coincidences and think the cases are connected. I especially believe that after I interviewed someone you know maybe a little too well -- Queenie."

I add, "That poster child for obesity damn near suffocated me by lying on my face."

"I hear you paid him back pretty good. Anyway, I learned what I wanted from him and wanted to share that information with you and your partner, Powers.

"The same man who tried to kill Powers and Dr. Cherokee is back in Boston to finish the job. He is also the man who blackmailed me to keep you in jail and who put my son in a coma after you were released.

"I'm on my way up to Boston. I have a plan I'd like to share with you and Powers. I'll be there first thing in the morning if you'll meet with me at a location of your choosing.

"And by the way," the ex-AG continues, "Queenie is on his way up to the Boston area too."

Washington, D.C. and Wiscasset, Maine: "Holy Expletive Deleted," celebrates Jimmy Ma as he wins another pot of money in Chinatown playing "Go." "I'd rather be lucky than good any day."

A bell chime rings and Jimmy looks down at his text message. "Get out, now. Call me ASAP." It is from his boss, Tucker Cherokee. The casino proprietor's thugs are approaching his table, so Jimmy stands up and loudly announces as he looks into a surveillance camera, "I'd like to thank the house for their generous hospitality, and will donate twenty per cent of my winnings to the proprietor as a show of my appreciation."

The thugs hear something in their earbuds and stop. Jimmy drops his tip money and scrambles down the steps and out onto 'H' street. That was the last straw; he is going to have to find out where on his sacred body they implanted a tracker. While walking down the street he calls Tucker back.

"Yes sir, what exciting assignment do you have for me? Will I have to parachute into enemy territory or go undercover as a John in a house of ill repute?

"Jimmy," says Tucker, "the phone is on speaker and Maya is here with me."

"Oh! Sorry!"

Maya says, "Tucker and I have been on the phone with Powers and Tank developing a plan to prevent another murder -- mine. Tucker, my sister, and I would greatly appreciate it if you would accept your role in this plan."

Wayland, Massachusetts: The eleven year old Winter Green Jeep Cherokee sits alone in a parking lot of a major defense contractor's office complex at 2:00 A.M. A late-model white Honda Odyssey with Maryland plates turns into the same parking lot, parks ten yards away from the Jeep and flashes its lights three times.

Queenie waits a good two minutes before he attempts to roll out of the Honda. His movements are slow, deliberate, and calculated. He begins to walk, feet wide apart, in the direction of the old Jeep. Queenie winces in pain from the crossbow injury with each step; his gait is unnatural, even for him.

The crack of the rifle fire in the dead of the night amplifies the deafening head shot. Queenie stays erect for what seems like an impossibly long time.   He is a statue in contrast with the reality of the event before the mountain of a man collapses on the parking lot pavement.

"Well I'll be damned," the ex-AG says, "It worked."

Powers says, "I guess I'm going to the Celtics-Lakers game tomorrow. Good thing Tucker has season tickets."

Boston, Massachusetts: Powers and I have front row seats in the Garden, and watch the tall guys warm up before the game. Though I was the largest guy in my high school, I sucked at basketball.   Instead, I became an all-State football defensive tackle on a losing-record team. Standing on the court with seven footers makes me feel normal. But Powers and I are probably the only ones near the court wearing a tiny communications device comprised of a micro-sized earphone, a transmitter necklace and a microphone connected to a cell phone. The micro-earphones are wireless and weigh only one gram.

The Garden is stacked with undercover Boston Police Department Officers, *White Knights*, and scores of interested civilian parties on the lookout. Powers and I are merely bait to attract the Rook.

The game starts.

There is no sign of the Rook.

Powers and I have a Sam Adams and act like normal fans enjoying the game, jumping up, high-fiving each other when a good play is made by the Celtics, but staying vigilant.

There is no sign of the Rook.

305

WHA-CKED   JED O'Dea
(White House Attorney-Counsel Killed)

In the second quarter, I begin to wonder if the Rook is going to show. Powers called in a lot of chips to get the Boston PD to allocate so much in police resources on overtime.

After a dog and fries during half-time I do a short roll call. All are accounted for and no one has seen anyone matching the Rook's description.

I say to Powers, "I need to hit the head. This will make me a large target but I got to go." Powers informs the team and puts everyone on the sting in high alert.

I walk up the stairs to the next level and into the Men's room. I stand at the urinal but just pretend to unzip my fly and urinate. I notice that a couple of the stalls are being used. With my back to the stalls, I recognize that **I** have put myself in a perfectly vulnerable position; especially if I was in the process of relieving myself.

He comes out of the stall like a thoroughbred out of the gate at Churchill Downs, with a five-inch serrated blade Fox Attack Tactical Dagger. It never reaches anything vital, as my left foot is planted into his solar plexus with enough force to stop a water buffalo. But the knife does cut a painful wound into my calf.

This pisses me off.

If I hadn't remembered that we need him alive, I would have broken his neck right there and then. Instead, I grab his head and pound it into the American Standard ceramic urinal. As he is falling to the floor, two of Boston's finest rush in and place handcuffs on the Rook while he is still in La-La-Land.

The ex-Maryland Attorney General flashes his credentials in front of the two arresting officers and tells them that the prisoner is wanted in the State of Maryland on murder charges.

The arresting officers ignore the AG and tell him to pound sand, and that **they** have jurisdiction. That is, until the senior arresting officer receives a call from his captain.

306

Somerset, Massachusetts: The Rook tries not to be sea sick with his mouth duct taped; he doesn't want to die choking on his own vomit. But the slow roll is getting to him, and he is gagging with remnants of his last meal coming out of his nose. When his eyes start to roll and his face exhibits a bluish tint, the ex-AG pulls the duct tape off his mouth. The Rook retches blood with his digested food this time, and struggles to get air into his lungs.

Powers admits to the ex-AG, "You know, we've just taken enhanced interrogation to the next level. We need to tell the CIA about this. We should call it Puke Boarding -- waterboarding with upchuck."

The Brayton Point Power Project receives bituminous coal from the nation of Colombia via barge. The empty barge on which they are meeting is scheduled to return to Colombia in three days.

The ex-AG asks, "Duke, you disgusting piece of shit, you almost killed my son -- you put him in a coma just to make a point. I want to know who gave you the order. Unless you want to die in the most undignified of ways via regurgitating a liverwurst sandwich with bananas that we feed you, I'd start spilling the beans now."

Though it is impossible for the Rook to remove himself from the restraints with which Powers is controlling him, he makes a show of trying.

The ex-AG says, "Suit yourself; I have nothing better to do for the next couple of days but to enjoy your suffering.

"Go ahead, Powers; put the duct tape back over his mouth. I'm going food shopping."

Rook capitulates, "I don't know who gives me jobs. I don't know who pays me. I get a call. It rings once. That's my signal to go to a library. I get a text on my phone that tells me what web site and what password to use to get orders. I do what I'm told; that's all. I'm told what to do and he doesn't care how I do it."

Powers says, "I took your phone from you when you were senseless in the Garden. It's been delivered to a super-nerd to perform cyber forensics.

"There are a couple of Fischer Men left unsupervised out there. What are their assignments? What did you order them to do?"

Rook, enjoying air in his lungs but feeling the seasickness coming on answers, "Our jobs were to kill you, Maya Cherokee, Tank Alvarez, and Richard Kingsley. My job was to kill you. Queenie's job was to kill Tank. It's Bishop's job to kill Maya."

Powers says, "OK, I'll leave you two lovers alone. I know you have a lot to talk about. Hopefully, Rook, I won't see you on the other side.

CHAPTER 51 -- KILL-BLADE

Shanghai, Peoples Republic of China and Boston, Massachusetts: Carmen Brave sits in Tucker Cherokee's *Entropy Entrepreneur*'s office late in the evening waiting for Meng Wong, President of China Methyl Ester Ltd., to answer the phone. Dr. Maya Li Cherokee sits closest to the speaker phone, to help in the event that translation is required between Tucker and Meng.

An angelic, almost childish voice answers and says something only Maya understands. But it is Carmen who speaks first, "Carmen Brave of *Brave Chicken Corporation* calling from the United States."

The melodic voice says, "Very well, Miss Brave; I will let Mr. Wong know."

In no more than fifteen seconds, Meng Wong answers the phone and says, "This is quite a surprise, Miss Brave; I thought you were avoiding me. I assume you are calling to agree to cover our loss in the deal you dishonestly brokered."

"I have you on speaker phone with the CEO of *Entropy Entrepreneurs*, Mr. Tucker Cherokee, and the former U.S. National Science Advisor, Dr. Maya Li Cherokee. I have shared with them the history of Brave Chicken's relationship with China Methyl Ester and Mr. Cherokee has an offer to make to you."

"Mr. Wong," says Tucker, "*Entropy Entrepreneurs* has a patented and proprietary technology which can accept the animal fats from Brave Chicken and other Maryland Eastern Shore poultry companies and produce biodiesel fuel at costs very competitive with today's petroleum-based diesel fuel costs. We will license the technology to you at no cost if you will ensure the safety of Carmen and Elliott Brave."

Meng says something in Mandarin before he returned to English, "Mr. Cherokee, I am not God. I cannot ensure the safety of Miss Brave or her father. I am, though, interested in your license-free technology."

"As an alternative," Tucker continues, "*Entropy Entrepreneurs* is interested in buying out your share of the joint venture with Brave Chicken at a fair and reasonable price."

Meng says, "Can you promise to sell us chicken at the agreed price offered by the Vice President of Brave Chicken?"

"I'll look into that. It just so happens that a poultry supplier I know out of New Zealand might be able to fill the gap."

Meng speaks to someone in his office for ten seconds and finally says, "We'll draft an agreement in principal for your review."

Tucker demands, "Call your negotiators off."

"My negotiators?"

"Your muscle!"

"Ah, I'll see if I can reach them. Ha. Ha."

The phone disconnects.

Tucker looks over at Carmen and says, "If I were you I'd stay close to Lucas at the Wiscasset guest house until this deal closes. Meng doesn't sound very trustworthy."

Maya says, "That's an understatement. In Mandarin he said to his assistant to send Niu Boa to Entropy."

Tucker lifts the intra-office phone and says, "Tony, can you find out who Niu Boa is? He may be on his way to visit with us."

"Sure, boss."

Tucker then pulls out a satellite phone and calls Powers who answers on the third ring, "I overheard Sonja tell you that she planted a tracker on the Chinese guest who crashed our dinner party in Wiscasset. Can you find out for me where he is at this moment? How long will it take him to get to Boston? And where is Sonja, by the way? Did she ever tell you how she knew the Fischer Men were about to ambush you and Maya?"

Powers answers, "I will. I don't know. I don't know at the moment, and Yes.

"Is Maya near you?"

Tucker answers tentatively, "Yeah, why?"

"She's on the last standing Fischer Man's hit list, the Bishop's list."

Boston, Massachusetts: Tony assigned the cyber forensic task to Casey Robinson, his most reliable scientist. She is a workaholic with the temperament of a pit bull on hormones; she won't let go until she solves whatever problem she is given. The fact that she stands in the doorway to Tony's office means the problem has been solved already.

Tony smiles and says, "Please, Casey, come in and tell me the good news."

With no preamble or explanation as to how she solved the problem she says, "Calls from the Rook's phone originated from San Diego, Baton Rouge, Key West, Caracas, Venezuela, and right here in Boston -- Cambridge to be exact."

"Fantastic," says Tony, "I assume you connected the origination locations with a timeline."

Casey says, "Of course!"

"Great," adds Tony, "Now all we have to do is cross link the whereabouts of the short list of persons-of-interest with your findings, and we've narrowed down who is directing the Fischer Men to murder Powers, Tank, Maya, and Richard."

Casey says, "Already done. It's a short list of one."

"My God, Casey," says Tony, "you solved it, you know who is giving the orders to the Fischer Men?"

Casey says, "There's only one person in this universe who gets out even less than I do. That person doesn't watch the news, read the newspapers, or check his Facebook page for weeks at a time."

Tony says, "Who's that?"

"You, you hermit!

"Did you know that Viktor Soroson committed suicide in Caracas, Venezuela? Did you know that some Russian chess master and priest is under arrest for allegedly driving Soroson to suicide? Did you know that his wife controls his fortune and apparently has for several years?"

"Casey, damn it," Tony says impatiently, "will you maneuver to the bottom line here sometime before the day is over?"

"Take a look at this photo of Soroson and his wife in the *Wall Street Journal*. Does she resemble anyone on our list of suspects?"

Tony says, "Judas Priest!"

Salisbury, Maryland: "Dad," says Carmen, "I'm in Maine as we speak and I'm safe for the moment, but I'm afraid for you. Can you take an extended vacation or something and hide for a couple of weeks -- in say Katmandu or someplace you can't be found? The Chinese thugs followed me all the way up here. I spoke with Meng and I sense he's more evil than even we suspected. Please, Dad, take a vacation."

"Carmen, darling, I've never run from a fight. I've re-hired *White Knight* which is protecting me day and night. I'll be damned if I'm going to let these Chinese thugs keep me from executing my responsibilities. What would your mother have said in this situation? She would have sung that Tom Petty song, "Don't back down. Stand your ground!"

Boston, Massachusetts: The wind bit right through the Bishop's New England Patriots nylon jacket and made his whole thin, wiry, body shiver -- making it difficult to focus his field glasses on the entrance to the *Entropy Entrepreneurs* office building.

His target, Maya Cherokee, had gone into the building, so she must come out eventually.

"Where da fuck are y'all?" The Bishop had lost communications with the mission leader, the Rook, a couple of days ago and hadn't seen any of his fellow Fischer Men in days. The hit-man, Bishop, had gone up to Wiscasset to scope out the Cherokee compound only to find it damn near impenetrable and zealously guarded by a large contingent of armed guards.

He concluded that the only way he was going to get to his target was when she went out for dinner.

"A high class babe like her has ta eat at a fancy place. I'll wait 'til the time is right."

The Bishop fanaticized at the opportunity to be alone with Maya. She is the most beautiful woman he has ever seen in person. He'd seen women more desirable to him in Victoria's Secret ads, but had never seen anyone who held a candle to his target in person. He made a decision right there and then -- he'd kill whoever got in his way. He was going to have her and she was going to like it.

"She's to die for."

Salisbury, Maryland: The dogs were not called off. The five Chinese Mafia thugs are on an uninvited tour of the Brave Chicken poultry processing plant. The leader of the Mafia, the man I referred to in the Wiscasset restaurant as Fuk Yuh, is actually Niu Boa who accepted his experience in the plant as a teaching moment. The Chinaman decides that he is going to use one of Brave Chicken's processing technologies on Carmen's father, the CEO of Brave Chicken, Elliott Brave.

Boa studies the kill-blade design to slit the throats of chickens and thinks it would be an easy concept to replicate and use on both of the Braves. Meng Wong's instructions were clear, "make them suffer."

The assassins also like the culture of cruelty applied to the process of ripping the heads off improperly shackled chickens, and tried to image applying the concept to the beautiful but dishonest Carmen Brave. They watched chickens being stabbed, clubbed and crushed. Boa saw other chickens stunned with electricity.

In a newer area of the plant, Brave Chicken operators use controlled atmosphere stunning which removes oxygen to kill the chickens in a much more merciful way; it bores the Chinese hit men to death.

Elliot Brave is surrounded by his new bodyguards in his chauffeured limousine. The armed driver has been fully vetted and is no threat risk. A backup car follows the limousine out of the parking lot to the plant gate.

The gate doesn't open. The back door to the limo does.

The backup vehicle explodes and a silenced pistol is used to neutralize the driver. Elliott Brave is dragged out of the limousine and Tasered repeatedly to total submission.

Edgar Allen Poe's *Pit and the Pendulum* has nothing on Niu Boa's plans for Elliot Brave. In his world, this is as good as it gets. "This is delicious; this is fun."

When Elliott regains consciousness, he finds himself tied to the kill-blade machine in his own plant. Niu Boa sticks his smiling face next to Elliott's and says, "I learn much from you chicken-man. I learn why the chicken crossed the road. To get away from you, ha, ha, ha."

The Chinese gangster places one man at the gate to prevent access from outsiders to the Brave Chicken plant, two men outside the kill-blade processing building, while two men support Boa for the intended torture of Elliott Brave.

The Chinese gate guard never senses it coming, never hears a sound, and never suspects he is in danger.

His head just explodes.

Sonja is only fifty yards away -- she is deadly from almost twenty times that distance.

The sound of the sniper rifle is deafening -- the two guards at the kill-blade plant know they are next, unless they dive for cover. Powers, Lucas, and I don't enter through the gate -- that's why God invented bolt-cutters. After cutting through the fence nearest the kill-blade processing building, we enter the back of the building and throw five flash-bangers and three tear gas canisters into the building. While the bad guys are diving for cover and air, Powers, wearing an air purifying respirator, cut a choking Elliott Brave loose.

One of the guards sprints from the building in an attempt to escape the tear gas, only to have his chest cavity evacuated by one of Sonja's 50-caliber death shots.

Coughing and choking, the remaining Chinese killers unwillingly give away their positions, but instead of surrendering, the three remaining men try to fight back in their weakened condition. One of them shoots Lucas in the chest, dropping him to the deck in a spasm of pain. I place a 9mm from my M&P into the culprit's forehead while a coughing Boa takes aim at me.

He misses.

I don't.

The final Chinaman lunges desperately at me with a knife but I torque my body and hit his throat with all the leverage I can muster with my 310 pounds. It is ugly -- there is no structure left to hold his head erect.

Powers and I run to Lucas to check on him, hoping that he is alive. We roll him over and I say, "Lucas, talk to me."

He says, "Who invented Kevlar, anyway? I need to write the inventor a thank you letter. Was it Tony?"

CHAPTER 52 -- FATEFUL DECISIONS

Wiscasset, Maine: In the end, most of us become products of decisions we made early in our "rose-colored-glasses" formative years. I made the decision to lead an "exciting" life of action and danger. My fate was set the day I took a job as a bodyguard and entered the personal security profession. That decision placed me between criminals and potential victims. I may have had a little too much excitement ... because I've been shot, stabbed, hit by vehicles, and badly beat up by gangs.

But, throughout my violent life, I've somehow managed to stay fearless -- maybe that's a reflection of how smart I am; I don't know. However, if you let fear grab you, it changes your critical response time which, in my chosen profession, generally results in pain or worse.

I've been fearless my entire life.

But today, I'm scared to death. My hands are shaking, my stomach is upset, and, hell, even my voice is quivering.

Today, I'm getting married.

I'm standing in front of the First Congregational Church altar with my best man, Tucker, who is standing next to me completely oblivious to my weakened mental and physical condition. He is too mesmerized with the appearance of Jolene who is walking down the aisle arm and arm with her surrogate father, Powers.

Jolene is absolutely gorgeous in her tight-fitting, lacey, white, low-cut, long-sleeved dress with a ten-foot train, the end of which is being carried by Star. Jolene's slimming dress is cut very low in the back which contains what appears to be hundreds of white pearl buttons and yards of lace.

Her long blond hair is pulled up on the sides to a crown and hooked with a diamond tiara veil which flows down her back.

The smile on her lovely face shines brighter than the new diamond necklace flawlessly wrapped around her.

Star wears a dress which is identical to Jolene's wedding dress except that it is pale light pink in color. Even her tiara matches Jolene's. She carries a basket of flowers over one arm while carrying Jolene's train with both hands. She is wearing a large pale light pink bow in her auburn hair. Ram follows Star, carrying a basket in his mouth as the ring bearer.

Maya, the maid-of-honor, wears a slimming, light turquoise satin dress down to her knees and a large pale light pink hat that matches the color of Star's dress. For once in her life, Maya is not the most radiant person in the room -- this is Jolene's day.

When Jolene reaches the altar, I suddenly understand why I am wearing a tailor-made white suite with a turquoise cummerbund, matching handkerchief, and turquoise corsage. We are a reflection of each other's love. When I look into her eyes, my butterflies disappear and I feel like the luckiest guy on earth.

The reception is held at our favorite Wiscasset restaurant, catered by Chef Rhino and organized by the androgynous Cossack-looking restaurant proprietor. It is comical seeing those two working together. Chef Rhino, not a whole lot smaller than me, took over the restaurant kitchen and is rolling over the restaurant manager like he/she isn't even there.

Everything is perfect – until it isn't.

The Bishop's Plan is to wait. He is a patient man and though he is simple, he understands that the later the evening gets, the more intoxicated the guests will become. He is pretty sure that at some point, Maya must exit the restaurant; after all, she doesn't live there.

He'll just have to wait.

The Bishop is not only planning to complete his assignment and eliminate Maya, he is planning to have some time alone with her so he can fuck her eyes out before he kills her. He is also planning an exit strategy. Frankly, killing Maya will be much easier than getting away with it. He has to trap Maya when there are not so many bad-ass men around. The reception is crawling with hard-looking bodyguards.

He decides to wait until Maya has to go to the Ladies Room. None of the *White Knights* would dare enter the bathroom with her. He could have his way with her, kill her, and escape through the bathroom window before anyone knows what has happened.

"That is a pretty good plan," he thinks.

He didn't quite appreciate what he was getting into when Maya entered the rest room with Jolene -- who had changed out of her wedding dress -- and Sonja.

The Bishop is lightning-fast with a knife. He thinks he can kill the other two women before Maya even has a chance to scream.

But all three women were well-trained in hand-to-hand combat. Both Maya and Jolene were trained by Powers, while Sonja was trained by Israel's Mossad.

The Bishop lurches out from a suddenly-opened stall door wielding a knife in the direction of the throat of the woman closest to him.

319

He is shocked -- this has never happened to him. "What da fuck; how did she take the knife away from me?"

Not only does Sonja take the knife away from the Bishop, she has it pressed against his neck, which is now bleeding.

Maya speaks first, "You must be the Bishop."

The Bishop doesn't answer.

Maya smiles a smile that scares him to the core. She never takes her eyes off the Bishop as she speaks, "Jolene, this is your wedding day. This piece of cognitively dysfunctional garbage tried to ruin it. If we ask Tank to join us, he'll get 'Bishop-blood' all over his new white suit. If we ask Powers to join us, he'll walk out of here with the Bishop's head in a bucket. If we ask Tucker to join us, he'll end up in jail for murder. God knows what would happen if we asked Lucas to come in here.

"So I suggest we handle this problem ourselves and tell our men about this tomorrow."

That's when the Bishop makes a fatal mistake; he tries a move on Sonja to recapture his knife. Jolene's elbow shatters the Bishop's glasses and continues into his right eye socket, while Maya stomps on his left kneecap forcing the knee in a direction which it wasn't designed to go, and Sonja drags the knife across his ugly face. Once he's on the ground, the three women take one turn each and stomp in the area of his genitals.

They leave the Ladies Room as if nothing ever happened. On their way back to the reception room, Maya whispers into the ear of one of the *White Knight* guards, asking him if he wouldn't mind discreetly cleaning up the mess in the Ladies' Room ... and she asks that he keep anyone else from entering until the task is complete.

The three women dance the night away as if everything is copacetic.

CHAPTER 53 -- THE TRUTH IS OUT THERE

Washington, D.C.: *The Drudge Report* website lists news magazines, publishers, reports, and recent editorials, as well as a current list of writers, listed alphabetically, with a link to their most recent editorial page or blog. Listed close to the bottom of the webpage between Cal Thomas and George Will is Forrester True. Those who choose to click on to the link are directed to an editorial in the *Tri-City Herald*.

Jolene Alvarez calls out to me, "You're not going to believe this. Please, come here; sit down with me, let's read this together."

I come in off the balcony of our Honeymoon suite in Key West, my happy-meter pegged, sat down on the bed next to my wife, put my arm around her and say, "I love you and I love to hear your voice, so please, read the article to me."

Jolene kisses me warmly and begins reading.

The Truth is Out There

By

Forrester True

"Justice can sometimes be very elusive. Law enforcement tools have not always been perfect in determining culpability for a crime. The two most significant forensic tools applied to achieve justice for victims have been fingerprinting and DNA profiling. Fingerprints were used as signatures in ancient Babylon in the second millennium BC and have been used in solving crime as far back as China's Qin Dynasty. DNA Profiling emerged as the modern-day forensic game-changer in 1985.

"Both forensic tools were used in the investigation into the death of a White House Counsel a couple of decades ago. At the time, neither technology was able to validate or invalidate the rush-to-conclusion that his death was a suicide. The investigation was sloppy, infected with incompetence, and a medical examiner, who recently committed suicide himself, conducted the autopsy as if under a felonious threat.

"Until now.

"I love science. A new scientific development equal in forensic importance to DNA Profiling has evolved and been used to conclusively determine the cause of death of the White House Counsel. In the responsible interest of protecting my source, the attached link is a shocking video and voice recording of a previous conversation between the deceased billionaire, Viktor Soroson, and a presidential candidate -- the former First Lady and law partner of the deceased White House attorney.

I watch and listen as Jolene clicks onto the link provided with Forrester True's editorial. The familiar voice of the former First Lady is easily recognizable:

First Lady: *Viktor, we need to talk.*

Soroson: *Is this call secure? Did you call from the encrypted satellite phone I gave you?*

First Lady: *Of course.*

Soroson: *Are you alone?*

First Lady: *Again, of course.*

Soroson: *Are you in the safe room, the room designed in accordance with specifications for a secure compartmentalized information facility? The room I paid for?*

First Lady: *God damn it, Viktor, yes. Now can we get on with it? Your inquisition is ridiculous.*

Soroson: *I'm sorry, but you have proven yourself to be unreliable with top secret information, so I assume you are even less reliable with merely confidential information. Now what do you want?*

First Lady: *I want you to advance additional funds to my campaign. Drop the money into the Berkley Political Action Committee account. The PAC wants to produce a video that makes the GOP candidates appear as Neanderthal women-haters, as I suspect they all are.*

Soroson: *To be brutally honest with you, I've decided not to support your campaign any longer. I'm now supporting the senator from Massachusetts as the Democratic nominee.*

First Lady: *You bastard. How the hell do you expect to be Ambassador to Germany if she's the nominee and ultimately elected?*

Soroson: *I'm sorry, but you have become too great a liability and you and your husband have been involved in way too many scandals. Frankly, I no longer think that you are electable. You're too old, too ugly, too mean, too sanctimonious, and unlikeable.*

First Lady: *You're calling me old?*

Soroson: *I'm not running for office.*

First Lady: *No, you're buying an Ambassadorship and I suspect eliminating anybody who gets in your way. How many people have you had murdered to achieve your ridiculous goal? My law partner and White House attorney, Kingsley, the first guy at the scene of the crime; the medical examiner; the pilots that went down in the Cherokee's jet; and who knows how many others? What, am I next?*

The recording was silent for a few seconds.

First Lady: *Why did you have my former law partner murdered? Was it because he was going to testify before Congress and you thought his testimony would damage your future chance to be assigned as Ambassador?*

Soroson: *Madame First Lady, your day has passed. Your constituents have figured out that you don't really care about the*

*'little people'-- you only care about the 'little peoples' votes.
Your nasty treatment of other people, your explosive temper and
your condescending attitude received the title as the most
detested person under the protection of the Secret Service.*

*"To answer your question, the White House Counsel was
killed trying to protect you, he was loyal to you; but you were
too clueless back then, too narcissistic, too self-absorbed to see
just how weak and vulnerable you were.*

*Not only did your husband cheat on you -- who could blame
him? -- but your lover betrayed you, too.*

First Lady: *What are you talking about Viktor?*

Soroson: *Surely you remember Kristen!*

The recording went silent for five seconds.

Soroson: *You see, Kristen video-recorded one of your
sexual encounters with her. It was well done. I've watched it a
couple of times. I see you can be quite aggressive in bed, too.
You make a classic alpha-male female partner. One of the
reasons I watched it was to make sure you are, in fact, female.*

*I really don't find that sort of pornography appealing, but
we thought it could come in handy in future negotiations.*

First Lady: *We?*

Soroson: *Kristen worked for me.*

First Lady: *You fucking asshole. What did that have to do
with anything? Why kill my law partner?*

Soroson: *Kristen had a drinking problem. She let it slip to
another one of her lovers that she was intimate with you. The
word got out. The White House Counsel was trying to get the
video so that it never saw the light of day. He thought he was
meeting Kristen at the Civil War Park to exchange the video for
hush money. **She killed him**. The rest is history.*

First Lady: *And Kristen ... was her fate sealed?*

Soroson: *She made her bed. She had to lie in it.*

Alexandria, Virginia: The "entire family of investigators" is celebrating and enjoying libation at the *Brown Leaf Cigar Bar.* Sonja is sitting at the bar privately confiding in Powers about the secrets of her life. Tony Vinci and Jimmy Ma are whispering with each other about a strategy to stop North Korea's counterfeiting of U.S. hundred dollar bills. Maya, Star and Carmen are introducing themselves to Melody. The ex-Maryland Attorney General and Tucker are sharing newfound information about Soroson's prior activities while Lucas listens intently. Richard, Jolene and I are commiserating with the long-lost attorney, Harold Andrews and the esteemed Washington Mystery Club members.

The two owners of the establishment, Clinton Auclair and Byron Chism, closed the *Brown Leaf* to outside patrons for this special meeting of the Washington Mystery Club and formally invited the attendees to celebrate the solving of the twenty year old and other mysteries. As background music, the attendees can barely hear the old 'Kool & The Gang' tune *Celebration.*

Gina Goodman, Chairman of the Board for the Smithsonian Institution and leader of the Washington Mystery Club stands up while Byron Chism taps the top of his crystal glass to quiet numerous on-going conversations. A few seconds later, the room is quiet as Gina Goodman holds up a glass, and says, "On behalf of my colleagues, I thank all of you here for taking the time out of your busy schedules to attend this rare and special meeting of our exclusive Washington Mystery Club.

"Secrets are hard to keep in this incestuous town with so many competing agendas, nosy reporters, loose-lipped staffers, and buyers of information. Washington is a place where it is sometimes, maybe all the time, impossible to separate fact from fiction, planted disinformation from real data, and editorial opinions from real quotations.

"Nonetheless, there are some real mysteries that sustain the test of time. Who was behind the assassination of John Kennedy; was it a conspiracy, plus who on the Warren Commission knew the facts and withheld the information from the general public? Has the Government been concealing the truth about the alleged alien find in Roswell, New Mexico in 1947? Or more recently, what happened to Saddam Hussein's weapons of mass destruction -- or was it a fabricated ruse?

"Our little club enjoys the pursuit of solving the myriad mysteries which infect Washington, and facilitating the answers by providing an occasional clue." A sly smile caresses her lips.

"We toast all of you in this room for the investigative roles you played in achieving the spectacular successes in solving one of Washington's many mysteries."

An exuberant "Here, here!" is heard around the room.

"As we Washington Mystery Clubbers see it, you, collectively, solved not only the twenty-year-old mystery surrounding the death of the White House attorney, but you also solved numerous subordinate mysteries, and achieved other amazing accomplishments which will survive with the works of those who write history.

"First, you solved the mystery about where Jolene Landrieu, now Jolene Alvarez, was being held captive."

"Here, here!"

"That was no small accomplishment, not to mention the spectacular success you had at rescuing her."

Everyone in the room is looking at Jolene. She stands up, looks around the room, makes eye contact with almost everyone and says, "I want to take this opportunity to thank all of you who risked your lives to rescue me out there in the middle of nowhere. It is with a heavy heart that I recognize my rescue cost the lives of two old friends.   Please, take this moment to remember General Ray LaSalle and Director Damian LaTorre. They were very special people and will always be with me in my heart."

All of us bow our heads; some of us pray silently, and all of us offer the respect that a minute of silence brings.

Clinton Auclair breaks the silence and says, "Secondly, you made sure the kidnapper of Jolene received justice."

"Here, here!"

I couldn't help but visualize the mess that Gunter Korf's body suffered at the hands of a crazy woman on a small remote British island in the North Atlantic Ocean.

"Thirdly," Clinton Auclair continues, "you collectively discovered the truth about the death of the White House attorney."

"Here, here!"

"That's right," adds Byron Chism; "many thanks to Tony Vinci and one of his scientists. I'm sorry, Tony, what is her name?"

"Casey Robinson."

Byron continues, "Right, and with the data provided by Jimmy Ma who followed the money, **you all discovered that the Park Police officer, Kristen Brown, committed the murder of the White House Counsel.**"

Tucker speaks up, "It didn't hurt in solving the crime that Tony applied the nano-drone technology to record the conversation between the former First Lady and that monster, Soroson, to hear about Brown's guilt."

"True," I add; "but it was Jimmy Ma and Tony who figured out that Kristen Brown was also the woman who claimed to be Viktor Soroson's wife. She pretended to be Soroson's student, mentor, lover, and ideological twin when she was merely manipulating the master manipulator."

"Congratulations," Gina Goodman says, "For solving one of this town's outstanding mysteries."

She continues, "You also discovered the truth about the death of Richard's father."

"Here, here!"

"Using heretofore unused interrogation techniques," Goodman theatrically hesitates as a broad smile crosses Powers' face, "the former, now reinstated, Attorney General for the State of Maryland learned that Duke Dillinger, the Rook, was directed by Viktor Soroson, to stage a vehicle accident for Robert Kingsley who insisted that the crime scene had been tampered with. Soroson did not want the death of the White House attorney to impact the career of the former First Lady and his ambitions to influence politics on the world stage."

All eyes are on Richard who just nods his head. The truth does not set him free.

"On the unpleasant subject of the Rook," I ask the ex-AG, "what is the status of your son?"

The AG smiles and says, "He is out of the coma, alert, still hospitalized, and in traction with broken bones, but otherwise good. The doctors say that he will walk again. He has absolutely no memory of being crushed by a truck."

The room erupts in applause.

"One of our accomplishments," I add, "is the total evisceration of the killer squad of Fischer Men."

"Here, here!"

"True," Maya adds, "but one mystery not yet solved is this: at what point did the Fischer Men stop being directed by Soroson, and when did Kristen Brown take over? Jimmy Ma proved he could pretend to be Soroson, and give the Rook new orders. As a result, it became obvious that Kristen Brown was giving the orders to kill Tank, Powers, Richard, and me.

"And, by the way, Jimmy, we never could have convinced the Rook to kill Queenie and walk into a trap without you. You learned how to pretend to be their benefactor, and how to give the Fischer Men new assignments."

Jimmy asks, "So, do I get a date with your sister, Suzanne?"

She says, "No."

That brought the house down.

Maya changes the subject and says, "Another mystery not yet solved, is how you, Sonja, knew to set up a sniper operation to kill two of the Fischer Men before we even knew they existed."

All eyes are now on Sonja.

Then several members of the investigative family's eyes move to Star to see if she is reading Sonja's thoughts on the subject. Star shook her head back and forth.

Powers interrupts the silence while everyone is waiting for Sonja to answer the question, and says, "Let's just admit that Mossad's intelligence gathering skills are very good, and leave it at that."

Tucker adds, "At least, Kristen Brown -- the killer of the White House Counsel -- has been brought to justice."

"Here, here!"

"How did that happen?" the Maryland AG asked; "we have no extradition treaty with Venezuela."

Jimmy Ma says, "It's all about money; it always is."

Tucker answers, "Let's just say that the Venezuelan authorities discovered, somehow, that Kristen Brown forged the marriage certificate which allowed her to be the recipient of Viktor Soroson's billions. That fortune has now found its way to the country's treasury while Ms. Brown awaits trial in a Venezuelan court of law. She may stay incarcerated for quite a while."

Again, the room erupts in applause with many echoing "Here, here!"

Tucker raises his hand deferentially to the Washington Mystery Clubbers and asks, "Is this a good time for me to add a major accomplishment by this 'family' as you put it, of investigators?"

"Please," says Gina Goodman, "just know that we have a couple more successes and mysteries solved to add to this already impressive list."

Tucker stands up and proudly says, "It is with great pleasure that I announce that the American Association for the Advancement of Forensic Science has awarded my brilliant and beautiful wife, Dr. Maya Li Cherokee, and *Entropy Entrepreneurs'* Chief Scientist, Tony Vinci, the *Scientists of the Year Award* for their discoveries in Subatomic DNA Profiling and Hyper-Nano-Particle fingerprinting. Congratulations to both of you."

More applause and "Here, here!" chants.

Gina Goodman says, "To add to these impressive accomplishments, you solved the mystery about who was responsible for downing the Cherokee Learjet in the area of the Bermuda Triangle which killed Willie Mays Robinson, the copilot, and would have killed Maya had she not been persuaded by her daughter, Star, not to get on that flight. You are a very lucky woman, Dr. Cherokee."

WHA-CKED   JED O'Dea
(White House Attorney-Counsel Killed)

Maya announces, "It didn't take long to connect the dots after Tony and Casey Robinson discovered that Kristen Brown was responsible for the attempt on our lives using Soroson's gang of thugs, the Fischer Men. What surprised, or rather, disappointed us was to learn that the former FBI agent-in-charge, Brian Richmond, was bought and paid for with Soroson's money. He apparently was in cahoots with Kristen Brown in the cover up of the murder of the White House Counsel."

Powers adds, "You know, an FBI agent learns all the tricks bad guys use to commit crimes. Agents that turn bad have more tricks in their bag than the average bear. When the National Transportation Safety Board called Tucker and informed him that Willie Mays Robinson was poisoned, we contacted the Medical Examiner for the NTSB. We learned that *Solanum dulcamara,* known as Deadly Nightshade, was found in the contents of the stomachs of both pilots. Deadly Nightshade is a slow-release poisonous berry plant which can take hours after ingestion to reach full toxic impact.

"It just so happens that Brian Richmond had investigated a similar case five years ago and had access to the research on the toxic chemical added to the pilots' meals before takeoff."

I blurt out, "This is a toast to Ram for his wisdom and decisive action to rid the world of a corrupt law enforcement agent."

Laughter and "Here, here's" fill the room.

It is Byron Chism's turn to stand up. He waits for the audience to quiet before he says, "Who knew that the investigation into the death of the White House attorney would result in a deep dive and diversion into chicken feces.

"I cleaned that up for the ladies in the room.

"Early on, Carmen's dad, Elliott, was high on the list of persons-of-interest for the kidnapping of Jolene. Following that thread led to the spectacular accomplishment of the saving of both Carmen and Elliott Brave's lives."

"Here, Here!"

"And finally," says Clinton Auclair, "probably the most amazing accomplishment of all by this impressive "family" of investigators is the ending of the presidential campaign by the former First Lady. Tony Vinci's use of nano-drone technology caught the former First Lady in true character and probably saved the country from an embarrassing legacy."

"Here, here!"

"Thank you, everyone, for all you've done," says Gina Goodman; "drinks are on the house."

"Time out," I say loudly, "there is one more impressive accomplishment resulting from these investigations. Eleventhly, is that grammatically correct? Eleventhly, and maybe the most wonderful of all our successes is the creation of a new U.S. Fish and Wildlife Animal Cruelty Division headed by Richard Kingsley with the support of the youngest FBI consultant in history, Star Cherokee, whose special and unusual skills will benefit animals of all kinds.

"Congratulations to Richard and Star."

All clap vigorously as Richard nods and Star curtsies. Tucker and Maya couldn't be more proud.

But the expressions on the faces of the Washington Mystery Club members and Harold Andrews show confusion. Finally, co-owner of the *Brown Leaf Cigar Bar*, Clinton Auclair asks, "I'm sorry for my ignorance, but what are you speaking about when you refer to Star's special skills?"

I quickly interject, "Before we answer that question, there are a couple of other mysteries which remain unanswered. Where did you Washington Mystery Clubbers get your secret information, the gun, and the photo? What was your role,

Harold, in the solving of the other mysteries? Whose blood was found at the entrance in your home in Clifton? We thought it was yours."

Harold Andrews speaks up for the first time and says, "I'm very sorry, but we are not allowed to disclose any of that information. You understand; I'm sure. Some mysteries are best unsolved. "

Star speaks up and says, "Those mysteries, too, have been solved."

The table erupts in laughter at the expense of Harold Andrews and the Washington Mystery Clubbers, whose inscrutable expressions will be forever imprinted in my mind.

Pentagon City, Virginia: While enjoying a final round of drinks at the Ritz Carlton Hotel before we all retire for the night; we sit in a semicircle around Star, anticipating the new information which she would impart to those of us unenlightened. Maya says to her daughter, "So, sweetheart, what did you learn at the *Brown Leaf Cigar Bar* from the Washington Mystery Club members?"

Star states very matter-of-factly, "The blood in front of Mr. Andrews' home was old blood from a Red Cross blood bank. It was used to throw the investigation away from Andrews.

"Mr. Andrews, Mr. Auclair, Mr. Chism, and Ms. Goodman were all four thinking about the same person. Mr. Andrews was paid directly by this person and the Washington Mystery Club members were getting their information from him through Mr. Andrews.

WHA-CKED   JED O'Dea
(White House Attorney-Counsel Killed)

"The former President of the United States, the husband of the former First Lady, doesn't want her to become the next president. He, more than anyone, knows how disastrous it would be to the country he loves, if she became president."

I boast to Tucker and Maya loud enough for everyone to hear, "Your daughter is going to make one heck of an interviewer for the U.S. Fish and Wildlife Animal Cruelty Division."

CHAPTER 54 -- BE CAREFUL WHO YOU MESS WITH

Caracas, Venezuela: The combination of heat and humidity in the stinking unventilated jail cell with dirt floors makes Kristen's unpleasant body odor hard for *even* her to endure. Her breath is so bad that she has to breathe through her mouth to avoid the aroma of food rotting in her teeth. She'd give damn near anything for a toothbrush. The prison workers intentionally fail to empty the stagnant toilet pot, and it has been too long since she has had a bath with clean water and soap. Six months in this Venezuela prison is enough punishment as far as she is concerned. If she believed in God, she'd pray to Him to help her escape.

She spends most of her wakeful hours formulating an escape plan. She decides to use a tactic which has served her well; she picks a guard to seduce. She first teases and convinces him to stick his manhood between the cell bars so she can bring him great pleasure. After about two weeks of daily pleasure-giving, she entices him into her cell to have uninhibited sex, if he arranges for her to have a warm bubble bath -- she'd even let him help to bathe her.

The disgusting-looking night shift guard she selected is absolutely perfect for her plan -- he isn't the sharpest knife in the drawer. A month after she first seduced him, he is in love with her. She shares with him, clandestinely, that she has a secret account with millions of U.S. dollars in it. If he would help her escape, she would be forever indebted to him, and agree to run away with him to be his sex slave.

Each night after sex in her cell, they discuss the elements of her plan and the things he needs to do to have his way with her forever. They settle on an exact time and the method of escape.

The mentally-challenged sex-sick guard surprises his fellow guards on his night shift and incapacitates them. Then he unlocks Kristen's cell and sneaks her out at 2:30 AM. They jump into the guard's 1998 VW bug and head for a shanty he has picked out for their initial hideaway. The plan is for Kristen to go to the bank tomorrow and secure enough cash from the secret account for them to safely hide for a few weeks, or until the manhunt for her wanes.

At least that is the plan.

After ten minutes en route to the "safe shanty" Sargent Brown says to the guard, "I think we're being followed." The guard looks into his rear-view mirror and takes some unnecessary turns to confirm that they are, in fact, being followed.

On a dark dirt road in the middle of the night, the VW has both its rear tires shredded by bullets. As the car skids to a stop, Kristen jumps out of the car and runs as fast as possible away from the shooter in the direction of the thick overgrown jungle tree-line twenty-five yards away.

The first shot hits her in the back of her left thigh. The second shot hits the guard in the right arm. The third shot hits her right calf. The shooter walks toward the unarmed guard and kicks him in the solar plexus to ensure his incapacitation.

She is bleeding and crawling in pain, not giving up, but there is nothing she can do, nowhere to go.

She hears a husky male voice announce, "Ms. Brown or Miss Von Braun or Mrs. Soroson or whatever your name is today, you must pay for your crime.

"Which crime, you might ask; the murder of the White House attorney?

"No, I'm not here for that crime.

"The fraud you perpetrated in your claim to be the wife of Viktor Soroson?

"No, I'll let the Venezuelan legal system take care of that.

"The crimes you committed using the Fischer Men who believed they were receiving instructions from their benefactor?

"No. Fortunately, they failed.

"The murders of the Learjet pilots?

"No.

"The extortion of money from Viktor Soroson's accounts?

"No.

"The attempted murder of my wife, Maya?

"Absolutely."

On his way back to Simon Bolivar International Airport, Tucker pulls out his encrypted sat phone and calls Tony Vinci, "It's time to remotely destroy the nano-drone in Kristen Brown's empty cell.

"Is the nano-drone in the Frankfurt home of the Chairman of the Deutsche Chamber still providing intelligence?

"Yes, and he has confirmed his bad intentions. Your MI-5 friend, Stone Garry, and the lovely Sonja McLeod are already waiting for you at the prearranged rendezvous location."

"I'm glad Sonja and Stone are going to join me there. The Chairman's decision to target **anyone** who may know about the Deutsche Chamber's shenanigans is about to bite him in the ass."

337

CHAPTER 55 -- FOUL PLAY

Wiscasset, Maine: I ask Powers, "Where were we anyway? I think I was ahead of you twelve to two."

Powers answers, "No way you ever got ahead of me, much less that far ahead. As I recall, you pulled a weapon on me and shot me in the fatty part my back in an attempt to gain advantage on the court. It took three weeks for me to recover from that shot and you destroyed the blue ball in the process. No, I'm sure I was ahead and serving."

I tease Powers, "Playing racquetball with you reminds me of Sun Tzu's ancient Chinese treatise, *The Art of War*. I always wondered: did you train Sun Tzu?"

"Sun Tzu was just a child when I trained him, you asshole."

"By the way, I heard from our old British friend, Stone Garry. I understand the guy who was trying to re-start the Irish Republican Army was assassinated. Do you or does Sonja know anything about that?"

"Why would **we** know something about that?"

I hear someone pounding on the Plexiglas back wall of the racquetball court. Not again. I look back to see that it's Director Clinton Auclair. Powers, in his Joe Cocker voice says, "I'm not '*feeling all right*' about this."

"What the hell is Auclair doing in Wiscasset? This can't be good news. This has to be the first time old Clint's seen the inside of a racquetball court."

I open the door to the court, duck down and climb through the opening and say with as big a grin as I can muster, "Well, well. To what do we owe the honor of this visit? Where's your racquet, Clint? Do you want to play cut-throat?"

Powers climbs through the doorway and follows up with, "Tank, I see we have a new victim. Really, Clint, you can't expect to get good traction on the court wearing dress shoes!"

WHA-CKED   JED O'Dea
(White House Attorney-Counsel Killed)

Director Auclair doesn't smile; doesn't react in his usual jovial way. Instead, he says, "It saddens me to tell you that Supreme Court Justice Antonio Scala is dead."

Though we are upset by the news, Powers and I wait for the other shoe to drop.

"It has been declared that his death was from natural causes."

Power concludes, "Let me guess. You don't believe it; you think the declaration is bullshit."

Director Auclair continues, "I am here on behalf of the Heritage Foundation. We have taken the liberty to wire transfer an advance payment to *White Knight Personal Security Services* to contract you to investigate the death of Justice Scala -- we believe he is a victim of foul play. We have absolutely zero confidence that a government-sponsored investigation will result in the discovery of the truth."

I ask, "What do you know that makes you say that, or more to the point, what does the Heritage Foundation know which makes them willing to retain us?"

Clint digs into to his jacket pocket and pulls out a thumb drive.

Powers says, "Déjà vu all over again."

I tell Clint, "I'm sorry, Director, but Powers is too old -- he doesn't have enough gas left in his tank -- pun intended -- to work an important case like this."

"Get the fuck back in the racquetball court, Tank. I'll show you who the weak link in this outfit is."

I think, "He took the bait -- we have our next challenge."

THE END

339

ACKNOWLEDGEMENTS

A Special Thanks goes out to *John Powers Mason.*

A Special Thanks also goes out to the cover and graphics designer, Sam Rotolo, *Lightyear Studios*, Leesburg, Virginia.

Thanks go out to ALL the WHA-CKED beta testers:

Betty Garry, Virginia

Brian Day, Florida

Dawn Allen, North Carolina

Jan Chappelle, Virginia

Ken Landon, Maryland

Michael Levine, California

Richard Nathan, Virginia

Steve Unthank, Virginia

A Special Thanks goes out to my wife, **Shere**, for her support, patience, and valuable contributions.

JED O'Dea's

Available in the Spring of 2017

Troy Vincent was unnaturally fast; his lightning reflexes allowed him to respond infinitely faster to an action than the average person. It made him a perfect short-stop, and allowed him to hit just about any pitcher's fast ball.

Troy was in Milwaukee when an irate gang of Brewers fans were tired of seeing him be the primary cause of another loss to the St. Louis Cardinals.

They beat him unmercifully.

What the doctors learned during the time he was in a coma was that no one in his family matched his blood type or DNA. At age 28, Troy learns that his parents are not his birthright parents, and that everything he had been told about his family is a lie.

In fact, in the world's data base there is no match to his unique DNA.

Though it takes two years for him to fully rehab, he uses his unnatural speed to excel in martial arts, the art of knife fighting, hand-to-hand combat, and weapons handling.

He becomes a private investigator in search of his real parents, in search of the criminals who beat him up and the truth about his early childhood.

He becomes a White Knight *where he earns the right to be a legend among legends. In his search for the truth, the adventures are endless.*